In Passion's Wake

Like a doe caught in the light of a hunter's lantern, she stood momentarily frozen in his arms. Confusion clouded her eyes. Slowly, offering her one last chance to escape, he lowered his face.

She didn't move. Her eyes were still staring into his when his lips brushed over her mouth. With a sound that was somewhere between a groan and a whimper, she sagged into his arms, and he was lost.

The taste of her was like whiskey to a drunkard. Like sin to a confirmed sinner. His flesh leaped eagerly in response to the sweet-salt flavor of her mouth, to the feel of her firm, delicately formed body. Just like that, he was fully aroused.

But then, he'd been aroused almost from the time he caught sight of her, so small, so alone on the vast empty shore.

Entwined

by

Bronwyn Williams

A TOPAZ BOOK

TOPAZ
Published by the Penguin Group
Penguin Putnam Inc., 375 Hudson Street,
New York, New York 10014, U.S.A.
Penguin Books Ltd, 27 Wrights Lane,
London W8 5TZ, England
Penguin Books Australia Ltd, Ringwood,
Victoria, Australia
Penguin Books Canada Ltd, 10 Alcorn Avenue,
Toronto, Ontario, Canada M4V 3B2
Penguin Books (N.Z.) Ltd, 182–190 Wairau Road,
Auckland 10, New Zealand

Penguin Books Ltd, Registered Offices:
Harmondsworth, Middlesex, England

First published by Topaz, an imprint of Dutton NAL,
a member of Penguin Putnam Inc.

First Printing, June, 1998
10 9 8 7 6 5 4 3 2 1

 REGISTERED TRADEMARK—MARCA REGISTRADA

Printed in the United States of America

Chapter One

It had been two years since he'd last been home. Maybe longer, he couldn't remember now. Liam had been trying to grow a mustache and get over a broken heart. But then, with Liam, neither condition was particularly new.

At any rate, it had been too long, and now he wished—oh, God, it would really make this easier—if he hadn't been away so long.

The hedges had grown shaggy. Absently, Brandon noted the fact, but his mind was on matters of far graver import. Not until he turned off the main road onto the long, hilly drive to the house did it hit him fully. The sorry condition of the land. The wind, cold, and wet as only a New England winter wind could be, howled around him, driving wet snowflakes down the back of his neck as he stared out across acres of rock-walled pasture to the barely visible hedgerows in the distance.

Startled by his presence, a peppering of blackbirds scattered over the treetops. There'd been a time when those same hills had rung with the sound of three boys, the smallest scarcely big enough to hang onto his new pony.

They'd been wild in those days. Wild, unconquerable young heathens, racing headlong over hills and fields, flinging challenges back and forth.

Poor Liam. The news was going to crush him. He'd

always idolized Galen. The youngest by eleven years, Liam had been the tenderhearted one. Spoiled by their mother, his boyhood battles fought by his two elder brothers, he'd had an easy time of it growing up.

Maybe too easy, Brandon admitted, adding guilt to his other burden.

Shoulders sagging under a burden of grief and exhaustion, he continued on his way, searching his mind for a gentle way to break the news.

He'd been searching for the same thing ever since he'd left the coast. There was just no gentle way to tell a man that his brother was dead. That Galen was lost at sea. That the *Mystic Wings* had gone down somewhere in the North Atlantic with all hands.

Scheduled to make a stop at Dublin on her way to Liverpool, she'd been a month overdue when his office had received an inquiry. That had been the start of it, the first inkling.

Galen had never been more than a week or so overdue in the year and a half he'd been commanding the *Wings*. But there'd been a series of storms that season. More than a few ships had been reported lost.

Brand had set out immediately they'd got word, following the course she would have taken. For four months he'd searched, hoping against hope to find some trace of her—or at the very least, some word of her crew.

He'd found nothing. The sea had swallowed up the last hope. And now, in spite of a nagging sense of uncertainty that persisted against all reason, he could no longer withhold the truth from Liam.

They would hold a memorial service—he, Liam, and Liam's new wife, Fallon, whom Brand had yet to meet. And perhaps their few close neighbors. Marshall Kondrake came to mind immediately. He and their father had grown up together, their properties adjoining. The staff, of course. Old Everette, the farm manager, had taught all three brothers to ride. He'd been as close as family.

But, God, he wished there was some way he could cushion the blow.

Perhaps the woman, Fallon—the girl Liam had been so hellbent to marry he couldn't wait for his brothers to come home for the wedding—perhaps she could offer some comfort. According to Galen, who'd been in great demand by the ladies ever since he'd grown out of knee pants, a woman's touch was a purely magical thing.

Personally, Brand wouldn't know. Except for one short-lived love affair, plus a few brief relationships that had involved comfort of an entirely different sort, he'd been far too busy building his own small empire to learn much about the species. He'd left that particular area of expertise to his two younger brothers.

Noticing a gate hanging by a single hinge, he frowned. Come to think of it, it wasn't the first sign of neglect he'd noticed since turning off the main road. Evidently managing a large farm, even with a reliable staff, wasn't quite the sinecure Liam had imagined.

At nearly twenty, he'd been eager to take over after their father's death. They'd waited, though, Brand and Galen. Waited until his twenty-first birthday to sign over their shares in the prosperous stud farm and set out to build their own future.

Congratulating each other on their selfless generosity, they had headed east to Mystic, first Brand, and a few weeks later, Galen. Both confident that Liam would manage just fine once they quit looking over his shoulders.

The truth was, they'd both been far more attracted to their mother's seagoing heritage than to their father's legacy of horse breeding.

Marriage should have settled the boy, Brand told himself, frowning. Any man old enough to marry was damned well old enough to manage his business affairs without letting things get in this sorry condition.

Brand had never met his new sister-in-law. According to Liam's letters, she was beautiful and passionate beyond belief.

And expensive, opined Galen, who had met her shortly before he'd finished up his own affairs and headed east to join Brand.

They'd both had a laugh over that, both finding it hard to picture their baby brother wed and settled. He'd barely achieved his majority. Even now, he was only . . . what?

Twenty-two?

Twenty-three?

Time, Brand told himself, feeling vaguely guilty for staying away so long, moved too damned fast to keep up with when a man was busy building a shipping business.

"Wait until you meet her," Liam had written. "You'll love her once you get used to the way she looks."

Get used to the way she looks?

But then, even Galen had said she was stunning, and Galen, for all his easygoing charm, had always been levelheaded where women were concerned.

Distracted, Brand rode up to the house, dismounted, and looked about for someone to come and see to his horse. He waited several minutes, then shrugged and walked the exhausted animal toward the vast rock-and-timber barn.

The barn was deserted. Not a single creature, four-legged or two-legged, to be seen anywhere. A feeling that had been quietly growing in the back of his mind ever since he'd turned off the main road could no longer be ignored. Something was wrong.

Something was terribly wrong.

The coach car reeked of stale cigar smoke and unwashed bodies, but with sleet beating against the windows, fresh air was out of the question.

The train began to move. Ana braced herself, still half expecting to be dragged out onto the siding. The porter had pointed out an empty seat near the front, but then he'd been called away.

Anamarie, it's up to thee.

This was no Pullman car. It was only coach, but it would serve. It would have to serve. It was all she could afford.

Clutching her valise with one hand, she took a tentative step forward, steadying herself on the seat backs as the train picked up speed. Careful not to hurry, not to do anything that would arouse suspicion, she swallowed her fear, only to have it stick like a dry biscuit in her throat.

Outside, the steam whistle broke into a scream. Ana gave a startled yelp.

Someone laughed.

Someone else made a sly remark, vaguely salacious.

Ignoring the clammy feel of wet petticoats slapping against her limbs, of wet shoes squelching with every step, she made her way down the aisle to the empty seat at the front of the car, imagining dozens of pairs of accusing eyes boring into her back.

But then, why should anyone accuse? How could they know?

Dear Lord, how could they *not* know? Surely something so horrendous couldn't be hidden so easily.

With cold, trembling knees, Ana Gilbretta—no, Ana Hebbel now—lowered herself onto one of the empty seats.

A woman across the aisle turned away and stared pointedly out into the inky darkness rushing past the window. Ironically, it was the same woman who had prompted her to buy a ticket to a place she'd never even heard of.

There'd been only moments to spare before the train pulled out when Ana had dashed into the station, breathless and terrified, to demand a ticket for the train that was just now ready to depart. She hadn't cared where it was bound as long as she was on it. Her only thought had been to get away.

"End of the line?"

"Yes, please," she'd gasped.

"That'll be twenty-nine dollars, then."

She'd stepped to one side and was digging in her reticule for the wad of money she'd brought with her, counting it for the first time, when a slender, heavily veiled woman had hurried up to the window.

"One way to Elizabeth City in North Carolina." The woman had sounded agitated. She'd glanced over her shoulder toward the door, ignoring Ana as if she weren't even there. "Did you hear me? Hurry, you dunce!"

Under any other circumstances, Ana might have been offended by such rudeness. But compared to what she had done, rudeness was a very small sin. Tallying up the amount of money she had with her, she'd stepped forward the moment the veiled woman had hurried away to board the departing train and said, "Elizabeth City, one way, please, and hurry."

The ticket agent had gawked at her. "Land's sakes, I never even sold a single ticket to that place before this. Now all of a sudden everybody wants to go to Elizabeth City. You ladies having a convention down there?"

Ana had forced herself to smile and nod, but feared it was a ghastly effort. Still shaking his head, the agent had taken her money and handed over a strip of cardboard just as the train had let loose one short blast, signaling its imminent departure. Grabbing the ticket, she'd snatched up her valise and run.

Where on earth was Elizabeth City? She'd never even heard of the place. What would she do there?

Survive.

Turning her head toward the window now, Ana closed her eyes in an effort to shut off her thoughts. What was done, was done. The die was cast, as her husband would say.

Would've said.

Her late husband.

Oh, Lord . . .

Up ahead, the engineer cut loose with one short and one long, mournful blast as they rocked and swayed their way noisily through the darkness. In spite of the crowded coach and the small coal stove at the rear, Ana shivered. She felt cold to the bone. Cold, wet, terrified, and alone in a way that even she could never have imagined before tonight.

With stiff fingers, she unlatched her valise and removed the shawl she'd crammed in on top of the few belongings she'd managed to grab before she'd left. Carefully, as if it mattered, she smoothed it over her lap.

It was then she noticed that the woman across the aisle had folded back her veil and was staring.

Ana stared back. At first, in the dim light of the wall-mounted lamp, she saw nothing but a pair of eyes that were . . . somehow not right.

And then, gradually, she saw beyond the eyes—the mismatched eyes, one hazel, the other a startling shade of blue—to a face that was almost a mirror image of her own.

The other woman was far prettier. Beautiful, in fact. And younger. They stared at each other with unabashed curiosity, neither speaking, and then each turned away. Until the other woman called her attention to it, Ana didn't even notice when the shawl slipped from her lap to lie crumpled around her ankles.

She leaned over to retrieve it and it was then she saw the widening stain. The shawl, a cashmere that had belonged to her mother, was pale ivory. The stain was dark. Not soot, for the windows were tightly shut.

Both women stared at the ruined square laying there on the filthy floor. The stranger with the mismatched eyes said something about cheap dyes bleeding when they got wet, and numbly, Ana nodded.

Bleeding. She snatched up the shawl and folded it so that the stain wouldn't show, and the other woman turned and continued her study of the passing night.

Blood?

Dear God, blood.

She shivered. Nausea rose in her throat. The same

feeling had followed her all the way to the station. She swallowed hard and forced herself to breathe slowly.

Don't think. Whatever you do, Ana, don't think about it.

She thought about it.

It had been an accident, but who would believe her? With her husband dead of a gunshot wound, and his wife nowhere to be found? With her father's gig left unattended at the train station?

The ticket agent was a stranger to her, but he was bound to remember a distraught woman traveling alone late at night, demanding a one-way ticket on the southbound.

Or perhaps he would remember two women, both bound for the same unlikely destination, and think they were traveling together. To—what was it?

A ladies convention?

Oh, yes. Oh, heavens, yes, she was bound to a convention in some place she had never even heard of. Why else would a wealthy young woman be running away in the dead of night, in the middle of a sleet storm, with blood dripping off her clothing and barely enough money to keep body and soul together once she'd paid her fare?

As the train clattered through the night, saluting each town and village with a mournful wail, Ana struggled to come to terms with what had occurred, and what was likely to happen in the future.

This couldn't be happening to her. Not to a sensible, responsible woman who had prided herself on being a dutiful daughter when it hadn't always been easy.

Had hardly ever been easy.

Oh, she'd been impatient at times, but then, years of caring for an invalid father who had grown steadily more peculiar, not to mention more irascible, could try the patience of a saint. She'd never pretended to be that.

Oh, Papa, how could you have done such a wicked thing? I never wanted to marry him. I could've taken

*care of myself, I told you so, over and over. Haven't I
been taking care of both of us for years?*

She shook off the shameful thought and wondered
if riding three or four days in the same wet underwear
might prove fatal. She would hate to be laid out in a
bloody gown and sodden petticoats.

*Here lies Anamarie Gilbretta Hebbel, the old drab.
She got what she deserved.*

The woman seated across the aisle was wearing
black, too, but hers was black silk with flounces, the
excellent cut apparent even beneath her short sealskin
cape. She wore several rings and a bracelet over her
black kidskin gloves, and a gold locket that sparkled
with the swaying movement of the train.

Self-consciously, Ana twisted the narrow wedding
band she wore under her gloves. She might have to
sell it if she couldn't find work right away.

She'd sell it anyway. She could hardly go on wearing
it now.

The woman across the aisle lowered her veil again,
and Ana wondered if she was in mourning. It was an
unusually heavy veil, and veils weren't even all that
fashionable this year.

Not that Ana was any authority of fashion.

Perhaps the woman simply didn't want to have to
deal with curious strangers striking up a conversation,
which suited Ana just fine.

She sneezed. She would catch her death of cold.
That would solve everything.

Had she thought to bring another pair of shoes?
She couldn't remember. The valise was too small to
hold much. Numb with terror, she had simply raced
to her room and crammed in whatever she could easily
lay hands on. It was a good thing she'd already
scraped most of the housekeeping money into her reticule before Ludwig had barged into the library, else
she'd soon be ragged, hungry, and begging in the
streets.

Or ragged, hungry, and behind bars. Did prisoners
have to pay for any food they ate?

Were they given clothes to wear?

Sleet continued to pelt the side of the passenger coach. In other cars, more affluent passengers would be sleeping soundly by now, lulled by the rhythm and the noise of a fast-moving passenger train.

Sighing, Ana rested her head against the back of the seat, oblivious to the stains of hair oil left there by previous travelers.

She'd got away.

Got away with murder. With shooting a man to death, never mind that she hadn't meant to. Never mind that he'd married her solely for her money, neglected her for months, not even bothering to come home for her father's funeral.

Never mind that he had beaten her and used her until she had feared for her very life.

Ludwig Hebbel, the man her father had bribed to marry her, the man who had wedded and bedded her and then left her to return to his mistresses and his gambling friends—oh, yes, she did know that about him. He'd actually bragged to her about it. Lugwig had showed up five days after she'd laid her father to rest, just in time for the reading of the will. Mr. Quillerby, her father's lawyer and confidant, had been out of town at the time of her father's death. Or so he'd said. Ana wouldn't put it past him to deliberately prolong the whole miserable affair. He was a spiteful little man.

On learning that her father's money had been left not to Ana, but to any children she might bear, Ludwig had been wild. After raging for hours, he had grabbed her by the shoulders and shaken her until her teeth rattled.

She had made the mistake of trying to reason with him first. Next, she'd told him he was drunk and would regret his behavior come morning.

It had been the wrong thing to say. He had started beating her then, using his fists instead of the flat of his hands. Dragging her upstairs, he had thrown her on the bed, torn off her clothes, and raped her.

For two days he had kept her locked in her room, beating and raping her repeatedly, saying hideously frightening things to her, telling her if she didn't give him a brat he would kill her.

The entire household had been frantic. Sally, the maid, had run home, crying her silly little head off. Ana could hear her all the way upstairs. Samuels, bless him, had gone for Mr. Quillerby, who had promised to come back with the sheriff, but neither of them had ever shown up.

Ludwig had said they wouldn't. That a man was king in his own house, and regardless of what was written on a scrap of paper—if it was written there at all—the house was now his.

When Samuels and Etta, the housekeeper, had hammered on the bedroom door, Ludwig had chased them down the stairs, raging like a maniac, driven them outside and then locked all the doors.

That had been the night Ana had shot her husband.

What, she wondered now, would become of Etta and Samuels? What would happen to the house now that both Papa and Ludwig were dead and she was gone, and there was no one left to inherit all the wealth accumulated by generations of Gilbrettas?

Too late to think about it now. Far, far too late.

Ana didn't have to look over her shoulder to know that most of her fellow passengers were asleep. The sound of snoring could be heard even above the clatter of iron on steel. Her own eyes refused to close, probably because she was afraid if she closed them she might see Ludwig again, see his pale eyes widening as he realized that the gun he'd tried to snatch from the drawer had gone off and the blood that suddenly covered the front of his starched white shirt was his own.

"Damnation." It was no more than a whisper, but it carried quite clearly across the aisle, bringing Ana out of her waking nightmare.

"I beg your pardon?"

"I've broken a damned stay," the veiled woman said. "It's jabbing me in the bosom."

Ana wondered if she could have misheard. No decent woman would dream of speaking of such personal matters to a stranger, much less swearing. Certainly not in a train car filled almost entirely with men. At least no woman in her right mind, unless she was the worse for drink.

She swallowed the wild urge to giggle as it occurred to her that drunk, insane, or immoral, the woman would be horrified to know she was traveling through the night with a murderess.

"I don't suppose you have a handkerchief I can borrow, do you? Mine's lace. Wouldn't do a speck of good as padding."

Bemused, Ana felt in her reticule and found a crumpled linen square. Wordlessly, she handed it across the aisle.

Wordlessly, the woman took it and in the dim light of a single lantern, Ana watched as she fumbled at the front of her gown.

"I'm hungry," she announced a moment later, fastening the last button and patting her generous bosom. "Where do you suppose the butch is?"

"Butch?"

"You know—the peddler. The boy who sells fruit and peanuts and newspapers. There's always one around to pester you when you want to be left alone, but the minute you need him, he's nowhere to be found. Lazy, pesky lot, if you ask me." She uttered a curse word that Ana had never before heard from a woman, and seldom from a man. "At least that damned stick of whalebone isn't sawing my bosom off. For two cents, I'd take the miserable contraption off. My boobies might not sit so high, but under my cape, who'd even know? Are you going far?"

"Elizabeth City." Dazed, Ana spoke without thinking.

"You're not!" Ana started to say she was, too, but the other woman rushed on to say, "But that's where

I'm going. What are you going to do there? Do you have family?"

Ana gave up. She was too keyed up to sleep. Talk might help to fight off the terror that still threatened to engulf her. She had no way of knowing how far Elizabeth City was from Pomfret, but she did know that North Carolina was hundreds and hundreds of miles from Connecticut, and at twenty-five or even thirty miles an hour, the journey would be tedious beyond belief.

And so they talked.

The woman's name was Fallon, which Ana thought lovely, and said so. Fallon Smith lifted her veil, and in the barely lighted coach, Ana—Ana Jones, she decided on the spur of the moment to call herself—tried not to stare at the face that was so like her own except for the color of her eyes and the fact that Ana's face was thinner, older, and not nearly as pretty.

"We look almost like sisters," the younger woman said. "Shall we tell everyone we're sisters? That would be fun, wouldn't it?"

"Tell who?"

"Oh, you know . . . anyone who asks. We could be sisters traveling to visit our father—a minister. How does that sound!"

It sounded crazy to Ana. Childish.

But then Fallon said, "I don't suppose you noticed any, um—any strange men lurking around the station, did you? You boarded after I did."

"Strange men?"

"If you must know," she leaned across to whisper, "I'm being followed."

Ana didn't want to hear this, she really didn't. She had more than enough troubles of her own.

"The man I ma—was engaged to marry is dreadfully jealous. When I broke our engagement, he started following me. He won't leave me alone."

"That's dreadful," Ana murmured. But not as dreadful, she added silently, as being followed by the

police and dragged off the train on a charge of
murder.

Some hundred-odd miles away, Brandon McKnight
stared out at the driving sleet as another shot of the
hotel's best brandy burned a path down his gullet.
Physically, he was as comfortable as he'd been since
he'd commenced his search for the woman responsible
for his brother's death.

Emotionally, he would never be comfortable again.

First Galen and then Liam. In a single year he had
lost everyone in the world he held dear. Lost any reason to go on building and expanding in an attempt to
make the McKnight name as big in shipping as it had
been until recently in horse breeding.

Not even learning of Galen's death had hit him this
hard. He'd ridden into the courtyard back in Litchfield, still trying to frame the words in the least hurtful
way possible to tell Liam that the *Mystic Wings* had
gone down with all hands, when it had hit him.

Something was wrong. Something was terribly
wrong. The house had been empty. Not merely deserted, but empty of nearly all the contents.

Oh, there'd still been a few things left. The gate-
legged table Galen had taken a saw to when he was
nine, that their mother had refused to replace, saying
that having to look at it each day would be a far more
effective lesson than a belt applied to his tender
backside.

The parlor sofa was still there, its cover shabby and
badly stained. A few odd chairs and end tables.

But his mother's pedal harp was missing, as were
the paintings of prize blood stock that had once graced
the walls of nearly every room in the house. His seagoing grandfather Dalton's collection of jade carvings
was gone, along with the étagère where they'd been
displayed. Gone were every one of his father's valuable first editions.

In less time than it took to tell it, Brand had
dredged up dozens of memories of curios and one-of-

a-kind pieces collected by generations of Daltons and McKnights. Things he hadn't realized he valued until they were no longer there. It was as if one more part of his life had suddenly gone missing.

At first he'd thought something terrible must have happened while Liam and his bride had been traveling. The boy had mentioned in one of his letters that Fallon loved to travel.

But where had the staff been? Surely, he'd thought, his brother wouldn't have given them all holiday and then gone off and left a stableful of prime breeding stock unattended.

Not that he'd found any evidence of livestock, prime or otherwise.

Methodically, he'd searched the house, trying to find a clue to the mystery. Most of Liam's clothing was still there, scattered and stained with filth and what looked like wine. The boy had never been much of a drinker. He'd never had a head for strong spirits, a fact that his two older brothers, to Brand's shame, had exploited more than once for their own amusement.

Two years. Was it possible for a man to marry, go to seed, turn into a drunkard, sell off everything he possessed, and then disappear, all in less than two years?

Where was the beautiful and passionate Fallon?

Why hadn't the damned woman kept him in line?

If Liam had taken up gambling, or some other potentially ruinous pastime, why the hell hadn't she written to his two elder brothers and asked for help?

Brand had ridden to the home of the nearest neighbor, three miles away by road. By the time he'd reached the Kondrake place, he'd been practically frozen to the saddle, but the snow on the ground was no match for the growing coldness inside him.

Marshall Kondrake, who had tolerated three young heathens trespassing to hunt and trap on his land as they grew to manhood, had ushered him into a warm, book-lined study.

"What the devil is going on at Pa's place?" Brand

had demanded before he'd even removed his wet overcoat.

"Sad business, Brandon, my boy." The elderly law-yer hadn't seemed at all surprised to see him after several years. He poured him a drink and said, "Where the devil have you been? I expected you long before now. We couldn't wait, you know. There was that thaw, and what with more cold weather on the way, we went ahead and buried him three weeks ago tomorrow."

"Buried? Buried who? Buried what?"

The old man had frowned. "Your brother. Liam."

Brand had dropped into a chair as if poleaxed, the whiskey forgotten.

"Drink it, son," the elderly lawyer ordered gruffly, and numbly, Brand obeyed. Without further comment, his host poured him another drink and proceeded to relate how Fallon had led her young bridegroom down a short, straight road to destruction. "Wild, she was. Everybody knew it. Her cousins up near Torrington couldn't wait to be shed of her. Didn't Galen tell you? He knew her. It was right after you left that she showed up—met him at a party, I believe. Some said she set her sights on Galen right off, I wouldn't know. Don't socialize much these days. At any rate, after he left home to follow you down to the coast, she took up with Liam."

"Why the devil didn't anyone tell me?" Brand demanded.

"Galen didn't mention her? But then, I suppose he left before she got her hooks into Liam. I wrote when things got bad. Wouldn't be surprised if a few others did, too, but your secretary said you'd gone to sea and he didn't know when you'd be back."

"I was looking for Galen. The *Mystic Wings* went down with all hands. I've been searching ever since we got word."

"Godamighty, son, I didn't know. Why didn't you write?"

Ignoring the question, Brand demanded to be told

everything. "I want to know what happened to the house—to Mama's harp and the paintings. To . . . to Liam."

The telling didn't take long. Before it ended, there were tears in the eyes of both men.

Fallon Webster, professing to have been recently orphaned, had come to live with her elderly cousins near Torrington. Beautiful and ambitious, she had promptly set out to lead every man for miles around on a merry chase.

"Like I said, she set her cap for Galen right off, but he was too wily for her. When he left, she turned her sights onto young Liam. He was always a favorite with the ladies. Nice manners, and I don't mind saying he was the handsomest of you three lads by a long shot. The fact that you and Galen had just signed over your shares in the most prosperous stud farm in these parts didn't hurt, either."

"You're saying she married him for his money?"

"Not necessarily. Liam was a fine lad. Nobody ever had a harsh word to say against him—at least, not until right lately."

Brand started to swear, but the older man ignored it. "A woman like Miss Fallon, she just naturally wants a man she can manage. And when a boy's set on rutting, he's not thinking with his brain. I doubt if you could've stopped him marrying her, even if you'd tried."

And so the story had unfolded, about how the young newlyweds had started hosting wild parties that lasted sometimes for weeks. Neglecting the farm. Gambling. Drinking to excess. One by one, the staff left, saying they hadn't been paid in more than six months and refused to put up with such shameful goings on.

"God, why didn't I know?" He'd been wild with shock, wild with grief, cursing his own negligence. "My secretary said something about some letters that had come while I was away, but I'd been gone since late summer. With Galen lost and Liam still to be told, the last thing on my mind was a bunch of business correspondence."

The truth was, he'd spent his first night back in Mystic alone in his rooms, wondering how he could bring himself to break the news to Liam. Wondering if he should wait a while longer, at least until he could rid himself of the feeling that somewhere in the world, Galen was still alive.

Having made up his mind in the small hours of the night that Liam had a right to know how things stood, he'd ridden out just after daybreak, still wearing the same salt-encrusted boots he'd worn for the past four months.

To find . . . this.

"She was what we called in my day a high-kicker. A greedy, wild woman is bad enough, but you take one as beautiful as Miss Fallon, and the devil never had a better handmaiden. They started selling off stock right away. I reckon it never occurred to her before she married the boy that farms, even the most prosperous, don't always have a lot of ready cash. I thought it was a shame, myself, but then, it was none of my business. Your pa's manager had been talking about retiring ever since your pa died. Liam, for all he was a fine boy, never had your pa's feeling for horseflesh."

A log settled in the fireplace, sending out a cheerful spattering of sparks. Brand hunched over his empty glass as pain and bitterness curdled inside him. "Tell me the rest," he said grimly. "I want to know exactly what happened."

"It was the race. They had the usual bunch of folks over there. Freeloaders, if you ask me. I was never invited to join them. Wouldn't have gone, even if I had been."

"The race," Brand prompted.

"Well, like I said, there was this house party in progress. They used to race your father's broodmares, and even that blue roan of his—"

"Mac the Knight," Brand supplied. McKnight Farm's

reputation had been built largely on the stallion's off-spring. "He's old. His eyes are bad. Liam knows—knew that."

"Still, he was a handsome animal. That bunch of high-living parasites were probably so drunk they'd have bet on a billy goat and never known the difference. Story is that Fallon dared your brother to race the Knight across the south field, all the way out to the main road and back, and then bet against him. Bet a whole lot of money, the way I heard it—more than she could afford to lose."

"She bet against her own husband?"

"They say Liam was drinking heavy that day. Even sober, though, he'd have likely done whatever she asked, he was that crazy about her. She probably knew the stallion was nearly blind, but the others didn't. Figured it was her ace in the hole, you might say."

"The bitch should be horsewhipped."

"I don't hold with woman-beating, but if ever a woman deserved it, then that one does. They say the Knight missed his footing at the second wall and went down with Liam under him. The boy landed on the wall, the way I heard it. Ruint his leg, busted his head, and did something to his back. Some of the men brought him home on a plank and sent for Doc West-fall. Doc stayed there three days, never slept a wink, they said, but in the end, he had to tell the boy he'd likely never walk again. Lucky he even survived. Ever-ette put the Knight down, and cried, they said, for a week afterward."

"But why didn't you—?"

"Do something? I tried. We all tried, but Liam begged us not to send for you until he'd had chance to come around. I figured about all the boy had left by that time was his pride, and even that had taken the devil of a beating. Promised he'd write you himself as soon as he got things back in shape around there. I thought I'd give him time to sort out his marriage, hire on a new manager, and start rebuilding."

"You should've let me know!"

"Do you think I don't know that?" Both men were yelling by then. "Do you think I haven't blamed myself a hundred times a day since then?"

The older man's anger served as a rebuke. At least Kondrake had been there. He'd tried. Brand hadn't bothered to come home for nearly two years. For that he could never forgive himself.

"Hindsight's a wonderful thing, son. Miss Fallon swore she was interviewing nurses to help her look after him. Instead, she turned off what few servants were still there, sold off everything that wasn't nailed down, and disappeared not two weeks after it happened."

"Didn't you even try to track her down?"

"I did, as a matter of fact. Her cousins over near Torrington didn't know where she'd gone. Didn't seem to care as long as she stayed away. Liam was in a bad way. I'm not sure he even knew what had happened. If I'd known how things were going to turn out, I'd have taken the boy home with me and locked him in until he came to his senses, but she took us all in. Standing there in the door whenever I went over, saying Liam was sleeping and couldn't be disturbed."

Brand groaned and buried his face in his hands.

"She was a fine little actress. Or maybe it was just those eyes of hers. I don't mind saying, I'm seventy-one years old, and I've never seen eyes like that before. Man gets so caught up in staring at her, he loses all sight of common sense."

Brand didn't want to hear all over again how beautiful she was. The woman was hideous. If it was the last thing he did, he would see her hang. "How long . . ."

"How long after she left did he shoot himself? Month, month and a half. Poor boy, he drove off anyone who came through the gate. Took to shooting at 'em. Shot at me more than once, but I knew he didn't mean it. It was when he didn't shoot that I knew something was wrong. I'd gone there after that hard blizzard we had, figured he could use some firewood. The boy managed to hobble around better than anyone ever thought he would, but that didn't mean he was up to chopping firewood."

Marshall smoothed back his thinning hair, his heavily veined hands none too steady. It occurred to Brand that his father would have been about the same age, had he lived. "Like I said, I knew something was wrong. I went in and found him in the library. At first I thought he'd fallen asleep." Looking tired and defeated, the old man sighed and shook his head. "Seated at the desk, he was. Gun on the floor beside him. He'd written a letter for you and Galen. I saved it for you. That and the picture of him and his wife they'd had taken when they eloped to New York."

Silence settled over the room, broken only by the snap of the fire and the muffled thud of wet snow sliding off the roof.

"I'll kill her," Brand said quietly.

"First you'll have to find her."

"I'll find her, all right. I'll find her if I have to search every mile of dirt between here and the Pacific Ocean."

And search he had, he thought now, stretching muscles stiff from weeks of travel, from following first one slender lead and then another. He hadn't found Galen after four months of searching. He hadn't found the woman responsible for Liam's death, yet, but he would. If he died trying, he would find her and make her pay.

Curiously enough, he'd discovered along the way that he wasn't the only man seeking her. Someone else was on her trail. Someone connected either to the fancy gambler she'd robbed and run out on in New York, or the politician she'd had a brief fling with in Washington, whose wife had threatened her with a lawsuit.

With a grim smile, Brand lifted the framed miniature he'd carried with him during weeks of travel and stared down at the sepia-toned image of his brother, sporting a new mustache and a proud grin as he stood beside a seated woman. A beautiful, high-breasted young woman in a seal-skin cape, with exquisite cheekbones, laughing eyes, and a smile that would tempt the serpent right out of the Garden of Eden.

Chapter Two

By the end of the third day of travel, Ana would have sold her soul for a bath and a change of clothing.

But then, she had already surrendered her soul to the devil.

Fallon Smith was an entertaining companion, for all she was a liar, a flirt, and possibly far worse. She teased and flirted with all the male travelers, but could turn cold and haughty in an instant if any one of them became too encroaching.

Ana knew she was a liar because the initials on the locket she wore were F.W. McK, not F.S. When Ana asked if the locket had belonged to someone in her family, Fallon admitted her name was actually McKnight, but she preferred to travel incognito because of her jealous fiancé.

But then, Ana had lied about her own name. The first time Fallon had called her Miss Jones, she had looked around for another woman. And when one of their fellow passengers had asked if they were sisters, Fallon had immediately said they were. Dear Ana, she had confided, was newly widowed and the two of them were traveling south to say good-bye to their beloved father, a highly respected minister who was leaving to join a foreign mission.

Ana had nearly strangled at that, but at least they'd been on a first-name basis from then on, which made it easier to remember who she was supposed to be. Scrupulously honest, she had always despised lies, considering those who resorted to lying cowardly and lacking in character.

And now she was not only living a lie, she was having trouble keeping her lies straight. Some women, no doubt, were suited to a life of high adventure. Unfortunately, she was not among them. Despite all the times she had chaffed at the limitations of her own dull existence, she would go back to it in a minute if only that were possible.

They were passing through Virginia when the sleet gave way to rain. Outside the windows, the world was a dismal shade of gray. Inside, it smelled like a cross between a stockyard and a cheap diner.

Not that Ana had ever experienced either. But if she never again smelled three-day-old sausage and onion sandwiches, it would be too soon.

Several times a day the butch came through hawking his wares. Fallon bought pies and sandwiches, fruit, candy and newspapers. Surprisingly enough, she spent hours each day poring over yesterday's news.

Ana counted out her pennies and bought apples and boiled eggs. She waited until Fallon was finished with the papers and then scoured them for a mention of a murder in northeastern Connecticut.

There was none. Which didn't mean Ludwig's body hadn't yet been discovered, it only meant that it wasn't tremendously important to the world outside Pomfret, especially in light of the terrible drought in the Plains and the continuing trouble with Chinese immigration.

It was cold. She didn't dare wear her shawl until she could wash it and try to remove the stains. Bloodstains were rather distinctive. They were also the very devil to bleach, especially in woolens. Now that the stains on her gown had dried, they didn't show, except in a certain light.

She wondered if the bruises on her body had begun to fade.

It didn't seem possible, even now, that someone had actually lifted a hand to her in violence. That sort of thing didn't happen to people in her circle.

Not that she even had a circle any longer. Even so,

people in Pomfret didn't resort to violence. Or if they did, no one ever heard about it.

Traveling, she thought, swaying as the train sped along at breathtaking speed, was dreadfully exhausting. She couldn't help but wonder why a woman like Fallon, a woman who dressed expensively and spoke disparagingly of the kind of men who could only afford to ride coach, wasn't traveling in the relative luxury of a Pullman car.

Although she herself was an heiress.

At least, her children would have been.

Not that she would ever have children now, and even if she should, she could never go back and claim their inheritance for them.

They had just crossed from Virginia into North Carolina early on the morning of the fourth day when Ana learned that Fallon was on her way to take a position as companion to an elderly couple who lived in an isolated area near Elizabeth City.

If she'd claimed to be on her way to meet a royal lover, or perhaps to a career on the stage, she might have believed her, but a mere companion?

Hardly.

Evidently she failed to hide her skepticism. Fallon shrugged and said, "Don't laugh, sister, dear, they're rich as Midas. Even you must have heard of Merriweather's Department Stores, they're all over New York. They say old man Merriweather sold out a few years ago and moved to some godforsaken place down south because his wife's crazy as a bedbug and it was either hide her somewhere or have her locked up in the loony bin."

Extending her limbs, she flexed her ankles in the stylish spool-heeled high-tops. "I don't know if I believe that or not. You know how gossip is. Still, I know for a fact the old stick's desperate for a nursemaid for his wife because I met a woman who had worked for him for a few weeks. She hated it. Not the work. That was easy. But the place is awful, she said."

Ana must have made some suitable response. Like most of her comments, it was ignored.

"Anyway, she said the old man has a bad heart or something like that, which means he doesn't have much to live for anymore, down there with nothing but a few noisy seagulls and a handful of servants to keep him company."

In growing dismay, Ana listened as the brash young woman went on to describe how she'd dashed off a letter and enclosed another one purporting to be a letter of recommendation. "Clever of me, wasn't it? All I did was slant my letters backward, and you'd never know they were both written by the same hand."

"But . . . but why on earth would you want to?"

"Maybe I felt sorry for the poor old stick."

Somehow, Ana found it difficult to believe Fallon was capable of feeling sympathy for anyone except perhaps for herself.

"Just imagine having all that lovely money and not being able to enjoy it. Besides, if you must know, I was looking for a place to lie low until my—until my fiancé loses interest, so when I heard about this opening for a genteel companion, I thought to myself, why not give it a whirl? Who knows, six months and I could be set for life if I play my cards right."

Ana cringed, but by this time little the younger woman did or said could shock her. A genteel companion? Hardly. Fallon was—

Well, she was simply Fallon. Brash, openly avaricious, but so striking she got away with saying things a less beautiful woman would never dream of saying.

Just how much of it was true, Ana wouldn't even venture to guess. One thing was growing more evident all the time, however. She was running away from something.

Or someone.

Each time they pulled into a station, Fallon would drop her veil, probably to hide those unusual eyes of hers, and study the face of every newcomer who boarded the train.

At least, every man.

Oddly enough, now that she'd grown accustomed to them, Ana hardly even noticed them anymore. A pair of mismatched eyes faded in comparison to her total lack of inhibitions.

Still, she was grateful for one thing. The puzzle of Fallon McKnight was so intriguing that for hours at a time she was almost able to forget the fact that she herself was a murderess, albeit an accidental one.

Not to mention the fact that she had barely enough money in hand to keep her until she could find work, and no skills to speak of except for taking care of a cantankerous old man who had sworn for years that he was on the verge of dying, thus keeping her chained to his bedside.

Marcus Gilbretta had used his illness to prevent his only child from cultivating a life of her own. In her rare free time while her father slept, she would stride alone across the countryside, dreaming of all the places she would travel if only she were free, and of the fascinating people she would meet there.

Ana was good at dreaming. If nothing else, she'd always been good at that.

On days when it was too wet to venture outside, she would shut herself inside her mother's old music room at the back of the house and pound on the piano. Mostly march music, badly played because she'd never had the patience to practice, even as a child. On bad days she simply played crashing chords. It was her own way of railing at fate. Afterward she felt relieved, if somewhat guilty.

But not all the pianos in the world would have brought her relief on the day her father had summoned her to his bedside to inform her that he had chosen her a husband.

Naturally, she'd protested.

Just as naturally, he had used the threat of his imminent demise to coerce her into obedience. The pattern itself was nothing new.

Ludwig Hebbel, Marcus had told her, was the son of an old friend who had died several years earlier. With the help of his lawyer, he had written and laid the proposition before him, and Ludwig had agreed.

"For God's sake, Papa, you're asking me to marry a man I've never even met?"

"Don't blaspheme, daughter. The boy's father was my dearest friend. We were at Exeter together. Besides, it's an accepted fact that women aren't capable of managing their affairs without the firm guidance of a man."

"It's never been accepted by me!" she'd all but shouted, horrified that he would do such a thing to the daughter he'd once professed to love.

The daughter who had stayed home to look after him all these years as one by one, her old friends married and settled down to have families of their own.

As usual, at the first sign of discord, Marcus Gilbretta had turned red as a beet. Ana had rushed to mix up his medicine. Meekly, he had swallowed the dose, and then informed her that everything had been settled. That she would be well looked after. That now he could go to his grave peacefully knowing she wouldn't fritter away his fortune on frivolous geegaws within the year.

"Geegaws! Papa, I haven't frivoled away a penny in years, and you know it!"

Ana had tried to argue, but Marcus had commenced to wheeze. She'd been left with two choices: she could stay and marry Ludwig and make her father happy. Or she could run away.

She had stayed, of course.

And ended up running away after all.

Now she flexed the tired muscles of her back. She would almost rather get out and walk the rest of the way than ride one more mile on the miserable, thinly padded seats. Daydreaming was one thing she did well. Walking was another, thanks to years of running upstairs and down, fetching whatever her father demanded, be it fried liver and onions for his blood, or medicinal brandy to ease his pain.

Etta's knees didn't take kindly to stairs. Sally was scared to death of the old man, and poor Samuels wasn't at his best in a sickroom.

She sighed and closed her eyes. Outside, the steam whistle sent a plaintive cry echoing over the countryside. Sitting up again, she flexed her shoulders and stared out through the filthy window at the strange, flat landscape, wondering if they were going to stop long enough for her to get off and stretch her limbs.

The brakes screeched and grabbed. The train began to slow down. A few minutes later the conductor stuck his head through the door to announce, "Libbacity!"

"We're here? This is it?" Ana clutched the armrest as the train jerked to a final stop. She wasn't sure she'd be able to stand, much less walk, after four days of traveling.

"Thank God! I'm so tired I could sleep for a week," came from across the aisle. Once again Fallon extended her shapely limbs and flexed her ankles. "The next time I go anywhere I'm traveling first class. No more cattle cars for me, thank you. I might even take a cruise. I've always wanted to see Paris."

Ana crammed the apple she'd just bought and barely tasted into her valise. Waste not, want not, her father had always said when she'd tried to convince him to spend money on improving the heating system or piping hot water up to the second floor.

So she'd wasted nothing and wanted a lot, but right now, all she wanted was a soft bed, a hot bath, and an enormous supper.

Oddly enough, the farther she'd traveled from Pomfret, the easier it was to forget the horror she'd left behind. It was almost sinfully easy to pretend that Ana Jones had sprung to life full grown somewhere in the middle of the country aboard a noisy, smelly train.

Libbacity—Elizabeth City—was a river city. More

of a town than a city, actually, although there were a
number of shops lining the main road and a bustling
waterfront near the depot. Once they left the train,
Fallon took out a letter, scanned it, frowned, and then
waved over a hackney.

Ana stood by uncertainly, her one valise in hand.
"I suppose I'd better find myself a room and start
inquiring about a position."

"You might as well come along with me," Fallon
tossed out carelessly.

"Won't the Merriweathers mind?"

"Not all the way, stupid. They don't live here in
town, they live on an island. I'm to let them know
when I get in and they'll make arrangements for me
to travel the rest of the way. In the meantime, they
not only bought my ticket, they wired money for a
hotel room, so you might as well come along while
you look for a job. We're sisters, remember?" She
grinned, and Ana thought with surprise, *I could almost
like her.* "Just in case anyone asks."

She was hardly the sort of woman Ana would have
chosen as a friend under normal circumstances, but a
thousand miles from all that was dear and familiar, it
was nice not to be entirely alone. By the time Fallon
left for her new position, Ana would have found work
and would be on the way to building a new life,
God willing.

A new life. Heavens, what a terrifying thought.

She had tried so hard not to think about all she was
leaving behind, but in her exhausted state, she was far
too vulnerable. Before she could help it she was picturing the worn, chintz-covered wing-backed chair
where she'd spent so many hours reading.

The little pear-wood desk that had belonged to her
mother, where she'd dashed off notes that her friends
had gradually ceased answering.

The forbidden novels she had squeezed money from
the housekeeping account to buy and then hidden
from her father. Etta had discovered them one day,
and after that they'd read them together each night

after her father fell asleep, sighing like a pair of moonstruck girls enjoying a guilty secret.

At the moment, however, Ana's biggest concern was not whether or not she would ever again enjoy such innocent pleasures. It was how long her money would last and whether to place an advertisement, post a notice in the village square, or seek out an employment agency. Those were decisions that would have to be made as soon as she'd had time to shake the wrinkles from her best dress, to bathe, and do something about her hair.

People milling about the siding stared at Fallon before she lowered her veil, glanced at Ana, and then back again to the vivacious younger woman.

Ana found it amusing, or would have done so if she hadn't been so very tired. It never occurred to her to resent it. No one could fail to be fascinated by a beautiful woman with eyes that didn't match—a woman who flirted as easily as she breathed, who changed her name at the drop of a hat and who made the most shocking statements as if she enjoyed being outrageous.

She was certainly entertaining, and at the moment, Ana welcomed any distraction from her own discouraging situation.

Of frame construction and questionable style, Brokerman's Riverside Hotel was far from luxurious, but according to the hackney driver, the town's premier hotel was filled with folks here for the christening of a new excursion boat.

Ana made a mental note to inquire tomorrow about a position either at the busy hotel or aboard the new excursion boat. She wasn't entirely sure what an excursion boat was, but any new enterprise seemed a promising place to look for work.

Fallon swept through the dozen or so men loitering in the lobby, fully aware of the effect she created. She was veiled again, but even so she had a way of carrying herself that called attention to her feminine attributes. "Your best room for my sister and me," she demanded.

The desk clerk blinked, stammered, and nearly swallowed his Adam's apple. "Bed and a trundle, ma'am. Best I can do. We're full up, what with the big party to launch the new excursion boat. She's fixin' to set out on her maiden cruise tomorrow. Band's down at the courthouse square right now, practicing for the send-off, if you'd like to go down and listen."

Ana wouldn't have walked across the room to hear the grandest band in all the world. A bed, even the meanest trundle, sounded heavenly.

The second-floor room was located halfway along the hallway. The wooden floors were uncarpeted, the walls unpainted and darkened by years of smoky lamps, but at least the place seemed reasonably clean. Fallon followed the boy struggling under the weight of her trunk and three hatboxes while Ana hurried to keep up, her single valise slapping against her legs.

Surveying the room's meager furnishings, Fallon pointed an imperious finger at a door in one wall. "What's that, a water closet?"

"Connecting rooms, ma'am. All the best hotels has 'em now. Stays hooked less'n the parties wants to un-hook 'em."

"I want a key."

"Yes, ma'am."

"And an extra blanket. A clean one. And bring a tub into the room and plenty of hot water—and make sure it's hot, not lukewarm. And I'd like my dinner served in my room, too. Bring up a bill of fare when you bring the hot water."

The boy took off his cap and wiped his brow. "Be cheaper in the dining room."

"Don't be impertinent. Hurry with that hot water, and don't forget my blanket."

Meanwhile, Ana had discovered the trundle, which was nothing more than naked gray canvas stretched over an iron frame. "Might I have bedding for this, please?" she inquired timidly, and the bell boy tugged his forelock and promised to fetch it quick as a tick.

Her stomach growled. She wondered if meals were expensive. Never having stayed in a hotel before, she had no idea of costs, but she was heartily sick of boiled eggs.

Brandon spent the night in Norfolk, betting that Liam's widow would have left the train there, even though she'd bought a ticket to a small town a few miles south of the North Carolina line.

He was on to her tricks by now. She liked big cities. The bigger, the better. Either for the entertainment afforded there or because it was easier to hide, he wasn't sure which, but it hadn't taken him long to discover that she invariably took an indirect route to reach her destination.

He had managed to corner the senatorial candidate whose career she had nearly ruined before his aides could buy her off. After showing her photograph and claiming to be a distant relative, he'd been told that she'd been offered her choice of a lawsuit or a hundred dollars and a one-way ticket to New Orleans.

Accepting the latter option, she had promptly sold her ticket to an unscrupulous conductor who slipped her onto a train to Boston instead. The conductor had resold her ticket, pocketed the money, and been fired for his troubles.

Fallon had gotten clean away, and Brand had wasted valuable time showing her picture around the train station in New Orleans before backtracking and picking up the Boston lead.

The lady didn't miss a trick. If he hadn't hated her so thoroughly, he might even have admired her ingenuity. When the trail had led him from Boston back to Connecticut, he'd taken time to go by his office in Mystic, hoping against hope for some word from Galen.

There'd been no word, of course, but at least he'd saved his frantic assistant from brain fever by making a few vital business decisions and signing all the documents awaiting his signature. With half an hour to spare before his train left, he'd paid up the rent on his rooms and set out again.

It was after following a zigzag trail across the state that he'd learned that two women, both strongly resembling the photograph he carried, had boarded a southbound train in Pomfret after buying tickets to a small town in North Carolina. Certain he was finally on the verge of finding her, he'd run smack into the tale of two sisters.

To his almost certain knowledge, Fallon McKnight's only relatives were the two spinster cousins near Torrington. If she had a sister, Liam had never mentioned her.

But then, she could have lied to Liam. Had most definitely lied to him. He was coming to believe her whole life was a lie.

God, what a wretched mess! Cursing under his breath, Brand stirred sugar into his coffee in a Norfolk hotel dining room. His own business was in danger of falling apart, and he couldn't drum up enough interest to care.

Two things drove him: grief and a thirst for revenge.

Later that same evening, ignoring the sounds of wheels on cobbled streets that filtered through his second-story window, he concentrated on what he knew and what he had yet to learn.

First of all, was he chasing two women, or one? Was Miss Smith, Miss or Mrs. Jones and Miss McKnight one and the same person?

If there was another woman involved, who the devil was she?

Who was the other man he kept hearing about, the one who was following the same crazy trail he'd been following ever since he'd left Litchfield Hills after visiting his brother's grave?

He'd heard various descriptions of the man who managed to stay a few days ahead of him, inquiring after a woman who fit the description of Liam's widow. One man said he spoke with a midwestern accent, looked like a farmer, and claimed the woman was his wife who had lost her memory after their child had died of the diphtheria.

A ticket agent in Baltimore had described him as a good-looking young fellow, but called him a bad sort. Trouble on two legs.

Brand couldn't see his brother's widow wasting her time on a hayseed farmer, good-looking or not, unless he was extremely well-heeled. By now he'd concluded the man must be one of the parasites Marshall Kondrake had described, who had sponged off Liam's goodwill until the money and the liquor had run out. Who knows what his relationship with Fallon had been? She certainly hadn't been his wife. She'd been Liam's wife, although not necessarily a faithful one.

By midmorning, Ana realized that she'd made a mistake in coming to a town so small. Other than ship-building and shipping, there was no industry. Women's work, other than the domestic sort, was impossible to find. She wasn't particularly good at cooking, but she could do it. She could certainly manage a household. She'd been doing it since she was fifteen, but she'd had Etta and Sally to help her.

Poor Etta. Poor Samuels. Where were they now?

Sally lived with her family. She would be taken care of, but Etta had only an elderly sister, and Samuels had no one. It hurt terribly to know they thought her a murderer.

The excursion boat idea hadn't worked out. The woman doing the hiring was the daughter of the boat's owner. Miss Aster Tyler had made Ana stand in the center of the room and then walked around her, examining her as if she were a cow at the county fair. The questions she'd asked had been more about her personal life than her accomplishments.

"How old are you?"

"Twenty-seven."

"You look older than that."

"I'm not. I was twenty-seven on my last birthday."

Which had been nearly a year ago.

"Have you been ill?"

"I'm not sure what you mean."

"Are you hard of hearing?"

"No."

"I asked if you'd been ill. You don't look healthy to me."

For goodness sake, what would you expect, Ana had been tempted to exclaim, after losing my father, being repeatedly beaten and raped, and then killing my husband to keep him from killing me?

She had worked it out in her mind that way. Self-defense. Escaping Ludwig's brutality had been her only intent. When she'd managed to break out of the room and race downstairs to her father's study, her only thought was to grab the housekeeping money and get away.

Somewhere.

Anywhere!

Shaking so hard she could barely grab the knob, she hadn't even thought about her father's pistol. The drawer jammed. She jiggled it to force it open. The cash box slid back and the pistol skidded sideways. Ludwig had burst in and lunged for her just as she had shoved the thing out of the way to reach for the cash box. Her hand had fallen on the walnut grip, and evidently he'd thought she meant to use it. He'd tried to snatch it away, and she'd been terrified that he would use it on her, so she'd held on to it.

If only he hadn't struck her then . . .

But he had. And the gun had exploded. They'd both stared down at the blood blossoming on the front of his shirt, and then Ludwig had crumpled to the floor, his pale eyes silently rebuking her.

Suddenly she'd become a murderer.

Dear God in Heaven . . .

"My father died recently," she said quietly now. "I nursed him for the past several years. It was . . . a rather exhausting period."

"You're in mourning? That's why you're dressed the way you're dressed? It won't do. I need pretty women who know how to wear good clothes and make the gentlemen forget how much money they're losing."

Ana gazed down at the plain woolen gown she had dyed black. It had once been dark green. At least this one didn't have bloodstains on the sleeve and skirt tail. "I look nice in green," she murmured hopefully.

At least she'd looked nice in green back when she'd had color in her cheeks and luster in her brown hair, and a few more pounds both above and below her waist.

"Come back next week. If I don't find anyone else, I might give you a try. You'll have to learn how to walk and speak like a lady, but at least you know how to stand."

Speak like a lady! You mean learn how to speak with my mouth full of molasses the way you do? Ana wanted to ask. As for her posture, she couldn't have stood any straighter if she'd had a board strapped to her back. Temper always did that to her. Stiffened her spine.

A pigtailed maid no bigger than a minute rapped on the door frame and said, "Miss Aster, yo' Papa said to tell you to don't go hirin' no mo' ladies less'n he sees 'em fust."

Miss Aster said a bad word.

Ana made her escape. "Miss Aster, indeed. *Dis*aster is more like it," she muttered on the march back to Brokerman's Riverside Hotel.

Now what? See if either hotels needed a housekeeper? Inquire if there were any elderly gentlemen in town in need of a general dogsbody to fetch and carry for them, to play chess and read the newspapers to them, hear their complaints, tend their ailments, and accept the blame for all the world's ills?

No thank you. She'd sooner sell sausage and onion sandwiches on the coach to hell.

* * *

Two days later she was almost ready to give up and throw herself on the mercy of the courts. At least prison would provide her with a roof over her head and something to eat until she took her last dreary walk to the gallows.

Oh, for Heaven's sake, Anamarie, don't be so melodramatic!

"I'm taking the steamer first thing tomorrow. What are you going to do?"

Ana sighed and continued darning Fallon's silk stocking. Rather than part with the few dollars she had left, she had agreed to serve as lady's maid to the younger woman in exchange for the trundle and her meals.

"I don't know. Would you give me a reference as a lady's maid, or should I write my own?" It was said half in jest, but Ana knew it might come to that. She was desperate enough to take the most menial position at this point, and not be any too particular about how she got it.

Fear and hunger did that to a woman.

Lucky Fallon. Not only had her new employers paid her fare and her room and board until the thrice-weekly steamer sailed, they had sent her enough money to buy anything she might need before she left town, as there were no stores at Merriweather's Landing.

"Oh, by the way, the clerk said someone was asking about a woman with eyes like yours." Ana had stopped by the desk to ask if there'd been a reply to the one-line advertisement she had placed in the Elizabeth City daily paper.

A hairbrush clattered to the floor. Ana glanced up and was shocked to see the expression on Fallon's face.

"He's here," she whispered.

"Who's here? Fallon, who is this man who's following you? And don't tell me he's a jealous fiancé, because I won't believe it."

"Would you believe he's my husband?"

She looked ghastly. All color had fled her face, leaving circles of rouge standing out like red bruises. "I might," Ana ventured.

"Oh, God, why didn't that blasted boat leave yesterday? If he finds me, he'll kill me! One more day, and I'd have been in a place he'd never even dream of looking."

"Can't you reason with him? If you truly don't want to be married to him," and Ana could certainly understand that, "then I'm sure there must be a way—"

"You don't understand, he'll kill me! I ran away! I was only sixteen, and he was so handsome, but I *hated* being married to a poor man. I'm too beautiful to bury myself in the Kansas dirt and work myself to death, everybody said so." She was sobbing too hard to tell the rest of the story.

Not that Ana wanted to hear it. Beset by her own problems, she couldn't take on any more, she simply couldn't. Here in this place that was so very different from all she'd known before, she had been able to go for hours at a time without remembering, without being overcome by the sheer horror of what she had done and why she had done it.

The days were bad. The nights were worst of all. She was afraid to fall asleep at night for fear of the nightmares that beset her.

As suddenly as they'd begun, Fallon's tears ended. She stared at Ana through those disconcerting mismatched eyes and said, "You're the sensible one. I always fall apart at the first sign of unpleasantness, but you're older. You'll simply have to reason with him. If I don't go to meet him, he'll come up here, thinking he's finally tracked me down, only it won't be me, it will be a woman who looks like me."

She beamed just as if she hadn't been crying a moment before. "Of course, you're taller and skinnier and not as pretty, but maybe he won't remember. And we'll have to think of something to do about your eyes. I don't suppose you have a pair of tinted eyeglasses? Never mind, I'll lend you a veil."

She began rummaging through a dresser drawer. Now that she had handed over her problem to someone else, she was all smiles.

Ana stood, clutching the half-mended stocking to her bosom. "Fallon, I couldn't possibly—"

"Yes, you can. You owe me that much. If it weren't for me, you'd be sleeping in alleys, starving to death, or selling yourself for the price of a meal."

"Indeed, I would not!"

"Yes, you would, and you know it. Look at you— you go for an interview and come back dragging like the ragtag end of the world. You put an advertisement in the paper that all but says you can't do anything worthwhile."

"I did no such thing."

" 'Refined lady seeks position.' Ha! If that doesn't spell it out, I don't know what would. Position as what? Typist? Cook? Seamstress? You couldn't say any of those because you can't do any of those things."

"The paper charges by the word. I was only being frugal."

"Yes, well, you can have my room all to yourself tonight. And supper sent up. It won't cost you a penny, is that frugal enough for you? I'll sleep in the next room. It's empty. I happen to know because I went in there to see if the couple who rented it had left anything behind."

"But what if it's rented out again?"

Fallon shrugged. "If anyone comes to the door, I'll tell them they've made a mistake. Hotels never like to have a wrangle in the hallway, not even dumps like this. It gives the place a bad name."

And thus it was that when the hotel caught fire that night and nearly burned to the ground, Fallon and Ana were sleeping in separate rooms.

It was one of the clerks who brought her the sad news the next morning. The guests—at least the ones who'd survived—had been carried to a nearby boardinghouse, and were settled on pallets on the floor while a physician examined those who'd been injured.

Ana, dazed and suffering from smoke inhalation, was unable to speak. The physician told her she would recover her voice in a day or so, but warned her not to rush things.

And then the hotel manager came by, knelt beside her, and took her grimy hand in his. "Miss McKnight, I'm afraid I have bad news for you. Mrs. Jones is—that is, she was—what I mean to say is, I'm terribly sorry to have to tell you, but your sister didn't survive the fire."

Chapter Three

It was as if fate had picked up her life, toyed with it the way a bored child would toy with a ball, bouncing it and catching it, whacking it with a stick, and then moved on to another toy, the ball forgotten.

What did it all mean? Here she was, in a strange Southern town with no money, no prospects, no chance of ever going home again. She'd lost everything, and now the hotel manager had broken the news of *her death*?

Ana had opened her mouth to correct him and started coughing so hard the physician had hurried to her side to caution her about straining her throat. "You had a very close call, young lady—a very close call, indeed."

And so the error had gone uncorrected. In a few short weeks she'd gone from being Ana Gilbretta to Ana Hebbel, and from Ana Hebbel to Ana Jones. And now, through no conscious decision on her part, she was Miss McKnight. Fallon McKnight. Brash, shameless, flirtatious Fallon McKnight. Young, beautiful Fallon McKnight.

Frightened Fallon McKnight.

Merciful heavens, wasn't it obvious to the most casual onlooker that she was taller, thinner, years older, and nowhere near as pretty?

True, their features were remarkably similar, as was the color of their hair. Although Ana's hair was more chestnut than auburn and thicker than Fallon's, a fact of which she'd been secretly proud. Perhaps because there was so little else she could take pride in.

But the eyes alone should have given her away. Ana's eyes were brown. Once a warm, gold-flecked amber, they were now bloodshot, dulled by grief, smoke, fear, and too many sleepless nights. In all the chaos, no one had noticed.

But the thing that had tipped the scales was that Ana had been sleeping in Fallon's bed. Not knowing where she'd be sleeping once Fallon left town, she'd been unable to resist the temptation of a decent night's sleep in a real bed. The thought had occurred to her that perhaps the nightmares wouldn't follow her there.

And so, in the middle of the night, after twisting and turning on her miserable canvas cot, trying to discover a position that wouldn't leave fresh bruises on unhealed old ones, she had crawled up onto Fallon's feather bed and slept soundly until she'd been wakened by the smoke and the sound of screams and someone pounding on her door.

Although she had dreamed . . .

It must have been a dream. The face of a stranger distorted by lamplight, peering down at her—his look of disbelief when she'd opened her eyes and blinked up at him, and then his exclamation of frustration.

It had to have been a dream. Part of the nightmare her life had recently become.

"Ma'am, there's a man from the newspaper here. He's talking to the folks that wants to talk." It was the maid assigned by the boardinghouse to look after their unexpected guests. The girl who had helped her bathe away some of the grime. Ana opened her mouth to reply, started coughing, and shook her head. *I don't want to see anyone,* she mouthed silently.

"Then don't you fret none, I'll keep 'im away," the maid declared earnestly. "They been takin' pitchers for the newspaper. Miz Hollowell done run 'em out, but they were a-snappity-snapping all over the place with that pitcher-taking machine. Me, I wouldn't want my pitcher in the papers, not if I was looking as awful as . . ."

The girl blushed and broke off. Ana managed a smile. Even looking her best, the last thing she needed was to have her face plastered all over the front page of the newspaper where anyone could see it and discover where she was hiding.

Awkwardly, the girl smoothed the dingy sheet provided by the establishment over her shoulders and backed away, twisting her hands in front of her. They were red, callused hands, the fingernails chewed to the quick. The colorless rag she was wearing under her filthy apron had been patched so many times it looked like a crazy quilt, but she wore a stringy pink ribbon bow in her orange hair, a brave statement that brought a fresh flood of tears to Ana's eyes.

Poor child. Was she hoping some fine young man would recognize her true worth by her brave show of femininity and rescue her from a life of drudgery?

Ana could have told her that life didn't work that way.

"Is there anything else I can do for you, ma'am?"

Ana opened her mouth, wheezed, and shook her head. *No thank you,* she mouthed.

Sooner or later she would have to write to the Merriweathers and explain what had happened. Right now, all in the world she wanted to do was hide her face under the covers until the world began to make sense again.

"I'll bring you some water, then. We're havin' soup for supper, and I'll be sure you get a chunk of meat in your bowl."

"Water," someone called hoarsely.

"Yessir, jest a minute."

"I need a preacher. Can someone find me a preacher?" another asked.

"He's around here som'ers, I'll see if I c'n find him," the maid replied.

"What about my clothes? I had a brand-new outfit from Baltimore—and my jewels! Who's gonna replace my jewels?"

That brought on a flurry of queries concerning any

luggage that might have survived the fire, and Ana, once more alone in her cramped corner of the lobby, turned away and allowed the tears to come.

Luggage?

Forget her luggage, what about her life? What was she supposed to do now? Even if she'd had the courage, she lacked the funds to go back home and face the authorities. Did that mean she was fated to go on running for the rest of her life?

She couldn't even afford to do that.

Two days later, using the funds she found among Fallon's possessions, Ana paid for a simple marker for a woman named Anamarie G. Hebbel, b. September 9, 1860, d. March 11, 1888.

Half expecting to be damned to hell for her lie, she was almost disappointed when no one challenged her.

But then, what harm could it possibly do? Poor Fallon was beyond all earthly help. According to her own account, she had no family. Then, too, she reasoned, if anyone had followed her from Connecticut, the trail would end here.

As the only mourner at her own funeral, Ana wished she'd thought to buy a wreath. Wished she could have said good-bye. She had a feeling Fallon would have understood why she'd allowed the mistake to go uncorrected.

Fallon's clothes and hers had all been thrown in together. The sealskin cape, singed and reeking of smoke. Rings, bracelet and hairbrush, slippers and that pretty monogrammed locket Fallon had worn so proudly.

Dear Lord, it hurt. What made it even worse was that she could grieve far more for someone she had known only a matter of days than she had for her own father.

And then she'd opened the locket and found . . .

Nothing. It was empty. And somehow, that was sadder, still.

God forgive me, she prayed when she should have

been praying for the immortal soul of the woman who had died so tragically.

Dragging a sleeve across her wet eyes, she knelt and dug a small hole in the dark damp clay, dropped in the locket and bracelet and covered it up again.

Fallon had been wearing her ring when she'd died, but her hands—her face—

Oh, God. "I'm sorry," Ana whispered. "I'm so very sorry."

It had been misting rain all morning. Turning her back on the bleak scene, she wiped the mud from her bare hands, pulled her stained shawl closer around her shoulders, and trudged toward the hackney driver waiting outside the wrought-iron fence to drive her to the docks.

It was late morning before they set out on the first leg of the journey to Merriweather's Landing. A misty rain still shrouded the cypress-lined banks of the Pasquotank River as the *Curlew* pulled away from the busy waterfront. Ana stood apart from the other passengers, lost in thought.

Have I done the right thing?

Did you have any choice?

One always had choices. The last time, allowing panic to direct her course, she had run away.

This time she had followed the line of least resistance.

Watching a bit of refuse floating on the surface of the river until it was caught up in the churning wake and lost, she felt a certain sense of inevitability. She could fight the currents, or she could allow them to take her where they would.

It was a choice, perhaps, but hardly an encouraging one.

Most of Fallon's belongings had survived the fire. Ana had given the clothing to the young maid in the boardinghouse, who'd been pathetically grateful. The fur cape she had asked to be donated to the local relief fund. She could have certainly used a warmer cloak, but her conscience would never have allowed her to wear it.

However, the steamer ticket was another matter. It seemed only sensible to make use of that, the overnight reservation at a hotel, and the passage reserved for her aboard a smaller ferry for the last leg of the journey to Merriweather's Landing.

If she hadn't impulsively allowed the mistaken names to go uncorrected and buried poor Fallon as Anamarie G. Hebbel, she could still have confessed and eased the burden on her conscience.

She could still . . .

No, she couldn't. A poor, desperate man had hired Fallon McKnight to serve as companion to his invalid wife. Fallon McKnight was not about to disappoint him. If there was one thing in the world Ana was capable of, it was caring for an elderly invalid. Perhaps in some small way she could make restitution for all the deceit.

Throat raw, chest aching, she stood near the stern of the chunky little steamer and watched Elizabeth City fade into the misty rain. Later on, once she'd had time to recover and think about it, she would decide how much to tell the Merriweathers. At the moment, all she wanted to do was sleep for a year.

It was early the next morning after a largely sleepless night in a small beach hotel, when Ana handed her valise to Pam the ferryman, who took one look at her wan face and made her a place to lie down inside the sheltered cuddy, out of reach of rain or sea spray.

Ana went willingly. Yesterday's trip aboard the steamer hadn't particularly bothered her, although she'd never set foot on a boat before.

A small sailboat was another matter. Aboard the *Curlew* she hadn't been so close to the water. There'd been noisy boilers, splashing paddles, and at least a dozen talkative passengers to distract her.

Here she felt far more vulnerable. The boat was too small. There were no other passengers, only the crack of canvas overhead and the rushing sound of water to distract her from a growing sense of unease.

That and the constant rolling and pitching.

She groaned, closed her eyes in the cramped, musty quarters and wondered what fate had in store for her next.

The sun broke through while Brandon McKnight stood outside what remained of Brokerman's Riverside Hotel. Half of the structure still stood, a smoke-stained bedroom and part of a stairway looking incongruous in the watery sunlight. The rear portion had collapsed, the second floor falling in on the kitchen and dining room below. The fire, someone said, probably started in the kitchen from a faulty flue. Someone else said it looked as though it had started in one of the second-floor rooms.

Brandon didn't particularly care. He had too many unanswered questions of his own. Why was Fallon McKnight traveling with a woman who claimed to be her sister? A woman who went by the name of Ana Jones, but had been buried as Anamarie G. Hebbel?

Why, indeed? Once again he had the uneasy feeling that something was wrong. But what? And why? And what did the fire have to do with anything?

A young man wearing a bell boy's cap sidled up beside him, looking as if he hadn't slept in days. "Shame about the McKnight sisters. The one with the eyes was prettier, but the one that died was a heck of a lot nicer."

"Eyes?" It wasn't the first time he'd heard mention of the woman's eyes. The photograph he carried didn't show much detail, but evidently there was something memorable about her eyes. "What about her eyes?"

"The crazy colors."

"What crazy colors? Pink? Burgundy?"

"Ha! That'd be something, wouldn't it? Funny thing though," the young man went on, "after a while you don't even notice it anymore. She was a real beauty, even if she was sort of snappish. Treated her sister like she was some kind of a maid or something, always ordering her around, making her sleep on that trundle."

That certainly sounded like the Fallon he had come to know, Brand told himself with grim satisfaction.

"Never did figure out what they were going to do at Merriweather's Landing," the youth added thoughtfully. "You wouldn't think a lively woman like her would cotton to a place like that."

Brand promptly forgot about the eyes. "Merriweather's Landing?"

"Down near Oregon Inlet. Nothing there but the old man's castle. Funny thing, though—if the older one hadn't snuck into the room next door instead of sleeping in the trundle, she might've still been alive. Not that I blame her, what with an empty bed in the next room going to waste. Our trundles aren't nothing but canvas on a stretcher. Myself, I'd sooner sleep on the floor. Costs thirty-five cents a night with a blanket and pillow, too. They say she was burned real bad. I didn't see her, I was over at Doc's place getting my hands fixed up, but believe me, from now on I'm only going to work in brick hotels, even if I have to go all the way to Norfolk to find me another job."

Brand glanced at the fellow's bandaged hands, made a perfunctory remark, and continued to stare at the place where he'd come so close to catching up with his quarry. He supposed he was sorry about the sister, but he hadn't known her. And if she was anything like Liam's Fallon, he wouldn't have wanted to.

Merriweather's Landing. He'd never heard of the place, but every mariner along the eastern seaboard knew where Oregon Inlet was.

Still, the clerk had a point. Just what the bloody hell was a woman like Fallon McKnight doing in a place like that?

It occurred to him that the description of the place might offer a clue. A castle? If there was money involved, that would do it. If there was one thing he'd learned about the woman his brother had married and

then died for, it was that she liked money and men,
in that order.

And that she was totally heartless, strikingly beautiful, and incredibly avaricious.

And that there was something about her eyes that
attracted notice. Whatever it was, either it didn't show
up in a photograph, or he was immune.

He was immune, all right. So damned immune he
intended to wring some answers out of her and then
haul what was left of her to the nearest court of law
and let them finish the job.

*Merciful heavens, Ana, what have you gotten youself
into this time?*

Not for the first time, Ana forced back the panic
that threatened to engulf her. By the time they ap-
proached the low, marsh-edged island late that afternoon, most of the clouds had disappeared. A watery
sun glinted off the surface of the dark, choppy Pamlico Sound.

Yet, oddly enough, she felt rested. For the first time
since she'd left home she had slept without dreaming.
She, who had never taken naps, had slept away the
entire afternoon, lulled by the motion of the boat and
the sound of water rushing past the hull.

Her throat was still sore, her chest still ached, but
she'd discovered, somewhat to her surprise, that she
was a fairly decent sailor. With so little to be proud
of, she would snatch her pride where she could find it.

The scent of Pam's pipe tobacco drifted past, reminding her of the happier times before her mother
died, when her father would lean on the gate, pipe
cupped in his hands, and watch her jump rope, or
throw sticks for her puppy to retrieve. Anamarie, he'd
called her. He always called her by her full name.

Anamarie, come to tea.

Anamarie, get down from that tree.

It had been a game they played. Rhyming. But then
her mother had taken a sudden illness and died, and
almost overnight her father had turned into a stranger,

a brooding man who had no time to spare for a lost and grieving child.

"Poor baby," Etta had murmured, gathering the gawky adolescent Ana on her lap. "He'll get over it, give him time."

But he never had. Instead, he'd grown more and more withdrawn and eventually he'd taken to his bed.

And now Anamarie was dead and buried near the edge of a deep, dark river near a stand of dripping cypress trees, and Fallon McKnight had become a woman with no past and no future.

A woman who had precisely eleven dollars and seventeen cents, two gowns, two pairs of shoes, a badly stained cashmere shawl, and barely enough underwear to get by unless she washed it out each night.

Anamarie, it's up to thee.

"Landin' off to th' sta'board. See the castle from here. If I'm not mistook, that's Miss Drucy out there a-waitin' for you, poor lady. Don't let on like you notice nothing. It upsets her."

Filling her lungs with damp, salt air, Ana gripped the rail and watched the shore approach. There was indeed a woman waiting. A woman waving something that looked like . . . a stocking?

The little sailboat glided up to the wharf, bumped gently, and then a line snaked out to wrap itself around a piling. "Good luck to ye, Missy. They're fine folk, even if they are Yankees."

And what do you think I am? Ana wanted to say, but didn't.

It was called Pea Island for a wildflower that covered the dunes in late summer, that much Pam had told her when she'd emerged from the cuddy earlier. There were two structures visible from where she stood, a shed and a tall, turreted building called the castle, sunlight glinting off its dozens of windows and spanking-white gingerbread trim.

According to the ferryman, who delivered freight and mail along this section of the Outer Banks, there was a Lifesaving Station manned entirely by a Negro crew near a shallow inlet that opened and closed according to the whims of nature. Beyond that point, there were still more in the long chain of barrier islands.

It was Pam who introduced the two women once Ana and her valise had been set ashore. Then, shifting his pipe between his few remaining teeth, he cast off, allowing his sails to fill again.

Ana watched with a growing feeling of panic as the weathered little skipjack veered out into the channel. It was all she could do not to call him back. Now that she'd committed herself to this course of action, she was beginning to have serious doubts.

Doubts that felt remarkably like panic.

And then she heard her father's voice. *Anamarie, it's up to thee. Sink or swim, which will it be?*

Well.

"Now, who did you say you are?"

Turning, Ana forced a smile for the elderly woman who barely came up to her shoulders. There was an elflike quality to Miss Drucy Merriweather, with her wispy white hair, her sparkling blue eyes, and her flowered, bedraggled gown. She was wearing a man's tweed coat and holding a stocking in one hand.

She was barefooted.

Taking a deep breath, Ana said, "Mrs. Merriweather, I'm Fallon. Fallon McKnight."

At least, she was doing her best to think of herself as Fallon until she made up her mind what to do about her identity.

"I don't know you, do I? I can't always tell, you know. People change."

And then she was off on a tale about someone named Tom and some children who . . . rode wild horses in the ocean?

Ana thought about Mr. Carroll's tale of a girl named Alice who suddenly found herself lost in a strange world peopled by even stranger creatures.

"I'll take you to see them tomorrow," the woman who'd been introduced as Miss Drucy confided.

"Tom and the children?"

"What children? I'll tell you a secret. I'm going to ride one tomorrow. The one with the white nose. Now, what did you say your name was?"

Utterly confused, Ana could only repeat the lie. Trudging through the deep sand, she tried desperately to keep up with the older woman, a task which was easier to manage physically than mentally.

Riding sea horses with white noses? And who was Tom? Who were the children? She could've sworn Fallon said there was no one here except for an old man, his wife, and a handful of servants.

It didn't take long to learn the answers to most of her questions, for both Merriweathers were inclined to be talkative. The servants were treated almost like family, which Ana found unusual, but not at all disagreeable. She'd always considered Etta and Samuels part of her own family, even if her father hadn't.

She explained about her voice and about the fire, but somehow she never quite got around to mentioning a woman named Ana G. Hebbel.

Thomas, she learned, was the Merriweathers' widowed son who lived with his two children in a small town near Buffalo, New York. Fallon hadn't mentioned those. Probably hadn't known about them.

There was also what was called an all-around man named George Gill, who had been called back home to his father's bedside in upstate New York, leaving the Merriweathers shorthanded.

She also learned that there were indeed wild horses on the island. And that Miss Drucy considered them her own special province.

In his elegantly furnished, well-stocked library, Maurice Merriweather explained her duties as companion to his wife. "Mrs. Merriweather's needs are quite simple," said the thin, well-dressed gentleman in the wheelchair. "We've lived here for several years now, but I'm afraid my wife is still lonely. I believe she misses her friends. We enjoyed a rather active social life back in Buffalo."

Ana thought it was far more likely that it was he who missed his friends, but said nothing. It was plain to see that Miss Drucy was a rather special woman with special needs. "I understand," she said tactfully, thinking it was no wonder a body grew lonely in this bleak and desolate place, especially having come from a large city.

Right from the first she found herself drawn to the elderly couple, partly because of their need, but mostly because of her own. Their obvious loneliness struck a responsive chord in her own heart.

"If you're a reader, my library is at your disposal. I'm afraid I'm rather short of fiction, but I'm perfectly willing to order any titles you wish, and I do subscribe to a number of periodicals and newspapers, which you're welcome to share. Of course, they're sometimes weeks old by the time they arrive."

Ana thought of the way she used to have to pinch pennies to buy books and then sneak around to hide them from her father. She could have wept if she hadn't already wrung herself dry.

"Oh, and we've a piano, though I'm afraid it's somewhat out of tune. I've sent for a tuner, but so far he hasn't arrived. My wife used to play. Lately, though . . ." The old man's gaze drifted away to a time and place Ana could only imagine.

And then he brightened again. "Chess. Now I don't suppose you play chess, do you? Or a rousing game of pinochle?"

She was struck by his whimsical smile. "As a matter of fact, I used to play both cards and chess with my father." Ana's voice was still hoarse, but her cough was much improved. "I'm a better chess player than I am a musician, Mr. Merriweather, but that's not to say I'm particularly good at either."

"Wonderful, wonderful! Please call me Mr. Merry, my dear, and I do hope you'll be happy here."

As easily as that, it seemed her immediate future

was settled. She was to keep Miss Drucy company, play the piano for her when and if it ever got tuned, walk with her, talk with her and then, after dinner, once her charge was settled for the night—if she had any energy left—she might indulge Mr. Merry in a game of chess or perhaps cards.

At least her nightmares hadn't followed her. That alone made it easier to come to terms with her circumstances.

Easier to forget that she had a home in Connecticut to which she could never return, an inheritance she would never be able to claim, a few friends she hadn't seen in years and now would never see again.

Her honor was already lost. If she returned to Connecticut she could very well lose her life, and Ludwig simply wasn't worth it.

Given a moment alone to take stock, she summed up her situation. At least here she was not only wanted, she was needed. Miss Drucy, as everyone called her, was sweet, gentle, vague, untidy, and inclined to wander. Both mentally and physically.

Mr. Merry hadn't mentioned his own condition, but evidently it left him somewhat breathless and unable to move about freely. Much of his time, it seemed, was spent in a wheelchair in his extensive library. From the looks of it, he had books on every subject from astronomy to zoology. Surely there was room for a few novels.

It was plain as day that he adored his wife and was extremely protective of her, which made it all the harder that he was totally dependent on servants to keep her from wandering away.

That would be Ana's job. "Not that there's anyone here to hurt her, you understand," he'd assured her.

She'd asked about the dangers of being so close to the water, not to mention the miles of desolate beach where a body might wander for days and not be found, and he'd nodded in agreement.

"There's that, of course. Which is one of the reasons I hope you'll be content to stay with us for a while."

Ana hoped so, too. She couldn't keep on running forever.

Aside from the Merriweathers, the household was composed of Maureen the cook-housekeeper, who was round of figure, kind of heart, and as Irish as her name implied even though she'd left Ireland as a child a long, long time ago.

There was Evard, a shy young man of sixteen who was cousin to Simmy the maid, who was even younger and pretty as a fawn. Both came from one of the villages on the island just south of Pea Island. They'd been recruited by the absent all-around man before he'd left.

Other than that, there was only Mr. Hobbs, the elderly valet who attended to Mr. Merry's personal needs, and Pam the ferryman, who brought over mail, supplies, and the rare visitor.

Although, strictly speaking, the ferryman could hardly be counted as a member of the household.

After the meeting with her employer, Ana had been sent to bed to rest before dinner. It was nearly dark by the time she found her way downstairs again, feeling considerably rested if still somewhat rocky from the long boat trip.

"I'm so terribly sorry. I never meant to sleep so long," she apologized.

Maureen scolded her as if she were a child. "Whisht now, girl, a body needs sleep to mend. You set down here and eat every bite of your supper. I kept it warm for you, knowing you'd wake up starving hungry. It's the salt air. I'm thinkin' ye're skinny as a knitting needle, that's the Lord's truth."

And thus, without quite realizing how it happened, Ana became a part of the household before she'd even made up her mind to stay.

The letter came less than a week later. Addressed to Mr. Maurice Merriweather of Merriweather's Landing on Pea Island, near Oregon Inlet, it advised them that a Mr. Neil Dalton, civil engineer, would be in the area for the next few weeks studying the navigational hazards of the inlet, and would take the liberty of calling on Mr. Merriweather if that was agreeable.

It was more than agreeable. Ana couldn't help but be touched by the change that came over the old man at the prospect of male companionship. She suspected that despite his own infirmities, he had sacrificed greatly to bring his wife to a place where she would be relatively safe.

Maureen, who had moved south along with George Gill and the Merriweathers, confided that Miss Drucy had gone funny in the head and taken to wandering in and out of strange houses without so much as a by-your-leave. Once she'd been missing for nearly eighteen hours and to this day, no one knew where she'd been.

Mr. Merry dashed off a reply that very morning and sent Evard out to hail Pam on his return journey to the mainland. "He'll stay here, of course. Maureen, see about airing a room if you will. The southwest wing, I believe, don't you?"

Ana thought he had the look of a boy on Christmas Eve, and was touched.

"Evard, you'd better set the big net in the morning," Mr. Merry added. "We'll be needing more fish once our guest arrives. Miss Fallon, I'd appreciate it greatly if you would see to entertaining Miss Drucy while Mr. Dalton is here. She tends to become overexcited sometimes and . . . well, I'm sure you understand."

He wheeled himself across to a large table that had been specially designed for his use. "Now, where do you suppose I put those charts? I was studying them just the other day. . . ."

Ana had quickly come to understand her responsibilities. She watched Miss Drucy and entertained her, and whenever possible, pitched in and helped with whatever else needed doing. With a guest on the way, there was much to be done.

Between taking up oysters and fishing his net, Evard

had his hands full. Maureen set to work in the kitchen while Simmy dashed upstairs to see to readying a room.

Even Mr. Hobbs, the dapper little gentleman's gentleman, seemed to take on a new vitality.

It was impossible not to be affected. A cheerful feeling of excitement hummed throughout the household. Snatches of song came from the kitchen. Linens were aired, rugs were beaten, delicious scents filled the air.

It was contagious. For the first time in weeks—in months—Ana felt a surge of optimism.

It was in the midst of all this that Miss Drucy went missing. Leaving her charge in the kitchen with an old newspaper and a pair of blunt-tipped scissors, Ana had hurried upstairs for their shawls. She'd promised a walk as the weather had turned off so fine, but evidently the lady had grown impatient. When Ana came downstairs again, she was nowhere to be found.

It was nothing out of the ordinary, Ana was assured, but with the March weather so fickle, cold and wet one moment, bright and blustery the next, she would have to be found in case she decided to go in search of her sea horses.

That had been known to happen. According to Maureen, she'd been brought home dripping wet more than a few times, usually by George or Evard, but once by one of the men from the Lifesaving Station.

"She can't have gone very far," said Ana, trying and failing not to feel guilty. "I was only gone for a minute. I'll start with the soundside—we were going to walk there to see if there were any horses today, and she probably went on ahead."

The ferryman dropped the mains'le and glided alongside the rough plank wharf. Brand uncoiled the line and waited, scanning a marshy shoreline riddled with narrow creeks, ponds, and small bays. He'd spent too many years on boats and ships of all sizes and descriptions to stand on ceremony. Tossing the line over the nearest piling, he made it fast and began gathering up his gear, trying unsuccessfully to subdue the simmering excitement that had been building in him for the past several days.

He had tracked her down. Finally, after weeks of racketing up and down the eastern seaboard, following one false lead after another, he had her right where he wanted her, trapped on a tiny island with nowhere to run for cover.

She'd arrived a week ago, according to the ferryman, after journeying from Elizabeth City to Nags Head aboard the same steamer Brand had taken. She had actually stayed in the same half-deserted beach hotel. He'd even seen her name on the register.

And short of swimming or hitching a ride with a passing fisherman, there was no way in hell she could escape. There were a few small boats out in the sound now that the weather had cleared up. According to the ferryman, there'd be even more later in the season, but few of them stopped at Merriweather's Landing.

Breathing in the familiar pungent smell of salt air, Brand shoved back his impatience. He felt like storming the damn castle, prying her out of her hiding place and—

Easy, man, easy—time's on your side.

It was sweet, indeed. Now that he had her where he wanted her, he could afford to wait, to hint at his true identity and watch the fear grow in her eyes. He'd gone over it a hundred times in his mind, planning ways he could reveal himself to her.

Not right off, though. He wasn't above playing cat and mouse.

Wasn't above watching her squirm. Watching the panic creep into those crazy colored eyes of hers.

He would let her beg and then savor her terror once she realized she couldn't manipulate him the way she'd done all her other men. And if that made him a sadistic monster, so be it. Such a woman didn't deserve to live.

Lucky for her he didn't simply break her treacherous neck. Unfortunately, there was no law against a woman's driving a man to take his own life, and if he lost control and took matters into his own hands, he'd only hang for it.

Not that his life held much meaning now that both Liam and Galen were dead, but he refused to give the bitch the satisfaction of claiming yet another man's life.

His craggy face giving away no hint of his angry thoughts, he paid the ferryman, took up his bundle, and stepped out onto a small, weathered wharf. Time was on his side, he reminded himself once again. On this narrow, all but deserted sandbar there was nowhere she could hide that he couldn't find her.

"There's Miss Fallon now," the ferryman said as he prepared to cast off again.

Brand stared. He felt an odd prickling sensation come over him. The last time he'd felt anything like it, he'd been trying to break up a knife fight among the crew of one of his ships. He'd waded in unarmed and nearly had his throat cut.

This time, he thought with a surge of quiet satisfaction, it wasn't his own life that was hanging in the balance. He stood for a moment watching the wind catch her gown and press it against her body.

She was thin. Thinner than she'd looked in the picture.

Sunlight splintered rainbows in her hair. It highlighted those cheekbones he remembered so well from the photograph. He couldn't see her eyes from here, but . . .

Judas priest, she was actually coming to meet him.

For the first time it occurred to him that she might recognize him. True, he looked nothing at all like Liam, but there was a strong family resemblance between him and Galen despite the difference in coloring, and she'd known Galen.

From behind him, the ferryman called out, "Afternoon, Miss Fallon. Ain't that Miss Drucy down by the point?"

Halfway along the path that led to the wharf, Ana shielded her eyes against the sun and followed the ferryman's gaze. "Oh, dear, I believe you're right." With only a cursory glance at the man who'd just stepped ashore, she hurried toward a lump of something she'd taken for a stump or a heap of eel grass cast ashore by the tide.

The lump moved. It was Miss Drucy, all right. Now that she was closer, Ana recognized that blue-flowered bottom. She was on her hands and knees in the wet marsh grass, and thinking she must have tripped and fallen, Ana gathered up her skirts and broke into a run, only dimly aware that the man who'd come in on the ferry was following her.

"Is something amiss?"

Without slowing up, she glanced over her shoulders. "I'm not sure," she panted.

It occurred to her that he might not be their engineer. He could be the all-around man. He could even be the piano tuner.

No, not the piano tuner. Not with those shoulders.

But what, she thought with a stab of fear, if he was a policeman, come to arrest her for murder?

With the sun behind him, she could see little of his features, nothing at all of his expression.

Whoever he was, at the moment she didn't have time to worry about him, policeman or not. Saw grass whipped past her ankles, stinging her legs through the thin stockings.

"Miss Drucy, stay right there, I'm coming!"

The stranger was right on her heels. Catching up with her, he matched his stride to hers. "Neil Dalton," he said, not even breathing hard. "I believe I was expected?"

At the sound of the familiar New England accent, Ana's heart did a flip-flop in her breast, but then, there was Miss Drucy, and she was in trouble. There was simply no time now to sort it all out.

"An—Fallon McKnight," she gasped without slowing. Neil Dalton. That was the engineer's name, wasn't it? "Listen, she might not want to go back with me. I'm not sure what to do . . ."

"Who is it?"

Quickly, Ana sketched in the circumstances. "I don't want to upset her, but I don't really know her well enough yet to know how to handle her when she's—um, like this."

For a civil engineer, the man seemed to radiate a lot of anger, but then, what did she know about engineers, civil or uncivil? With Miss Drucy bent double in the muck, with all the broken shells and knife-sharp grass, she had more to worry over than a surly stranger.

"Miss Drucy, are you—?"

"Shhh, they've been drinking. Oh, is this your young man?" Her expression totally guileless, the elderly woman beamed up at them. "How lovely. Fallon, I think . . . I think . . ." She hesitated, as if searching for the next word. "Oh, yes. My sea horses have been drinking again."

Limp with relief, Ana knelt beside her charge on the wet turf. "Have you been digging, Miss Drucy? Oh, look at your poor hands. We'd better go wash them and let Maureen put something on the cuts."

"No, no, no!" Drucy pulled away and Ana was forced to kneel there, knees sinking slowly and painfully into the wet turf, while the old woman gave a disjointed account of the drinking habits of wild horses.

"They dig with their hooves to find fresh water, because they can't drink salt water. I asked Tom, and he said—well, he said something, I forget what. The leader's called Caliban. I gave him his name. He already had one. I'm sure his mama must have named him when he was born, but I keep forgetting what it is."

Ana nodded, nothing in her expression even hinting that there was anything out of the ordinary in what Miss Drucy was saying.

Off to one side, the stranger stood perfectly still.

Watching. She caught a glimpse of his face, angled as it was to the sun, and was struck by the strength of his features.

He was a Northerner. There was nothing at all in that to trigger her suspicions. The Merriweathers were Northerners, too. So were half the population of the country, in fact.

Besides, if he truly had been following Ana Hebbel, the trail had ended elsewhere.

He continued to study her, his eyes conveying little besides a certain coldness that Ana marked down to her raw imagination.

Or her guilty conscience.

Tiring of the mud hole, Miss Drucy plopped back on her seat in the wet turf, her skinny bare legs sprawled out before her, and gazed from one face to the other, a bright, expectant look in her faded eyes. "My, he's a handsome boy, isn't he?"

Still kneeling, Ana stared openly at the man who towered over her. He wasn't handsome. He was certainly no boy. Even so, there was a something about him—a heightened masculinity, for want of a better description—that triggered a peculiar sort of excitement inside her.

Surely an odd reaction for a woman whose experience with men was both limited and painful.

He was staring at her as if she were one of his engineering projects, and he had suddenly discovered a serious flaw in the plans. Was it something she'd done? Something she'd said? As they'd hardly exchanged more than a dozen words, and all those had been about Miss Drucy, Ana told herself it must be some inherent lacking in her own personality.

Which was rather sad, but there you were. Ludwig hadn't liked her, either.

Shaking off the odd sensation of being studied like a bug pinned to a corkboard, Ana turned to the old woman. "Why don't we go home now and ask Maureen for a carrot? Perhaps if we left a treat here by the edge of the, um—the drinking fountain, we could watch from the window upstairs and see if your horses can be lured from their hiding place."

Mr. Dalton snorted. Or at least, she thought he did. Turning, she glared at him over her shoulder. "Don't let us keep you, sir. I believe you're expected up at the castle?"

He smiled then, reminding her of a German shepherd that had turned up unexpectedly one morning at her back door back home in Pomfret. The creature had probably only been hungry, but it had had a way of growling and lifting the corners of his mouth at the same time that was disconcerting, to say the least.

"I have all the time in the world, Miss Fallon," he said quietly. "All the time in the world."

Chapter Four

Halfway between the castle and the landing, having gone back for his luggage, Brandon stood with a canvas bundle slung over his shoulder and watched the two women make their way to the castle.

Something didn't add up here.

At the moment, he couldn't put his finger on what was wrong, but something was definitely out of kilter. If there was one thing he'd learned early in life, however, it was that a rider who valued his neck never rushed his fences.

He could wait. He'd waited this long; he could wait a bit longer until she gave herself away. As inevitably, she would. How long could such a creature be content to hide out here in a place where there were few men, no wild parties, and no riches to rake into her own pocket?

Personally, he rather liked what he could see of the place. He could understand how some might call it barren. Bleak. Even desolate. A few weather-beaten shrubs huddling protectively near the cupoloed, shake-clad dwelling. Patches of wild grass here and there. Straggling, all-but-leafless vines hanging on for dear life against the winds. The usual stretches of marsh on the soundside.

Other than that, there was only sand. Sand and water, as far as the eye could see. Eastward, a few hundred yards away, lay the Atlantic, her breakers clearly visible from where he was standing. To the west lay the largest sound on the East Coast, the Pamlico.

Someone had put out a net. A small sail skiff was pulled up on shore, her mast bare, her canvas rolled neatly around the boom. Some fifty or so feet offshore was a brushy shelter that was probably a duck blind.

Which meant there were fish and fowl. Probably not much else in the way of game, but still, a man, if he were determined enough, could live comfortably in a place like this.

As for how a woman would manage, that was a different matter. Women, at least the breed of women he was familiar with, required more care than a hothouse rose.

Brand stroked his jaw thoughtfully. It might be interesting to see just how long the little bitch would last.

Out over the inlet a shoal of gulls hovered, their sun-gilded wings tilting with the wind. Brand looked about for a sheltering dune, but found none. He'd come fully prepared to camp out if he had to, but he'd hoped for an invitation. Having done his homework, he knew that until a few years ago, Merriweather had led a busy and successful life, traveling extensively to expand the business his father had begun, turning one small shop into a growing number of fine mercantile establishments.

Then suddenly, for reasons that were never fully explained, he had turned everything over to his son and a select few shareholders, pulled up stakes, and removed with his wife and a handful of servants to a place so barren and isolated it didn't even have a name.

Since then, a series of companions had come and gone, none able to withstand the loneliness and the harsh conditions. Fallon, curiously enough, was the latest of those.

And while Brand was reluctant to impose himself on the hospitality of strangers, he was determined to do what had to be done to achieve his ends. There was a moral law, if not a written one, against a woman using her beauty to drive an innocent man to his destruction. Before he left this island, he promised himself, she would be on her knees begging his forgiveness, if not actually pleading for her life.

As if a few crocodile tears—or even his own forgiveness—could bring back the man she'd driven to suicide.

Shifting the heavy canvas bundle that contained a bedroll, a change of clothing, and a rudimentary tent, he followed the path taken by the two women.

She was a clever piece, he'd hand her that.

Liam's Lorelei. Easy to see how the poor lad had been taken in. The way she handled the old woman, anyone who didn't know her would almost believe she had a heart.

Filling his lungs with the pungent salt air, he was reminded of another coast, one that lay far to the north. God knows when he'd see Mystic Harbor again. He'd given his assistant a power of attorney to do business in his stead until this thing was finished. It was either that or see the remains of what he'd built there go under. If only for the sake of his grandfather's memory, he was reluctant to see that happen.

The civil engineer ploy had been the first thing that had come to mind once he'd discovered where Fallon was hiding. As a ship owner and mariner, he had a basic knowledge that would have to serve until his business here was done. Unable to come up with a better excuse, he'd dashed off a letter, sent it by the first boat headed in the right direction, and followed it as quickly as he'd dared, still seething with the anger that had driven him for so long.

Now that he'd arrived, however, it was time to bank the coals of his anger. Although come to think of it, what he was feeling at the moment was not so much anger as a sense of accomplishment.

Almost, in fact, a feeling of anticipation.

The house did indeed resemble a sand castle. He couldn't imagine what would prompt anyone to build such a fanciful structure in so isolated a location, but then, someone had once asked him the purpose of a figurehead on a ship and he'd had a hard time coming up with a reply that hadn't sounded pretty idiotic.

Here goes, he thought, and rapped on the door frame.

Someone called out for him to enter. "Oh, it's you. Please do come in." On her knees, Fallon was toweling sand from the old woman's bare feet and listening to a rambling discourse on devil's pocketbooks.

She glanced up at him, then back at the woman. "Excuse me a moment, Miss Drucy," she said, and then, turned to look over her shoulder again. "Sorry we ran off that way. I was afraid Miss Drucy would take a chill. Did you get everything? I could send Evard down to collect whatever you left behind."

Brand watched as an array of emotions flickered across her expressive face. Amusement, apology—an artless smile that might have been convincing if he hadn't known her for what she was.

Clever, he thought. Damned clever. He'd always relished a challenge.

It occurred to him that with a thick crop of chestnut hair tumbling down her back where the wind had whipped it free, her face flushed by the same wind, and those famous gold-shot eyes of hers glowing as if she'd been lit up internally, she was even more beautiful than her photograph.

Beautiful, greedy, and deadly, he reminded himself forcefully. But then, certain qualities were impossible to transfer onto a cardboard image.

Lowering his compact bundle, he used the few moments it took to wipe his boots free of sand to solidify his defenses. Unlike Liam, he was no green youth to be taken in by a pretty face and a few seductive tricks.

"Miss McKnight, where do you suggest I leave my equipment?" He deliberately called her Miss instead of according her the status of widow to see if she would correct him.

She didn't. Still holding a damp foot in her hand,

she feigned confusion. "Oh, I—that is, I'm not sure. You could leave it here for now, I suppose. But we've aired out one of the guest rooms if you'd rather take it directly upstairs."

With that she turned back to her charge. "Miss Drucy, I think we'd better have ourselves a nice hot soak, don't you? Your hands and feet are like ice." Miss Drucy, for all she'd been bright as a button down at the shore only a few minutes earlier, now appeared tired and docile.

The two women disappeared inside the house, leaving Brand entertaining an unbidden vision of Fallon soaking in a tub of hot water, her face damp, her breasts and shoulders dripping soapsuds.

Swearing softly under his breath, he glanced around the enclosed porch, wondering whether or not he was supposed to follow her inside.

He could camp here if he had to. The walls came only halfway up, but at least there was a roof overhead. Several pairs of boots in assorted sizes were aligned on a shelf. Rain gear hung from hooks mounted on a rafter, as did two lanterns. Other than that there was a small table, painted grass green, two chairs painted to match, a fishing pole, a bucket and a dip net.

Casual and comfortable were the words that came to mind. More like a fishing camp than a castle.

Which made Fallon's presence here all the more puzzling.

On the other hand, if a woman wanted to hide from a pursuer, she could hardly do much better.

He gathered up the bundle that held his camping gear—a roll of canvas, pegs, lines, and a sleeping roll—and stashed it in an empty corner. As for his clothing, he'd brought along only enough to get him through a few days. A week should be more than enough time to achieve his ends.

Upstairs, she'd said. Was he supposed to barge ahead or wait politely to be shown the way? Never one to stand on ceremony, he drew the line at entering a strange house without the owner's permission.

So much for storming the castle and capturing the enemy before she'd had time to shore up her defenses.

The thought brought with it a fleeting smile as he pictured three tattered, grimy boys, the youngest only five, the eldest all of sixteen and too old for such play. As soldiers, they had stormed many a castle, slain many a dragon, and rescued many a fair maid.

God, so long ago. . . .

The quiet passage of rubber-rimmed wheels along bare wooden floors alerted him to the approach of his host, and he braced himself to lie to a man whose hospitality he was about to abuse.

"Mr. Dalton, I'm delighted to see you. Fallon said you'd arrived. Come in, come in, we don't stand on ceremony around here. I expect you could do with a warming drink after your crossing."

Brand shook hands with the elderly gentleman whose clasp was surprisingly strong for an invalid. Briefly, the two men remarked on the weather, on Brand's passage out from Elizabeth City, and on his supposed mission.

"You'll stay here with us until your work is completed, of course."

Feeling the screws of his conscience tighten another few turns, he said, "I don't want to impose, sir. I'd be perfectly comfortable—"

"Nonsense. If it will make it any easier, suppose we make a deal?"

A deal? He was in no position to make a deal. Something of his wariness must have shown on his face.

"I assure you, it won't require much of your time. None at all, I sincerely hope, but the thing is, we're rather shorthanded here since my bailiff left to be with his father—the poor man's gravely ill. Naturally, I don't expect you to take George's place, but one never knows when an emergency might arise. I'd feel far easier in my mind knowing there was another able-bodied man within call."

Brand found his modest, self-deprecating smile enormously touching. "I'd be delighted to be called on, sir. I'm only here to observe and make notes, which shouldn't require too much time. I'll look forward to an opportunity to make myself useful."

What he looked forward to was a chance to ease his conscience. If he'd thought things through more thoroughly before foisting himself off on Merriweather's hospitality, he'd have insisted on begging only a place to pitch his tent.

Not that he favored a lumpy bedroll over a dry, comfortable bed. But this way he'd be close at hand to set his trap and watch while she blundered into it.

"Shall we toast our agreement with a glass of wine? Or something stronger if you'd prefer. Maureen will have dinner directly. We're rather informal here, you'll find. We all sit down together." Again that apologetic smile. "Maureen and my dear Mr. Hobbs have been with me forever, and as for the other two members of the staff, they're only children. Children, I've always held, can best be taught properly by example."

"That sounds fine to me, sir."

"Well now, that's all settled. Do you know, I was just looking over a collection of old charts before you arrived. You might be interested. Early sixteenth century, right up to modern times. Amazing thing, the way inlets come and go for no apparent reason. Something to do with the littoral currents, I expect. Now, you take the one to the south of us. According to these old charts it's literally a case of here today, gone tomorrow."

Thus, for the next hour or so, Brand found himself sipping a regional wine made from the native scuppernong grapes, studying old maps and navigational charts, and discussing shipping and politics with his erudite host. Gradually, without his even realizing it, some of his burden of grief and anger began to loosen its grip.

He yawned and asked to be pardoned.

"Yes, of course. Understandable on a day like this, with a crackling fire on an open hearth." The old man remained in his wheelchair, a lap robe arranged over his knees, but there were several comfortable chairs scattered around the long, many-windowed room. Brand had chosen one well away from the fire.

"These new furnaces are all very well, but when it comes to putting a man at ease, there's nothing like an open fire, I always say."

Brand nodded. The combination of heat, wine, and the feeling of having finally arrived at his destination after so long was beginning to make him feel drowsy.

Or perhaps it was a case of too many sleepless nights.

Outside, the wind whistled around corners, eaves, and cupolas, accentuating the coziness inside as dusk settled over the island. Lest he fall to snoring right where he sat, he rose and moved to stand beside a window, hiding another yawn.

Obviously, the ploy didn't work. "It is rather warm in here, isn't it?" Again that twinkling smile. "With George gone, Mr. Hobbs has taken over the duty of laying the fires. He tends to overdo it. I do enjoy a driftwood fire, though. It takes more heat to warm old bones, though I like to pretend it's only to keep away mildew."

Brand nodded. "The books, you mean. My father used to have trouble with mildew, and we didn't even live on the coast."

He'd thought his father's library was impressive. It couldn't compare to this one. He said as much and was touched by the look of pleasure the words brought.

The entire castle, or what he'd seen of it so far, seemed to be a comfortable blend of styles, elegant but unpretentious. The juniper-paneled walls had been left unvarnished so that the spicy smell of the wood blended with salt air, the scent of leather and burning wood, and the subtle aroma of beeswax. A few of the floors were covered with handsome Persian rugs, but most had been left bare for easier access by wheelchair.

Picturing his own shabby rooms in a boardinghouse one block off the Mystic waterfront, rooms that had been furnished in his landlady's taste, Brand told himself it was time he began looking around for something more comfortable, something more permanent.

And then he felt guilty all over again, for even thinking of his own comfort when Liam and Galen were . . .

Unexpectedly, another yawn overtook him. "I assure you, it's not the company, sir. It's just that I've been traveling for weeks now. Hotel beds aren't always the most comfortable."

"You must lead a fascinating life, young man. Perhaps when you've had time to catch up on your rest and get started on your task, you might find time to share a few of your adventures. As you can see, I live a somewhat circumscribed life these days." It was said so wistfully that Brand felt like the lowest form of life.

Damn the woman for what she'd forced him to become!

Ana waited until the two men were once more cloistered in the library after supper and Miss Drucy was settled for the night before she allowed herself to take out the handful of impressions she'd collected and examine them, one by one.

Neil Dalton. My, what a striking gentleman. Even to a woman in her situation, bereaved and guilty of not only a crime but a mortal sin, there was something about him that made her feel . . .

Well. She wasn't entirely certain what it was she felt, but she felt *something* in his presence.

She most definitely felt *something*.

All during the evening meal his gaze kept returning to her. Not that he stared openly. Nothing quite so obvious. All the same, she would sense his gaze on her, and her cheeks would catch fire and she'd find herself dropping things. Spoons. Her napkin.

Even now the thought of it was enough to bring a rush of heat to her face.

And at the moment, Fallon McKnight was extremely tired. Miss Drucy had been even more distracted than usual tonight, probably due to all the excitement. Wearing one of her prettiest dresses—she had dozens of gowns, all the finest quality—with her wispy hair teased into a pompadour and anchored with pearl-trimmed combs, she'd looked witty and bright and charming.

She would smile at some remark of her husband's, but the smile would remain fixed on her face long after the moment had passed, accompanied by a growing look of confusion, almost of panic.

Ana had felt like gathering the poor old dear in her arms and comforting her as she might have comforted a child.

Not that she'd ever had the chance to comfort a child. Nor was she ever likely to.

To his credit, Neil Dalton had treated both Merriweathers with the same unfailing courtesy. He and Mr. Merry found scores of topics to discuss. But unless she was imagining things, his manner toward her had been considerably cooler.

Could she have imagined it?

No, she most definitely had not. She'd been far too aware of everything about the man.

Still was, even in retrospect, more's the pity.

But she was quite sure of one thing: she had not been mistaken in the glacial quality both his eyes and his voice took on whenever he'd addressed her.

As in, "Are you enjoying your stay at the seacoast, Miss McKnight? That is *Miss* McKnight, isn't it? We were never properly introduced."

The challenge in his tone had been so blatant she'd

been amazed that no one else had seemed to notice. She had prayed for the meal to end so she could escape, all the while wondering if she were being overly sensitive.

Possibly.

Of course she was. The man had no earthly reason to dislike her. He'd only just met her. Even Ludwig had pretended to like her for the first few days.

Her thoughts drifting like wisps of morning mist, she went about getting ready for bed, a simple matter of a hundred strokes, a slathering of the lavender-and-lemongrass lotion Maureen had given her when she'd noticed the condition of her hands, and kneeling to say her prayers.

Dear Father, I've done the best I could today. If it's not enough, I'm sorry. I promise to try harder tomorrow. Bless Miss Drucy and Mr. Merry and—

She sighed.

"Amen," she whispered. Folding her arms on the bed, she rested her forehead for a moment and allowed the impressions to flood in on her.

Mr. Hobbs dyed his hair. The white roots showed quite plainly. Starchy little man . . .

Maureen had taken off the white collar she wore during the day, that was tied at the back with tapes, and put on a lace collar, fastened in the front with a cameo.

Mr. Merry didn't eat enough to keep a bird alive. He looked as if he weighed no more than Miss Drucy, and Ana could have carried poor Miss Drucy, soaking wet, in her arms if she had to.

It had nearly broken her heart to see the way the poor dear would bravely hang on to a panic-stricken smile long after she'd forgotten what she was smiling about.

Tonight she had suddenly pushed away from the table, mumbling something about finding her shoes. "I left them down on the shoreside."

"No, Evard brought them home and we left them in the vestibule to dry, remember? That's why you're wearing your black kid slippers tonight." Ana had half risen, ready to lead her upstairs and settle her for the night when Mr. Dalton had stood to pull back her chair.

In the process his hand had brushed her shoulder. If a spark had snapped up from the fireplace and landed on her naked skin, the effect could not have been any more startling.

Judging from the way he'd stared at her, he'd felt it, too.

How strange, she thought after finishing her prayers and folding back the covers on her bed. Evidently the fortress she had carefully erected to protect herself still had a few serious flaws.

He didn't like her. Not one bit.

Now why should she think that? He didn't even know her.

With a sigh, she set it down to her own guilty conscience and crawled into bed. He'd be gone in a few days. After a few more days, she would have forgotten all about him.

Brand left the house shortly after breakfast the next morning. He had some thinking to do, and it was hard to think when at any moment Fallon might swirl into a room. It had happened already twice this morning.

The first time she claimed she was looking for Miss Drucy's shawl. He'd been standing beside the table, one of the old charts spread out before him—the things were damned interesting, even to a man who had no real interest in the region—when she'd popped in, stopped short, and stammered out an apology.

"You don't need to apologize, *Miss* McKnight." He'd deliberately stressed her title again. She was no more a Miss than he was President Cleveland, dammit! She knew it. *He* knew it.

What's more, he wanted her to know he knew it.

He'd been struck all over again by certain subtleties that could be masked by the impersonal lens of a camera. She looked older than he knew her to be. Physically beautiful, but in a different way from what he'd expected. The hollows under those flawlessly sculpted cheekbones were more pronounced than in the picture, but then, being on the run for so long might do that to a woman.

In the photograph, under a hat roughly the size and shape of a birdbath, her hair had been not all that impressive.

Now, without the hat, it was thick, lustrous, with a tendency to curl, the color a perfect match for her eyes.

As for the eyes themselves, he wasn't quite sure what all the hubbub had been about. They were large, expressive, and heavily lashed, the color nice enough, but hardly unusual. He'd expected brilliant blue, or possibly emerald green. Even purple or aqua.

Something, at any rate, more spectacular than light brown.

Although there were those gold flecks. Not visible from a distance, but fascinating at close range.

"Were you looking for this?" he inquired, his voice even, his face a polite mask. He handed over the shawl that had obviously fallen from the back of a chair, and she snatched it as if she'd expected him to jerk it away at the last minute.

Ah-ha. He had her on edge.

With a grim sense of satisfaction, Brand had told himself he had her on the run now. It was a start.

But the next time he'd seen her, it was he who'd been left wondering. She'd been in the kitchen, holding both Miss Drucy's hands while the old woman had twisted and tried to pull away.

"No, dear—it isn't safe. Evard just sharpened it and you might accidentally cut yourself."

"But I won't! I never, ever cut myself! I need to cut through the roots so my sea horses can find water. Evard said their hooves are dull from the sand, and that means they can't cut through the roots."

Fallon had succeeded in making her drop the knife, but by then the old woman had been sobbing pitifully and looking lost again. While Brand watched from the doorway, Fallon had gathered the weeping woman to her breast just as if she were a child, and spoken softly for several minutes. In the end, Miss Drucy had sniffed, wiped her nose on the back of her hand, and said, "You promise? You won't forget? Can we go now?"

"Yes, dearest, we can go right now. Let's put on your old boots so you won't ruin your pretty slippers, shall we?"

He'd backed away and silently closed the door. Lacking any notion of what she was up to, much less what it was she'd prevented Miss Drucy from doing, he had to admit she had dealt well with what could have been a dangerous situation. Not with force. Not with demands. Not by stamping her foot and threatening to leave if the woman didn't hand over the wicked-looking butcher knife this minute.

For a spoiled, selfish young woman, he had to admit she had handled it well. Fallon McKnight, it seemed, was playing a deeper game than he'd suspected. He'd thought she was merely hiding in an attempt to elude her followers.

Now he was beginning to wonder.

He also wondered, not for the first time, just who her other follower was?

Had the fellow given up?

What if he should turn up here, demanding whatever satisfaction he sought? Which one of them would take precedence when it came to exacting revenge?

First come, first served, Brand thought as he let himself outside, a notebook, pencil, and a pair of binoculars tucked into the pockets of his canvas coat.

While Ana stood on the shoulders of the spade until it sunk into the sand, cutting through the roots of the marsh grass, Miss Drucy prattled aimlessly about roses and teaching Tom to ride a bicycle. There were times when her mind was clear as a bell, when she knew who she was and just how she fit into the three generations of Merriweathers.

There were other times when she forgot she had a son, much less grandsons. Forgot she even had a husband. Forgot that the wild horses that roamed the beach weren't the same as the sea horses that swam—somewhere, if not here—beneath the surface.

Ana was exhausted. Her feet were damp, her cheeks were chapped by too much wind and sun, but they stayed outside until Maureen clanged the ship's bell mounted just outside the back door because Miss Drucy hated to be inside when it wasn't actually raining cats and dogs.

Gratefully, Ana put away the spade and the two women went inside, still discussing the bed they were preparing for roses.

"The big pink ones with cream-tipped petals. I forget what they're called, but we must have those."

"Yes, dear, of course. And perhaps some of those lovely deep rose-colored ones, too, if they'll grow in sand." Ana brought up the rear, lugging bucket, boots, bonnet, and shawl, all discarded over the course of the morning. Some things, she was discovering, were worth fighting over—others weren't. With the sun blazing down from a cloudless sky, it was warm despite the damp wind. Ana's back might be broken and her skin felt as if it had been parched in a hot oven—indeed, she was turning brown as a gypsy. But Miss Drucy was as chipper as a sparrow. The woman was far hardier than she appeared.

They had nearly reached the house when they met Neil Dalton coming from the direction of the inlet, his Harris tweed coat slung over one shoulder. His boots were damp and sandy, his head bare, and Ana felt the familiar tug at her senses. It occurred to her, not for the first time, that for a man who was not strictly handsome, there was something about him that stirred a woman's imagination.

Even a woman whose imagination had no business being stirred.

Mercy! She still had bruises, albeit they were faded to a liverish shade of yellow by now, from her last encounter with a man. That was something she never, ever intended to invite again, even given the opportunity.

"Mrs. Merriweather." The gentleman touched his hatless brow. "*Miss* McKnight."

Again that subtle emphasis. Now why should she find it so objectionable? He certainly couldn't know anything about her past, else he'd be calling her Mrs. Hebbel.

"Did you learn anything of interest, Mr. Dalton?"

"Of interest? Oh . . . you mean the inlet. It's swift, all right. Runs deeper than I'd expected."

"I thought it was still waters, not swift waters, that ran deep," Ana countered. Her pulses stumbled and she thought, good heavens, did I say that? He'll think I'm flirting. I wouldn't know how to flirt if my life depended on it.

"They do, indeed, madam," was all he said. Turning on his heel, he stalked back the way he had come, leaving her staring after him.

"And red ones, too. They're not my favorites, but William always loved the red ones best. He's such a passionate man, my Billy." Miss Drucy sighed, and Ana felt a heaviness in her heart that had nothing at all to do with the exertion of spading up a garden plot that might or might not ever get planted.

Honestly, if she didn't soon pull herself together, she'd never manage to survive. Her monthlies had finally come and her emotions were all over the place. She'd always been regular as clockwork. This time she'd been a week late, which had given her nightmares of yet another sort. If she'd been carrying Ludwig's child after all, she didn't know what she might have done. Thrown herself into those swift, deep waters, perhaps.

Well, of course she would never do that. It wouldn't have been the fault of a child that its father had been such a wretch.

All the same, she hardly recognized herself lately.

It was as if Ana Gilbretta had indeed been buried in a lonely grave beside the Pasquotank River, and some-one she hardly knew had taken her place.

Which wasn't all that far from the truth.

Chapter Five

Life was not always easy at Merriweather's Landing.

But then, life had never been easy, Ana thought a few days later as she sorted through an untidy stack of sheet music.

At least, not since she'd been a child. As an only child in a privileged household, she'd taken all the pleasures for granted. Endless days in which to play, to explore, to climb trees and skin knees, confident in the knowledge that even if she stained her dress and ripped her pinafore in the process, all would be forgiven. Her parents loved her. She had accepted that love, taken it for granted, only slowly coming to realize just how fleeting love could be.

First her mother had died and left her. As clearly as if it had happened only last week, Ana could remember the way they'd laughed while her mother helped her dress for a friend's sixteenth birthday party. She'd looked at herself in the mirror and made a face, and her mother had made a face right back at her.

Ana had hated her braids, hated the childish dresses and white cotton stockings she'd been forced to wear. She remembered declaring fervently. "The day I turn sixteen, I'm going to dye my hair with henna and wear pink silk stockings with red clocks on the sides, and be the most beautiful girl between Canterbury and North Woodstock."

"Well, of course you will, my darling." Her mother had gently teased her out of her sulks until both of them were giggling like a pair of schoolgirls.

Two days after the party, Ana had come down with sniffles and sneezes. A few days later her mother had taken to her bed with the same complaint, along with feverishness and aching bones.

A week later she'd been dead.

Marcus Gilbretta had shut himself in his study for a week, coming out only for his wife's funeral. Then he'd shut himself in again, and judging from the number of bottles a disapproving Samuels had carried back and forth from the cellar, drowned his grief in brandy.

It was a stranger who had emerged, days later.

Ana had loved her father even after he'd grown querulous and peculiar. It had been hard to like the man he'd become as illness invaded his body and mind, but she'd loved him. Loved him enough to devote her life to taking care of him, her only comfort being the knowledge that he was not responsible for what he'd become.

But she didn't think she could ever forgive him for making her marry Ludwig. That had been unconscionable. The man had been a libertine, a gambler, and worse. He'd been a cruel fortune hunter who had never bothered to pretend he cared for her.

And she had killed him. However much he might have deserved it, she would bear that burden on her conscience till the day she died. One day—perhaps one day soon—she would have to go back and face the consequences of her deed.

But not yet. Not just yet.

Miss Drucy began to pat her feet and clap her hands, reminding her of why she'd been dragged to this particular room in this particular wing of the house. The piano tuner still hadn't showed up, and Miss Drucy, never patient, refused to be put off any longer.

So here they were, for better or worse. Ana feared it would be worse than anyone could imagine.

"Ah ha," she exclaimed, having finally found a piece that wasn't beyond her abilities. At least not terribly far beyond. "Here's one of my favorites."

She plopped the leaflet on the music rack, tilted the top of the Steinway, and fluffing her skirts, took her place on the bench. "Last chance, Miss Drucy. Are you sure you don't wish to take my place? I'm certain you play far better than I do. Most people do."

Drucilla shook her head vigorously. "Bless us all, I haven't practiced since Thursday last."

Too many Thursdays last, according to Mr. Merry, who didn't play at all but had hoped to encourage his wife by having her piano shipped along with the rest of their household furnishings.

"Well, here goes," Ana said cheerfully. "Don't forget, I warned you." Flexing her hands, she launched an enthusiastic assault on her favorite among Mr. Sousa's marches.

Squatting beside a worm-eaten timber uncovered by the last high tide, Brand lifted his head at the raucous sounds coming through an open window in the castle. Unless he was very much mistaken, that was a piano he was hearing.

And unless he was very much mistaken, it was being dismantled by a wrecking crew who took great pleasure in their task.

Jehosephat! Was she trying to startle the birds from the sky?

Brushing the sand from his hands, he sat back, wiped a bare forearm across his sweat-dampened forehead, and shook his head. Evidently, Miss Drucy fancied herself a musician. No person in his right mind could call that cacophony music, but if the lady was having fun, who was he to begrudge her the pleasure?

The sun beat down from a cloudless sky, the early spring weather being nothing if not fickle. Brand had been at Merriweather's Landing for five days now, and was no closer to his objective than he'd been the day he arrived. He couldn't swear to it, but he was beginning to suspect the wicked widow of deliberately avoiding him.

True, he'd had to make some slight pretense of

studying the inlet, but each morning he lingered as long as he dared over breakfast, discussing everything from politics to the new Woolworth stores, to the project at Niagra Falls with his host. He kept expecting Fallon to join them.

She never did.

He always came in promptly for the midday meal after hours of walking along the shore, scribbling bits of nonsense in his notebook in case anyone was watching. He kept expecting her to be there.

She never was.

"Fallon and Drucy are having an *alfresco* luncheon over on the ocean side in honor of the break in the weather," Mr. Merry had told him yesterday when he'd hurried back in time to wash and change his shirt. The day before, the two women set up a telescope in an attic window and were taking their bread, cheese, and apples there while they watched the horses digging for fresh water.

Every day it was something. Some excuse. Oh, he saw her now and then. She would pass him in a hallway smelling of some crisp, clean feminine scent, her hair as often as not untidy from being outside with her charge. She would smile at him as guilelessly as if she hadn't driven at least one man, and possibly more, to destruction, but she never lingered.

"I'm sorry, I can't stop to talk now," she'd said just yesterday, or maybe the day before. "Miss Drucy's waiting for me. We're making a rose garden."

Clever little tramp. Not even to himself would Brand admit his disappointment. When she'd missed dinner last night for the third night in a row, he'd told himself it was because she was growing uneasy. She probably sensed exposure in the offing and wanted to postpone it as long as she could.

If the mere presence of a stranger, supposedly here only to study the inlet, could make her this edgy, then he must be on the right track. A guilty conscience was a tool he could work with.

It was Maureen who had inadvertently set him

straight. "Poor bairn, she do suffer with her woman-lies," he'd heard her confiding to the young maid of all work, Simmy. "You take her this mug o' my hot spiced poteen and tell her I said to drink it down. Sure, and it'll settle her belly right enough. Miss Drucy is busy threading needles at the kitchen table. She'll keep just fine, the poor old dear. I'll get her to bed meself."

So much for his theories.

Rising now, Brand gazed thoughtfully down at the half-buried timber, a section of keelson from the look of it, riddled with ship's worm and barnacles. Having uncovered it just that morning, he couldn't help but wonder if someone a hundred years hence on some foreign shore would dig up a timber from the *Mystic Wings* and spend a few moments pondering the fate of her crew.

When Ana opened her eyes early the next morning sunlight was spilling across her pillow. Her head felt as if it might explode at any moment from the hot spiced whiskey she'd gulped down before falling asleep, but at least her belly no longer ached. Maureen had been right about that. Funny how a woman could live for years with discomfort and not be aware of such a simple remedy.

But then, her courses had barely begun when her mother had died. Etta, for all she was a wonderful friend, had never held with strong spirits.

Poor Etta. Poor Samuels. To be turned off at their age without a reference. She would have to find out where they'd gone and how they were managing before she turned herself in.

But not just yet. She couldn't very well leave The Landing until someone could be found to look after Miss Drucy, and that would take time. Perhaps next week she might give notice.

Perhaps then she would write to Mr. Quillerby about Etta and Samuels.

And perhaps not. . . .

It was with a rare sense of well-being that she shoved her feet into her slippers and hurried to the bathroom, to a heated bath of rainwater from the huge cypress cistern under the eaves. She had come to love the smell of it, and the way it made her hair shine. Once she was dressed and had herself a cup of Maureen's strong black coffee, she would be ready to face the day.

Even a day that included Neil Dalton.

She was far too aware of the man. It was a totally new experience for her, one she didn't quite know how to deal with, but deal with it she must.

What choice did she have?

For the first few days she'd been wary of him, especially after hearing his northern accent. Then, too, he had a way of looking at her as if he knew something she didn't, which was somewhat off-putting.

On the other hand, she was probably being overly sensitive. The week before her monthlies she was always that way. Temperish. Bursting into tears at the drop of a hat.

Besides, Miss Drucy liked him. Maureen liked him. Simmy blushed all over herself when he spoke to her, and Evard, when he wasn't jealously watching over Simmy, seemed to enjoy his company.

The two men had gone fishing in the surf together, and taken turns shooting at a target with Evard's shotgun, and Evard had come in bragging on the other man's skill.

However, just because a man possessed a few masculine skills, not to mention a few masculine charms, that didn't mean he couldn't turn vicious in the blink of an eye. Before she'd reluctantly let herself be talked into marrying him, she'd even convinced herself that for an older man, Ludwig was rather charming.

He'd dressed well. Expensively, if a bit flashily for her taste. Of course, he'd made an appreciable dent in her father's cellar the weekend he'd come for a visit to look her over, but at least he hadn't belched at the table or picked his teeth with his fingernail.

That had been the only time they'd been together before the awkward bedside ceremony. For her dying father's peace of mind, Ana had accepted her fate and even managed to convince herself that for a gentleman approaching middle age, her bridegroom was rather attractive.

In a jaded sort of way.

There was nothing at all jaded about Neil Dalton. There were no pouches under those piercing eyes of his, no lines of dissipation bracketing that wide, firm mouth. No sagging muscles, flabby waistline, or padded coats. In trousers, boots, and shirtsleeves, he looked fit as an oak tree and twice as strong. A woman would have to be blind not to see what a strikingly attractive man he was.

Still, Ana knew to her sorrow that looks could be deceiving.

Stop it, Anamarie! You've been given a new chance—don't you dare waste it.

Deliberately closing her mind to the past, she rolled up the sleeves of her flannel nightgown. The sun was shining. It was going to be a beautiful day. She was gainfully and happily employed, and best of all, she was not carrying Ludwig's child, which meant that until she decided to go back, her past was no threat to her immediate future.

She even began to hum under her breath as she laid out her freshly laundered underclothes. It was going to be a wonderful day for walking. Miss Drucy enjoyed walking as much as Ana did, and wherever they went there was always something new and interesting to discover.

Long-necked, long-legged wading birds.

Tiny crablike creatures with lobsterlike claws.

Perhaps today they might walk around the point of the inlet and see what they could discover there.

"Ta-da-da-*da*, ta-boomp, ta-boomp!" she chanted as she brushed her hair, twisted it, and anchored it on top of her head.

Yesterday while she'd been playing the piano for

Miss Drucy, she had seen him down on the beach near the inlet. He'd been sitting on a log, staring out over the water. After a while he'd stood, dusted the sand off the seat of his trousers, and turned toward the house.

At that point, she'd clean lost her place. When he'd stretched, lifting his arms over his head, and then proceeded to tuck his shirttail back under his belt, she'd fumbled a few notes and gone back to the beginning to start all over.

"That's not the way it goes," Miss Drucy had complained. "It's supposed to go like this. Bump-diddy-bump-diddy-bump-bump-bump!"

So she'd bumped some more, even though fully a third of the keys didn't sound at all and those that did twanged dischordantly. As long as she kept the proper beat, Miss Drucy didn't seem to care, which was a good thing, because, while she'd often found release in playing the piano, she'd be the first to admit she didn't possess one iota of talent.

Her mother had claimed it was because she was too impatient to practice, but her father had said lessons were a waste of money, that she had a tin ear and no amount of practice would ever change that. She suspected her father had the right of it.

Now, hopping into first one slipper, then the other one, she hurried to Miss Drucy's room, only to find it empty. "Oh, no . . . not again," she muttered. Spinning around the newel post, she took the stairs two at a time.

It wasn't the first time her charge had slipped out of the house before anyone else was awake. And while there might not be any streets or city traffic to worry about, that didn't mean life here was entirely without danger.

Could the woman even swim?

And dear heavens, there were those swift currents. . . .

"Miss Drucy?" she called softly. She tried the dining room first. It was empty. "Miss Drucy?"

"Mislaid something, have you?"

Slapping a hand over her breast, Ana spun around. "Don't ever sneak up on me that way! Neil, have you seen Miss Drucy? She might've gone out looking for her horses. You know how she is about those horses—I can't seem to make her understand that they're wild, and not to be trusted."

A wintry smile crossed his face for a moment before it disappeared. "Not to be trusted, hmm? And what about you, Miss McKnight. Are you to be trusted? Do you like horses? You strike me as the kind of woman who might enjoy a good . . . horse race."

"A horse race?" Confused, she blinked her eyes.

"You know—pitting the speed of one animal against another? I understand it helps if you happen to know something about one of the animals. A weakness, perhaps?"

What a strange thing to be discussing, she thought, struck by the way the sun slanted through the tall window, emphasizing the strength of those masculine features. "I—no. That is, I don't know the first thing about horse racing, and at the moment I'm far more concerned with Miss Drucy's whereabouts."

"I'm sure you are," he murmured, sounding sure of no such thing. "I believe you'll find Miss Drucy just outside the kitchen door. When I last saw her she was drawing off squares in the sand with a stick. I believe she said something about . . . spreading horse manure?"

"Oh, lord, her roses," Ana muttered as she hurried out the back door, leaving a bemused man staring after her.

Brand slowly shook his head. For all he'd been here a week, which was five days longer than he'd expected to stay, he was no closer to pinning the woman down and forcing her to admit her guilt than when he'd first landed on this desolate stretch of nowhere. Time, he'd rationalized, was his ally. Time and her own guilty conscience.

But he was fast becoming aware of another prob-

lem. The witch was doing things to his mind. At the
advanced age of thirty-four, he had had some experience with women. Not a whole lot—certainly not as
much as Galen had—but enough. Besides that, what
he knew about this one should be more than enough
to put him off women forever.

Yet in spite of all he knew about her, he'd been
forced to remind himself more than once of what he
was supposed to be doing here. It was becoming just
a bit too easy to lose sight of his mission.

Day after day he watched her playing with the old
woman. They were like a pair of children, romping
around on the shoreside, cutting paper dolls, banging
on that wretched piano—

Dammit, something didn't fit! No matter how many
times he reminded himself of what a vicious, heartless,
greedy bitch she was—of what she had done to Liam,
not to mention to any other man fool enough to come
within her range—he kept finding himself caught up
in her spell.

All it took was a whiff of her scent, or a glimpse of
her breasts when she lifted her arms to shove back
her hair, and he'd catch himself wondering what it
would be like to strip her down to her bare skin, to
lay her on his bed, and—

Her face was turning a golden tan from being out-
doors so much. It was hardly fashionable, yet on her
it looked good. She even had a few freckles. Half a
dozen across her cheeks, a few more on her elegant
little nose.

As for the rest of her body, it would still be pale
as buttermilk. Pale and soft, and . . .

Swearing under his breath, he snatched up his notebook, pencils, and binoculars and stalked out the door,
his stomach growling its protest of going unfed.

For a change, both Ana and Miss Drucy joined the
two men for supper that night. Maureen had outdone
herself in preparing a local delicacy. "Evard got three

trout, some croakers, and a nice puppy drum this morning. I cooked the drum."

Brand eyed the heaping platter skeptically. If there was anything nice about it, it escaped him. He'd eaten fish baked, broiled, stewed, and fried, and once even raw.

He had never tried it muddled into a lumpy gray mass with brown specks of—something.

However, he bravely ladled a spoonful onto his plate and served Ana, who was seated beside him at the oval table. She met his eyes, interpreted his expression, and her gold-shot eyes twinkled up at him.

"It's better than it looks, I promise you," she murmured. "Fish, potatoes, onions, and bits of crisp, fried salt pork. Simmy taught Maureen how to make it this way. Simmy's from across the inlet—a place called Chickie-something or other."

"Chicamacomico," Simmy put in shyly. She seldom spoke more than a word at meals.

It occurred to Brand that his own family would have been aghast at the idea of dining with staff. Personally, he was enjoying it. He'd dined with family, with friends, with the men on whatever ship he happened to be serving on before he left the sea.

There was a gaping hole in his life that could never be filled, but this helped. Oddly enough, in some small way, it helped.

They talked about names. Place and people names. Simmy, it seemed, was named Simone for her father, Simon, only she pronounced it Sea-*moan*-ee. Evard's name was actually Edward, but no one had ever called him that.

"And your name, Miss McKnight . . . am I correct in assuming your first name is Ann?"

"Why no, why would you think that?" She blinked, and he noticed the length of her thick, golden-tipped lashes. He was beginning to see why her eyes were considered remarkable. The effect was subtle, but it was there, all the same. If he didn't know her for what she was, he might even have been taken in, himself.

"That first day, when we met down at the landing, you introduced yourself as Ann Fallon McKnight, remember?"

"Oh, but I . . ."

"Dalton," Mr. Merry said thoughtfully. "I once knew of a family named Dalton. Shipping business, I believe. I don't suppose you've relatives along the New England coast?"

"I'm afraid not," Brand said. And while it was literally true—he no longer had a family at all, either Dalton or McKnight—he couldn't help but feel guilty for piling one lie on top of another.

As he concentrated on shaping the dubious fish mixture into a mound in the center of his plate, he thought of several applicable clichés concerning the weaving of tangled webs and being hoist by one's own petard.

In his case, both came uncomfortably close to the mark.

That night after everyone had retired, Brand sat alone in his room, gazing out over the spectacle of a half moon behind a bank of clouds, casting a silvery streak on the horizon. Having seen the same effect from another window, on another portion of the sea, he indulged himself in a moment of nostalgia, then shook it off.

He had work to do. This was no time to dwell on the beauties of nature. A direct man, this playing of games didn't suit him. Better to lay out his options and choose the best among them.

The obvious thing would be to face her with what she'd done. Accuse her and then watch her squirm and try to lie her way out of it. The woman was possibly the most skillful liar he'd ever encountered, and in rough ports both here and abroad, he'd met his share of liars.

Her whole life was a damned lie.

According to her cousins, Fallon's mother had run away from home at an early age and been disowned by the family, none of whom had ever set eyes on her again.

And then, one day a young woman turned up on their doorstep with a family Bible and a faded tintype of a woman she claimed was her mother; their own first cousin.

Evidently, she'd managed to convince them of the validity of her claim. Something about the family eyes, the older one had said.

Those eyes again. What the devil was it about her eyes?

So they were beautiful eyes. Hell, she was a beautiful woman, if not quite in the style he'd expected.

But brown eyes weren't all that uncommon. Even light brown eyes with flecks of gold embedded in their clear depths. Even large amber eyes set in dense beds of gold-tipped, curling lashes.

Flexing his shoulders to ease the knotted muscles at the back of his neck, Brand went over it in his mind once more. All the things he'd heard about her. The things he'd observed personally. He had more than enough to indict her, but now that his initial rage had cooled down, he could afford to be more deliberate.

He was after more than an indictment. He was after a conviction.

The woman thrived on excitement. Men were as necessary to her as the air she breathed. The question was, how much longer would she be content to bury herself in this deserted backwater?

The answer was, not much longer. Sooner or later she was bound to grow restless, and the minute she slipped up, he'd be right there to catch her. The first thing he intended to do was force her to admit she was a widow.

God knows, she owed Liam's memory that much.

Pam the ferryman came on Wednesday, bringing supplies, mail, and a passenger from across the sound. Brand, who'd seen the boat turning into the slough as he strolled down to collect the mail and whatever sup-

plies had been ordered, watched as a dapper little man
with a greenish complexion staggered ashore, clutching a worn alligator case to his concave chest.

His first thought was that Fallon's other follower
had caught up with her. Hardly a worthy opponent,
was his second.

Both notions were quickly dispelled when, after taking several deep gulps of air, the visitor announced
that he had the honor of being Alphonso Smythe,
piano tuner by profession. "Not that it'll do a smidge
of good to tune any instrument in this wretched climate," he added self-righteously.

Brand hid his amusement and offered to carry the
heavy case. The poor fellow looked as if he might still
cast up his accounts a time or two between the wharf
and the castle.

His offer declined, he collected the bundle of newspapers and mail, and two sacks of supplies and then
steered the gentleman toward the house.

He was halfway up the path when the ferryman
called after him, "Tell Miss Fallon a man come around
asking after her last week. Didn't give his name."

The piano tuner, plodding beside him, was in the
process of listing all the reasons why he should never
have set out on such a miserable, totally pointless
journey. By the time Brand could break away and
follow up with a question for the ferryman, it was too
late. The stem of his corncob pipe clamped securely
in the gap between his teeth, Pam had already poled
the bow away from the wharf and hoisted his mains'le.
With one hand on the tiller, he saluted the two men
on shore and veered away, bound for the Lifesaving
Station and points south.

Mr. Smythe remained at the castle for three and a
half days. Quickly recovering from the journey out,
he was first to arrive at the table for every meal. In
his own unique manner, he did flattering justice to
whatever Maureen prepared. Laughing uproariously at
his own joke, he boasted that he never touched a fork

except in his work, eating only what he could balance on the blade of his knife.

Which, to Ana's amazement, included peas, tapioca pudding, and raw oysters. He informed them proudly that he'd inherited the trait from his grandfather, who had been a world-famous knife smith in his day.

Ana's lips quivered with amusement. Meeting the eyes of the man seated beside her, she murmured, "I'm certainly impressed, aren't you?"

For a single instant, before the shades came down, she caught a glimpse of a different Neil Dalton. The corners of his mouth twitched. His gray eyes gleamed with laughter.

The illusion was quickly shattered as the familiar chill returned. Sighing, she turned away, determined not to let anyone, certainly not a humorless stick of a man who didn't even pretend to like her, spoil what had turned out to be a perfectly delightful day.

Miss Drucy had been on her best behavior. They had ordered roses from a catalog, and Evard had promised to whistle up his pony, which roamed with the wild ones, hitch up the cart and collect manure to compost along with the seaweed that washed up on the sound shore.

All that had taken place before noon. That afternoon they had both been allowed to sit quietly in the music room while Mr. Smythe finished tuning the piano. Then, with a flourish, he had invited Ana to test the results.

He hadn't been particularly impressed with her skills. Far from being insulted—after all, she did know her limitations—she had been amused. So many things amused her lately, she had to wonder if she'd left her common sense behind when she'd boarded the train back in Connecticut that awful, icy, February night.

Well, of course she had. That had never been in question.

A few minutes later she'd been leaving the music room, promising to make a pan of cocoa, when Neil Dalton had caught up with her in the back hall.

"You go ahead, Miss Drucy, I'll be right there."

"I forgot to tell you earlier," he said, "The ferryman sent a message."

"For me? Who on earth . . ."

"He said to tell you there was a man asking about you."

If the floor had opened up and she'd suddenly fallen through, she couldn't have been any more shocked. "A man? Are you sure he was asking for me?"

"A man was asking about Fallon McKnight, that's all I know. Pam was gone before I could get any more details."

The wheels had spun so fast she'd had to reach out and touch the wall to keep from reeling. Did they know? Had someone found out who she was?

"A creditor, perhaps? Or a suitor? What about a husband? Surely you weren't careless enough to leave one of those lying around?" He'd made out like he was teasing, but Ana hadn't been fooled. Neil Dalton hadn't a teasing bone in his body. Now and then their eyes might meet in a moment of shared amusement, shared understanding, but *only* for a moment. Then the anger would return. The anger he seemed to reserve only for her.

She tried to tell herself she was being fanciful. That he couldn't possibly know about her. If he'd come all this way to arrest her, then he would have done it that first day and not spent all this time playing cat and mouse. Policemen didn't do that sort of thing . . . did they?

Of course they didn't. The man was exactly who and what he claimed to be, no more, no less.

She'd do better to worry about the other man, the one who was asking questions about her.

So she'd fretted until dinnertime, and now she fretted some more. At the head of the table, Mr. Merry had launched into another story about his young days as a store clerk, learning the family business from the ground up. A genial and gregarious man, he was in his element with an expanded audience.

Ana was determined not to cast a pall over the occasion. She'd quickly come to realize how very lonely he must have been with no one to talk to except for a handful of servants and a wife who was not always entirely present.

It was possibly the most romantic thing she had ever heard of, for a man to give up everything for the sake of the woman he loved. Compared to the brief travesty of marriage she had endured, it was nothing short of heroic.

She sighed, and felt Neil's gaze focused on her. Against all reason, it felt warm, like sunshine on her naked skin, and she savored the illusion, knowing it was only that. A fleeting illusion born of need.

"Something wrong?" he murmured.

Picking up her spoon, she shook her head. "No, everything's lovely," she said and saw the familiar mocking light reenter his eyes.

Tonight they were having oyster stew and turtle hash. She sipped the broth, carefully avoiding the oysters—she could never abide squishy food. But she made short work of the hash, which was delicious. Rather like veal, only sweeter.

Miss Drucy, as usual, peppered the conversation with *non sequitors*. By now Ana was used to it. It occurred to her to wonder how the real Fallon would have managed.

Not particularly well, she suspected. In the short time they'd spent together, Ana had come to realize that Fallon had been unhappy, and that her unhappiness had taken the form of restlessness, which frequently showed itself in a lack of patience.

Poor Fallon.

Mr. Smythe, considerably mellowed by several glasses of wine, yawned, wiped his knife on his napkin, and shoved his chair back from the table. He belched, begged pardon, and said, "I'm for an early night, one and all. Ferry's coming for me bright and early in the morning, and I'm dreading it some kind of bad, I can tell you. Never been a good sailor. No stomach for it."

Maureen said, "Sure, and gingerroot's what ye're needing. I'll cut off a bit for you to chew on yer way across the waters."

Mr. Merry was disappointed, but he covered it well. "It's been a pleasure, sir. I'm sure we'll be enjoying the results of your visit for a long time to come."

"I'll give it a month. Less'n that, if it rains overmuch."

There followed a discussion of climate, geography, and the feasibility of keeping several lamps lit in the music room. Once the piano tuner left, Mr. Merry turned to Neil to suggest a game of cards.

"I might be a bit rusty, sir, but if you're willing to risk being bored, I'm game."

Miss Drucy clapped her hands and said, "Games! Oh, lovely, a party!"

"Yes, dear," Ana said, "we'll have our own party upstairs, with slippers and bathrobes and hot cocoa, shall we? We can lay out our rose bed. The yellow ones, I was thinking, might do better next to the house, and perhaps the red—"

Bright-eyed, Miss Drucy clapped her hands again. "Oh, yes! And perhaps the red!"

It was Neil Dalton who held her chair for her to rise. Ana, thanking him with a wary smile, led her charge from the room. For reasons that quite escaped her she suddenly felt like crying.

But then, it had been a long day. For such a supposedly quiet place, Merriweather's Landing was turning out to be quite a bustling thoroughfare.

Hours later, she was in the kitchen heating tinned milk for another cup of cocoa when the door opened. "I thought I heard someone in here," said Mr. Dalton. "Have you remembered?"

A bustling thoroughfare indeed. Mr. Hobbs, dressed for once in a paisley dressing gown instead of a drab three-piece suit, had been just leaving when she'd entered. She'd smiled. He'd blushed and hurried away. Poor sweet man.

She turned and glanced over her shoulder, stirring the milk to keep it from scorching. "Have I remembered what?"

He had loosened his collar and removed the coat he'd worn to dinner. His hair, ruffled as if it had been combed with his fingers, was so dark it seemed to absorb the light. His eyes were the color of the slate on her father's roof. Dark, cool, with a hint of blue.

"Pam's message. I just wondered if you'd remembered who might be looking for you."

Ana forgot to stir until the scent of scorched milk reminded her. Hastily, she sat the pan aside. "No, I—that is, it could've been most anyone, I suppose."

He leaned his back against the wall, crossing his arms over his chest, and studied her thoughtfully. "I believe you said you were from somewhere in New England?"

Ana's breath caught somewhere in her throat. "No," she whispered.

"You aren't?"

"I didn't say."

"Oh."

They were sparring. She'd never been good at that sort of thing. If he wanted to know where she was from, why didn't he just come right out and ask?

He wasn't a policeman. She was almost certain of that by now. Who ever heard of sending a policeman so far, even to capture a murderer?

On the other hand, she was beginning to wonder if he was actually who he said he was. She wasn't entirely sure what civil engineers did, other than to design bridges and roadways, but he'd been here for more than a week and so far, all he'd done was walk along the shore scribbling in that notebook he carried with him.

She'd come across it in his room the other day when she'd been helping Simmy change the linens, and absently flipped it open, not expecting to see anything, really—or perhaps a few structural drawings. Engineering-type things.

Instead, she'd seen drawings of another sort. The first one had been of a young man's face. Little detail, but enough to know that whoever he was, he was remarkably handsome. For some reason it had struck her as terribly sad.

Unable to stop there, she'd looked further. There'd been several drawings of ships with detailed sketches of rigging in the margins. One of a fancy bowsprit with a nameplate. *Mystic Wings*. It had a lovely sound. Mystic, Connecticut, perhaps? That would explain the familiar accent.

And then she'd turned a page and seen her own face staring up at her, only it hadn't been quite right. Something in the expression . . .

She'd snapped the thing shut and dropped it like a hot biscuit, ashamed of herself for snooping, but more curious than ever.

Who are you? she'd wondered at the time.

She wondered now. "Was there something you wanted, Mr. Dalton? Hot milk, perhaps, to help you sleep?"

"Thank you for your kind offer, Miss McKnight, but I never have trouble falling asleep." He looked pointedly at the pan of scorched milk. "You, on the other hand, do, I take it?"

"Not at all."

"Liar," he taunted softly, and suddenly, she was shaking with anger. Who was he to come here and threaten her, to accuse her of—

Well, whatever it was he seemed to think she'd done.

"Then I won't keep you, sir," she said, struggling to regain the upper hand.

As if she'd ever had it.

An upper hand.

She certainly hadn't with her father, nor with Horatio Quillerby, nor with Ludwig. And not with Neil Dalton, either.

She was pathetic.

Evidently she'd been born lacking an upper hand.

He left without another word, and Ana forced herself to finish what she'd begun. The cocoa was only warm, not hot, and tasted of burnt milk. She made a mess of pouring it from pan to cup, mopped it up, and swore.

And then swore some more when she went to pick it up again, and her hand shook so hard the cup rattled in the saucer.

But then, swearing was better than weeping. Didn't do a bit more good, but at least it didn't clog up her nose.

A few minutes later, propped up in bed and scowling at the skum on her cup, she reassured herself with the thought that no one could possibly know where she was.

And if by chance someone should find out, how could he know *who* she was?

Chapter Six

Three wind-tossed blossoms still clung to the vine, their bright gold color contrasting sharply with the weathered shingles of the shed. Head pounding, Ana leaned on the handle of the shovel and wondered whether or not to pull up the vines to make way for Drucy's roses.

In the end, she decided to leave them all. The delicate yellow jasmine, the thrifty wild peas, and the stubborn catclaw briars. Anything that could survive in the barren sand deserved a place under the sun. Live and let live, that was her motto.

God, what irony!

Still leaning on the splintery hickory handle, she pressed one hand against her throbbing temple. She had woken with a headache that was growing worse.

"Digging a grave?"

The shovel handle shifted under her weight, and she might have been pitched facedown in the sand if Neil Dalton hadn't leaped to catch her.

His hands on her shoulders felt startlingly warm and hard. It took all the willpower she possessed not to press her face against his shirtfront and allow his strength to absorb her pain.

But of course, she did no such thing. Stepping away, she said dryly, "Why no, I simply enjoy digging. Some people play croquet, some paint pictures, some do needlework. I happen to enjoy digging holes in the ground."

It was a test of wills not to look away. Ana knew it, and suspected he did, too. The man frightened her

as much as he attracted her. She wasn't sure if either
was deliberate, but thought both probably were.

"Your head hurts," he said. It wasn't a question.

"How can you tell?"

"Those furrows on your brow. The pinched look
about your eyes."

"It hurts like the very devil, if you must know."

"So instead of lying down with a cold cloth over
your eyes, you come outside to dig holes in the
ground."

"Digging takes my mind off my pr—my headache.
Besides, it's far too lovely to stay inside."

He glanced at the sky. It was overcast again. There
was a cold, damp wind blowing in off the ocean.

"I needed the air," she cried, sounding shrewish and
hating it.

What she'd needed was to get away from Miss
Drucy for an hour. This had not been one of her better days. After insisting that Ana play the same piece
of music five times, she'd lapsed into one of her fussy
spells and finally flounced out.

Ana had counted to fifty and then gone after her.
She'd found her in the kitchen cutting a fringe around
a picture torn from the *National Geographic,* as sweet
and peaceful as anything.

Maureen had taken one look and poured her a cup
of tea, to which she'd added a few drops of something
from a small brown bottle. "Here, child—it's slow ye
should sip it, though."

Ana had tasted, shuddered, and made a face. "It
might cure my head. Heaven only knows what it'll do
to my stomach."

"Whisht, girl, it's only paregoric. Now go along and
walk your miseries off, it'll do ye good. Herself will
come to no harm."

And so she'd grabbed an old coat off the back door
and gone outside, but instead of walking, she had tack-
led the plot set aside for Miss Drucy's roses.

But her head still throbbed. The dull ache that had
started that morning had grown worse as the day pro-

gressed and clouds moved in from the west. There was a limit to what even fresh air, paregoric, and blessed silence could achieve.

"Sorry," she whispered. "I didn't mean to bite your head off."

Neil lifted his hands toward her face. It was a mark of her distraction that she reacted instinctively, flinching away as if to protect herself.

"What the devil did you think I was about to do, madam? Strangle you?" He look greatly offended.

"Of course not, I wasn't thinking at all."

"Do it yourself, then. Pressure sometimes helps ease the pain. Walk your fingertips around your eye sockets. Press harder where it hurts most."

"I—it was—I thought I saw a bee." A lame excuse, but all she could come up with.

His expression told her quite clearly just how lame he thought it was, but she could hardly explain. If she even tried, she would probably end up confessing every last one of her sins, because as much as her head ached, her conscience ached even more.

He stared at her intently. Ana bore it stoically, seriously considered screaming at him even though screams weren't in her repertoire, but then, without another word, he turned and left. She scowled at his back and wondered what there was about the man that set her teeth on edge, even knowing he was only trying to be helpful.

Honestly, between her nightmares and her daydreams, it was no wonder she had the headache.

Somewhere in a distant room, a clock struck two. Brand closed his notebook, raked a hand through his hair, and flexed his stiff shoulders. He couldn't sleep. Hadn't slept a whole night through since he'd set out on this self-imposed mission of vengeance.

Liam's Lorelei. The clever, conniving bitch with the lying, golden eyes.

It was no wonder men remembered her eyes. Even knowing what he did about her, it was hard to gaze into those amber depths and still believe she wasn't the innocent she appeared.

He'd come here fully prepared to find a flashy little strumpet whose beauty was barely skin deep. Instead he'd found a curious blend of kindness and sensitivity, humor and intelligence. Not to mention a maturity that was both unexpected and dangerously attractive.

If he hadn't known better . . .

"But, dammit, I do!"

And even if he hadn't been quite certain, the shadow of guilt he'd glimpsed in her eyes more than once would've given her away.

He was beginning to wish he'd never tracked her down.

A chunk of driftwood settled in the small fireplace, crackling noisily for a moment. Outside, the wind howled around the corners of the wing where his room was located. The house had been planned to catch the crosswinds from any direction, which was no doubt a great advantage during the muggy summers.

Of course, it could be just as great a disadvantage with a cold wind howling in off the Atlantic.

Still, he liked the place. Liked it rather a lot. Paneled almost entirely in fragrant juniper, carpeted with a number of Persian rugs and furnished in an assortment of styles, it was a every bit as comfortable as it was attractive.

But tonight, neither comfort nor attractiveness held any appeal. Pausing before one of the dormers that faced out on the ocean, he closed his eyes against a churning mixture of anger, frustration, grief, and guilt.

Not to mention a large portion of unwanted and totally inappropriate sexual arousal.

God, what a mess he'd made of things!

Part of it was that he was out of his element. He was good at dealing with men—with shipbuilders, seamen, brokers, stevadores, and the like. He did well enough with charts, ledgers, logbooks, and the endless regulations dealing with trade tariffs and such.

Unfortunately, none of that was any help when it came to mapping out a course of revenge.

Especially against a woman.

Hell, he'd never even been able to hold a decent grudge.

And as if all that weren't enough, he'd even gone and caught her headache. Massaging his throbbing temples, he attempted one more time to sort out his feelings into some sort of orderly pattern.

Grief? Only natural. He'd lost two brothers, after all. His entire family had been wiped out in the space of a few months.

Arousal? Well, hell—no man with eyes in his head could help but be affected by such a woman.

"Beautiful and passionate beyond belief," Liam had written shortly after their marriage. "I took her to Manhattan for our wedding trip. Whoo-ee!!! You wouldn't believe some of the things your baby brother is learning! Fallon says we're going to Paris next spring. Can hardly wait! Wish now I'd paid more attention in French class."

Brand wished he had paid more attention to common sense. Before anyone even knew what was going on, the scheming little jade had seduced the boy into marrying her, squandered his inheritance, destroyed his pride, and robbed him of his will to live.

And all without either Brand or Galen suspecting anything was amiss.

Damn it all, if only Liam hadn't jumped the gun and eloped! Either Brand or Galen—any man, in fact, with any knowledge of women—could have told him that a female's sense of honor was about as substantial as a politician's promise. Aside from his mother, Brand had yet to meet a single woman worthy of a man's trust.

Well . . . perhaps one, but he hadn't wanted her. The woman he *had* wanted had accepted his gifts and his foolish declarations, only to turn around and marry a doddering old fool with twice his money and three times his years.

To Brand's certain knowledge, not a one of his mistresses had ever been faithful once the door had closed behind him.

Not that he'd expected, or even wanted their loyalty.

Poor Liam. They could have helped if only they'd been there. Instead, both he and Galen had chosen to go their own way shortly after their father had died, priding themselves on their generosity.

Oh, they'd been a pair, all right, congratulating themselves on their wisdom in giving the boy room to grow, to learn to shoulder responsibility like a man.

To which Galen had added words to the effect that, having been spoiled rotten all his life, it was time the boy grew up, and the best thing his elder brothers could do was leave him to the task.

Pure bilge, every last word of it. The truth was, neither of them had ever been interested enough in horse breeding to devote their lives to it. Instead, they'd both been fascinated by ships; the building of them and the sailing of them.

Brand had first felt the lure of the sea when his grandfather had shown him a heavy, crudely formed gold cross set with rubies and told him it had come from the wreck of a pirate ship that had once sailed the Spanish Main, right off the mid-Atlantic coast.

What kind of a ship? he'd wanted to know. How many sails? How fast could she go? How many guns could she carry?

Dammit, he should have stayed home. With both parents gone, he should have stayed home and married Margaret Kondrake and made a decent home for Liam.

Instead he'd chosen to go haring off after his own dream.

Margaret would have made him a good wife. She was older than he was—a few years, at most—but it had seemed a generation at the time. Some women were simply born older than others.

Still, she was pretty. Her disposition was everything

any man could want in a wife. Over the years Brand
had fallen into the habit of driving her to church, of
escorting her to socials. He had kissed her and they'd
both enjoyed it. He'd fondled her, too, but in the end,
he hadn't done more.

He could have had her. She'd made that quite clear,
but the truth was, he'd always held out hope of finding
the one woman in all the world who could make his
head spin and his blood sing with a touch or a glance.

Less than a year later he had found her, only she
hadn't proved any more faithful than the rest. With
tears in her lying eyes, she had told him she would
have missed him so much when he was at sea that it
would have broken her heart.

Then she'd gone off and married her rich old
banker.

So now he had no one. No parents, no brothers—
no wife, no children of his own. And damned few
friends, for he'd been so busy building his empire
these past few years he'd allowed them to drift away.
Which only went to show that for all his vaunted maturity, he was no wiser than poor Liam had been.

Oh, yes, he told himself with a derisive chuckle,
he'd made his share of mistakes, all right. More than
his share. He was making another one right now, and
he didn't know what the devil he was going to do
about it.

The plain truth was that he was increasingly attracted to his brother's widow. He wanted to believe
it was the same kind of horrified fascination he'd felt
the first time he'd watched a snake capture and swallow a baby bird. Revolted at something both so
wicked and so innocent, yet unable to move away.

But it was more than that. He had only to touch
her, to catch a hint of that crisp, warm fragrance that
always seemed to surround her, and his body would
react the way old Mac the Knight used to react whenever a new mare was turned into his paddock.

Damn. Maybe he should take time to go up to Norfolk for a spell. Like every seaman in every seaport

in the world, he knew where to find the right kind of women. Or rather the wrong kind. Word about such things spread quickly from crew to crew.

Turning to the rosewood desk, he opened the notebook and idly thumbed through the sketches, most of which had been done when he was supposed to be studying the inlet currents.

There were several of ships he'd sailed on, two of ships he still owned, and one of the *Mystic Wings,* the way he'd last seen her. Tall, fast, proud as an eagle. A 746-ton three-master, she'd been stern to, hull down, and racing before the wind, with a cargo of rice and cotton and a deck cargo of machinery, bound for Liverpool by way of Dublin.

Thumbing through the pages, he paused to stare down at the face of a woman who was both familiar and unfamiliar. He'd done the original drawing from the wedding photograph, then altered it after meeting the woman herself.

Yet, still it wasn't right.

Brand was no artist, had never pretended to be, but he'd always had a certain flair. An adequate marine draftsman, he was usually able to render a passable sketch of a face that interested him.

And hers did. God help him, it interested him far more than he cared to admit, considering what he was planning to do to her.

It had come to him earlier, when he'd watched her flinch from his touch in the garden. Or rather, the weedy patch of sand she was attempting to turn into a garden.

Which was another thing that puzzled him. The woman he'd come to know solely through Liam's letters and the shredded reputation that had followed her after she'd stripped him bare and left him injured and helpless, would no more grow her own roses than she would soil her hands brushing mud from an old woman's feet.

Yet, he'd seen her do both.

Not that it changed anything. She was merely biding

her time, playing yet another role. Either hiding or trying to find a way to dip her greedy fingers into the Merriweather coffers. Every bit as convincing as a snake-oil salesman at a county fair, her kind could make a man believe black was white and up was down.

Just as long as he kept that thought firmly in mind, he should be safe.

Closing the notebook, Brand fingered the letter he'd received yesterday from his office, concerning the latest maritime ruling and increase in tariffs. Whether or not the absent all-around man showed up, he couldn't afford to stay here much longer. Doing business under a growing burden of regulations was a constant challenge that required constant attention.

On the other hand, he'd always thrived on challenges.

Which was the reason he'd made up his mind to court his brother's widow, to play on her weaknesses, hinting at all he could offer her both physically and financially.

It wasn't much of a plan, but it was the best he could do. Under any other circumstances, he wouldn't bet a copper penny on his chances. His face was more the kind to frighten small children than to set a woman's heart to beating faster. Liam had been called beautiful. Galen had been called handsome.

Brand had been called tough.

Wealth? His was mostly tied up in his two remaining ships. The insurance money on *Mystic Wings,* when and if it was paid out, would cover the cargo, the rest being distributed among the families of the men lost.

As for his physical prowess, while he'd never had any complaints, vanity had never been one of his failings. He could only hope that with the dearth of competition, the bait would prove sufficient. She should be getting bored by now. Restless enough so that he could interest her in his supposed wealth, if not in his manly charms.

Once he had her right where he wanted her, he

would have the pleasure of introducing himself properly and watching as horrified realization crept into those famous eyes of hers.

"Brandon McKnight, madam. Does the name ring any bells?"

Oh, yes. And that would be just the beginning.

"We're to be treated to a concert tonight in honor of the newly tuned piano," Mr. Merry announced at breakfast the next morning.

"Before it goes out of tune again," Ana put in, laughing.

Eyes twinkling under his bushy white brows, the old gentleman nodded. "Miss Fallon has generously consented to play for us."

"Miss Fallon," corrected Ana, "has apologetically, and with greatest reluctance, allowed herself to be blackmailed."

"Blackmailed?" Brand speared her with a sardonic look. "Now, that's a curious way of putting it. Are we to guess what it is you've been hiding from us, *Miss* Fallon?"

"Perhaps bribed is a better description," suggested Mr. Merry, enjoying his third cup of Darjeeling.

"If you must know, it's my birthday. Maureen promised to bake me a cake if Miss Drucy and I chop all the dates, nuts, and currents. We're going to start right after breakfast, aren't we, Miss Drucy?"

Mrs. Merriweather lifted her teacup and smiled brightly in response, but it was heartbreakingly plain that she'd forgotten all about the project.

Ana dressed carefully for her performance that evening. Under any other circumstances, she would have been cowering in a pantry, but Mr. Merry knew her limitations. He'd been warned in advance. Whatever pleased his Drucy pleased him, and as they both knew, Miss Drucy liked anything with a beat that she could accompany with her clacking clam shells.

Even Maureen was looking forward to the evening.

She'd reminisced at length about the music parties she dimly remembered as a child back in Ireland, where all the babies, only she called them babbies, were piled into a single bed while their elders sang and drank and raised the roof with the finest music in all the world.

"Just don't expect any miracles," Ana warned the housekeeper. "I'm loud enough to raise a few shingles, but not very fine."

Maureen laughed and said, "Go along wi' ye, girl," and Simmy shyly professed herself looking forward to it.

As for Neil Dalton . . .

Well. That was neither here nor there.

She sighed. There'd been a few times when she thought he was almost coming to like her, but then she'd catch him looking at her in that funny way he had, as if he weren't quite sure which species of animal life she belonged to.

Not for the first time, she reminded herself that his opinion of her was irrelevant, if only because of who she was. Or rather, who she wasn't.

In other words, Anamarie, he's not for thee.

The green dress she had dyed black for mourning was beginning to look more than slightly tarnished. She had washed it in cold water to remove the bloodstains, only it had removed some of the dye along with the stains.

Come summer, she'd be in a sad state, with two gowns, one of tarnished marino, the other of heavy gray twill. Not that she'd ever had all that many. But then, with no social life, she'd hardly needed them. Her father had even grumbled at the two new gowns she'd had made up for her trousseau, before he'd remembered that he was supposed to be dying.

But Ludwig had torn the bronze silk, and the violet had never fit right because it had been so hurriedly made. With her summer clothes all packed away, she had fled with only what she could snatch in a hurry and cram into her one small valise.

She gave one last tug to her sleeves, patted her

hair, which she'd knotted and anchored with four pins, praying it would hold for the duration of the concert.

"Sit up straight," her mother used to scold. "Don't slump, don't twist about, and for heaven's sake, don't stare out the window and lose your place."

She'd never been good at recitals.

"Carry yourself like a lady, Anamarie," her mother used to say when she would dash inside the house looking like a cat that had been chased up a tree by dogs. "Back straight, head high, dear," she'd admonished the year Ana had turned fourteen and put up her hair. Her bosoms had just begun to sprout. Acutely embarrassed by her changing shape, she had rounded her shoulders whenever anyone glanced her way.

Her mother had died the next year. Ana's breasts never had grown all that much, but now, at least she could get through an entire evening without her hair falling down. For a twenty-eight-year-old woman, her accomplishments were pathetically modest.

The chairs had been arranged in rows for the occasion. Mr. Hobbs was wearing a different cravat, one with black and gray stripes. His others were all solid black.

Mercy, Ana though, what a signal honor.

Maureen was wearing her lace collar and cameo. She smiled and nodded encouragingly as Ana swept aside her skirts as if they were the finest silk taffeta, and took her seat at the keyboard.

Mr. Merry patted his wife's hand, looking like a gentle, white-haired elf. Simmy and Evard sat stiffly side by side, as if not quite knowing what to expect, and Neil . . .

Ana tried not to look at Neil, but it didn't help. He was the largest person in the room, and even dressed plainly as he was in tan woolen trousers and a short frock coat, with a somewhat rumpled tie, he was magnificent. Not handsome—his features were too boldly hewn for that, but strikingly, uncomfortably, irresistibly masculine.

She dropped the first piece of music she had selected to play. It sailed across the floor and Neil leaned forward and scooped it up. With a mocking bow, he replaced it on the music stand. Ana tilted her head to thank him and felt her hair begin to slide. It was that kind of hair—too slick and heavy to support its own weight.

It was that kind of night, she thought, as half amused, half terrified, she braced herself to begin.

A triumph it was not, she told herself some fifty minutes later. But neither was it a complete failure. She had started with one of Beethoven's simpler pieces, one even she had been able to master after years of practice. That was followed by two of Mr. Sousa's marches, both of which she'd had to repeat several times at Miss Drucy's demand. In the middle of the first one, Miss Drucy had darted over to a shelf and snatched her clam shells, and from then on, no matter what the tempo of the piece being played, it was accompanied by the rapid clacking of home-made castinets.

After that, her carefully planned program fell apart. She settled for taking requests, everything from "Froggie Went A-courting" for Simmy, to an Irish air for Maureen, a sentimental ballad for Mr. Merry, and a lullaby Ana remembered from her early childhood. Half remembered. Without the music, she'd made a tentative stab at it, and been stunned to see Maureen mopping her overflowing eyes.

"Sure, and if that wasn't the sweetest thing ever I heard," the housekeeper said. "With a name like Fallon, ye're bound to have a touch of the Irish in ye."

Mr. Hobbs cleared his throat several times and went so far as to smile at her. After that, there was no point in going on. Everyone had had their fill of her playing, and in no time at all, Maureen had the birthday cake all set out in the dining room.

Brandon waited until the others had filed out and then escorted her down the hall. "A woman of many talents," he remarked after they'd all been served their cake and punch. He was tempted to bring up the matter of her name, but he didn't. It was her birthday. The sniping could begin again tomorrow.

Maureen's notion of punch was powerful enough to lay a stevedore out cold, he suspected, sipping carefully from his cup. "What is this stuff, do you know?"

"I'm not sure—prune juice and Irish whiskey, I think."

"Holy horn spoon!"

"Well, what do you expect at short notice? Oranges don't exactly grow on trees around here."

"You're sounding chipper for someone who just spent an hour torturing an innocent piano."

Instead of taking offense—Brand wasn't entirely sure he even meant to offend—she grinned. A smile he might have resisted, but not that grin of hers. It was entirely too disarming.

"Sorry. I'm truly awful, aren't I? Tone deaf, my father always claimed. But don't say you weren't warned."

"I thought your disclaimer was false modesty," he said, recalling her earlier offer to relinquish her position to anyone who cared to take her place.

"Nope. It was the genuine article. I might not know much about music, but I do know my own limitations. Lucky for me, Miss Drucy's not at all critical as long as it has a good fast beat. Boom-diddy-boom-boom-boom." She went to set her empty punch cup on the table and nearly missed. He caught it just in time.

"How much of this stuff have you had?"

"Two—no, three cups. I sneaked one before the concert for courage."

"Was that wise?"

"Wise? If Solomon had no more talent that I have—if he had to wear a dress that was not only faded, but seven years out of fashion, with his hair threatening to fall down over his face every time he searched for a key, he'd have drunk the lot, bowl, dipper and all. Now, *that*, sir, would be wisdom."

Brand laughed. Couldn't help himself. The woman

was irresistible. When she laughed right along with him, it was all he could do to remember his mission—which was to seduce her one way or another, not to fall for her wiles.

"Yes, well . . . I suppose we'd better mingle. I think Evard is getting soused."

"Lovely. Before he sobers up, perhaps I can worm a promise from him to haul me another cart load of manure."

Brand nearly choked on his punch. "Miss Fallon, you astound me."

She nodded sagely. "Sometimes I even astound myself. I think I'm probably going to have the most awful headache again tomorrow. At least I'll have earned this one."

"Not to mention a bellyache, if you're right about those ingredients." Taking her arm, he escorted her across the room to a chair, and when she swayed against him, he wrapped an arm around her waist. To steady her. Only to steady her, he assured himself.

The party ended shortly after that, with another round of birthday wishes. Simmy blurted out the hope that if she ever got to be as old as Miss Fallon was, she hoped she would get around as well. Fallon giggled. Simmy blushed. Brand found himself actually laughing for the second time in nearly a year.

Glancing down at the woman at his side, he looked for a single gray strand in her wealth of chestnut hair and found not a one. There were a few fine lines at the outer corners of her eyes, but instead of making her look older, they only made her appear more fragile.

Again he felt that disturbing sense that something wasn't right. This time he had a feeling it was more than Maureen's potent birthday punch.

Long after she crawled into bed that night, Ana lay awake, sifting through an assortment of impressions, some of them ludicrous, some touching, and a few wildly inappropriate. The last time she'd celebrated a birthday she'd been fifteen, embarrassed because she was the tallest girl in her class, and because her bosoms jiggled when she walked, and because she wasn't as popular as her two best friends.

Tonight she'd hardly been any more poised. Although after a few cups of Maureen's punch, she hadn't worried about it too much.

Maureen had said something that sounded like a frog in the throat, but was supposed to be a Gaelic birthday wish for a lovely young colleen. Which was sweet, but a bit embarrassing.

She wasn't entirely sure what a colleen was, but she suspected she wasn't qualified. She'd been tempted to confess to being a widow, only if someone were to ask her how her husband had died, she wasn't sure she could deal with it.

Random thoughts wafted in and out of her mind like clouds on a summer day. She settled deeper into the comfortable feather mattress, picturing flocks of small white clouds drifting lazily over familiar farms and fields, all framed by low rock walls.

Roses . . . tomorrow she would have to see about placing another order from the seed catalog. Evard had promised her another load of eel grass and manure, and she'd pinched his cheek. Actually pinched his cheek.

Oh, my . . .

And Neil. She had called him that tonight. He had called her Fallon. She'd wanted him to call her Ana. There wasn't an Irish bone in her body, she was English and Italian and sick to death of pretense.

Oh, how she wished she had never set out on this wicked, crooked road. . . .

Mr. Hobbs was brewing up feverfew tea for the Merriweathers when Ana made her unsteady way to the kitchen the next morning. "If you're troubled with indisposition, madam, I'd be glad to offer you a cup," he said. "Mr. Merriweather swears by it for the headache." He was the only one in the household who referred to his employer by his full name.

"I'll try anything. I never used to have headaches at all," she said plaintively. "It must be all this humidity."

It was partly the heavy atmosphere, partly Maureen's potent punch, and partly the fact that she'd been up half the night with Miss Drucy, who had been tearful and angry by turns. Ana had ended up singing to her, and through some miracle, it had done the trick. Not that her singing voice was any more musical than her touch on the piano.

She had looked in on her before coming down to breakfast, tucked the covers up under her wattled chin, and on impulse, leaned over and kissed the old dear on the forehead. The thought occurred to her that if this was the closest she would ever come to having a child to care for, she might as well make the most of it while she could.

After breakfast, she collected the darning basket and several pairs of stockings, both hers and Miss Drucy's. Briars, vines, and saw grass were hard on hosiery. She had barely slipped the darning gourd into the first stocking when Neil came into the room. She glanced up and caught him watching her from the doorway.

"Well, for heaven's sake, why not scare a body to death?" she snapped, thoroughly disgusted at the way her pulses leaped at the sight of him. Even more disgusted at the visible heat that flooded her cheeks.

He laid a bundle of mail and newspapers on the parlor table. "Evidently, birthdays don't agree with you," he said dryly. "Would it help to know there's a gentleman at the landing waiting to see you? Advanced age doesn't seem to have diminished your charms. I invited him in, but he said he'd rather wait for you outside, that he needed to speak to you privately."

"To speak to me?" Ana dropped the stocking. The gourd rolled unnoticed under her chair. She'd always known that one day her past would catch up with her, but not now. Not yet. She wasn't ready. "Are you sure he asked for me?"

"He asked for Fallon McKnight, and said to hurry, please, as the ferry was to collect him on his way back from the station."

Fallon McKnight. Of course.

Well, whatever the poor woman had done, it couldn't be as bad as what Ana had done.

Nervous, she stood too quickly, dumping the tangle of stockings in the process, and hurried from the room without a word. Brand watched her go, her skirts swaying around her hips in a way that was probably intended to have just the effect on any man within range that it was having on him.

Damn her. He had a fairly good idea the man was just one more of the poor fools she'd left bleeding in the trenches after she'd fled from Litchfield Hills. A smarter man would have chalked it up to experience and considered himself lucky to get off with nothing more lost than his pride and pocketbook, but evidently this poor sod wasn't too smart.

Without a shred of guilt, he moved to the window that looked out over the landing, waiting for her to appear. The man was young—surprisingly young for a woman who admitted to having turned twenty-eight.

And that was another thing that puzzled him. He could have sworn Liam said the girl he'd married was only nineteen years old. He'd known women to subtract a few years, but never to add them.

He was half tempted to go after her himself, but he didn't. Arms crossed over his chest, a scowl on his face, he waited for her to join her young man.

Chapter Seven

Brand continued to watch from the window, only dimly aware of various household noises. The clash of crockery being dried and put away. Maureen's melodious, if untrained voice singing one of the songs Fallon had played for them.

Or rather, tried to play.

God, she was bad. The surprising thing was that she freely admitted it. With no pretense whatsoever of false modesty, she'd given in to their demands and cheerfully sacrificed herself on the altar of entertainment.

As much as he hated to admit it, there were other qualities in the woman that he was reluctantly coming to admire. Qualities Liam had never bothered to mention, possibly because he'd been too young to appreciate them.

Outside, sunlight slipped through the clouds, glinting off the ruffled gray surface of the water. Waiting for her to appear around the corner of the house, he pictured the way the same light would glint from her unruly hair.

Could she have dashed upstairs to pin it up again before meeting her young man? As early in the day as it was, she was already beginning to fall apart.

And against all reason, that was just one more thing he had come to enjoy about her—the way her hair behaved.

Or rather, misbehaved. More than once while she was out digging in the sand or walking with Miss Drucy along the shore, he had watched her yank the remaining pins from that knot she started out with each day, cram them into a pocket, twist the unruly mass into a rope, knot it, and go about her business.

Where the devil was she? he wondered. How long did it take a woman to tidy herself and pinch some color into her cheeks?

Not that she needed to do much pinching. He hadn't missed the way she'd colored up when she'd seen him in the doorway. He'd like to believe it was in reaction to his manly charms, because if his campaign of seduction had any chance of succeeding, she would need to meet him halfway.

Were women at all like men in that respect? Could they enjoy sex for the sake of sex, alone, without caring two-penny's worth for their partner?

A few did, but not many, at least not in his experience. He'd brought a few of the women he'd known to pleasure, and enjoyed it all the more himself, but most weren't able to let themselves go enough.

Still, if Fallon was one of those rare creatures who truly did enjoy the pleasures of the body, then once experienced, perhaps it had became habit-forming. And from all he'd heard about her, she had definitely formed the habit.

Where the hell was she? If she wasted much more time, her fellow would be gone. It didn't take Pam all that long to off-load freight at the station and head north again.

Belatedly, it occurred to Brand that she might be packing to go with him. Swearing under his breath, he was just headed for the stairs when Mr. Merry emerged from the library. "If you've a minute, Neil, I've run across something that might interest you."

He hadn't a minute, only he didn't want to have to explain why he was in such a tearing hurry. The old gentleman liked her. He was going to hate like hell having to disillusion him.

On the verge of making up some excuse, he turned from the window and said, "Don't tell me you found that book you mentioned yesterday?"

"Not only found it, but found a newspaper clipping listing all the ships that have wrecked in the inlet since it opened back in forty-six, and a description of Fort Oregon."

Taking time only to poke her head in the kitchen and ask Simmy to look in on Miss Drucy now and then, Ana hurried out the back door, being careful to keep the house between herself and the landing until she was safe and out of sight behind the row of low dunes that bordered the ocean.

It had to be Fallon's young man. What on earth could he want with her? Didn't he know Fallon had died in the fire?

But Fallon hadn't died. It was Anamarie G. Hebbel who had died, her grave clearly marked for all to see.

Oh, God, what now? Anyone who had known Fallon would know at a glance that she wasn't who she was pretending to be. Was that why he'd come after her? To expose her to the Merriweathers? Then why not go directly to Mr. Merry instead of asking to speak to her privately?

Unless he intended to demand payment for his silence.

That was almost funny, only she didn't feel much like laughing. The truth was, if he could afford the ferry fare out to Pea Island, he had more money than she did.

Think, Anamarie, think!

She didn't want to think. She was sick to death of thinking. She would much rather lie down on the soft, cool sand and allow the wind to blow and blow and pile sand over her until she disappeared from sight. Maybe then the world would ignore her until she could figure out what to do next, where to go . . .

The wind had already made a ruin of her hair. Impatiently, she plucked away the loose strands that skeined across her face. Her cheeks were burning, too, but only because she'd stayed out too long yesterday digging up a bed for roses where no roses were ever likely to grow.

One more in a long line of fruitless exercises.

Skirts swishing with every vigorous step, she strode along the shore, trying as she had done so many times in the past to outwalk her troubles. Her heels dug deeply into the soft sand, kicking up grains that would inevitably find their way into the hem of her skirt, her petticoat ruffle, her shoes, and even her stockings.

Not to mention her bed.

One of the few pleasures she'd been able to afford over the years she'd been a prisoner in her own home was walking. Walking, taking out her frustration on her mother's old piano, and squeezing enough money from the household account to buy books. Purple, passionate prose, the more lurid, the better. According to her father, fiction was a waste of time, but then, life itself had become a waste of time. He'd said it so often she had almost come to believe him.

Vague fears and fragments of memory drove her on, plowing through the soft sand. She lost track of time. Not until her boots filled with the stuff did she slow down, and then, dropping to the ground, she unlaced them, stripped them off, and emptied them out, setting them neatly beside her.

She wriggled her toes, relishing the small pleasure. Then, propping her elbows on her knees, she squinted against the glare of morning sun on the water and willed nature to work its magic spell.

Come now, sky—come now, ocean—surely you can help me put my tiny problems in perspective.

That perspective being, she thought ruefully, that she was appallingly small, her troubles of no great significance to anyone outside her immediate circle.

Did she even have an immediate circle anymore? If she dropped from the face of the earth this very minute, would anyone know or care?

Would Neil?

Hardly.

How the devil had she got herself embroiled in such a mess?

"Don't ask," she whispered. "Just go ahead and wallow in self-pity. Pretty soon you'll be weeping, and then your nose will stop up and your eyes will start to burn, and then you'll really have something to complain about, won't you?"

Sighing, she reached for her shoes, cradled them in her lap for a moment, and then set them down again. Better wait a few more minutes just to be sure he'd gone. Whatever it was he wanted, she couldn't help him, poor man.

Offshore a flock of noisy seagulls squawked and dived for their dinner. A string of pelicans flew past, and Ana marveled that such ungainly birds could look so graceful. Perhaps all God's creatures were lovely in their element. It was only when they tried to escape their destiny that things went wrong.

"Well. As pleasant as all this is, Anamarie, you can hardly sit here forever."

For one thing, she was hungry. For another, the wind off the water was chilly, despite the sun's heat. If her caller were any sort of gentleman at all, he'd be gone.

And if he was still here, she would simply have to come up with a plausible story to explain why she had borrowed Fallon's name.

Ha! And while she was at it, she might explain why the tide followed the moon, or was it the other way around? And why light shone out through a window, but darkness didn't shine in.

And why she was so attracted to a man who couldn't make up his mind whether she was friend or foe. Whether to like her or despise her. Who could laugh with her one minute and freeze her with a single glance the next.

She was reaching for her shoes again when someone spoke from over her head. "At a guess, I'd say it's rum and molasses headed north, coal headed south, and lumber bound for the West Indies."

With a startled yelp she twisted around to glare up at the man who had come up silently behind her. "Why do you insist on trying to scare me to death? Does it give you some perverse kind of pleasure?"

"I was speaking of the three freighters offshore. Sorry—did I startle you?"

"Not at all, my heart always jumps around this way. Of *course* you startled me! You do it on purpose!"

With a casual grace that was rare in so large a man, Neil Dalton dropped to the sand beside her, grinning just as if he hadn't deliberately frightened her out of a year's growth. "I was expecting you to come inside again after you saw your young man off."

"He's not—that is, I didn't—"

"He left. Came up to the house looking for you, but no one knew where you were. Said to tell you he'd be back. I think he was hoping to be invited to stay, but Maureen took a dislike to the poor devil and sent him packing. Said he looked shifty to her."

Brand watched curiously as she dug her toes into the sand, refusing to meet his eyes. "Yes, well . . . I don't really know him."

"No? Then aren't you even curious as to what he wanted?"

She shrugged. "Not really. Probably a salesman of some sort."

"What if you needed whatever it was he was selling?"

"I don't waste money on things I can do without," she snapped.

"My, aren't we frugal? I'd have thought there were several things you might need. A new gown, for one. A pair of shoes that aren't ruined from salt-water baths for another. Maybe even a few more hairpins."

Brand reached out to touch her hair, now in utter disarray.

She jerked away from his hand, and then tried to pretend she hadn't. He watched curiously as she brushed sand from her skirt and then went on to pinch tiny pleats in the dull fabric with her fingers.

He was half tempted to relent. It went against the grain to torment a woman, but dammit, there were certain things he needed to know.

Could she really be as poor as she tried to pretend? She had certainly cleaned out Liam's pockets. Sold everything that wasn't nailed down. And what about those other poor devils she'd lured into her web? What had happened to the sealskin cape she'd worn in her wedding picture? He was no expert on women's clothes, but he'd lay odds the thing had set someone back a tidy bundle. Probably Liam.

Give her some leeway, you jackass. She lost everything in the fire.

She refused to look at him. Instead, she scowled at the three ships passing offshore, as if a lugger and two schooners were of great interest.

Several strands of her hair blew across his face. It felt like silk. Shorter strands curled around her face and her small ears. He'd never seen hair quite like it. Liam had called it auburn, but what did the boy know about such things? Those glinting depths weren't red. Not even gold. They were more like the yellowish amber from the Baltic Sea.

Like her eyes.

Wrapping his arms around his knees, Brand dug his boot heels into the sand. "Miss Drucy was asking for you."

Aha! That got a rise out of her. With a stricken look she tried to scramble to her feet and in the process, stepped on her skirt tail, let out a yelp, and tumbled awkwardly onto his lap.

He caught her around the hips. "Whoa, easy there."

One of her hands had landed dangerously near a particularly vulnerable part of his body. Off balance, she struggled to right herself, making matters worse.

Brand wasn't quite ready to let her go. When one small fist slid off his inner thigh, he caught his breath, inhaling the scent of the sea mingled with the tantalizing fragrance he'd come to associate with her. Crisp, lemony, sweet, womanly. A fragrance that reminded him of things he'd just as soon not be reminded of at the moment.

Fat chance of that.

"Oh, for heaven's sake, let me up," she grumbled. She shoved against his knee with one hand, his shoulder with the other.

He didn't make it easy for her. A slight shift of his legs and she lost her balance again, giving him another moment to enjoy her slight weight just where he wanted it, cupped against his aching groin.

He took a deep breath, savoring the scent of her skin, and said meekly, "Sorry, I was only trying to help."

"Then thank you kindly, but I'm perfectly capable of standing on my own two feet if you'll only let me go."

"Oh, I can surely do more than that," he said, and without releasing her he got to his feet, lifting her with him so that she stood in the circle of his arms, flushed face, wild hair, sandy gown and all.

Like a doe caught in the light of a hunter's lantern, she stood momentarily frozen in his arms. Confusion clouded her eyes. Slowly, offering her one last chance to escape, he lowered his face.

She didn't move. Her eyes were still staring into his when his lips brushed over her mouth. With a sound that was somewhere between a groan and a whimper, she sagged in his arms, and he was lost.

The taste of her was like whiskey to a drunkard. Like sin to a confirmed sinner. His flesh leaped eagerly in response to the sweet-salt flavor of her mouth, to the feel of her firm, delicately formed body. Just like that, he was fully, embarrassingly aroused.

But then, he'd been aroused almost from the time he caught sight of her, so small, so alone on the vast empty shore.

This hadn't been a part of his plan—this reaction to her—but it had happened, all the same.

She didn't pull away. She had to know the condition

he was in, because there was no way in hell of hiding it, yet she wasn't frightened by him.

But then, why should a woman who had been married—a woman who'd probably slept with more men than she could remember—be frightened by a perfectly natural physiological response?

Ana was terrified. Petrified, yet unwilling to end it. His body was moving against her—down there—and his tongue was inside her mouth, and yet she didn't feel threatened. Terrified, but not threatened. As if her mind and her body were separate entities.

It was easy to see which side was winning.

She told herself that he wouldn't hurt her. Not Neil. Not the man whose eyes so often met hers in moments of shared amusement, shared understanding. Other men had hurt her, but Neil never would.

His hands moved over her back, cupping her here, stroking her there—making her wish she had a few more curves for him to explore.

I've lost my mind, she thought. I've completely lost my wits.

Excitement bubbled inside her like boiling water. She felt incredibly strong and incredibly weak at the same time. She felt . . .

Hungry. *Starved!*

Needy. *Desperate!*

She felt things she couldn't begin to understand. Things a few of her novels had hinted of, but not a one of them had ever described.

Certainly nothing she'd ever felt with Ludwig had prepared her for what was happening to her now.

With the warm sun beating down on her bare head and a cool wind pressing her skirt against her body, she stood there on the empty beach and let herself be kissed senseless. If she'd known how to kiss back, she would have done it, but it was all so new to her.

This gentle persuasion, this blossoming, aching, demanding pleasure when his lips moved down her throat to find a sensitive spot she'd never even known she possessed.

Ludwig's few hurried kisses had been wet, messy, and hurtful. She had endured them because she hadn't known any better. Because it was her duty as his wife. He'd told her that, and more.

He'd done that, and more—far more.

It had been nothing like this, nothing at all like the way Neil was touching her, holding her, kissing her.

Heavens, what was he *doing* to her? He really shouldn't be touching her there!

One more second and she would pull away, she really would.

Just one more . . .

Was that ragged sound his breath or her own? Was the hammering between them her heart or his? Or only the beat of the surf against the shore?

Still holding her tightly against him, he lifted his head and stared down at her, and Ana blinked, trying to bring his face into focus. His eyes—had she ever thought them cold? They were beautiful. Like dark, sunlit slate. Warm, intense, and . . . puzzled?

"Neil, what is it? What's wrong?" she whispered, but even as she watched, the warmth fled and once again his eyes were as cold and empty as the North Atlantic Sea.

Wary, confused, and yes, disappointed, she shoved against his chest with both hands. He let her move away, but he didn't release her. Not completely.

"Nothing's wrong, Fallon. Why would you think something was wrong?"

"I don't know, I only know it is."

"Should I apologize?" he asked, and she wanted desperately to think she was only imagining the note of mockery in his voice.

"I—no, I suppose—"

Whatever she might have said went unspoken. No sooner did she manage to gather her wits than he scattered them all over again by capturing her hand and lifting it to his lips. Then, as she continued to stare at him like a bird in thrall to a snake, he turned her hand over and began to trace the calluses at the base of her fingers. Calluses formed by years of carrying scuttles of coal up to her father's room, and more recently, of digging and raking and chopping briar roots to make a rose garden in a barren, desolate place where nothing except for a few wild vines could possibly thrive. . . .

"Let me go," she whispered.

"I'm not holding you."

And he wasn't. His arms were at his sides. Arms that only moments ago had held her. Hands that had caressed her. She tried to think of something devastating to say, but she'd never been any good at that sort of thing.

"No, I don't believe I'll apologize after all. A man would have to be made of stone not to take advantage of a woman who literally tumbles into his lap, and I'm hardly that. Well, not all of me."

His laughter was the kind she'd always hated. The kind meant to embarrass or to hurt.

Brand watched her shoulders stiffen, saw the proud lift of her head, watched her turn and walk away. He'd proved what he had set out to prove. That she was willing. More than willing, in spite of her pretense of reluctance.

He should have felt satisfaction. Instead he felt . . . something else. A troubling mixture of tenderness, anger, and lust that had no place in his plans.

Next to the kitchen and the library, Ana's favorite room in the castle was the one they called the parlor. It was just the sort of room her mother would have loved. A lady's room. It had obviously been furnished with Miss Drucy in mind, though she wasn't sure the woman appreciated it. After hastily brushing, braiding, and pinning up her hair, she collected Miss Drucy and led her there, arming her with a magazine, her blunt-tipped scissors, and a pot of paste.

Settling into the chair by the window, she picked up the darning basket she'd left so hastily less than an hour ago.

Gracious, had it only been an hour?

She glanced at the tall, wag-tailed clock. Fifty-seven minutes. A life could change irretrievably in less time than that. Hers had, more than once.

Darning was safe, comforting. Squinting, she threaded a needle and felt about in the basket for the darning gourd. Across the room, Miss Drucy, her pale lips pursed, carefully cut pictures from old copies of *The Ladies Journal* and pasted them in a ledger as though they were photographs in an album.

No gourd. Voicing a mild oath, Ana knelt and retrieved the thing from under the chair where it had rolled, then picked up a stocking, one of the delicate silk ones Miss Drucy treated as carelessly as if they were dust rags.

Both hands grew still and she gazed out the window toward the inlet. He had kissed her. Oh, my. . . .

She could count on one hand—on three fingers, in fact—the number of men who had kissed her. Abner Butler didn't count. He'd been nine, she'd been ten. He'd done it on a dare.

There'd been another young gentleman when she was fifteen, the summer her mother had died. They'd played spin the bottle at Sara Dozier's birthday party while Sara's parents had been playing bridge in the next room, and Ana had received what she'd thought of at the time as her first grown-up kiss.

It had been no more than a dry peck of puckered lips on puckered lips, but years later, when Ludwig had kissed her on their wedding night, she had remembered it longingly.

Remarkable, she thought dreamily, how kisses could differ. A mother's kiss. A friend's. A father's for a daughter who had fallen from her pony and landed in a pile of manure, hurting little more than her pride.

Anamarie, you're a sight to see!

Left with her thoughts, Ana darned rips, snags, and ladders. Miss Drucy muttered to herself. The clock ticked away an hour, and then another, and Maureen came in to see who wanted hot tea and who wanted cold, now that spring had finally arrived.

"Pity you weren't here when your young man came to call," she said, lingering to straighten the folds of a linen drapery that didn't need straightening.

"Yes, isn't it?" Ana murmured.

"Said he didn't care to leave a message. I asked him."

"Hmm."

"Didn't even leave his name. I offered to let him wait until Mr. Hobbs had done shaving Mr. Merry, but he said he had to get back."

"I expect he was in a hurry."

"Sure, and didn't I just say so? Not that I was sorry to see the backside of him. I'm thinking I'd not be trusting a daughter of mine with the likes of that one, not that I ever had a daughter, but you mark my words, girl, you'd do a sight better to play up to Mr. Neil. Now, there's a gentleman any lady would be proud to wear on her arm."

Ana had to laugh, in spite of herself. "Somehow, I can't picture any woman wearing Neil Dalton on her arm."

"Well, then, there's always Mr. Tom. He's coming to visit, him and the boys. Letter came today on the same boat as brought your friend."

Mildly exasperated, Ana laid aside a half-mended stocking. "I keep telling you, he's not my friend. I have no idea who he is, much less what he wants, and don't you dare try any of your matchmaking tricks with Mr. Merry's son."

"Sure, and didn't Mr. Tom's wife pass to her reward more than a year ago? And here you are, an unmarried lady? He's not all that much older than you are, and them two boys needs a mother."

"Maureen," Ana warned, and the housekeeper climbed on her high horse and wrapped her hands in her apron.

"All right, all right, but I'll have me say, and don't you forget it. A hot water bottle's not near as nice to snuggle up to of a cold winter night. Just you remember that before you get too old to do anything about it."

Laughing in spite of herself, Ana threw the stocking at her. Maureen retreated, still muttering under her breath, and Miss Drucy said, "Cold."

"Oh, please—not you, too. A stack of quilts and a nice hot water bottle are far less trouble, believe me."

"Tea. I want mine cold."

Ana closed her eyes and leaned her head back against the chintz-covered wing chair. Could she have slipped through the looking glass again, like poor Alice? It seemed more and more likely.

"We'll both have cold tea, and perhaps toasted cheese sandwiches, and some of Maureen's lovely ginger wafers."

"And pickles."

"Yes, dear, and pickles. Let's see how it looks." Setting aside her basket, she joined Drucy, and after admiring her neat handiwork, showed her how to draw a fancy frame around each picture. "I'll need you to help me get the trenches ready for your roses this afternoon. They'll be here before you know it."

For the next three days Ana managed to avoid being alone with Neil. It was bad enough sharing a table with him at mealtime, feeling his gaze on her as she cleaned her plate and urged Miss Drucy to do the same.

Her appetite was better now that she no longer suffered nightmares. It had been nearly two weeks since the last one. She put it down to being so far away from home, from anything that might remind her of the past.

Now all she had to worry about was her daydreams. Those were almost as disturbing, if for a different reason. Especially after what had happened on the beach. Still, even the daydreams could be managed as long as she was careful to fill every waking hour with some activity or another.

Which wasn't always as easy as it might seem. She and Miss Drucy drew pictures in wet sand, built sand castles, decorating them with bits of broken glass and shell, and walked for miles, following the elusive wild horses. The day the roses came, thorny dry sticks bundled in burlap, they planted every last one and then sent off for seeds for a vegetable garden.

Yet still she found time to dream. Gazing now at the tiny woman hovering over neat stacks of clippings, it occurred to Ana not for the first time that this was as close as she would ever come to having a child of her own to care for. To play with, to keep safe, to comfort when the tears came, often for no discernible reason.

Oh, lord, in her own way, she was every bit as fanciful as Miss Drucy. No wonder the two of them got along so well together.

On the day Tom and the boys arrived, Ana and Drucy were wading in the shallows, searching for clams. There were none to be found, of course. Evard warned them that it was far too early in the season and the water was still too cold—as if she didn't know that; her feet ached all the way up to her hips.

But Miss Drucy insisted, and Ana had long since learned that it was easier to give in than to argue unless real danger was involved.

And so, skirts tucked up around their hips, they waded through the shallows with buckets, collecting shells and the occasional bit of driftwood, drenching petticoats and splashing shirtwaists.

Ana wondered what she was going to do about clothing now that summer was nearly upon them. Thank goodness fashion was not a priority here at Merriweather's Landing.

Of course, Maureen had her lace collar, and Mr. Hobbs his bright paisley bathrobe and his three-piece suits. Mr. Merry had his handsome smoking jackets and his fine tapestry and cashmere lap robes. But as for the rest of them, Miss Drucy included, they were more often than not tattered, faded, sandy, and damp. This was not Pomfret, or even Elizabeth City.

Somewhere in northeastern Connecticut there was a trunk filled with muslins, dimities, and light summer voiles, all perfectly adequate, if a few years out of fashion. Her father had seen no reason to spend money on new dresses as long as she was decently covered. From the man who had once indulged her every childish whim, from pony to sled, to ice skates and china-headed doll, it had been hard to endure, but she'd had no choice.

Not that she'd had anywhere to wear new finery even if she'd been able to afford it. Where financial matters were concerned, Marcus Gilbretta's head had remained clear almost to the end. With Horatio Quillerby's help, he'd seen to it that she had to beg for every penny she spent, and once spent, to account for it to the lawyer's satisfaction.

At least she no longer had Mr. Quillerby to contend with. Now, all she needed was her first paycheck.

Standing knee-deep in water, Ana shaded her eyes with one hand and watched the small skipjack glide alongside the wharf. Two boys leaped ashore, yipping like wild animals. A tall, thin man tossed several bags onto the wharf and clambered over the sides.

"Hello, Mother," he called, just as if there were nothing out of the ordinary in seeing an elderly woman wearing a pink gown and a flower-bedecked bonnet wading up to her knees in the sound, and it not even summer yet.

"William, is that you?"

"It's Tommy, Mother. Come give me a hug!"

"Oh, blessed saints, he would have to catch me like this," Drucy exclaimed. "Now he'll fuss and tell me I'm going to catch my death. I've done it to him more times than I can count."

Her mind had been clear as a bell all day. Ana never failed to marvel at the way she could slip in and out of reality with the ease of a child playing "pretend." Sometimes it was hard to tell just where she was, mentally, which made for some comical moments. More than once Ana would be left wondering which one of them was supposed to be caring for the other.

Only after they had slogged toward the landing through knee-deep water did it occur to Ana that they could have waded ashore and arrived with a speck more dignity.

Well, no . . . hardly dignity.

She brushed her wet skirts down over her blue-tinged ankles while Tom swept his mother up in his arms and swung her around in a circle. Drucy giggled like a schoolgirl. Ana, pretending to a composure she was far from feeling, waited for an introduction.

"Hello. You're Mama's wonderful Miss Fallon, I presume. I'm Tom Merriweather. I know all about you from Father's letters. Those two wild bucks racing off over toward the ocean are Billy and Caleb. Don't let them take advantage of your good nature."

"You're assuming I have a good nature," she said. Allowing her hand to be clasped, she thought, if you knew all about me, dear sir, you'd be beating me about the ears with your Gladstone bag instead of entrusting your family to my tender mercies.

He had nice blue eyes and sandy hair beginning to go gray at the temples, although he was hardly what she would have called middle aged. He was dressed too formally for the occasion, but his grin was engaging, and without knowing any more about him, she liked him for the way he treated his mother.

"There's ginger pudding, if Fallon hasn't eaten it all," Drucy confided as the three of them headed toward the house. "Someone's been sneaking into the kitchen every night and eating all the cakes and puddings. We're not sure who it is, but I have my suspicions." She glanced pointedly at Ana.

Gone again, Ana mused. Sometimes she wished she could escape reality with as much ease and as little pain.

Neil was just going out the door, notebook in hand,

when they met him. Ana made the introductions, uncomfortably aware of looking far from her best.

Not that her best was any great improvement.

"Good to meet you, sir," Tom Merriweather exclaimed cheerfully. "Father writes me that you're
standing in for George while you're here studying the
inlet. With a view to bridging it, I sincerely hope. The
ferry ride can occasionally be daunting to those of us
who suffer a weak stomach."

"I doubt it'll be bridged in my lifetime. Hardly
enough need."

With a piercing look that moved from Tom Merriweather to Ana and back again, he turned and strode
away, leaving Ana to wonder if her imagination was
playing tricks on her again. For a moment he had
looked at the two of them as if they were parts of a
puzzle and he was trying to determine just how and
where they fit together.

Chapter Eight

If Ana's youth had ended abruptly when her mother died, it was restored to her with the coming of Billy and Caleb Merriweather. The four of them ran wild, the two boys, their grandmother, and Ana. Like a pack of playful puppies, they skipped shells, splashed after minnows, and raced yipping and yelling up and down the shoreside, scattering the herd of wild ponies that grazed on the sparse beach grasses and exploring an old, deserted fisherman's camp a few miles down the beach. The boys, simply because they were boys. Miss Drucy because—well, for whatever reason. And Ana, because it was the only way she could keep up with the other three. It was wildly inappropriate for a woman her age, and she loved every minute of it.

Well . . . almost every minute. Nights, when she crawled into bed, sandy, exhausted, sunburned, sporting a multitude of cuts, scrapes, and splinters, she thought she must have utterly lost her mind.

More often than not, Neil Dalton happened to be somewhere nearby. More than ever, she simply didn't know what to make of the man, and so for the most part, she tried not to make anything at all. He was almost frighteningly attractive. She couldn't look at him without remembering how they had kissed. He was invariably patient with the boys and kind to everyone else, but now and then when she caught him looking at her, there was something in his eyes more like anger—or puzzlement—and she reminded herself that Ludwig had seemed kind enough at first, too.

Or rather, he hadn't seemed openly *un*kind. Not until he'd learned the terms of her father's will.

Wisdom, she warned herself, was the better part of valor.

Or was that the other way around?

Either way, she was neither wise nor brave where Neil Dalton was concerned. The more she tried to ignore him, the more aware of him she became. Something about the man invariably spurred her into some outrageous act whenever she knew he was watching. It was almost as if she wanted to shock him. Wanted to force a reaction from him.

Mercy. Lately, she didn't even recognize herself. If anyone had asked her a year ago what she'd be doing a year hence, she would have said without a second thought, dosing her father with cascara and Hostetter's Stomach Bitters, defending her weekly household expenditures to a toadying little lawyer, and remaking another of her mother's old gowns by adding ten inches to the length and subtracting five inches from the bust.

It was Caleb who interrupted her unrewarding thoughts with another question, one of the hundreds he asked each day. Caleb was all wide, hazel eyes, big ragged teeth, and avid curiosity.

"Did you know you can eat muskels, Miss Fallon?" He was clutching a muddy clump of shells in his grimy hands. "Do you think Maureen would cook these if I asked her and said please?"

It had taken Ana less than an hour that first day to learn that he was alarmingly adventurous. "I'm sure certain types of mussels are edible, but—"

"But those, young man, are called horse mussels. Don't ask me why, but I'm pretty sure it has nothing to do with horses. They're probably filled with mud and little else. I doubt they'd be worth the trouble of shucking, much less cooking." Neil had silently come up behind them, his hair, grown shaggy in the weeks since he'd arrived, almost as untidy as Caleb's. "Now, if you're determined to have shellfish for lunch, Evard can show you where to take up some oysters."

Caleb went whooping off after Evard, and Ana, aware that once again he'd caught her looking like something that had washed up on shore, tried to appear composed, gave it up, and looked irritated, instead.

"I believe that's Miss Drucy, isn't it? Did she say she was going to wade out to the duck blind? If I were you I'd try to talk her out of it. Tide's in."

"Oh, lord," Ana muttered. Gathering her skirt in one hand, she kicked off her shoes and hurried down to the water's edge. "Miss Drucy, come see what I've found! You'll never guess!"

Brand watched as she went to head off her charge. It was a constant marvel to him, the way the woman could disguise her true nature. After nearly three weeks, he was no closer to catching her out than he'd been when he'd first arrived, much less to seducing her with his supposed riches and his manly charms.

If anyone was being seduced, it was poor Tom Merriweather. The man was smitten. As his father's heir, he was no doubt sitting on a fortune, which should make him a prime target for a woman like Fallon McKnight.

And as a widower with two sons to raise—sons she was going to great lengths to cultivate—he was just about ready to fall into her greedy little hands like a piece of overripe fruit.

Which was a damned shame. Although a bit of a prig, the fellow seemed a decent, likable sort. Brand was torn between wanting to warn him off and wanting to watch Fallon go into action, if only to prove that he'd been right about her all along.

The trouble was, the longer he was around her, the more doubts were beginning to creep in. It didn't stand to reason that a woman could play such a demanding role twenty-four hours a day, week after week without giving herself away.

So he'd waited for her to slip up, and yesterday he'd
been rewarded for his patience.

Sweetness and light, my foot. She was no more
sweetness and light than he was. He'd caught her ring-
ing a peal over one of the mule-eared kitchen chairs
when her pocket had snagged on it once too often,
tearing a rent in her skirt.

And not three hours later he'd seen her take out
after Evard's pony with a carpet beater when the half-
wild beast made a mess of her newly planted garden.

On the other hand, he'd never seen her lose patience with Miss Drucy. Or the boys. And God knows,
they were wild as ticks.

Then, too, there was the way she tactfully deflected
Tom's attentions when they became a little too warm.
Either she was cleverer than he'd given her credit for
being and was angling to lure the poor besotted fish
even deeper into her net, or she was trying to salvage
his pride by letting him down easy.

He preferred to believe the former, because to believe the latter would be to undermine his very reason
for being here.

Damned if he knew what to believe at this point.

He did know, however, that as long as Tom and the
boys were here, his own campaign would go nowhere.
For one thing, he could never get her alone. Either
she was in the kitchen conferring with Maureen over
meals—the staff already deferred to her as if she were
the lady of the house—or she was out racing up and
down the shore with those two boys and Miss Drucy.

Swearing softly, he seriously considered leaving on
the next ferry despite what she'd done to poor Liam.
If he hadn't promised to stand in for the absent
George Gill, he would do just that.

It wasn't as if he didn't have anything else to do.

But if he went back, it would all be there waiting
for him. The emptiness. The loss. God, he missed
Galen. A year and a half apart in age, nothing at
all alike in temperament, they'd still been closer than
most brothers.

He missed Liam, too, even though they'd never been all that close as adults.

Another mark against him. The boy had needed his guidance, but he'd been too wrapped up in the excitement of building a shipping business to notice. If he'd given the matter any thought at all, he'd probably have concluded that he was doing it for the sake of his brothers. Galen needed something to get involved with. He was inclined to be easygoing, without a whole lot of ambition.

And Liam surely needed to learn to stand on his own two feet, without someone looking over his shoulder every minute.

Besides, what else were achievements for if not to be shared with loved ones? There were enough ships available to transport all the world's products to all the world's markets without his modest fleet.

Digging his fingers into the taut muscles at the back of his neck, Brand sighed heavily and swore some more. A week. He'd give it one more week. Then he would tell her who he was, tell her straight out what he thought of her, damn her wretched soul to hell, and leave.

Maybe if he worked hard enough for the next fifty years, he might even forget her.

Or rather, forget who she was and what she'd done.

For the next few days the house was overrun with noise and laughter and sandy, smelly little boys bringing in things better left outside. Fallon was everywhere, serving as both captain and crew. If it occurred to him that now and then there was almost an air of desperation in her laughter, in the tireless way she kept her three charges going until everyone was ready to drop, he dismissed it as wishful thinking.

He wanted to believe he had her on the ropes, but did he? Did he truly?

At night, once the boys were settled and the ladies had retired for the evening, Mr. Merry invariably invited her to join the gentlemen for a glass of wine and perhaps a game.

And just as invariably, she declined.

Once or twice, he wondered if it was because she was ashamed of the condition of her gowns. They were nondescript at best, downright bedraggled at worse.

Brand had never paid much attention to ladies' fashions, but it was hard to ignore the fact that everything she wore looked just like everything else, and none of it was pretty.

If only she weren't so damned likable!

Not to mention so damned desirable.

They were sitting around the dinner table one evening after one of Maureen's splendid baked oyster casseroles, followed by an iced gingerbread. Conversation was dilatory. Everyone was pleasantly tired. Brand had spent the day securing loose shutters and replacing the sand that had scoured away from the foundation on the northeast corner of the house.

"Market was down seven points last week," Tom remarked.

"That's a serious dip. Perhaps I'd better get in touch with—"

Miss Drucy laid a thin hand on her son's sleeve. "Who is his wife?" she whispered loudly, pointing at her husband.

Tom smiled indulgently. "Why, Mother, you are."

The elderly woman looked thoughtful for a moment, and then nodded. "That's nice."

Brand happened to glance at Fallon at that moment and saw her eyes fill with tears. She bit her lip and blinked them away, and the moment was swallowed up by Tom's announcement that he and his sons would be leaving two days hence to continue their trip to Charleston.

"Grandma Billings said I could sleep out on the balcony next time we came to visit, and this is next time."

"She did not, you're not big enough."

"She did so, didn't she, Papa? I am, too, aren't I?"

"Boys." Their father's rebuke settled the two in their chairs, but there were a few aftershocks. The odd twitch. A lurch or two.

Recalling his own boyhood, Brand had a feeling there was a battle underway beneath the damask-covered table.

It was Fallon who affected a cease fire with a single look. His lifted eyebrows said silently, "Well done."

Her regal nod replied, "It was nothing."

He looked from Fallon to Tom and back, awaiting another announcement, but none was forthcoming.

He refused to admit that it was relief he was feeling.

And then the moment passed. Maureen said something about hoping tomorrow would be a good drying day, and Miss Drucy began beating out rhythm with her knife handle on the rim of her Waterford tumbler until Fallon gently removed the knife from her hands and suggested a cup of cocoa before they went up to bed.

It was Fallon who helped get the boys' clothing washed, dried, and ready to pack the next day. She seemed subdued. Brand told himself it was because she hadn't been able to bring young Merriweather up to scratch.

Yet. There was still time.

So he made a point of staying around the house to watch her, hating the feel of what he was doing. Snooping. Spying.

Hating what he had become.

To his relief, he could detect nothing more than a hint of sadness as she packed clothing, the cookies Maureen had spent hours baking, and all the salty treasures the boys had collected during their visit.

On the morning of their leave-taking, he remained in the background, feeling guiltier than ever over his own deceptive role. He saw the old man halt his wheelchair in the doorway to watch wistfully as the others set out along the sandy path to the wharf, and it came to him that there was one thing he could do before he left that might help assuage his conscience.

So he followed them down to the landing, and while the others said their good-byes, he had a word with Pam, handed over a few folded bills, and stepped back while Fallon embraced both boys and turned to Tom. "It's been lovely. I hope you—"

Whatever it was she hoped, Brand missed it when the boys began shouting back and forth.

"Grandpa Billings said I could drive the pony cart all by myself this time," Caleb crowed.

"I get to drive first," Billy insisted.

"You do not, because he promised me first!"

"He did not!"

"He did, too!"

Fallon moved to take control—oh, she was good at control, Brand thought rancorously—by grabbing first one boy and then the other and planting a noisy kiss on each tanned cheek. While they were uttering sounds of disgust and wiping away her kisses with small grimy fists, Tom embraced his mother.

Then, with a last, lingering look at Fallon, he stepped aboard the ferry and collared his two sons before they could come to blows again.

Embarrassed and angry, Brand stalked back to the house, hands shoved deep in his pockets. He wasn't jealous, dammit. Far from it. Whether he knew it or not, young Merriweather had had a narrow escape. God knows how the boys would have fared with *her* for a stepmother. They'd have ended up in a reformatory, either that or the poorhouse.

Beautiful and passionate beyond belief, Liam had written.

The beauty, Brand would concede, if hardly in the usual style, but passionate? If she was passionate about anything, he had yet to see it.

Passionate about her own welfare, he amended. About looking after her own interests.

Although, he had to admit . . .

No, dammit, he didn't have to admit anything.

*   *   *

It was a Monday when the young Merriweathers left to continue their trip south. The following Thursday the lumber Brand had ordered was delivered, and with the few available tools and Evard's help, he set to work building the boardwalk that would run between the house and the landing.

He was going to have to leave soon, George Gill or no George Gill. The project helped ease his conscience, and besides, there was a bonus he hadn't counted on. Miss Drucy was fascinated by the project, which meant that Fallon was usually somewhere around, giving him further opportunity to study her.

Although, by the end of the first day's work, he wasn't sure it could be counted as a bonus. With her laughter, her easy chatter and her disheveled beauty, she was a constant distraction. He knew for a fact that she was only a couple of years shy of thirty. Yet, seeing her with both hands clasping her blowing hair, skirts billowing in the wind, her head thrown back as she laughed at something Miss Drucy said, he would have sworn she was no more than eighteen.

The two women dug in the newly planted garden, replanting the rows destroyed by the half-tame pony Evard used to pull the cart. They brought out a tray of tumblers and a pitcherful of cider and plopped down on the stack of cypress boards, freely offering comments and suggestions.

"Did you know oxen won't swim an inlet?"

"No, I didn't know oxen won't swim an inlet, and since there're none about, I don't see where it matters." He sounded surly.

He felt surly.

"Miss Drucy says so, and they do have oxen, too. At the Lifesaving Station. To pull the boat."

Brand shot her a sour look, suspecting she knew precisely what she was doing. Distracting him. Taking his mind off what he was supposed to be doing.

Well, dammit, it wasn't going to work.

He whammed down with the hammer, the nail bent, and he bit off an oath.

"What if a tide comes, will your boards float away?"

Without bothering to reply, he took out his frustration by pounding even harder, bending more nails, and working up a thoroughly unjustified temper.

The sun blazed down from a cloudless sky. Sweat dripped off his hair, ran down his brow to sting his eyes. He went on pounding nails, more carefully now, ignoring the soft murmur of female voices. When Fallon asked about building a fence to keep the ponies from ruining her garden again, Brand heard Evard assure her that there would probably be enough lumber left over, as they'd overordered so as not to run short.

Impatiently, Brand stood up, tore off his shirt, and flung it aside. If she wanted a damned fence, then he would build her one!

At this rate, he'd be here all summer.

Off and on all day, Mr. Merry watched from the doorway. The staff came and went, monitoring the progress, enjoying the unusual activity. Even prim Mr. Hobbs lingered outside to watch the progress, not even sweating in his three-piece suit.

Late that evening, they gathered outside in the warm spring air to watch the sun set over the sound. Brand's temper had cooled by now, leaving him embarrassed and ashamed of himself. To make up for it, he set himself forward to be as pleasant as possible, all around.

It wasn't hard to do. Dammit, he liked these people. Genuinely liked them, Fallon included. Which made what he had to do all the more difficult.

Evard watched Simmy more than he watched the setting sun, and as if to make up for his earlier shortness, Brand caught Fallon's gaze and nodded at the young pair perched on the stack of boards.

"What d'you think, love in bloom?" he murmured.

She gave him a wary look, but whispered, "He's her cousin. And besides, she's only fourteen."

"Didn't you ever hear of kissing cousins? Maybe I'd better warn the boy to be on his guard."

"I hardly think he's in any danger. If anyone's in danger, it would be Simmy. She's so tiny, and for all he's only a couple of years older, he's as strong as a grown man."

The sun sank in a splendid blaze of color, and as the western sky rapidly dimmed, they all trooped inside, Fallon bringing up the rear. Brand watched as, hands locked behind her back, she followed the others and stepped up on the half-finished boardwalk.

Then he set out to catch up with her, feeling for once no more than a pleasant mixture of tiredness and relaxation. "Hold up, will you?" he called softly after her, and she did.

Catching up with her, he inhaled and savored the scent of her hair—clean, warm, and sweet, like a pasture full of clover.

"Did you want something?"

"That was a strange remark."

"What was a strange remark?" She kicked first one heel and then the other on the edge of the boards, to remove the sand.

"About the boy being so much stronger." Brand had the oddest feeling that he was on to something, if only he could pin it down.

Ana gave up on getting all the sand off her shoes and moved on toward the house, one part of her wanting to linger outside and bask in the last gleam of daylight.

The trouble was, that wasn't all she wanted to bask in.

Foolish woman! "There's nothing strange about it," she said, a little more sharply than she'd intended. "Men are usually more powerful than women."

"He's only a boy. Besides, women more than make up for the difference with guile. I should think a woman of your experience would know that there's more to strength than mere physical prowess."

"What experience is that?"

"For one thing, I think you're not quite what you'd have us believe. For instance, I'm pretty sure—"

Whatever he might have been going to say was lost when Maureen poked her head out the door and told them to hurry inside and wash for dinner.

Ana snatched at the reprieve, thinking, Dear Lord, what did he know? How had he found out? What was he going to do?

What was *she* going to do?

She did what was expected of her, staying busy, trying not to think. Only when Miss Drucy was washed, brushed, neatly dressed, and calmly buffing her ragged fingernails did she pause long enough to go over that brief, puzzling exchange again.

Once in her own room she moved to stand at the window, gazing down on what had become a familiar view. Water. Sand and a bit of marsh, but mostly water. She loved seeing the reflection of the sky on its surface, but now it reflected only her own troubled thoughts.

He was only fishing. He didn't know anything. He would have said so right away if he knew anything. He'd been here almost as long as she had. How could he possibly have discovered who she was, much less what she'd done?

He was only needling her, trying to get some sort of a reaction from her for his own purposes, whatever they were. Even his kiss had been something like that. The way he'd looked at her.

The trouble was, she knew so little about men.

And didn't want to know the things she *did* know.

Discouraged, she peeled off her gown and washed, taking care not to splash her underclothes. Sooner or later, she was going to have to do something about her wardrobe. Woolens were all very well for winter and early spring, but soon it would be summer.

It would help if she knew when she could expect to be paid. Fallon hadn't mentioned whether it would be on a monthly or a quarterly basis.

She would have to do something to her hair, too. Cut it, perhaps. She could do that. Anyone with a pair of scissors could cut hair. It would be far cooler and easier to manage.

There was little she could do about her unfashionable sunburn or all the freckles she was collecting. She hadn't freckled since her tree-climbing days, when she used to run wild in the orchard, much to her mother's dismay and her father's delight.

Who would ever have believed, she mused as she dusted off her shoes and fastened the last two buttons at the back of her neck, that the Gilbretta heir would end up serving as paid companion in a place like Merriweather's Landing?

And who would have thought that, after committing a crime and running away—after exchanging her identity with a chance-met stranger—she would be able to go for whole days without even thinking about her past?

Dinner was fish again. Fresh vegetables other than the root variety were in short supply, which was why Ana had decided that, as long as she was committed to digging up vast sections of what passed for a yard to plant roses, she might as well plant a kitchen garden, too.

"I miss those boys," Mr. Merry said with a sigh.

"Sure, and they're growing like weeds, they are," said Maureen. The two of them talked about the boys, and how children changed as they grew up, resembling various family members at various stages.

Ana thought, amused, I have my mother's features and my father's stubbornness. Better that than the other way around, I suppose.

"Somebody's stealing my horses," Miss Drucy announced. "Pass the potatoes, please."

And so it went, a pattern that had grown comfortably familiar over the past few weeks. It was almost like having a family again, thought Ana, though she could hardly remember what it had been like to sit down with both her parents at mealtime.

Nor would her mother ever have dreamed of invit-

ing Etta or Samuels to join them, much less whatever
daytime help they happened to have.

Carefully avoiding so much as a single glance in
Neil's direction, she served Miss Drucy a boiled po-
tato, cut it up, and added a pat of butter. Her own
meal had scarcely been touched. At first she'd been
afraid Neil would corner her and pick up where he'd
left off out on the boardwalk, but evidently he hadn't
been serious.

Needling her. That's all it was. He'd simply been
needling her, the way Mr. Quillerby used to needle
her, hoping she would say something he could use
against her.

All Neil said was things like, "Please pass the salt,"
and "I'll get started on your fence as soon as I wind
up the walkway," and then he and Mr. Merry started
talking about politics, and Ana relaxed again, allowing
her mind to wander.

For some reason, she felt unusually homesick tonight. Leaning back in her chair, she stared out the
east window at the purple-streaked sky, remembering
all the years she had eaten her meals from a tray in
her father's bedroom. All the years spent dreaming of
places she would never see, people she would never
meet. . . .

"Full moon rising out over the ocean," Mr. Merry
observed.

"Don't forget to make a wish before it sets," said
Maureen, who believed in wish-making at every possible occasion.

Ana rose and collected her plate and Miss Drucy's.
Many hands, as Maureen often said, made for short
work. Neil stacked the plates on his side of the table
and handed them over to Simmy. Rising, he said
"Anyone for wish-making? I think Miss Fallon is missing someone."

"I'm missing a button on my drawers," Drucy declared. "I told you I wanted ties."

Ana snatched up a handful of silverware and escaped to the kitchen, where Neil found her a moment later. "Do you need a wrap?" he inquired.

"You go ahead. I'm going to stay here and help Maureen."

"Ye'll do no such, young lady. With a full moon coming up o'er the ocean, ye'll go along and make yer wish. And don't tell me there's nothing ye're wanting, for I know better, that I do."

Sometimes it was safer to be with Neil than to be with a woman who saw romance in the most unlikely places.

"Just for a minute, then. Not that I have a wish to make."

Neil grinned, just as if he hadn't been taunting her a few hours earlier. "You might wish for something around your shoulders. It's turned off cool now that the sun's gone down."

"No, it hasn't, it's warm."

It wasn't all that warm. *She* was warm. But then, she usually was whenever he was around. He could bring her temper boiling to the surface quicker than any man she'd ever known, and that was saying a lot. She could tell the exact moment he entered a room, could sense even before he spoke whether he was in a teasing mood or one of those puzzling dark moods that came over him more and more often lately.

Lord help her, she was allergic to the man!

The spectacle of a full red moon lifting majestically from the ocean, spreading a path that reached all the way to the shore, was breathtaking. In spite of her plan to remain unmoved, Ana was completely enthralled. A single star hung low in the sky, and she made her wish and told herself it didn't matter, that it wasn't going to come true, anyway. She didn't believe in Maureen's pookas and fairies and fairy trees and wish-making nonsense.

"If a hundred people lined the shore, the moon would lay its highway directly at the feet of each one, did you ever notice that?" From the whimsical note in his voice, one would never dream that only a few hours ago he'd been accusing her of—

Well, whatever it was he'd accused her of.

"How could I? I have only my own perspective to go by." A current of cold air drifted over her. Crossing her arms over her breasts, she shivered.

"And what perspective is that? Tell me, Fallon. I'm really curious."

Knowing full well they were talking on more than one level, she played along, if only to prove to herself that she wasn't affected by a moon and a man. "Only what I can see in front of me, from where I happen to be standing at the time."

"And what do you see?"

"A moon. A star. Some water. I grew up in the country. I've seen moonlight before, you know. On snowy meadows and wet slate roofs, and even on a winding stream. It's all nice."

"Nice," he mused.

But then, I didn't have a tall, handsome man beside me making mincemeat of my common sense.

"It's pretty. All right, it's lovely, does that satisfy you?"

He laughed, and reluctantly, she did, too. It was all so silly, this constant sparring. Just this once, she vowed, she was going to forget the past, along with whatever the future might hold, and live for the moment. Surely every woman deserved one recklessly romantic encounter.

She didn't notice when the others went inside. When his arm went around her waist, it seemed the most natural thing in the world. She leaned her head against his shoulder and together they watched as clouds skeined across the sky, casting a nacreous veil over the face of the moon.

"I wish . . ."

"You wish?" he prompted.

"I wish I could follow that magic path all the way across the ocean, around the world."

"I expect you do. Instead, you'll have to be content with another kind of magic."

She thought, he's going to kiss me. Oh, Lord, if he doesn't, then I'll have to kiss him.

"The two of us are casting a single shadow on the sand, have you noticed?"

And, of course, she had to turn her face to see their entwined shadows. He took the opportunity to cup her chin and lift her face to his, and the kiss that followed, just as she'd known it would, was a part of it all. A part of the magic. A part of the exquisite tension that had crackled between them almost from the first.

Or so it seemed to Ana. This time she needed little encouragement. When his fingers pressed gently on her jaw, she opened her mouth to him eagerly. Her knees nearly buckled when his tongue began to explore, but it was more a caress than an invasion, and she caressed him right back, learning along the way. Except for the other time he had kissed her, nothing in her past could have prepared her for the experience. All she'd known of a man's passion before coming here had been hateful, hurtful, and in the end, disastrous.

This was a whole different realm. Heat pooled in her loins, swelled her breasts until they ached for his touch. She could actually feel her nipples harden against the soft lawn of her chemise.

Could he feel it? Was he as aware of what was happening to her body as she was of what was happening to his?

Oh, my . . .

It went on and on—she couldn't get enough of him. Hard and warm, his masculinity, far from being a threat, seemed to issue an invitation she understood only dimly.

His hands roved over her body just as if he could read her mind, as if he knew where she ached for his touch. Her own palms pressed the sides of his face,

moved through his hair, and slid down over his wide
shoulders, reveling in his strength.

Actually reveling in a man's strength!

Even when he dragged his mouth from hers, she
could still feel his heart pounding against her breasts.
Burying his face in her throat, he groaned. "What are
you doing to me? God, woman, we can't—this isn't
supposed to happen."

"I know, I know." Was that thready voice hers?
"What happened?"

"I think it's called spontaneous combustion." He
laughed, the sound raspy, uneven. His hand fit perfectly over her bosom. She could feel her own flesh
swelling against the heat of his palm.

He made no attempt to remove his hand, and she
didn't know how to call his attention to it without
embarrassing them both.

Spontaneous combustion, indeed! If the part of him
that was pressed against her belly moved against her
one more time, she might truly burst into flames.

"Neil, I think—"

"Yeah, so do I," he said hoarsely.

"What?"

His arms eased so that he was no longer holding
her quite so tightly. When his hand fell from her
breast, she wanted to snatch it up and put it back
where it belonged. "I think we could both do with a
long walk on the shore before we go back inside. Either that or a cold swim. Or . . ."

"Or?" she prompted with a boldness that was totally out of character.

"You want me to spell it out for you?"

"No, I—that is, you don't have to make excuses.
I'm hardly an inexperienced girl."

By then he had taken her hand and started walking.
At her words, his fingers tightened painfully on her
own. "Is that an invitation? Are you saying you've
taken lovers before?" There was both a steeliness and
a silkiness in his voice that hadn't been there a moment earlier.

Feeling oddly defensive, yet still not threatened—not physically threatened, at any rate—she tried to explain, "I'm a widow, Neil."

He went utterly still. Stopped in his tracks, and she waited for him to either go on or say something.

He did both. "That doesn't answer my question."

"Your question doesn't deserve an answer," she said with a quiet dignity. She removed her hand from his. Head held high, she turned and started walking back, not daring to look and see if he followed her. Hoping he had. Hoping he hadn't.

Hardly knowing what she hoped.

By the time she let herself in the door and hurried upstairs to her bedroom she was on the verge of tears. She tried to convince herself that it was only because she missed the children. Because she missed—

Oh, everything! All the things she'd once dreamed of having, things every young girl dreams of. If she was crying, it was because she had a right to cry. Because she was falling in love with Neil Dalton, and it wouldn't serve. It simply would not serve.

Taking a deep breath, she knuckled her eyes, blew her nose, and proceeded to ready herself for bed. In her nightgown, with her hair neatly braided and a dab of Maureen's lavender and glycerine balm rubbed into her hands, she tiptoed into Miss Drucy's bedroom and peered in at the sleeping woman.

Moonlight reflected off the white counterpane, revealing a slight form, a pair of frail hands clasped over a flat bosom, one thin white braid trailing across the pillow.

Are you dreaming of the years past with your sweet William? Ana asked silently. *Dreaming of nights filled with passion, of days filled with the boisterous laughter of children? Days filled with love?*

"Perhaps after all, you're the lucky one, my dear," she murmured softly, settling the covers over a pair of bony shoulders. "You got to live all the things some women never do. Remember those things for as long as you can. Surely you'll always have your dreams."

Chapter Nine

The letter came the very day the boardwalk was finished. The entire household, including Mr. Merry, was on hand for the maiden voyage. With several pleasure boats passing in the offing now that spring had arrived and tourists were beginning to flock to Nags Head and Kitty Hawk on the other side of the inlet, there was an air of celebration about the entire procession. Maureen had hurried back to her room to put on her lace collar. Simmy slipped away to pin up her hair, and then looked so self-conscious that Ana wanted to hug the child to her bosom.

Young Evard, having had a hand in the construction, stood proudly beside Neil Dalton. Miss Drucy, her faded eyes round and suspicious, stood silently beside Ana, her flowered muslin skirt billowing in the light breeze while Mr. Hobbs, wearing his festive black and gray cravat, majestically set out to steer the wheelchair down the ramp.

It was Maureen who started the cheers, and then everyone including Miss Drucy joined in. Halfway down the four-foot-wide construction, Mr. Merry waved hands-off and took control of his own locomotion.

"Looks bumpy to me," said Simmy.

"Quit your blathering, girl," Maureen scolded. "What's a bump or two compared to being cooped up inside forevermore?"

"There now, not so fast, sir" cautioned Mr. Hobbs, who trotted two steps behind, his hands poised to pounce if the wheelchair showed any signs of running away.

It was, indeed, a bumpy ride, but it was a triumphant occasion, all the same. Mr. Merry was openly jubilant at his newfound freedom. "Look yonder! Pam's coming to help us celebrate," he called over his shoulder, and sure enough, the ferry was just then pulling into the slough that led to the landing.

The ferryman went so far as to tie up his skipjack fore and aft, walk the length of the boardwalk, and then accept a celebratory glass of cider. "So that's what all that lumber went for," he said more than once. "If that don't beat all. Hope the contraption don't wash away come spring tide."

"That's a consideration, all right," the contraption's builder admitted. "We're working on a way to anchor it down."

The bundle of mail lay forgotten on the hall table while they all went out to see the ferryman off on his rounds. Evard counted sails in the offing. Maureen mentioned a new excursion boat that plied the nearby waters in the summer months, and Ana thought, mercy, where would I be now if I'd succeeded in landing a position with Miss Disaster Tyler all those months ago?

One thing was certain—she would never have met Neil Dalton.

When they turned to go back to the house, Mr. Hobbs insisted on pushing the wheelchair. Mr. Merry was obviously tried from all the excitement, but he pronounced it was a pleasant sort of tiredness, and indeed, the twinkle in his eyes was only slightly dimmer than usual.

Once back in the house, he began sorting through the mail that had been left on the hall table. "Fallon, my dear, here's one for you."

Ana, on her way up the stairs to fetch a pair of dry shoes for Miss Drucy, who had grown bored with admiring the boardwalk and gone chasing mud-fiddlers, turned with a wary look. "For me? Are you sure?"

Retracing her steps, she cautiously extended her

hand, as if half expecting a poisonous spider to emerge from the envelope and bite her on the finger.

Which was little less than the truth.

Who on earth could be writing to her? No one even knew where she was.

But then, the letter was addressed to Fallon McKnight, not Ana Hebbel. Just for a moment she'd forgotten who she was supposed to be.

She took it up to her room, unaware of one man's cool regard as he lingered in the doorway, watching until she disappeared into her room at the head of the stairs.

For the longest time, she stared at the childish handwriting on the front of the envelope. If she'd had the courage, she would have burned the thing and put it out of her mind, but then, she'd already proved she lacked courage.

It had to be from the same man who had come here looking for Fallon. Which led to more questions than she could list, much less find answers for.

Did he know about her? Had he come here to expose her, perhaps even to blackmail her? Heaven knows he had grounds. At the rate her sins were piling up, there wasn't enough money in the world to buy his silence.

But then, why had he addressed the letter to Fallon if he knew Fallon was dead?

Because, you ninny, if he'd addressed it to Ana Hebbel, Mr. Merry would have sent it back, saying there was no one here by that name.

Hands trembling, she ripped open the cheap envelope and shook out the single sheet. There were only two lines, badly written and quickly read.

"Meat me at the hut by the stomps at sunset or I'll tell thim everthing." It was signed, J.W.

The letter fell to the floor. Ana stared out the window at the figure striding toward the inlet, sun glinting off his dark hair, wind plastering his loose white shirt against his chest. She would give her soul for the right to call him back and dump the whole frightening business in his capable hands, and then seek shelter in his arms.

But, of course, that was out of the question.

Anamarie, it's up to thee.

Forcing herself to retrieve the letter from the floor where it had fallen, she smoothed it out and reread the brief message.

Who on earth was J.W.? She didn't know any J.W.

But then, hadn't Fallon been a W.? Among all the other names she'd called herself hadn't there been a Webber? Or a West?

No, it was Webster. She'd mentioned a Webster once in the litany of names she'd adopted. Smith, McKnight—Lord only knew what her real name had been.

The hut by the stomps. The stumps? It had to be the deserted fishing camp. The boys had discovered it when they'd noticed an osprey carrying bits of eel grass in his claws and followed its flight along the shore to a dead pine tree beside the ruins of an old shack. There'd been a few blackened stumps near the water, vestiges of trees killed either by fire or flood.

The boys had wanted to climb the tree and explore the nest, but she'd managed to talk them out of it. No amount of warnings about snakes and rotting wood could keep them from exploring the shack, however. It had been all she could do to keep Miss Drucy from following them into the place.

Meet him at the shack. Why in the world would he want to meet there? Why would he want to meet her at all? And even if he did, why not simply come to the house and ask for her?

Because he'd come once before, and she'd run away.

Because whatever it was he wished to speak about was private. Which meant it was something to do with either her own past or Fallon's. Lord knows, her own was bad enough. Fallon's could hardly be worse.

*   *   *

They'd planned to go out onto the boardwalk and watch the sun set over the sound—sunsets and moonrises were an important part of the local entertainment—but by late afternoon a dark layer of storm clouds had moved in from the west. In view of the frequent flickers of lightning, the excursion was canceled.

Which was just as well, considering that everyone was tired. It had been an exciting day.

After an early supper, Ana took Miss Drucy upstairs and got her ready for bed. She sang "Oh, Susanna" once and "Darling Clementine" twice, and read an article about children's clothing from *The Ladies Journal.*

Not until her charge was sound asleep did she creep into her own room and retrieve her shawl and hurry down the stairs.

Near the bottom, she paused to listen. Evidently, Maureen and Simmy were in their rooms in the servants' quarters. Evard had probably gone out to put hay in the manger in case that pesky half-wild pony of his came around.

There was a light under the library door. At the sound of low masculine murmurs, she recalled that a game of chess had been mentioned earlier.

Good. It was safe, then.

Quietly, she let herself out the back door and hurried down the boardwalk to the shore, wondering if she'd delayed too long. What if he'd grown tired of waiting and left?

Was J.W. the same man who had come before, asking for Fallon?

Of course he was. It would be too coincidental for two different men to show up, asking for Fallon.

The flashes of stark white lightning only made the intervals darker. A breeze, neither warm nor cool, lifted her skirts as she stepped off the boardwalk onto a narrow band of pale sand that followed the edge of the water.

Arms crossed over her breasts, she hurried along,

telling herself it would be over in no time at all. She would find out what he wanted and send him on his way, and that would be the end of that.

Fool. Hardly a week goes by without reading about some poor soul being set upon and murdered.

Yes, but that was in the big cities. Things like that didn't happen in places like Merriweather's Landing.

Thank goodness the tide was low.

Or was it? Everything looked so different at night, even without the confusing bursts of light.

What if she were to trip and fall into the ocean? She wouldn't be missed until sometime tomorrow. Everyone would assume she was asleep in her own bed. The powerful currents flowing out the inlet would probably carry her miles out to sea.

If the fish didn't devour her first.

For heaven's sake, Anamarie, why not frighten yourself to death while you're at it?

Winding creeks cut through the marsh. There were small ponds where wildfowl gathered to feed. She wished now she'd paid more attention to their location.

Just think, not long ago you'd have jumped at the chance to explore a distant shore.

Yes, but not with a storm growling and flashing overhead.

Well, you always wanted to have an adventure, so you might as well make the most of it.

As a means of cheering herself up, the thought failed miserably. A drop of rain struck her forehead. Somewhere nearby, a night heron croaked. Adventure or not, she would count to twenty and then she would turn back. No sane man could possibly expect her to come out on a night like this.

He appeared in a flash of lightning. One minute she was alone; the next minute he was looming in front of her. She cried out and he grabbed her wrist and told her to hush up, and suddenly she was far more than uneasy.

She was terrified.

"Don't touch me!" Pulling her arm free, she jumped back. Dear Lord, how could she have been so stupid as to come alone to meet a strange man on the basis of a semiliterate scrawl? She didn't *do* things like that.

Step by step she backed away.

Step by step, he followed.

She turned to run when he called out, "Wait—come back! *Please.* I'm not going to hurt you."

It was the "please" that did it. Warily, she stood there, poised to flee at the first sign of danger.

"I didn't do it, you know. Leastwise, not on purpose. It was an accident."

"What was an accident?" she whispered.

There was a bright flash and in the moment before her eyes could adjust to the darkness, he caught her by the arm, his fingers like a steel manacle. She tried to scream, but all she managed was a pathetic whimper. He wasn't tall—hardly taller than she was, but he was strong, and there was something about him that wasn't . . . right.

A cold sweat broke out on the parts of her body that weren't already wet from the rain that came in soft, penetrating waves. It made a sound—the rain sweeping across the water. Enclosing her with this terrifying monster.

She tugged at her wrist. His fingers bit harder. "Didn't do what?" she croaked.

"Set the fire."

"The fire?" She forgot to breathe and then had to gasp for air. Torn between the desperate need to get away and the equally powerful urge to stay and discover once and for all what this was all about, she thought, *I'll give him one minute to say whatever it is he came to say, and then I'll break away and run.*

"I can't spare more than a minute. They're waiting for me at home. If I'm not back—" His fingers tightened on her arm, and she thought, I'll be black and blue by morning.

But then, it wouldn't be the first time.

It was raining harder now, hammering down so that

she had trouble hearing his soft-spoken words. Rain dripped off her hair and into her eyes, carrying with it the salt of her own sweat. Lightning captured and held them in its cold brilliance for one endless moment, and she took advantage of the chance to peer at his face.

By the time thunder shook the earth and the world went dark again, she as quite sure of one thing: she didn't know him. Had never laid eyes on him before.

And yet . . .

Like a half-remembered dream, something tugged at the back of her mind. He was young, several years younger than she was, although it was hard to judge accurately under the circumstances. For one thing, he was as wet as she was. Any possible outstanding features were disguised by a grizzle of whiskers. Dark hair, possibly red, plastered his skull, and when he raked it from his eyes she saw that the index finger on his left hand was missing.

"You came to tell me something," she prompted, making a valiant effort to sound calm, and even somewhat bored.

Which wasn't easy when she was trembling in her sodden clothes, but she remembered hearing that when dealing with strange animals one must never show fear.

"Get on with it then, if you please. My friends are waiting for me to—to make up a fourth at bridge."

"You're not her sister. I thought and thought about it, but Fallon never had a sister. She had two old maid cousins somewhere up north, but I'm the only other family she ever had." He frowned as if something puzzled him, and Ana pressed her advantage.

"And you are . . . ?"

"James. Her husband. James Webster."

Husband. Fallon had claimed a jealous fiancé. Later she'd admitted to a husband. Ana didn't know who to believe at this point. Fallon had lied so much, never telling the same tale the same way twice in a row.

"All right, so you're her husband. What do you want with me?"

"Then she's—she's really gone." Light flickered around them again, and she saw that he looked genuinely puzzled. "You don't know me, do you?"

"Of course I don't. We've never met."

He looked relieved, and yet the feeling came over her again that she had seen that face before. Uneasiness gave way to panic, and she tugged at the hand he was gripping. Something was terribly wrong. If she didn't get away quickly . . .

He must have sensed her panic. His hands moved up to her arms, biting painfully into her flesh. "Don't go. Please don't run away again."

"No, no. Of course I won't," she assured him, feeling guilty because that was exactly what she intended to do the minute she could catch him off guard.

His eyes were opened too wide. She could see the whites all around his glittering irises. It made him look . . . dangerous. Irrational. "Please—I have to go now."

"I don't want you to go. *She* went away. I can't let you go, too. I told you I wasn't ever going to let you go, don't you remember? But you didn't believe me."

Dear God, he was mad. He truly thought she was Fallon.

Dealing with Miss Drucy's inconsistencies had given her a certain insight, but it wasn't nearly enough. This man knew Fallon was dead—he had admitted it. Yet he still seemed to be confusing them in his mind.

He shook her until her teeth rattled. "Didn't I tell you that? Didn't I?"

"Tell me what? James." She used his name, hoping to calm him down. He was beginning to fidget, either that or he was as chilled as she was.

"I told you I'd take care of you."

"Yes, you told me that."

"There, I knew you'd remember. Come on, let's go inside out of the rain. Your hair's getting all wet. You never liked that, did you? You see, I remember, too."

Ana's shoulders sagged. She couldn't run away, he was holding her too tightly. Her only chance lie in playing along, answering whatever questions he asked of her, and then running as hard as she could the minute she could break away.

He urged her toward the shack. "Your skin's cold, Fallon."

She was cold all the way to her bones, and it had nothing to do with the weather. He was mad. She'd thought Ludwig was mad, but he'd merely been evil. This poor man was truly . . . confused.

The shack sat up on pilings, three or four feet above the ground. It wasn't easy with a long, wet skirt tangling her legs, but she scrambled inside, wondering if there was any way she could go out the other side.

She couldn't remember.

Oh, God, not again. Was there something about her that invited men to misuse her?

Stop it. Don't even think that way. The problem is his, not yours.

But regardless of whose problem it was, it was up to her to solve it.

It was pitch dark inside. There were gaping holes in the roof where the rain fell through. Cautiously, she crawled toward the far corner, trying to remember whether or not there were any rotten or missing planks. Just her luck to fall through and break her neck.

He was no longer touching her, but that didn't mean she was free to leave. She kept on crawling, cursing the skirts that threatened to bring her down, until she felt the far wall.

He was right behind her. Oh, Lord, what now? she thought.

Turning, she pressed her back against the damp plank wall, drew her feet in as close to her body as possible, and wrapped her arms around her knees. It was something she'd learned during her mercifully brief marriage. To protect her vital organs.

"Mr. Webster, tell me what's bothering you and I'll

do what I can to help, but I really do need to get back to my friends."

It would have helped if her teeth weren't chattering so hard. She sounded like Miss Drucy's clam-shell castanets.

"You're not Fallon. You never told me who you are." He sounded petulant. Which was better than sounding angry.

"You never asked," she said gently. But before she could tell him her name, he shot to his feet and started pacing. She braced herself to jump and run the minute he fell through the floor, and then, against all reason, found herself feeling sorry for him.

He's not your problem! Good Lord, woman, use your brain!

"You're that Ana person, the one that was named on Fallon's tombstone, aren't you? You were sleeping in her bed that night, and—"

And then it hit her. The reason he looked so familiar. "I didn't dream you, did I?" she whispered. "You came into my room that night and woke me up, didn't you?"

He flung himself down in front of her. The floor creaked, and she began to sidle away. "I never meant to hurt her," he whined. "I loved her too much. I'd have treated her like a queen if she'd've only come with me, but she laughed at me. She laughed in my face, like I was dirt under her feet."

Goose bumps prickled down her arms. She, of all people, knew what it was to plead for mercy. This poor man was pleading with her, only she couldn't help him. She wasn't the woman he wanted.

Icy prickles of fear moved down her spine as she moved silently away, keeping her eyes on the lighter rectangle of the doorway.

She was nearly there when suddenly he lunged at her. "I told you not to leave me," he screeched. "I warned you! Didn't I warn you? I know what you did, Fallon. I know everything, all about your fancy men, and the lies you told about me. I know—I know—"

His voice broke. He started to cry and Ana thought, *Oh, Lord, he needs help even more than I do.*

"I can't let you go back, you know." Just like that, he was calm again. Too calm. She tried to crawl away, but he grabbed her hair. "Stop moving away from me! I told you you can't go! We'll stay here together tonight, and then tomorrow we'll go back to Kansas. I have a boat. I stole it, but it doesn't matter. I'll take care of you, Fallon, you know I will. I promised you'd never go hungry—promised I wouldn't let your papa beat on you anymore, and I kept my promise, didn't I? I never let you down."

Please, God, please . . .

"Sit down over here in the corner. There aren't no mice. I looked. I've been here all day, waiting. It's not dirty, either. You always hated the dirt, didn't you? But I cleaned it out real good while I waited for you, so you won't mess up your pretty dress."

There was no longer the least doubt in her mind that James Webster was mad. Totally, terribly mad. Afraid of staying, but even more afraid of triggering another outburst, Ana allowed herself be led back to the far corner. For all the entire place was no more than twelve by twelve feet square, the single door might as well have been a mile away.

"How have you been, um—James?" she asked, hoping to lull him into complacency. Perhaps he would fall asleep.

And perhaps an angel would fly through a hole in the roof and waft her away to safety. Perhaps one of the lifesavers from Pea Island Station would come and save her life.

"Sad. I've been real sad, Fallon, thinking you didn't love me anymore. That's why I followed you, so I could tell you we can move to the city if you hate the farm so much. I don't mind Kansas City, not if you're there with me."

"Oh. Well. That's nice."

"But that other lady, she saw me that night."

But I am the other lady, she wanted to say. *I'm not your Fallon.*

Oh, God, he had them all mixed up in his poor sick mind until there was no untangling them. Whatever Fallon had done to him, it was Ana who would pay.

"That other lady, she knows I went into your room. I thought it was you until she opened her eyes and looked at me, and then I knew. I didn't mean to say all those bad things to you, Fallon. I sure as heck didn't mean to holler at you, but when you said what you said, I got mad. You know how I get sometimes. And then you threw the lamp at me, and the fire started, and I was scared, so I ran. I thought you were right behind me—there were people pushing and shoving and screaming all around me and I thought you were right there, too, only you weren't."

His voice trailed off, and Ana shuddered. Poor Fallon. Poor, poor James. Was love always so destructive? Her father had been so shattered at her mother's death that he'd allowed bitterness to eat at him until he died from it.

Oh, yes, and he'd blamed Ana, too, because if she hadn't gone to that party and caught a cough, her mother never would have come down with a cold a week later that settled on her lungs. It was her fault her mother died. Her father had told her so more than once.

It was her fault Ludwig had died, too.

No wonder James felt guilty. All he'd done was to love someone, and look how it had turned out.

"Fallon?"

She felt his hot breath on her face. He was kneeling in front of her. With the rain droning down on the roof, dripping noisily onto the floor, she hadn't even heard him move. Her back was against the wall again, and once more she began to edge toward the door.

"James, you have to let me go now before someone comes to find me. I'm not Fallon, you know I'm not. I don't have her eyes, see?" She opened her eyes as wide as she could, but of course, in the darkness he couldn't see. And even if he'd been able to see, she suspected he was far past the stage of reasoning. "Listen, you must let me go home now, James. Fallon is safe. I'm sure she understands that the fire wasn't your fault. She knows you love her, that you'd never hurt her, not in a thousand years."

"You saw me, though. I was there in your room, and you opened your eyes and saw me, and I thought, Jimmy, she's going to tell on you, you know she is."

"I would never do that, I promise."

"Cross your heart?"

"Cross my heart," she whispered solemnly. For a moment, she hoped . . .

But then he said. "If I let you go, you'll tell on me, and they'll put me in jail again, and I don't ever want to go back there."

"Oh, please," she moaned.

She felt his hands close around her throat and began to claw at his arms, but he was incredibly strong. She choked—her lungs were on fire—and then somehow, panic lent her one last burst of strength. She managed to whack him on the side of the head with her arm, breaking his grip just long enough to scramble toward the door. She almost made it when there was a sudden blast of thunder and a brilliant, blinding flash. A sharp pain, and then—

Nothing. Peace settled over her like a warm brown fog.

Chapter Ten

Hell was surprisingly comfortable, except that her head ached unbearably. Ana thought about opening her eyes and then thought better of it. Whatever awaited her here, she'd just as soon put it off as long as possible. At least until her head stopped throbbing.

She's awake.

No, she's not.

Yes, she is, I saw her eyelashes twitch.

Lord love us, she is. Go fetch Mr. Neil, quick!

Maureen and Simmy, Ana thought, wondering how they'd come to be here in this particular place. She would have sworn the two of them couldn't come up with a single sin between them if they tried for a hundred years.

But then, you never knew about people. . . .

The next voice she heard was so achingly familiar she felt a heaviness in her chest that extended all the way up to her throat. Smoke inhalation, she told herself. Funny, if she'd thought about hell at all, that aspect of it had never occurred to her.

Brand rolled off his bed and hurried down the hall the instant he heard Simmy call his name. Not taking the time to put on his shoes, he opened the door cautiously and tiptoed across to the bed. Ignoring the housekeeper, he leaned over and examined the purple lump on Fallon's forehead. The swelling had gone down some, but not enough.

"Has the doctor come yet?" he whispered.

Maureen's round face gathered into furrows of concern. She shook her head. "Evard said not to look for him back until this evening." She spoke softly, but not in a whisper.

Bending over the patient, Brand said, "Fallon, can you hear me? Can you open your eyes?"

"Poor bairn, I've been keeping the room dark, but maybe if she was to see some light—?"

"Open the windows. It's stuffy in here."

"I'm thinking she's sure to take cold, being out all night in the rain."

"If a cold's the worst of it, she'll be lucky."

Right from the first, when he'd carried her up to her bedroom, the housekeeper had refused to leave her bedside. He'd finally dragged in another chair and the two of them had kept watch together. If one of them had snored away half the night, no one would ever learn of it from him.

The housekeeper had woken less than an hour ago with a snort and a few muttered words. She'd taken one look at his red-rimmed eyes and insisted he go to bed until the doctor came. "It's no better off she'll be, I'm thinking, for the two of us watching o'er her. I've had me own nap, now go before your eye sockets sink into your skull like two rocks in a bog."

"Do all the Irish have such a wonderful way with words?"

" 'Tis the best in the world we are when it comes to doing what's important. Talking's important."

"Among other things."

"Aye, among other things."

They'd both managed to smile, but then their eyes had turned back to the woman lying so still on the bed, and the smiles had faded.

But Maureen had been right. An hour, or even a few minutes of lying flat on a good bed had helped undo the damage done by too many hours in a chair that had never been designed for sleeping.

Not that he'd slept. Hadn't expected to. His eyes sockets were no better off than before, but at least his back no longer felt as if it were broken.

Dammit, woman, I'll not lose you this way, he vowed silently, touching her cheek. Tracing the bruise that ran from temple to jaw where the rafter had struck her. She'd been damned lucky, at that. The thing could have broken her neck.

A scattering of freckles stood out against her unnatural pallor, making her look younger than the twenty-eight years she claimed. Sick with anger, concern, and something else—something he refused to name— Brand was still staring down at her when she opened her eyes and gazed up at him, just as calmly as if she hadn't been unconscious for nearly eighteen hours.

"I never catch cold," she whispered. "Not since I was a child."

He nearly fell to his knees in surprise. "So you've finally decided to come back to us," he growled, to disguise the relief in his voice.

"Given the choice, wouldn't you? I take it I didn't die and go to hell?"

He glanced over his shoulder at the housekeeper. "She'll need something hot to drink," he said gruffly. "And you might pass the word that she's awake now, but no visitors until the doctor gives the all-clear." Waiting only until the woman left, he closed the door quietly behind her and returned to the bedside. "We're all alone now, Fallon. Is there something you'd like to tell me?"

He watched her try to swallow. She lifted a hand to her throat as though it hurt her. She had beautiful hands. Pale, long-boned, well-formed, for all the calluses in her palms. There were bruises on her wrist, a few on her upper arms and more on her throat, but none to match the one on her forehead.

"No," she rasped. "Yes. I'm thirsty. My head hurts and I need to use the pot. And I think there's a rock on my chest."

"Would you care to explain what you were doing out there in the middle of the night, and who the devil you were meeting?"

"I don't believe so." Sighing, she closed her eyes and he felt the cold finger of dread.

"Fallon? Don't go to sleep again. You've hurt your head. I'm not sure if you have a concussion, but you need to stay awake now."

"No, thank you." Her lashes didn't so much as twitch.

"Listen to me!" On his knees beside the bed, he gripped her hand tightly. "Fallon, open your eyes!" How the devil had she come by those bruises? The one on her head was easy—there'd been a rafter laying at an angle across her shoulders when he'd found her sprawled in the door of that old shack, one arm dangling almost to the ground.

But the others—three distinct finger marks on her wrist, with an opposing thumb mark. Not four, but three. And from the look of her throat, someone had tried to strangle her.

"Fallon, wake up," he repeated urgently.

"Name's not . . ."

"I don't give a damn what your name is, you're going to have to stay awake until the doctor gets here!"

"Tea an' pot. Pot first . . ."

Cursing softly, he surged to his feet, went to the door, and yelled for Simmy.

It was late afternoon before the physician arrived, having been summoned all the way from Currituck County. Maureen brought him upstairs and introduced him, and then remained in attendance while he examined the patient. After a thorough examination and a series of questions, all of which went unanswered, he said shortly, "At any rate, you're a very fortunate young woman to have survived a lightning strike with no more than a lump on your head and a bad cold. As for your other injuries . . ."

"A lightning strike?" Ana struggled to sit up. "I don't remember any lightning strike. What happened to—How did I get home?" Her head was threatening to burst wide open. She grabbed it with both hands and groaned, and the doctor snorted impatiently and pressed her back down onto the pillows. He handed Maureen a packet of powders with instructions to mix it with half a cup of water. Ana only hoped it was something that would make her sleep for the next few years.

And then Neil came in, looking like one of those mythical Norse gods—the one with a fistful of thunder bolts. She gulped down the dose and shuddered. Neil told the doctor that coffee and sandwiches were awaiting him in the kitchen, and that Evard stood ready to take him back across the inlet to where he'd left his horse and buggy.

The entire time he'd addressed the physician, his gaze had never once left Ana's face. She closed her eyes, but it didn't help. She could still feel him looking at her.

"Well?" Amazing how much expression a man could put into a single four-letter word. "Do you feel up to answering a few questions?"

"No, do you? I have some questions of my own," she croaked.

Evidently she'd been hit on the head by a falling timber and on top of that, caught a cold that had settled in her chest and throat. She felt horrible and probably looked worse, and for some reason, that made her feel like crying. What's more, the foul-tasting medicine wasn't doing her a particle of good. She was still wide awake, and she was still hurting.

Looking as if he might actually call down a few thunderbolts, Neil drew a chair up beside the bed. She stared doggedly at the ceiling. He cleared his throat. She tugged the covers up under her chin.

"Well?" he repeated.

"Oh, for heaven's sake, I got struck by lightning! What more do you need to know?"

"You remember, then?"

"I don't remember a blessed thing! All I remember is . . ."

"Yes? All you remember is what?"

"I remember that there was a lot of lightning and some rain. I remember how the rain sounded sweeping across the water. I remember thinking the worst of the storm had passed over, but evidently I was wrong."

"Is that why you decided to take a midnight stroll? Because you liked the sound of rain on the water and thought the worst of the storm had moved on?"

"It wasn't anywhere near midnight," she said sullenly. "It might have seemed later on account of the clouds, but it was only just after sunset."

"Ahhh," he said, as if that explained everything.

The light breeze that stirred the curtains brought with it the pungent aroma of seaweed, cedar, bayberry, and fish. Ana wondered distractedly if being struck by lightning could intensify a person's sense of smell.

She sniffed and caught a drift of something more personal. Something warm and masculine. Something that made her feel both safe and threatened at the same time, which made about as much sense as anything else in her life had made these past few months.

"What makes you think you were struck by lightning? You're not burned anywhere, are you?"

She shrugged. "The doctor said so. He said I was lucky."

"What were you doing in that place, Fallon?"

She clamped her lips shut and scowled at a flying insect that had come in through the window.

Where was James? Surely if the shack had been struck by lightining, he would have been hurt, too. He'd been one step behind her when the explosion had happened.

Had his body been found? Could he have survived and escaped? Had she truly opened her eyes and felt his hands on her throat, heard him sobbing, or had she only imagined it?

No, that was the first time—back at the hotel.

Only then his hands hadn't been around her throat. Oh, drat this miserable confusion! She really needed to know, but if she asked too many questions, she might have to explain who James was and why she'd gone to meet him, and then the whole ball of wax would come undone.

"Fallon? What were you doing out there at that time of night?"

"I like to walk. It gives me an illusion of freedom."

"That's a strange way of putting it. What makes you think you're not free?"

She rolled over, presenting him with her back, and winced at the pain even so small a movement caused. "Oh, for heaven's sake, it's only a figure of speech. I'm sleepy now, Neil, so if you don't mind—?"

She heard him rise, heard the rustle of curtain rings, and the room grew dimmer. Not dark, only shadowy. She heard his footsteps return, heard the chair creak under his weight, and she swallowed a painful lump in her throat. She'd been hoping he would leave.

Lie to others if you must, Anamarie, but not to yourself.

All right, so she didn't want him to leave. There. She'd admitted it.

Sleeping, rousing only long enough to swallow whatever was put before her, Ana soon lost all track of time. When at last she could sleep no longer, she stretched her stiff limbs, flexed her toes, and then her ankles, and remembered the way Fallon used to do the same thing when they both grew stiff from the interminable train ride.

She blinked her eyes several times, and the room gradually came into focus. She was awake. Stiff, sore, disoriented, and disgruntled, but finally awake.

Her head no longer ached. She swallowed experimentally and discovered that her throat was no longer sore. And the rock had finally rolled off her chest.

Maureen bustled in with a tray, took one horrified look and said, "Sure, and you're not about to get out of that bed, girl."

"If that's broth, I don't want it. I'm starving."

"It's oatmeal. You'll eat it and like it, and if you scrape your bowl clean, there's a bit of bread pudding to be found in me kitchen."

"I'm not an invalid. I got a bump on the head, that's all. But if I have to go without real food one more day, I might turn vicious."

The housekeeper plopped the tray on the bedside table and handed her a napkin and a spoon. "My, aren't we cheerful tonight?"

"Yes, we are. What did you make for dinner?"

"Mr. Merry wanted fried fish cakes, and there's some of yesterday's turtle hash left over. I put a pinch of salt in your oatmeal this time."

"You might as well take it away, I won't eat it."

"Then it's fish broth you'll be having. I boiled a puppy drum for the fish cakes."

"I don't want oatmeal and I don't want fish broth, I want real food. Please, please, Maureen?"

"Eat half your oatmeal, and we'll see. I might come help you to get up after dinner. If it's steady on your feet you are, then we'll think about going downstairs in a day or so."

"Yes, ma'am," Ana said meekly. Too meekly by far, if the woman only knew. Some twenty minutes later, her supper tray untouched, she stood shakily at the head of the stairs, fully, if somewhat carelessly, dressed.

Staring down the endless row of stairs, she thought, Maureen just might have been right.

On the other hand, she'd seen for herself what prolonged bed rest could do to a body. If there was one thing she refused to do, it was turn herself into an invalid.

Her stomach rumbled. She gripped the banister. She was halfway down the stairs when a wave of dizziness swept over her. Clinging to the railing, she waited to get her second wind.

At the foot of the stairway, the library door opened suddenly. Neil said something over his shoulder to someone inside, then turned and saw her swaying there, waiting for the spots to drift away from her eyes.

Swearing, he lunged, taking the stairs two at a time. "Where the bloody hell do you think you're going?"

"Where the bloody hell does it look like I'm going?" she shot back, willing her legs not to buckle. "I'm going in to dinner."

"You were ordered to stay in bed."

"Ordered?" It was hard to sound haughty when she was reeling like a kite in a high wind. She lifted her chin, but it didn't help.

"If you're going to be sick to your stomach, speak up. I'll get a bucket."

"Did I ever tell you how much I despise you?" Her grip tightened on the banister and she prayed she could make it all the way down to one of the two side chairs flanking the hall table. It didn't help to notice that even scowling, even with a jaw like the cow catcher on a train—with a nose that went south, then east, then south again—he was the most beautiful man she'd ever laid eyes on. The angel Gabriel should look so good.

"You're not strong enough to be out of bed."

"I won't get any stronger lying in bed and starving."

"If you're hungry, I'll bring a plate up to your room. Maureen's been feeding you. Everytime I look around, she's trudging up those stairs with a tray, won't even let Simmy take over for her."

"She feeds me oatmeal. She knows I hate oatmeal. So does Simmy. Cows eat oats."

"Horses."

"Whatever, at least they don't have to eat it in bed without cream and sugar. There's only one thing wrong with me. I need to use my muscles." To prove it, she let go of the banister and promptly began to sway like a drunken sailor.

Moving faster than a man his size had any right to move, he caught her before she could fall. Swept her up in his arms and then hesitated, as if wondering what to do with her.

She glared at him, trying to ignore the effect his touch was having on her breathing apparatus. "You take me back up there and I'll climb out the window and come in the front door. I'm sick to death of being sick, Neil."

Her eyes lifted pleadingly to his. It was like pleading with a chunk of granite.

"Please? I can't just lie in bed for the rest of my life being waited on." And then she grumbled, "Oh, for heaven's sake, would you listen to me. I've never whined in my life, and now I'm whining, and if there's one thing I can't stand, it's a whiner. I sound just like my—just like an invalid."

She was too close to miss the way his jaw tightened. It could have been the strain of carrying her this way, but she didn't think so. She'd seen it happen too often before, that telltale twitch when she'd done something to irritate him.

Or even when she hadn't.

"Please put me down, I can make it in my own."

She might as well have saved her breath. His arms tightened around her and he demanded softly, "Is that why you ran away?"

"Ran away?" she repeated.

"Because he demanded too much of you?"

"I shouldn't have said that. I don't suppose he could help it, really, but it was just such a waste. Such a needless, senseless waste." Gazing up at his face, it was all she could do to keep from laying her palm against the side of his face, shadowed now with a day's growth of beard. Her father had insisted on being shaved twice a day at first, but after a while he'd refused to let Samuels shave him at all. "How did you—?"

Before she could ask him how he knew about her father, because she was almost sure she had never mentioned him, Mr. Merry wheeled himself into the hallway.

"Fallon! My dear child, we've missed you. I'm delighted you feel up to joining us again. We've all worried about you, haven't we, Neil? Drucy wanders around the house looking like a lost lamb."

"I've missed all of you, too." Oh, blast and damnation, she was fogging up again.

And so they went into the library, and Mr. Hobbs poured them all a glass of scuppernong wine and took his customary place on a stool over by the reference books, and everyone said how glad they were to see her up and around again. Not a one of them mentioned how peculiar they thought it was that she would go out walking after dark in the middle of a thunderstorm without telling anyone where she was going.

Or that she should come home with more bruises than could be accounted for by a rafter falling on her head.

It was almost as if she'd been away on a long journey. Something in the atmosphere was different, but she couldn't put her finger on what it was.

At least Miss Drucy was still the same. Which is to say she talked about her horses and her roses, and then fell silent, staring off into the distance while the others talked all around the subject that was uppermost in their minds.

It was Neil who finally brought it up. They had just settled around the table for dinner when he turned to her and said, "I went out the next morning. There were no footprints—they'd all been washed away the tide, but I found a man's handkerchief near the shack. If Tom or one of the boys had dropped it, the tide would've carried it out by now. Is there something you'd like to tell us, Fallon?"

The fish cakes she'd been so looking forward to turned to ashes in her mouth. Carefully, Ana laid her fork on her plate and took a sip of water. "No. Not that I can think of," she said thoughtfully. "James must have dropped it before he left."

Oh, for pity's sake, she hadn't meant to say that. The medicine must had addled her wits.

"James?" Of course, Neil pounced on it right away. "The man I went to meet."

"My dear, you're perfectly free to invite your friends to visit you here at the house. After all, it's your home now." Mr. Merry looked so troubled she was tempted to pour out the whole wretched business, but that would hardly be fair. He had enough to contend with without taking on her troubles.

Not for the first time Ana wondered how she had ever managed to get her life so entangled. Tell enough lies and they twined together like those vines that covered half the shed, mixing and mingling until it was impossible to tell where one left off and the other began.

She took a careful sip of water, wishing it were wine—wishing it were something even stronger. Maureen's birthday punch would have done nicely just now. "Well. If you insist on knowing, I had a friend who traveled with me as far as Elizabeth City. Unfortunately, there was a fire and she . . . she didn't survive. James is—that is—he was her husband. They'd had a quarrel, you see, and she'd run away, but he wanted her back and so he came after her, only he was too late."

"But why would he come here?" It was, of all people, timid little Mr. Hobbs who asked.

"Now that's a very good question. Actually, I don't really know. That is, I never actually met him before. After the fire we were all taken to a boardinghouse, those of us who survived, and then I left to come here, and . . ."

Ana paused to collect her thoughts, and Drucy clapped her hands and said, "I just remembered where Tommy left his raincoat. He left it at the train station. I knew he would. That boy . . ."

Her voice trailed off and she frowned. Cutlery clinked. Cups rattled in saucers. And then everyone began talking about something else. Maureen said, "If he was the same boy-o who come here looking for you last week, you'll do well to send him packing. Me da had a cousin with eyes like that, with the whites showing all around. Walked into a bog, he did, and drowned himself to death."

No one said a word. An embarrassed silence seemed to have afflicted the entire company. Frantically, Ana wondered if something she'd said could have given her away.

Neil had asked her who James was.

She had told him.

She hadn't mentioned the fact that he was probably mad, or at the very least, badly confused, or that he had twisted her wrist, threatened her, and tried to strangle her. Or that even before that, he'd been involved in the fire that had killed three people, including his own wife. If she truly was his wife.

Not that it mattered any longer whose wife she'd been.

Poor Fallon.

Poor James. What on earth could have happened to him? Wherever he was, she hoped he would forget all about both her and Fallon. Then, perhaps he could begin to heal.

Suddenly, she was overwhelmingly tired. "If you don't mind, I believe I'll make an early night of it," she said. For all her troubles, she hadn't been able to eat more than a few bites.

"I'll take you upstairs," Neil said.

Her protest was lost in a flurry of good nights, and once again she found herself being swept up into his arms. With dreary amusement, she told herself that being an invalid had its rewards, after all.

For the next three days it rained steadily, beating her tender, newly sprouted seedlings into the ground. Ana mourned for all the work that was being undone, but Maureen wouldn't hear of her going outside in the rain to rescue her precious plants. Not that she would have known where to start. What little she knew about gardening she'd learned from one of Mr. Merry's books.

However, the very next day she insisted on resum-

ing her duties as companion, which was how she came
to be in the attic one afternoon with Miss Drucy, going
through one of the dozens of trunks stored there.

It was gloomy, the only light coming from the rain-
spattered dormers and the lamps Evard had lit for
them when he'd come up to clear away the spider-
webs.

Miss Drucy was having one of her good spells. She
chattered cheerfully of the past, pulling out dresses
that were dated and badly creased, but still lovely. "I
wore this the first time William took me to a horse
race. We bet fifty cents on a bay named Mortimer's
Dream." She giggled. "Lost it all, too, but I didn't
care. He was so wickedly handsome with his blue
broadcloth suit and his black satin waistcoat. My William, not the horse. On the way home he bought me
an orange ice and held my hand."

She lifted out a handsome purple brocade with jet
beads, and then several summer gowns of muslin and
taffeta and lawn in shades that were still as bright as
new. The scent of camphor and lavender mingled with
the smell of lamp oil and dust. Rain drummed down
on the roof, enclosing them in a cozy world of make-
believe and memories, and Ana tried to imagine a
past that was nothing at all like her own. A past filled
with dances and parties. . . .

And a war. There was a moth-eaten blue uniform
packed away in tissue. Carefully replacing it along
with a tarnished sword and scabbard, she watched as
the older woman opened another chest and began to
lift out pressed flowers, a pair of yellowed kid gloves,
and a pair of tiny crocheted baby stockings. Several
times she smiled, once she even laughed aloud. Ana
sat silently by and allowed her to explore her precious
broken memories.

And then she lifted out the doll, her matted hair
and painted simper untouched by time. "Oh, was she
yours? She's lovely!"

"She was for Alice. Alice would have been five
years old on her birthday." The faded blue eyes filled

with tears and overflowed, and somehow, the two women found themselves clinging together, crying for all the treasures and tragedies of their separate pasts.

Ana recovered first. She sat back on her heels, sniffed, and said, "There now, my nose is stopped up and yours is red as a cherry." With a broken laugh, she mopped her eyes on a monogrammed linen handkerchief that shed bits of dried lavender all down her bosom and handed a lace-edged one to Miss Drucy. "Dry your eyes and blow your nose and you'll feel better. Shall we wrap the doll and pack it away, or take it downstairs? If Tom should remarry, you might still have a granddaughter who'll treasure such a lovely doll."

"He won't. I'll be too old."

Ana didn't even try to sort that one out. Blowing out the lamps, she led the fragile old woman down the stairs. Neil met them at the foot of the stairs.

"I was coming up to tell you dinner's ready. Maureen says—Fallon, what's wrong?"

He looked so worried that she had to smile. Evidently they hadn't managed to erase all signs of their tears. "It's nothing, honestly. Just rainy-day blues."

"No it's not, our baby died," Miss Drucy said.

Ana looked at Neil, and it happened again—that odd meeting of minds. Of feelings, if not actual thoughts. "There's cocoa," he said. "It's a good day for cocoa."

Chapter Eleven

From the wide doorway of the shed where nets, oars, decoys, and an assortment of tools were kept, Brand watched as the two women attempted to lure the horses closer with a few shriveled turnips. Even knowing all he new about her, he found it increasingly difficult to picture Fallon McKnight as the type of woman who could marry a man, run through every cent of his worth, deliberately taunt him into doing something dangerously stupid, and then desert him when he was at his most vulnerable.

To see her now, standing out there whistling for all she was worth in an effort to entice a few shaggy wild ponies to eat from her hand, it was all but impossible to visualize her doing any of those things.

The pieces of the puzzle that was Fallon McKnight no longer fit where they were supposed to fit. It was like seeing an image through shattered glass.

He watched as she did her best to beguile a particular pony close enough to take a turnip from her hand. When the little stallion, a sorrel barely twelve hands high, stepped back, shook his head, and then stretched out his neck again, she passed the root over to Miss Drucy.

Brand told himself she was only afraid of being nipped.

But when the wary beast daintily plucked the turnip from the old woman's outstretched palm, it was Fallon who applauded. It was Fallon who looked as pleased as any new parent whose child had just showed off a brand-new accomplishment.

From a few feet away, Simmy and Evard grinned their encouragement. Simmy reached into the basket for another turnip. Miss Drucy peeled off her shoes and stockings and waded out after the pony, who had decided to take to sea.

Without a moment's hesitation, Fallow removed her own shoes, tucked two turnips into her pockets, and followed the old woman out into the shallow water.

"Oh, you sweet baby," she crooned as another pony splashed closer to take the lure. "Here, Miss Drucy, feed him this."

Leaning against the vine-covered shed, Brand stood in shadow and watched the two women until his attention was drawn to one of several small boats that had been cruising offshore. An open launch with a gaily striped canopy, she veered into the slough that led to the private landing.

It wasn't the first time one of the pleasure boats had ventured in for a closer look. The castle was considered a showplace along this section of the coast. The first time he'd inquired about Merriweather's Landing he'd been told all about the eccentric old Yankee who had come south and built a castle, complete with moat comprised of a sound, two inlets, and an ocean.

Each summer, according to his informant, people flocked to the islands north of the inlet, bringing with them milk cows, horses, chickens, and ducks, as well as an army of staff to see to their every comfort while they roughed it at the seashore. Sooner or later, even this early in the season, a few of them managed to find their way to The Landing.

But not today. It didn't suit his purposes for Fallon to be reminded of all the partying, the dancing, the harness races, dog races, and gambling to be found less than a day's journey away.

Nor did he care to have Miss Drucy distracted by a group of curious sightseers. On one of her good days she could have held her own, but this might not be one of her good days.

Stepping out of the shadows, he set out down the boardwalk and had nearly reached the wharf when three young gentlemen clambered ashore. They turned to help five young females disembark in a flurry of petticoats and giggles, clutching their chip-straw bonnets. A cigar-smoking helmsman handed out two large picnic baskets, then resumed his place under the gaudy canopy.

Quickly sizing up the group, Brand turned and glanced over his shoulder just as the herd of Banker ponies, evidently spooked by all the activity, took off, tails and shaggy manes flying in the wind.

Standing ankle-deep in the chilly water, her skirts tucked up about her knees, Miss Drucy stared after them while Fallon, Evard, and Simmy warily studied the newcomers.

Fallon's features took on a look of bulldog determination. He'd seen that same look on her face more than once. Turning to Miss Drucy, she gestured toward the disappearing horses in an obvious effort to distract her until Brand could dispatch the intruders. They might be at cross-purposes on most things, he mused, but when it came to protecting Miss Drucy they were of one mind.

"Yoo-hoo! Hallo, did you come to see my horses?"

Oh, hell. Miss Drucy had spotted the newcomers and was wading toward the wharf, waving the stocking she used to shoo away flying insects. Fallon slogged after her through the shallow water, still trying to distract her, but it was too late.

Brand vowed silently to break the neck of the first young hooligan who cracked wise at Miss Drucy's expense. From the way they were staring, that wouldn't be long in coming.

"Sorry, friends, but this is a private beach."

Someone snickered. One of the girls giggled. Then they all did. He glared at the boatman, who shrugged as if to say, "Don't blame me, I just haul 'em around."

A beardless young blade in a striped blazer stepped

forward and looked him over boldly. "I say there, old
man, they told us at the hotel—"

"I don't give much of a damn what they told you
at the hotel, boy, this place is off-limits."

"But all we're looking for is a place to—"

"There's a nice beach on the other side of the inlet.
I'd advise you to climb back aboard your launch and
head due north before the weather takes a turn for
the worse."

"Oh, but there's not a cloud in the sky." One of
the women, older and a lot bolder than the others,
emerged from the cluster of females, smoothing the
skirt of her blue and white resort dress over her hips.
Strikingly beautiful, she had a smile that implied
promises she might or might not be willing to keep.

"Yet," Brand said tersely. Arms crossed over his
chest, he waited for her to fire the first shot. He'd
been building up to a good brangle for some time. At
this point, he wasn't all that particular about his
opponent.

She put one directly across his bow. It was a good
one. Peeling off her white cotton glove, she laid a soft,
pale hand on his hard, tanned forearm. The look she
gave him was openly speculative. Using her eyelashes
to advantage, she said in a throaty drawl, "You're just
teasing about the weather, I can tell. Honestly, if I
never set foot in that smelly hotel launch again, it will
be too soon. Steam is so awfully noisy." She nodded
her head toward Evard's skiff. "I don't suppose you'd
care to take me for a ride?" She arched an eyebrow,
her smile never wavering. "That is your boat, isn't
it, Captain?"

She was good. Really good. Under any other circumstances, he might have been tempted. "Ma'am,
that boat's only used for fishing. Believe me, you
wouldn't like the way she smells."

Without once taking her eyes from his face, the
young woman unbuttoned the top three buttons of her
shirtwaist and fanned her throat with a languid hand.
"Gracious, it's warm in the sun."

Brand figured she must spend at least an hour a day standing before a mirror, practicing that trick with her eyes. Widening them ever so slightly, and then fluttering her lashes. "Um-hmm," he said.

"If we promise to leave peacefully, will you let me sit in the shade on your lovely porch just until I . . . cool off a bit?"

The younger girls were snickering. All three young men were scowling. Brand couldn't believe his own complete lack of interest, but there it was. Despite the fact that he'd been without a woman for more than six months, he wasn't even mildly stirred by the little minx.

A quick sidelong glance told him that Fallon had managed to distract Miss Drucy, and was shepherding her toward the house. A longer glance told him that Fallon's hair, as usual, was curling around her face, rapidly shedding the orderly restraints she tried so diligently to impose. The tip of her nose was pink from being out in the sun without a bonnet. There would be a few more freckles on her cheeks and a few more smudges of mud on her skirt. She was no match at all for the pink and gold blonde in the impeccable blue and white shirtwaist. Nothing even to warrant a second look.

He had to strain to hear what they were saying. "The ponies won't be back for hours, Miss Drucy, so we might as well go inside and have a nice cool glass of cider while we wait."

"But I don't want to go inside," that lady protested. "We have visitors."

Fallon glanced over her shoulder just as Brand turned her way. Their eyes met. He nodded toward the house and she nodded her understanding.

Get her inside, I'll handle things here.

I know. Thank you.

"Come along, Miss Drucy, they're not staying. They only pulled in to ask directions."

Funny, the way her voice, for all its softness, carried so clearly under all the high-pitched giggles and chatter. Brand told himself it was on account of the wind's direction. It had nothing to do with the fact that he always knew when she was somewhere nearby. Felt it in his bones. Or that he could pick out her voice in a roomful of chatter.

"Are they the ones who're coming to take me away?" Drucy quavered.

"No, dearest, no one will take you anywhere you don't want to go."

"Good. I don't want to go inside."

"Ah, but William's waiting for you. Shall we bathe and put on your lilac with the Brussels lace? And I'll do your hair the way you like it, with ribbons and a velvet rose."

Their voices faded as Fallon hurried her charge to the house, safely out of reach of the openly curious day-trippers.

"That old woman had a stocking in her hand," one of the girls said with a shocked gasp. "And did you see the way she kept picking at her wrist? They say when someone does that it means—"

"Shhh, she must be the one they were talking about at the hotel." Another one crossed her eyes and waggled a finger near her left ear. Brand wondered if there was a single shred of common decency among the whole noisy lot of them.

"Yes, but did you notice the other one? Isn't she the same woman whose picture was in the Sunday paper a few weeks ago?"

"Shhh, don't let her hear you, for heaven's sake!"

Brand tried to ignore the whispers and giggles, watching as Fallon, flanked by Simmy and Evard, hurried Miss Drucy through the back door.

Not until the launch was safely out into the channel again did he allow himself to think about what he'd overheard.

What other one?

What picture in the Sunday paper?

Which Sunday paper?

*   *   *

Miss Drucy was out of sorts for the rest of the day. As luck would have it, her lilac dress had been washed and was still wet. Ana laid out her blue and thought, What if all you had to choose from was bile green and dirt gray, Miss D.? Blue cambric would be a welcome change, believe me.

Drucy grumbled, but allowed Ana to braid her hair with blue satin ribbons and pin it into a coronet. "I want the drawers that tie, not the ones that button."

"I removed all your buttons and sewed on tapes, remember?"

No answer. Sometimes, Miss Drucy simply went off somewhere in her mind, and that was that. She would come back when she was good and ready.

Before going down to dinner, Ana slipped into her own room for hasty repairs. The green was becoming impossibly shabby. Not only that, it was damp with salt water, which she had learned to her sorrow would never dry unless it was first rinsed in fresh water. Her gray needed airing and brushing, but it would have to do. Perhaps tomorrow she could steal a few minutes to look after her own wardrobe.

If it didn't rain.

If Miss Drucy wasn't too restless.

If, if, if. . . .

It hadn't helped matters that the horses had failed to return. They had watched and waited all afternoon long as the sky clouded over and the wind began to pick up.

"You said they'd be back," Miss Drucy accused.

"And I'm sure they will. I'll tell you what, if they're not back by noon tomorrow, we'll go looking for them, shall we?"

"And take a picnic lunch?" After seeing the picnic baskets brought over by the group from the hotel, she'd been remembering picnics all the way back to her childhood. They had compared notes on favorite picnic foods, which had left Ana feeling somewhat depressed.

Chocolate for you, chocolate for me, and angel food for our Anamarie.

"Why don't we wait and see what the weather brings?"

That evening Simmy and Evard announced plans to go home for a brief visit to their families. They discussed aunts and uncles and cousins, and the possibility of a northeaster over the next few days. When Ana asked if that meant rain, Evard ducked his head and said shyly, "Even if it don't rain all that much, ma'am, we'll likely get a hard blow. Might be some overwash."

Neil nodded. Mr. Merry mentioned a northeaster that had done considerable damage while the castle was under construction. Mr. Hobbs nodded. As usual, he ate silently, putting away a surprising amount for an elderly man who couldn't weigh more than eighty pounds, soaking wet.

Maureen hadn't joined them this evening. Sometimes she preferred to eat alone in the kitchen where she could prop her feet up on another chair and look at pictures in the latest *National Geographic*. Sobbing noisily whenever there was a feature on Ireland.

Supper, then, was a quiet affair. While Neil and Mr. Merry discussed politics and Miss Drucy picked at a loose thread in the hem of her sleeve, Ana made a mental list of things to do tomorrow. Rinse out her green. Wash out her undergarments and hang them in the spare bedroom to dry. Embarrassment over their threadbare condition prevented her from hanging them out with the family wash.

She pretended it was only modesty.

She'd have to ask Maureen to make up a picnic basket and ask Evard if he would mind if she drove his pony cart while he was gone. She had yet to explore the other end of the island, and she was running out of interesting projects to entertain her charge.

It took three stories and several songs before she could slip away, confident that she had at least an hour or more before Miss Drucy would wake up needing to use the chamber pot. Occasionally she slept the night through, but when she'd had one of her fretful spells, or more than a single cup of tea in the evening, she was inclined to be wakeful.

Quietly, knowing that the men were probably still playing cards in the library, she slipped down the back stairs and into the kitchen, intending to locate a basket and see if there was enough ham left over for two sandwiches tomorrow. And perhaps help herself to another slice of chocolate cake. She could do with a spot of comfort, and chocolate helped when one was tired and somewhat depressed.

Instead she found Maureen standing at the sink in tears, drinking whiskey straight from the bottle.

Shocked right down to the soles of her worn-out slippers, Ana hurried across the room, put one arm around the woman's plump shoulder, and removed the bottle from her work-worn hand. "Maureen, has something happened? What's wrong?"

What was wrong, she quickly discovered, was that the housekeeper had a boil on her behind. She'd had it for more than a week now, and the pain was growing unbearable.

"But why on earth didn't you ask the doctor to lance it while he was here?"

"Sure, and I'm not a-a-about to let a strange gentleman look at me nether end."

In a garbled recital interrupted by hiccups and sobs, the story came pouring out. About how as a young woman she'd been all set to marry her young man when he'd got a boil on his ankle, neglected it for too long, and died of blood poisoning three days before they were to have wed.

"And here I went into service for a year to save for me dowry. The Lord's payin' me back," the red-haired, red-faced woman wailed. "For I never wanted to marry Conn Makim in the first place. I only said I would on account of another girl wanted him, and I never wanted her to have him."

More sobs. Ana handed her a dish towel, and she blew her nose and crammed it into her apron pocket.

"S-she had everything. We all come over together, but her pa got himself a fine job right off, while my poor old da got himself kicked in the head by a cart mule three days off the boat. Niver a day in his life did he work back home in Wicklow. Played cards, he did, and drank up every cent me ma and me brought home. And I hated her for it! Not me ma—me friend, Trina."

The tale was becoming muddled, not that Ana was particularly eager to sort it out. "You'll have to let me see to your boil, then. Come along now, it won't hurt and you'll feel better by morning, I promise. My father had bed sores. I used to tend those for him. Boils can't be all that different, now can they?"

She was leading the tearful woman from the kitchen to the servants' quarters, supporting her with one arm while she carried the proper surgical tools in the other, when Neil came through the other door. He eyed the housekeeper, the half-empty bottle she clutched to her ample bosom, and lifted a questioning brow.

"Don't ask," Ana murmured.

Maureen swayed and Ana staggered and nearly dropped her surgical implements, which consisted of a freshly whetted butcher knife, which she'd rinsed off with the whiskey, and a bottle of Porter's Healing Oil, guaranteed by its maker to heal all wounds and to prevent putrification.

Some forty minutes later, feeling as if she could drop where she stood and sleep for a month, she emerged from the staff's quarters, reeking of whiskey and healing oil. She rolled down her sleeves. Maureen was sleeping soundly on her stomach, her boil lanced, drained, medicated, and bandaged. By morning, Ana thought with a rueful smile, the poor woman's head would be aching enough to take the curse off her so-called nether end.

"You look tired."

She nearly jumped out of her skin. Wouldn't you

know he'd be waiting for her? The man had a way of turning up just when she was frazzled to a fare-thee-well, too tired to guard her heart, much less her tongue.

"Neil, do you happen to know if the French Foreign Legion takes women? Surely there must be an easier way to earn a living."

"Or to hide."

"Or to hide," she repeated wearily, crossing to the kitchen sink to wash the knife before she set it to boil. She'd been thoroughly drilled by her father's physician in proper sickroom procedure.

"Then you admit it?"

Glancing over her shoulder, she was struck by how handsome a dangerous man could look.

Or was it how dangerous a handsome man could look?

And devil take it, he wasn't even all that handsome!

"At this moment, I'd probably admit to setting the Chicago fire, shooting Mr. Garfield, and flooding the Ohio Valley. Do you suppose there's any coffee in that pot?"

They both reached the stove at the same time, both reached for the gray graniteware coffeepot. Brand lifted it, shook it, and then felt the top of the stove. It was barely warm. He selected a few sticks of pitch pine, tossed in a few lumps of coal, and watched a moment to see if it would catch up again. By the time he turned back, she was nearly asleep at the table.

He shook his head in amazement. She was puzzling, all right. He didn't know what the devil she'd done to the housekeeper, but whatever it was, coming on the tail end of a day that had started just after sunup, she was worn out.

"Go to bed, Fallon," he said softly. "You're exhausted."

She opened one eye just long enough for the lamplight to catch the golden shards buried there, shut it again and smiled, chin propped in her cupped palms.

"How'd you guess? What gave me away? Was I snoring?"

He studied the way her lashes curled on the high curve of her cheekbones, the scattering of freckles on her elegant little nose. If more women realized how fetching a golden tan could be, they wouldn't go to such lengths to protect their lily-pale complexion. "Oh, I don't know . . . could be the way you're sprawled out there, with your feet flopped over on their sides like a couple of beached bluefish."

"Not very graceful, huh? They hurt."

"In those things, it's no wonder. Feet need support. You need a new pair of boots."

"I need a new pair of feet, a new pair of hands, and a new back. And as long as I'm at it, I might as well send off for a new head, too."

"Headache?"

Drowsily, she denied it. "I think my old one must be worn out. It doesn't seem to work properly anymore."

Softening in spite of himself, Brand pulled up a chair and lifted her feet onto his knee. She was wearing a pair of paper-thin kid slippers, the kind meant to be worn inside. He knew for a fact that she had only the two pairs of shoes, and when her boots were wet, she wore these.

Peeling them off, he began chaffing her stockinged feet in his hands.

"Ohhh, that feels so-oo good." She sighed, wiggling her toes.

"You shouldn't allow me to do this, you know."

"I know. Tomorrow I'll be embarrassed to tears, but at the moment I'm enjoying it far too much to worry about propriety."

It occurred to him that in her vulnerable state, she might just admit to a long list of sins.

On the other hand, if he planned to woo her, win her, and then denounce her, this might be a good way to start. "I've been told I'm good with aching backs, too. Shall we adjourn to your room and let me work on yours?"

She opened one eye again. And then she opened the other one. He could feel the rising tension before she even spoke. "While I do appreciate your generous offer, I believe I'll just settle for a cup of coffee. It should be hot by now, judging from the way the pot's beginning to rock."

It was boiling. Strong as lye, black as tar, and she drank it straight, adding neither tinned milk nor sugar. "Mercy," she said with a shudder. "After that, I'll probably lie awake for all of twenty seconds."

She stood. He deliberately remained seated. She smiled down at him, ignoring his lapse of manners, and in that single moment he could have sworn she was everything she pretended to be.

He found himself wishing they could have met under different circumstances and damned himself for a fool.

He fully intended to destroy the woman. He might have underestimated her cleverness—might even have discovered a few admirable qualities in her—but that didn't mean he intended to let her off the hook.

Tilting back his chair, he stayed there after she left, breathing in the lingering aroma of fish and burned coffee, aware of the increasing thunder of the surf, more felt than heard.

Thinking about all that had occurred since he'd gone haring off on a mission to find his brother's widow and bring her to justice.

What had really happened in the shack that night? He'd been the one to find her there. At his wit's end once she was discovered missing, he had gone out in the driving rain with a lantern, searching the shed, searching along the shore—cursing the storm, the lack of light—cursing the wild streak in her that would send her outside on a night like that.

It had been just after daybreak when he'd found her. He'd damned near had a heart attack. Soaked to the skin, her body had been so cold and still that he'd thought at first she was dead.

Before he could move her he'd had to shift the tim-

ber that had evidently struck her on the temple and
settled across her back. It hadn't been all that hard to
figure out what had happened. Lightning must have
struck the peak of the roof and splintered down
toward the eaves. If it hadn't been raining so hard,
the whole place would have burned to the ground,
with her in it.

He sighed a heartfelt sigh, thinking that if ever a
woman attracted trouble, it was Fallon McKnight.
Fire. Lightning. God knows what else she'd survived.

Others around her hadn't always been so fortunate,
and yet Brand knew in his heart that if she'd died that
night, he would have been devastated. It didn't bear
thinking about, but he thought about it, anyway.
Thought about it for a long time, coming up without
a single answer that would satisfy the growing conflict
inside him.

Chapter Twelve

Sometime during the night the wind began to wail, the keening sound quickly gathering volume. Ana huddled under a quilt, wanting to sleep, unable to crawl back into her comfortable dream. A shutter banged on the far side of the house. Evard had been right about the wind, then. It had switched to another direction.

From somewhere down the hall she heard voices. She squeezed her eyes tightly shut, but then a door slammed and she gave up.

Reluctantly she sat up, blinking at the thin light that filtered through the dimity curtains. Another door slammed, and someone yelled, "Fetch ropes from the shed!"

Ropes? What on earth—? Why was everyone in such an uproar? Had something happened?

Miss Drucy. "Oh, please, no," Ana whispered. Throwing back the covers, she stumbled out of bed and flew to the wardrobe to grab her shoes and shawl. A moment later she was racing down the stairs in her nightgown.

According to Maureen, who was bustling between stove and table in her bathrobe, a ship had gone aground just before daybreak, not a quarter of a mile from the castle. Neil was already on the beach. Evard had come back for the pony cart and whatever ropes he could collect. Maureen and Simmy were making sandwiches and coffee, and Mr. Hobbs in his paisley bathrobe was entertaining Miss Drucy with a game of checkers, wincing whenever she cheated.

"What can I do?" Ana asked, suddenly wide awake.

"Blankets. They'll all be wet and chilled. And put on some clothes, child. Ye'll be naught but a distraction in your underwear."

Ana raced upstairs, flung on a dress, gathered up an armload of blankets, and then hurried outside, following the cart tracks down to the shore.

Topping the dunes, she stood and stared in horror. She didn't know what she'd expected to see—a ship high and dry on the shore, perhaps. There was no ship. At least, not a recognizable one. Clutching the quilts and blankets, she stared as massive waves battered a broken, capsized hull, crashing down on tangled lines, shattered spars, and shredded canvas. Two men were hanging onto the rigging, trying desperately not to be swept away before help arrived. A small open boat valiantly fought its way through the boiling surf. Twice in as many minutes it nearly foundered.

Recognizing Neil, Ana hurried to where he was lowering a limp form to the ground, well out of reach of the tide. Wordlessly, she handed him a blanket. He covered the man—hardly more than a boy, actually. She tried to think of something appropriate to say. "He's too young to die," was all she could come up with.

The look Neil gave her defied description. "They're bringing in a woman now. Go and see if you can help." He indicated a huddle of activity—surfmen in their dark winter uniforms, two ponies and a mule cart, dozens of lines and what appeared to be a big canvas bucket.

Someone was being lifted from the bucket contraption. Skirts all a-tangle, the poor thing was weeping and screaming while men shouted back and forth. Under a steel-gray sky she watched as two men, ropes tied around their bodies, more line coiled over their shoulders, waded out to sea.

Why didn't someone stop them? They'd be drowned! No one could survive in that maelstrom.

Neil passed her, striding toward the group of men and the screaming woman, and she hurried after him.

Salt spray stung her eyes until she could scarcely see. Blowing sand stung her skin and worked its way inside her clothing. She lent a hand where she could, but not until hours later, when there was time to talk, time to put the pieces together, did she gain some slight understanding of what had happened.

One crewman had been killed by falling debris, another swept down the beach and drowned. Of the remaining souls on board, four men and a woman had been plucked from the sinking ship alive. The men were taken to the Lifesaving Station.

Ana was given the care of the woman.

Neil drove them back to the castle in the pony cart while one of the surfmen drove the other survivors south. Evard stayed on the beach to help secure the station's equipment. It would be hours before the cart could return to haul it back to the station.

Meanwhile, Simmy had trudged back and forth with coffee and sandwiches for all.

"—daughter's wedding. Did I tell you she's getting married next week? Oh, Lordy, Lordy, what am I going to do? My clothes are all gone." The voice had been droning on and on, since even before the poor woman had been lifted from the breeches buoy onto the shore. "Young man, stop this contraption, we have to go back for my clothes. They were packed separate in a green trunk. See if they've brought the luggage ashore yet."

Neil met Ana's eyes over the woman's head. A silent message flashed between them. She's in shock, poor creature. There would be no luggage. The survivors were lucky to have escaped with their lives. The woman, wrapped in two woolen blankets, couldn't seem to stop babbling. Ana spread another quilt over her shoulders.

A few hours later they were all sitting in the parlor, their lady guest sharing a love seat with Miss Drucy while she related the details of her late husband's demise, not the least bit disconcerted when Miss Drucy broke in from time to time with a remark about horses or roses.

Across the room, Neil quietly told the others what he had learned from the first mate. Northbound out of Mobile, the schooner *Angeline Jane* had encountered a furious southeast gale off Cape Lookout. Hoping to clear Cape Hatteras, where the landmass itself would offer some protection, the schooner had been battling her way around the Cape when she'd lost part of her foremast.

Striving to reach the protection of Oregon Inlet, where he could lay over in the comparatively quiet waters of the Pamlico long enough to make temporary repairs, the captain had pressed on. Dusk had been falling when he'd sighted the inlet. Not daring to risk entering unfamiliar waters after dark on a falling tide, he'd anchored nearby to await daylight and floodtide.

But sometime during the night the wind had swung around to the northeast and gathered strength. The anchor lines had parted, and the *Angeline Jane* had been driven aground. There'd been time to launch only a single distress signal before she began to break up.

Ana sat quietly, hands folded on her lap, lulled by the sound of Neil's quiet baritone against a background of whistling wind, a ticking clock, and Mrs. Colvin's nasal drone.

"—I told her she could wear Mama's wedding dress, but she insisted on having her own. I told her over and over again to wait until June, but would she listen? Oh, no, not my Lucy, no siree. Takes after her dear departed father that way. Never listens to a word I say. He never did, either."

Maureen rolled her eyes a few times and slipped away to the kitchen. Simmy didn't wait long before following her. Evard poked his head in the doorway, lingered a moment, and disappeared. Then Mr. Hobbs mentioned the time and wheeled Mr. Merry from the room.

Mrs. Colvin never even broke her stride.

Neil grinned, and Ana thought absently that he should do it more often. He looked years younger and not nearly so . . . hard.

Poor Mrs. Colvin. She hadn't even stopped talking long enough to eat. As a consequence, no one else had lingered long enough to do justice to Maureen's ham and cabbage.

Ana tried to think charitable thoughts. The poor woman had lost everything she owned—at least, everything she'd had with her for the journey to Richmond by way of Norfolk. Of all people, Ana knew how helpless she must feel, battered by the winds of fate.

Miss Drucy was snoring softly. As soon as she could politely leave Mrs. Colvin, Ana would have to wake her and get her upstairs and into bed.

"—dog named Desdemona. I told her, I said, Lucy, you can't take a dog on a honeymoon trip. I'll keep the pesky little thing for you until—"

"Shall I carry her upstairs?" Neil asked quietly.

"Who, Mrs. Colvin?" Ana studied the woman's gaunt face. She was too pale, her eyes too bright, and her fingers had braided, unbraided, and rebraided the fringe on her borrowed shawl.

"I meant Miss Drucy, but I'll be glad to take them both upstairs if you'll show me where to go. One at a time, though."

Ana rose. "Mrs. Colvin," she said, interrupting the flood of words.

"So I said, if you won't take that . . . What? Were you speaking to me?"

"Perhaps you'd like to retire. It's getting late, and Simmy has a room all ready for you."

"Retire? Well—yes, but I'll have to leave early in the morning. I'm supposed to catch a train from Norfolk at two in the afternoon. My daughter's expecting me. She lives in Richmond now, did I tell you? She won't know how to go on without me there to tell her what to do."

*   *   *

It was nearly eleven the next morning when Ana allowed herself to be helped on board Pam's skipjack. She didn't want to go. She especially didn't want to go with Neil as an escort, but there was really no choice. Wedding or not, it was imperative that Mrs. Colvin leave the landing as quickly as possible before someone slipped up and told the woman to kindly hush her mouth. Maureen had been banging pots and pans all morning. Even the mild-mannered Mr. Hobbs had uttered a swear word.

The poor woman could hardly go alone. There was only Ana to go with her, and Mr. Merry wouldn't hear of sending two women off unescorted.

The widow sat on a fish box in the middle of the cockpit, her voice rising above the crack of canvas and the sound of rushing water. Wearing her borrowed clothing and clutching a borrowed reticule, she talked at Pam's back while Neil and Ana moved as far forward as possible to escape the sound of her voice.

"Pam's taking us all the way to Elizabeth City," Neil murmured in her ear, his lips brushing her hair. "It'll be a long trip, but at least we won't have to lay over at Nags Head."

Ana drew her shawl closer around her shoulders. With the clouds gone, the sun was warm, but the wind off the water was still cool. "Will he wait until we see her aboard the train and then bring us back?"

"I'm not sure of the train schedule. We'll probably spend a night in town and get an early start back."

Not for the first time, Ana considered boarding a northbound train and going home to face whatever awaited her there. Sooner or later she'd have to go back, but not yet. She wasn't ready yet.

Besides, she didn't have the price of a ticket.

Pam sang out a warning, hauled in the boom, and set out on a northwesterly tack. Without thinking, Ana adjusted her position, leaning only briefly against the man beside her.

"Good sea legs," Neil observed.

"I beg your pardon?"

"Sea limbs? Sorry. I only meant you've a way of keeping your balance no matter how rough things get."

It was choppy, but hardly rough. She said as much and watched the subtle change come over his expression. She would like to think it was admiration she saw there, but it looked more like a challenge.

Which didn't even make sense.

She turned away and stared at the low coastline barely visible in the distance.

The trip was tiresome. Maureen had packed sandwiches and cider, but no cups. Pam had one glass and a coffee mug, stained black inside. He claimed the mug. Mrs. Colvin drank from the glass and Neil and Ana shared the jug.

More than once their shoulders touched. Their hands touched. Their eyes met in flashes of laughter, flashes of understanding—occasional flashes of something else. One might even have thought they were friends except for the odd constraint that came over them from time to time as the afternoon wore on.

Ana would feel him studying her and grow self-conscious. Then he'd move to converse with the ferryman, and she would find herself staring, admiring the way he stood braced against the wind, his shirt blowing against his chest, his cuffs turned back to reveal the glint of hair on his sun-bronzed forearms.

Powerful legs spread to accommodate the roll of the deck, he was an impressive man. Ana, unable to tear her gaze away, wondered how a man who was not truly handsome in the traditional sense could be so beautiful, all shiny and tall and free under the brilliant sunlight.

They barely made the last train to Richmond. Neil purchased a ticket while Ana waited on the siding with Mrs. Colvin. "We'll send word ahead to your daughter so she'll know to meet you."

"Did I tell you about that little dog of hers? It belonged to her grandmother—did I tell you Lucy

lives with her grandmother? Yes, well, she insisted on
it. She's a good girl, my Lucy, but—"

"Ma'am, we'd better get you on board. The train'll
be leaving any moment now."

They stood and watched until the last car was out
of sight. Ana stared down the endless stretch of track,
gleaming like copper under the setting sun, and
thought about another train, another time. Any moment now she might awaken and discover that it had
all been a dream. Ludwig—that endless, terrifying
journey. Fallon.

Neil broke into her thoughts. "Fallon, we'd better
go find accommodations." He frowned at her. "What
is it? What's wrong?"

"Nothing, I—"

"Come along," he said gruffly, taking her arm and
steering her toward a waiting hackney.

Ana would have gone directly to bed and stayed there,
given the choice. She was as tired as if she'd walked
the whole way from Merriweather's Landing. While
she brushed her hair and pinned it up again, she listened to the unfamiliar sounds drifting in through the
open window. Instead of gulls and night herons, the
rattle of wheels on cobblestones. Instead of the constant whisper of surf to shore, a gabble of voices. Of
laughter. A barking dog.

And so many lights. Mercy, it was strange to be
back in a city again.

Neil rapped and called through her door. "Fallon?
I've bespoke us a table. We'll make an early night of
it. Pam says he'll meet us on board at seven tomorrow morning."

So they dined. And Ana, wearing the same gown
she had worn her first night at Brokerman's Riverside
Hotel months earlier, surprised herself by eating two
pieces of friend chicken, fresh garden peas, and three
buttermilk biscuits slathered with butter and black-
berry jam.

Neil didn't talk much. He nodded to one or two

people, making her wonder if he'd spent much time here. She thought about asking, because conversation of any sort would be better than dwelling on all that had happened the last time she'd been here.

But when she looked up to speak and found him studying her as if he half expected her to jump up onto the table and dance a jig, she completely lost her train of thought.

"What is it? Do I have jam on my mouth?"

Before he could reply, someone rushed up to the table and cried, "Ma'am, is that really you?"

The girl wore a black dress with a white apron, designating her as dining-room staff. She had bright red hair, and for some reason, Ana visualized a straggly pink hair ribbon instead of the starched white cap.

"I beg your pardon, were you addressing me?"

"It is you! I wondered where you'd got to. After the fire, I mean. Didn't nobody seem to know, but then, things was so confused there for a spell."

The girl from the boardinghouse. What was her name?

"I'm Louise, ma'am, don't you remember me? I sure do thank you for all them things you give me. Soon's things calmed down some, I put on one o' them fine dresses and come directly here to the Indian Queen, and they give me a job right off. It was the dress what done it. I looked real smart."

In spite of her exhaustion, Ana had to smile. "I'm so glad for you, Louise." If she'd ever heard the child's name, she'd forgotten it.

"And that fur cape you give me to give to the relief fund? Miz Stevens, she bought it, but when she couldn't get the smell o' smoke out of it, she give it back and let 'em keep her money, and they sold it all over again. Made a mint o' money on it before the smell went away. I don't know the name o' the lady what finally ended up with it, but I reckon she was some proud."

Brand didn't say a word. All through the brief exchange, he watched the play of emotions flicker behind those clear amber eyes. There was amusement, but also sadness. Caution? Certainly wariness.

Obviously, something had happened here that he didn't know about, but he would. Sooner or later, he would know everything.

"You're looking heaps better than the last time I saw you, ma'am," the cheerful little waitress declared. "You was wrung out worse'n a drowned rat."

Their eyes met and once again Brand experienced that odd sense of sharing. The lady was dangerous. In more ways that one. He watched the color rise to her cheeks, watched the sweep of her lashes as she lowered her gaze.

She swallowed. He could almost swear it was genuine. Almost swear she was feeling the same thing he was feeling—wanting the same thing she was wanting.

Back off, McKnight, you're way out of line.

It occurred to him that if he was going to stay the course, he'd do well to cut short the evening. Too many possibilities were beginning to occur to him.

Impossible possibilities.

They left the dining room, and when he declared his intention of walking down to the waterfront before he turned in, Fallon murmured her thanks for the meal and started up the stairs. Halfway up, she turned back. He hadn't moved. He'd been watching the seductive sway of her hips.

Did she do it on purpose?

Was she even aware of it?

"Neil, could we get up early enough in the morning so that I could go by the cemetery first?"

The cemetery. "Anamarie G. Hebbel?"

She nodded and didn't even question his knowledge. But then she was exhausted. They both were.

Brand started to speak and clamped his lips shut again. He'd come close to tipping his hand by reminding her that she had yet to visit her husband's grave.

She hadn't caught his first slip, but if he'd mentioned Liam, she would have been all over him with questions. He couldn't afford to explain. Not just yet. If he had one thing working in his favor, it was the single element of surprise.

Although, he was beginning to wonder just how long it was going to take to bring her to justice.

Revenge, as it turned out, wasn't quite as simple as he'd expected.

Chapter Thirteen

The following morning flew by with seldom a moment to spare. Thanks to overindulging in rich food, Ana had felt queasy all during the return journey, and had slept practically the entire time.

Just as well. It had thrown her off balance—being back in Elizabeth City. Seeing Louise again. Not to mention spending so much time alone with Neil Dalton. It was good to be back home again, where all she had to contend with were Miss Drucy's whims.

Shading her eyes, she watched Evard's little sloop head out the slough under a fresh northwest wind. Watched as it neared the channel proper, the sail fluttering, falling slack for a moment until the little sloop came about on a southerly heading.

If only it was that simple. Climb aboard, hoist a sail, and go with the wind, leaving behind all the woes, the worries, and fears.

Evard was seated astern, one hand on the tiller, the other controlling the single sail. Seated amidship, Simmy looked as solemn as a small brown owl in her Sunday best, with her hair pinned up on top of her head in the style she'd recently adopted. According to Maureen they were second cousins. Evard was only biding his time, watching over her until they were both old enough to marry.

Ana envied them their youth, their innocence, their family, and their future. Most of all she envied them their love.

Turning back to the clothesline with a sigh, she reached into the laundry basket and began to pin the day's wash. Before he left, Evard had showed Neil where his oyster bed was located, taught him how and when to fish the small gill net. Lacking a boat, he would have to wait until low tide and wade out. It was too late for hunting wildfowl, too early for clams, but there was always salt beef or ham if they grew tired of a diet of fish, and Evard had promised to bring back a few chickens.

It occurred to her to wonder how Fallon would have fared if things had not turned out the way they had. Judging by the few days they'd spent together at the hotel—the wet towels tossed down for someone else to pick up, the expensive clothing carelessly scattered about for someone else to gather up, brush, and put away, and the remains of all those delivered meals left for someone else to collect, one would have thought she'd grown up being waited on hand and foot. Which, if James Webster could be believed, wasn't at all the case.

Poor James. What would become of him? She hadn't dared ask, but surely if he'd still been on the island, she would have heard about it by now.

Reaching into the basket, she selected another of Mr. Merry's nightshirts and pegged it to the line. She envied him the fine linen garment. Her one and only nightgown was showing severe signs of wear. Not for the first time in these past few weeks, she pondered the vagaries of fate, marveling at the way her own life had turned out. Under other circumstances she might have been content to remain here caring for the Merrys. She was fond of them both. She liked the rest of the staff, and even Merriweather's Landing itself, for all its inconveniences, possessed a certain wild charm.

It was becoming more and more apparent, however—especially after the advent of James Webster—that she would have to return to Connecticut. It was more a matter of conscience than of character. Somehow or other she seemed to have developed the former, if not the latter. If she'd realized what an uncomfortable companion a conscience could be, she

would have refused to have one, but it had sneaked
up on her when she wasn't looking.

So. Sooner or later she would have to go back. She
couldn't run forever. That conclusion reached, she
pegged another bedsheet to the line, shoved a tendril
of hair from her face, and sighed again. She seemed
to do a lot of that lately.

She did a lot of things lately she had never done
before.

Through an open window came the low murmur of
masculine voices. Mr. Hobbs, it seemed, served his
employer in several capacities. At the moment they
were discussing Mr. Merry's investments. Over the
sound of the surf and of wet sheets snapping in the
wind, Ana caught only the occasional word. Interest
rates. Bonds. Stock shares.

Idly, she wondered how her father's investments
were prospering. She had offered, soon after he had
taken permanently to his bed, to help deal with his
voluminous business correspondence, only to be re-
buffed for her troubles. The female brain, it seemed,
had been designed to deal solely with matters concerning kitchen, parlor, bedroom, and nursery. She'd been
accused of squandering vast sums on novels and other
frivolous fare, driving them to the very door of the
poorhouse.

And then, one day Marcus had summoned Horatio
Quillerby, his lawyer and man-of-business, and the
two of them had remained closeted in the master bedroom for hours. Quillerby had left with a smirk and a
bulging briefcase.

Ana, emerging from the kitchen where she'd been
helping Etta plan a week's meals on three days' allowance, had been just in time to see Samuels hand him
his bowler and topcoat and show him out the door.

Not until a week later, when she'd asked her father
for money to buy a pair of house slippers and some
of the fresh fruit just coming into season, had she
learned what had prompted Quillerby's smug expression. The lawyer, it seemed, would henceforth be han-

dling the household allowance, along with all her
father's business affairs.

Ana had never been given a personal allowance.
She could buy groceries in moderation, but henceforth, if she needed funds for anything of a more personal nature, she must present her request at his office
and he would consider it, render judgment, and dole
out what funds he deemed appropriate.

She'd pitched a royal fit and threatened to walk out.

Which of course she would never have done. All
the same, she had charged up the stairs and into her
father's room after her first meeting with the nasty
little man, and raised the very devil.

Equally stubborn, neither of them had given an inch.
Finally, afraid her father would have a stroke, she had
stormed out, flung on her cloak, and set out at a furious
pace in a heavy downpour, marching for miles through
the mud, kicking stones out of her path, muttering to
herself, wallowing in a sea of self-pity, and vowing to
run away to someplace where her sweet nature, even
temper, and years of generous self-sacrifice would be
appreciated.

Hours later she had returned home, drenched to the
skin and thoroughly ashamed of her tantrum. She'd
tucked an extra slice of mincemeat pie on her father's
supper tray and not even fussed when he'd eaten both
pieces of pie and ignored the baked chicken and
green beans.

Instead, she'd meekly measured out his tonic,
cleared away his tray, brushed the crumbs into a dust-
pan, and settled down to read from his favorite collection of sermons until her growing hoarseness began to
irritate him. After that, they had played checkers and
she had allowed him to win three games she could
easily have taken.

In the end, all she'd had to show for her brief rebel-
lion had been a sore throat, a runny nose, and a nagging sense of guilt for being such a disrespectful
daughter.

Horatio Quillerby. What a wretched little toad. She

suspected he'd had a hand in dictating the terms of her father's will, because if Ana had inherited outright, Quillerby would have been dismissed out of hand.

Even Ludwig had despised the man. It had been the one thing they'd had in common.

Basket empty and both clotheslines filled, she turned to the vegetable garden. That, at least, was prospering, despite the hard rain. Neil had promised to build a fence around it to keep the ponies out, but so far he hadn't got around to doing it.

Nor could she bring herself to remind him.

Which was another reason why she couldn't stay here much longer. Neil Dalton. She was dangerously close to falling in love with the man, and that simply would not do.

Collecting the empty basket, she brushed her hair from her face and turned to take one last look out over the sound. Evard's sail was nearly out of sight. It occurred to her that Simmy at fourteen probably knew more about men than she did at twice that age. According to Maureen, the child came from a large, happy family that included numerous brothers, a grandfather, and several aunts, uncles, and cousins.

By contrast, Ana's sole adult experience with men before she'd come to The Landing had taught her that the creatures were to be obeyed for no other reason than that they were male.

That, she refused to accept.

Brand set out right after breakfast with his notebook, not because he felt like making any more sketches, or even felt a need to pretend to study the inlet currents any longer. His cover identity had holes big enough for a freight train to pass through. From one or two things Merryweather had let drop, the man suspected him of being a government agent of some sort. If the country had been at war, he might even have been suspected of being a spy.

The old gentleman was too well-bred to ask questions. In fact, Brand suspected he was rather enjoying the vicarious adventure. On more than one occasion he'd been tempted to confess his real reason for being here, but something always held him back.

For one thing, he wasn't looking forward to witnessing the man's disappointment when he learned what kind of a woman his precious Fallon really was.

For another—one that bothered him even more—he was having a hard time hanging onto his own objectivity. The more he saw of Liam's Lorelei, the better he came to know her, the more he wondered if he could possibly have misjudged her.

Arriving at a place where tide had exposed a section of shipwreck, he brushed off the sand and seated himself on the worm-eaten twelve-inch timbers. He had some serious thinking to do, and he could do a better job of it out here where he wasn't apt to be distracted.

As if his growing lust weren't distraction enough.

A stiff northeast breeze fought against the strong inlet currents, the resulting turbulence a perfect match for his thoughts.

Start at the starting place, that was what his grandfather had always advised back when he'd been eager to learn all there was to learn about life at sea.

First of all, he'd found her.

Second, he'd forced her to admit she was a widow.

The third step would be discovering why she'd lied about it in the first place.

Had she lied simply because lies came easy to her? Because lying gave her a feeling of power over her victim?

The trouble was he no longer knew who the real Fallon McKnight was. Was she the woman responsible for his brother's death?

Or was she the woman he was coming to know too well for his own peace of mind?

Up against an all-too familiar brick wall, Brand felt his mind skittering away. He found himself thinking about Liam, about Galen. Pondering the fate of the *Mystic Wings.*

Were her parts even now being cast ashore in some

distant land to be picked over, studied, and wondered at, the way he'd wondered about every half-buried timber he'd found washed up along this stretch of shore?

Despite their names, his three ships, the *Mystic Winds,* the *Mystic Wings,* and the *Mystic Lady,* had been named for nothing more mystical than the town where his grandfather had set himself up in the shipping business more than half a century before.

"Back to the problem at hand," he muttered, letting the wind take his words and carry them out to sea.

How the devil could he arrive at an answer when he couldn't even focus on the question?

"Question number one. What happened to change Liam's widow into the woman she is now?"

Because something had sure as hell changed her.

"Question number two. Which one of us is trying to back the other one into a trap?"

Brand knew which one of them was afraid to fall asleep at night, afraid of having the kind of dreams that left a man limp, spent, and thoroughly frustrated. He couldn't remember the last time he'd wanted a woman as fiercely as he wanted his brother's widow. Ten years ago, he'd have blamed it on his youth and either done something about it or put it from his mind. He was older now.

Older, but no wiser. He still found himself fantasizing about undressing her—sometimes slowly, sometimes tearing the clothes from her body—and gazing his fill at those treasures he saw so clearly in his imagination.

He wanted to touch her, to taste her, and pretend that no man had ever done those things to her before. He wanted to make love to her until he collapsed and died in her arms, and then rise from the dead and do it all over again. Once he'd spent himself in her body a few times he might even stand a chance of functioning like a rational being again.

Beautiful and passionate beyond belief. Liam had written that about her. Brand wished he hadn't. It made him feel like a damned voyeur, lusting after his own brother's wife. Or rather, his widow, which might have been slightly more acceptable, only in this particular case, it made it worse.

Burying his face in his hands, he let guilt wash over him, making no attempt to fight it. Having visited any number of foreign countries, he knew that among certain peoples, a man was expected to take his brother's widow as one of his own wives. Such an arrangement made sense in a culture when there were more widows than single men to look after them. There were other societies where such a thing was against the law.

In this particular case, it was out of the question.

Funny, how clear-cut it had seemed when he'd first set out to track her down. There was never any question of her guilt. Just because the law couldn't punish her, that didn't mean he was going to let her get away with it.

Only somewhere along the way he'd begun to lose sight of the big picture. And now the picture he saw was of Fallon helping an old woman feed turnips to wild horses. Fallon kneeling in the mud to examine the woman's hands where she'd cut them on mussel shells. Fallon laboring to mix mounds of rotted seaweed and horse manure into dry sand in an attempt to grow roses. An attempt that they both knew was doomed from the start.

And that concert. Oh, God, she'd been so bad he hadn't known whether to laugh, cry, or plug up his ears. All he knew was that their eyes had met in the middle of it all, he'd seen the laughter in hers, and he'd wanted to grab her and hold her and tell her it didn't matter that she was awful, truly awful. To tell her that he understood when he didn't really understand at all.

"It's crazy!" He picked up a broken clam shell and hurled it into the water.

The whole situation was just so damned crazy. The fact that he'd finally caught up with her, fully prepared to bring her to justice, only to find himself more often than not admiring her.

Even worse than that, wanting her in all the ways a man wants a woman.

So what now? Where did he go from here?

Ana took in the clothes and folded them on the kitchen table, except for the masculine garments. Mr. Hobbs took care of those. He would have washed and hung them out if she'd let him, but they compromised. He insisted it wasn't proper for a woman to deal with a gentleman's unmentionables. She insisted right back that she'd been doing it for years for her father, and so far as she could tell, it hadn't affected her morals.

She and Maureen had had a good laugh over it. "Don't let his proper manner fool ye. Back when he first commenced to working for Mr. Merry, he had a full head of black hair and the wickedest Kerry blue eyes ever I did see. I weren't so bad meself in those days. We had us a time or two together, that we did, but don't let on I told ye so. A man's got his pride, he has."

"I wouldn't dream of it."

"To be sure, your Mr. Neil's no laggard, either."

Ana blushed and changed the subject. "Do you think there's time for a cup of tea?"

"Sure and there's always time for that, child."

She got out the cups while Maureen set the kettle on to boil. There was a time for coffee and a time for tea. Just now, with the wash in and dinner cooking, with Miss Drucy in the parlor peacefully cutting up old magazines and pasting the pictures in an album and Neil still out doing whatever it was he did all day, it was time for a restorative cup of tea.

Ana was still dawdling over hers while Maureen picked over beans to soak for tomorrow's dinner. They both looked up when Neil came in through the back door, bringing with him the scent of fresh air, sunshine, and the clean masculine aroma that seemed to cling to his skin.

"Did you learn anything more?" she asked, not because she particularly cared about currents and erosion and such things.

"About what? Why do you ask?" He pulled out a chair uninvited and joined her at the table.

"About whatever it is you came here to find out," she said more sharply than she'd intended. She'd asked only because he made her nervous, and when she was nervous she was inclined to chatter.

"There's tea in the teapot, coffee on the stove." Maureen got to her feet with a great deal of grunting and groaning. "I'd better go look in on Miss Drucy."

Ana rose too quickly, rattling her cup in her saucer. "Let me."

"You'll do no such, you'll set and finish your tea. While I'm up and about, I need to change me slippers." There was a twinkle in her eyes that Ana found highly suspect. The last thing in the world she needed now was a matchmaker.

"I met one of the surfman from the Lifesaving Station on my way back," Neil said as soon as she'd left. He rose and poured himself a cup of coffee, added tinned milk and three lumps of sugar. "He said a small boat washed ashore a few days after the storm. Nothing in it. Looked like it might have capsized a time or two before it washed up, he said."

"Could it have been from the shipwreck?"

He shrugged. "He said it looked more like a local boat. He mentioned a builder over in Wanchese who built the same style boat. You don't suppose it could have belonged to your friend's husband, do you?"

Ana strangled on a swallow of tea and endured a helpful whack on the shoulders. "No, I—that is, why would you think that?"

"How do you suppose he got here? Pam brought him over the first time. How did he get here the second time?"

"I don't know. I didn't ask."

"You must have talked about something, you didn't waste any time hurrying out to meet him."

"I don't believe that's any of your business."

She was on her high horse. Brand did his best to ignore the elegant lines of her face, so at odds with the way she was dressed. He refused to think about her mouth in particular, because it distracted the hell out of him. No woman should look so vulnerable when she was on her high horse, unless it was a deliberate tactic.

"Why didn't he stay and help you after you got knocked out? If he couldn't bring you back here alone, he should have gone for help. What happened? Did you have a quarrel? Was he really your friend's husband, or could he have been one of your lovers? Maybe he was the same man who followed you all the way from Connecticut. Who was it who left those bruises on your arm and your throat, Fallon? Your friend's bereaved husband? Why would he try to strangle you?"

He was pushing too hard. He knew it, yet he couldn't seem to stop.

"Who are you?" she whispered, and he had the bitter satisfaction of seeing panic fill those hauntingly beautiful eyes.

Chapter Fourteen

There was more than a threat of rain, for all the air was mild as May. All night long the surf had been pounding. It didn't take a barometer for Brand to know the pressure was low and falling lower. Nor would it surprise him to see the tide washing over the entire north end of the island before morning.

Standing on the shore beside the wharf, he watched Evard's small sloop beat doggedly into the wind, then come about and glide alongside the wharf. Pam's ferry was not far behind, both vessels evidently wanting to get ahead of the weather.

Brand stood by at the ready. Ignoring his hand, Simmy leaped out, nimble as a doe. From the look on her face, the trip home had not been altogether successful. Evard dropped the sail, handed over her bundles, and then the two men eased the small sail-skiff along the wharf and off to one side, to her usual berth, just as Pam came alongside.

"Looks like you'd better come inside and stay the night," Brand called out as he caught the line tossed by the old seaman and quickly whipped it around the nearest piling.

Pam made fast the stern and began uncovering a stack of boxes. Tossing the tarp aside, he shouted over the whine of the wind, "Thankee kindly, but my old woman, she'd lay back 'er ears and take after me wi' a boocher knife."

"I doubt she'd be any too happy if you foundered halfway across the sound, either," Brand yelled back cheerfully. "We're in for a blow. More than a day's

worth, I make it," He passed another carton to Evard,
who stacked it on top of a growing heap on the weathered planks. A few drops of rain escaped the fast-
moving clouds, but with any luck they should be able
to get the lot under cover before the bottom fell out,
Brand assessed.

"For one o' them engineer fellers, you read the
signs right fair. Wind'll likely lay in a day or so, but
with a full moon, we'll have us a tide, all right. If I
was you, I'd tie that skiff off good, boy." He nodded
toward Evard's fourteen-foot sloop.

With the freight unloaded, Pam handed over a bundle of mail, saluted, and cast off again. By the time
Evard set out at a lope toward the shed where his
wheelbarrow was stored, the doughty little skipjack
had nearly reached the mouth of the channel.

The two men were stacking the boxes on the
wooden barrow when Fallon came hurrying down the
boardwalk, a waterproof coat flung over her shoulders.
"What in the world is all that?" she exclaimed, her
words picked up by the wind and carried directly to
Brand's ears. "Do you need any help?"

He gave up on securing the fifth box and lifted it
to his shoulder. There were five in all, each bearing
Merriweather Mercantile's distinctive label, and all di-
rected to Miss Fallon McKnight at Merriweather's
Landing.

Brand wondered if she intended to tell the Merriweathers the truth about her marital status. Not that
it mattered except as one more indication of her
honesty.

Or lack thereof.

"As if you didn't know," he muttered in answer
to her question. "Nice going, lady." Things had been
strained between them since the night he'd accused
her of being in league with James Webster. Her
stricken look was gone so quickly he told himself he
must have imagined it.

But he hadn't imagined the proud lift of her head
as she hurried along beside the wheelbarrow. Wind

lifted her skirts, swirling them in a flurry of white ruffled petticoats about her knees to reveal a flash of
black stockings that had been darned more than once.

Holding onto the raincoat with one hand and
steadying the load with the other, she leaned over to
examine the labels. "Oh, but this one on top is addressed to me," she exclaimed, just as if it were the
greatest surprise in the world.

Brand could understand a woman's wanting pretty
clothes. Hell, he wouldn't mind another change-out,
himself. He'd come here prepared to stay only a few
days.

"So are all the others. Excellent delivery service,
wouldn't you say?"

She ran awkwardly, leaning over to keep the parcels
from toppling, clutching the raincoat and trying to
read another label. If he didn't know better he might
have been taken in by her convincing display of
confusion.

Fortunately, he knew better.

Even so, he found himself admiring the lean lines
of her body. In both his ships and his women, he'd
always looked for good lines. Hers were flawless.

"But what is it? Where did it all come from? Who
sent for it? Why does it have Fa—my name on it?"
She sounded genuinely puzzled.

Tom Merriweather. He'd thought at the time the
poor devil was getting off easy. He didn't know how
she'd wangled it, but judging from the size and number of those boxes, somebody had spent a small fortune on clothes that would be wasted in a place like
this.

Which meant that she'd been up to her usual tricks.
Get while the getting was good, and then get out.

"As to where it came from, that's easy. It says so
right on the label. Who sent for it? I think we both
know the answer to that. I only hope he took your
measurements properly."

She could have made her fortune as an actress on
any stage in the world. With just the right touch of

confusion, she looked him in the eye and said, "Tom? You're thinking Tom sent all this? But why would he do that? We hardly know each other."

And then she frowned. It was a nice touch. He didn't understand what message she was trying to get across, but it was a very nice touch.

By then they had reached the house. Fallon held the door open and while Evard steadied the barrow, Brand lifted the boxes off and set them inside the sheltered vestibule. By the time he'd handed over the last box, he was wishing he'd asked Pam to wait while he packed his gear and left with him. He was sick of the whole business—of lying about who he was and what he was doing here.

Nothing seemed worthwhile. Liam was dead. Galen was dead. What difference did it make if he gave up his drive for revenge and let her go free? She wasn't the first woman ever to make a career of sucking a man's lifeblood and then casting his lifeless body aside. Nor would she be the last.

At least if he left now, he wouldn't number among her victims.

"Oh, this is too much," she exclaimed.

You're right, madam, it's far too much. However, I expect you'll manage to find some way to accept it, won't you?

By then the rest of the household had flocked out to discover what all the excitement was about. Maureen dusted the flour from her hands and it blew toward Simmy, who kept stealing worried looks at Evard, who, ignoring her, turned and stalked off toward the shed with his wheelbarrow.

Mr. Merry appeared in the doorway, beaming like a beardless, emaciated Santa Claus in a maroon cashmere smoking jacket. "Halloo, what have we here?"

Fallon, obviously determined to keep up the pretense, whirled around and exclaimed, "Mr. Merry, what is all this, do you know? They're all addressed to me, but that can't be right. There's been a mistake."

"Bless me if that'un don't look like a hatbox." Maureen reached out a floury finger to touch a tall, round carton.

"This one rattles," observed Simmy, who had picked up one of the smaller boxes and was shaking it.

"Did anyone find my crochet needle? I left it in the parlor, and that new maid must have found it and hid it from me. I never trusted her from the day she came here. Billy, I warned you she'd steal us all blind. Didn't I warn you?"

Fallon turned away from the box she'd been examining and knelt beside the old woman. "Was it a wooden hook or a steel one, Miss Drucy? Why don't we find Evard and ask if he can't whittle a new one? Did you see those lovely birds he whittled from scraps left over from the boardwalk?"

"Oh, yes, the birds . . ." Miss Drucy, her eyes puzzled, smiled her familiar heartbreaking smile, and Brand found himself meeting Fallon's eyes, sharing a silent message.

Care for her! She's so damned vulnerable, gray eyes demanded.

I do. I will, amber eyes replied.

Bloody hell. There it was again, that odd meeting of minds. Lust, he could deal with. Not comfortably, but he could manage plain, ordinary lust. He could even come to terms with the unexpected tenderness that came over him now and then, watching her gentle way with the old woman.

It was this feeling of affinity that threw him for a dead loss. This momentary melding of minds, as if they were two halves of a whole.

All he could figure was that the gods must be having one hell of a laugh at his expense.

"Why don't I take these things up to your room?" he said gruffly. Without waiting for a reply, he shouldered two of the larger boxes and headed for the stairs.

Before Ana dared open the first package, she had to know who was responsible. If these were clothes Fallon had ordered before she'd died, she didn't know quite how she was going to explain the fact that nothing fit. True, she could claim to have lost weight since she'd been here, but she didn't know how she was going to explain adding several inches to her height.

But before she could explore or explain anything, she had to settle Miss Drucy. And then it was time for lunch, and then the rain stopped and there were windows to open, and then it started up again and the same windows had to be closed. Even the ones on the off-side, because the rain came at them from all sides, swirling around the house as if trying to find a way inside.

By the middle of the afternoon it was dark as pitch. Between the wind, the rain, and the roar of the surf, she could hardly hear herself think.

Brand and Evard, protected by waterproof coats and hats, disappeared somewhere outside. Mr. Hobbs was wheeling Mr. Merry to his room to massage his brow with lavender water and his joints with tincture of aconite when Ana, on her way to see where Miss Drucy had disappeared to, caught up with them in the back hall.

The old man apologized. The lowering weather, it seemed, always brought on a variety of aches and pains. Personally, Ana had always found wild weather exhilarating. Given time to dwell on it, she might have worried a bit about their exposed location, but there was simply too much to do.

"My father used to be the same way," she confided. "He always seemed to suffer more than usual before a snowstorm."

"Drucilla is seldom troubled by headaches, but she's always more restless when the weather closes in. Never did take well to confinement. Poor dear, I'm afraid she never will."

"And I'm afraid you're right. She slipped away a few minutes ago. I'm on my way to find her now. But Mr. Merry, could you please tell me about the boxes? I haven't had time to open them yet, but you must know I could never afford so much, even on the generous salary you've agreed to pay me. Could there have been . . . um, a mistake?"

"There's no mistake, my dear. When it occurred to me that you must have lost all the things you'd purchased with the advance on your salary, along with all your other possessions, I thought that rather than waiting until next quarter, I'd simply take the liberty of having a few things sent out to tide you over, so to speak."

To tide her over! If every box was as full as its weight implied, it was more than she'd bought for herself in the past ten years.

"Maureen took your measurements from your gowns and boots, and Tom selected the fabric and styles after discovering your preferences. I hope you're not too unhappy with me. I'm afraid I find retirement rather boring. This entertained me for days. We must both hope Tom wasn't too far afield in determining your preferences in color and style."

Totally disarmed by such unexpected generosity, Ana knelt and laid her hand over his. "Is that what he was doing?" She had to laugh; it was either that or burst into tears. "I haven't had time to unpack a single box yet, so I've no idea what he chose, but at least I know now why he asked so many personal questions." She smiled through the quick moisture in her eyes. "I thought at the time it was strange that a man—a widower, at that—should be so interested in women's fashions."

"Ah, but don't forget, my dear—women's fashions make up a large part of the business. Even though neither of us takes an active part any longer, we're both major stockholders. And Tom . . . well, I'll admit I was hoping . . ."

"Sir, if we're to have time for a nap before supper, perhaps we'd better go along now," Mr. Hobbs suggested.

And Tom *what*? Ana wondered, watching them disappear into the private suite that had been set aside on the first floor. What had Mr. Merry hoped?

She found Miss Drucy in the staff's wing threading new shoestrings in every pair of shoes to be found there. Stringy things seemed to intrigue her, Ana had noticed before.

What with one thing and another, it was much later before she could even think about opening her packages. Simmy helped her, and despite the excitement of lifting out gown after gown, layer upon layer of lovely embroidered undergarments, two bonnets, and two pairs of shoes, Ana couldn't help but notice that the child seemed quieter than usual.

"Simmy, is anything bothering you? Sometimes it helps to talk about things."

"No, ma'am, ever'thing's just fine."

It wasn't, but then, it wasn't in her to pry. For all her youthful shyness, Ana told herself, Simmy knew her own mind. When and if she wanted to talk, Ana would find time to listen. And if possible, to advise.

"Then we'd better hang these up and go back downstairs. I left Miss Drucy in the parlor cutting strips of rags, but that won't last very long. She's edgy today. Heaven help us if she starts fretting over her horses in this weather."

The horses weren't mentioned. The afternoon, dark and blustery, seemed to go on forever as Ana read aloud and Drucy tied the ends of her strips together. A few of them had been cut from old curtains, saved for dusting, but most of them were cut from perfectly good bed linens. The two women together rolled them into balls for some nebulous future project, and Ana considered the day well spent.

Not until nearly dinnertime was she able to steal a few minutes to herself, and by then she'd almost forgotten her new gowns. Excited all over again, she chose the yellow muslin to change into, because yellow had always been her most flattering color.

She told herself she'd chosen it only because it was such a gray day.

"Mercy, and a bust improver," she murmured, holding up a deceptively fragile contraption designed to lift the bosom and rein in the waist. She was both amused and embarrassed, wondering if Tom had thought her so lacking in that department that she needed improving.

At the advanced age of twenty-eight, having been through one harrowing experience after another, she hoped she was sensible enough to accept with good grace whatever blessings came her way. And a new gown of butter-color Swiss muslin, no matter that she did have to wear a corset underneath to make it hang correctly, was definitely a blessing, as were the neat black patent slippers that fit perfectly over the new white lisle stockings.

Before going downstairs, she stopped by to help Miss Drucy get dressed before dinner, only to discover that she'd already gone downstairs. Sometimes she did that, dressing herself in whatever appealed to her at the moment.

Ana only hoped she wouldn't decide she needed a few balls of yellow for her latest project. Loving the soft swish of starchy new fabric against her legs, she hurried down the stairs and breezed into the library where the others had already gathered for their evening glass of wine.

"Oh, my, and don't you look a perfect picture?" Maureen, having already shed her apron and put on her lace collar, came to meet her and made her turn around twice for effect.

"Lovely, lovely, my dear." That from Mr. Merry. "Yellow becomes you."

Mr. Hobbs nodded. Simmy's smile flickered and disappeared too quickly. Evard looked equally distracted.

"Where's Miss Drucy?" Ana asked.

"I thought she was with you."

"No, I left her lining up her shoes all in a row and told her I'd be back to help her dress, but when I looked in, she was already gone. I thought . . ."

They spread out, one woman to each wing, with Mr.

Hobbs taking the fourth. Brand and Evard headed for the back door, and after a quick search of the first floor, the others met in the hall.

"I'm sure she's perfectly all right," Ana said a few minutes later. While the others had trooped up the stairs for a search of the second floor, Mr. Merry had waited downstairs in his chair, looking small and fragile and worried. "Why not look in the library again? She might have fallen asleep in that big chair over by the bay window."

He wheeled about, so eager to help her heart nearly broke on the spot. But she didn't linger, because it had just occurred to her—something Drucy had mentioned just that morning.

Oh, no—she wouldn't. Not in this weather!

Two of the raincoats were missing. Brand and Evard. She flung one of the smaller ones over her shoulders, eyed the row of boots, and with a shrug, hastily stepped out of her new slippers. Peeling down her stockings, she tucked them inside her shoes and set out barefooted down the boardwalk, calling as she went. Not really expecting a response.

So much for her new finery. The rain had slacked off, but the wind still howled. Neil had said earlier that afternoon that it was blowing at least thirty knots. Miss Drucy had immediately started counting the knots in her strips, and Ana had looked up just in time to meet his eyes. Once more, if only for a moment, something warm and welcome had flowed between them—a sort of understanding. And then it was gone, as quickly as it had come.

Alice and the looking glass, she thought not for the first time as she hurried through the darkness, trying to think the way someone with the direct mind of a child would think.

Someone with the cunning of a fox.

Clouds scudded rapidly across the sky, offering an occasional glimpse of a full red moon hovering on the horizon. It would have helped if she knew which direction Brand and Evard had taken. She thought she'd heard someone bumping around in the shed when she'd hurried past, so they'd probably started their searching there, which was as good a place as any.

All the same, she had a feeling where Miss Drucy might have gone. Earlier that day in the front parlor, they'd been talking about Tom's boys. Miss Drucy had mentioned the day they had all gone to explore the old shack.

Ana had no fondness at all for the old relic. "The place needs to come down," she said, collecting loose threads from all the cutting, tying, and rolling. "It was bad enough before, but now, with half the roof fallen in, it's a real hazard."

"My horses don't want it torn down."

"Miss Drucy, what possible use could that old shack be to your horses? They can't get inside out of the weather, it's too far off the ground. It wouldn't even serve to store feed because the roof, what little there is left of it, leaks like a sieve."

"Shade."

"Shade?" Ana eyed the odd streak of paisley in the ball she was holding. Could that possibly be . . . ?

No, of course not.

"There aren't any trees here. Billy says there used to be trees, but someone stole them and now the island is blowing away."

Someone stole the trees, leaving behind the stumps. Of course.

Mumbling to herself, Drucy knotted a few more strips and Ana rolled up the slack.

"I could leave some turnips, that might make it friendlier. If they smell the turnips, why then, they'll see the shade."

Ana had tried to follow, she truly had. It usually helped if she could keep up with where the woman was in her own mind, but at the time, she'd been distracted, wondering when she could find a few minutes to unpack all those boxes stacked on her bed.

Pounding along the narrow path that followed the

length of the island, she couldn't help but remember
another dark rainy night when she'd come this way.
At least this time there was no lighting.

She should have found Neil or Evard and asked
them to search the old shack, only then she'd have
had to explain, and it was easier just to go herself.
Conversations with Drucy were sometimes hard to follow—sometimes impossible, but if she concentrated
hard enough there was usually a thread weaving
through the random phrases.

Horses needed shade. There weren't any trees.
Stumps, but no trees. In the afternoon, there would
be shade on the north side of the old shack. Horses
lured to the site by turnips might discover the shade,
which might encourage them to linger on this end of
the island instead of farther south near the Lifesaving
Station where, according to Pam, they were offered
far tastier treats than a few shriveled turnips.

"Well, mercy me, there's shade enough there now,"
Ana panted. Skirt gathered up in both hands, she ran
as fast as she dared, searching the darkness ahead for
a looming structure. She jumped a narrow creek,
skirted around another one, and breathed a sigh of
relief when she reached the low, flat place Evard
called the mud flats. Not so much as a single clump
of grass would grow there, only a kind of flat, yellowish moss. It might be slick after a rain, but at least
there was nothing to trip on.

Knowing she was almost there and the going from
here on out would be easy, she put on a burst of
speed, skidded, and nearly lost her balance as water
splashed to her waist.

*Oh, for pity's sake, to think I once had a function-
ing brain.*

The rain, of course. It had all but stopped now,
however it had been raining cats and dogs all afternoon. "Miss Drucy," she wailed breathlessly, "where
are you? Please let me take you home."

Poor Mr. Merry. He'd be frantic. How terrible it

must be, to be so dependent on others. She wished now she'd had more patience with her father.

It took forever, even longer this time than it had the last, or maybe it only seemed that way. Not even the moon helped, for as soon as her eyes adjusted to the darkness, it would break through for a moment, only to disappear behind the clouds, leaving her stumbling in the darkness again.

Several times she caught the glitter of light on water where no water was supposed to be. Rainwater, she supposed.

Rainwater, she sincerely hoped!

A bush loomed up in her path, and before she could veer away, she was fighting off a tangle of briars and stubby branches.

Even knowing it was there, she nearly ran into the shack before she could catch herself. Bracing her hands on the wet shingled wall, she struggled to catch her breath. "I hate this place, I really, truly hate it," she panted.

The moon, still low but rising, lifted above the clouds to glitter on the wet floor inside. There was no place to hide. She'd found that out the last time.

"Where *are* you, Drucilla Merriweather?" It was half prayer, half plea, but it sounded more like a threat. "If you're hiding from me—"

The trouble was, even though she almost never played pranks, what would have been a prank in a child might seem perfectly rational to a woman whose mind followed an obscure path all its own.

Oh, this was a mistake. A silly, stupid mistake. She might as well go back, but she couldn't go another step until she caught her breath.

Hitching herself up to sit in the littered doorway, she thought, where now? What next?

Not the landing. Unless a boat came in, there'd be nothing to attract her there. Surely not out to the duck blind, although Evard had said he'd caught her wading hip deep in that direction one day last summer. She'd said something about Tommy and a tree house.

Squinting through the darkness, Ana tried to make out the lights of the castle. From here it looked as if lamps were lit in all the rooms downstairs, and at least two in the bedrooms upstairs.

She caught a glimpse of a flickering light in the attic, but it disappeared so quickly she thought she must have imagined it.

They had already searched the attic. They'd searched everywhere, but now they were probably searching all the nooks and crannies they might have missed the first time. Surely if they'd found her, they would have called off the search.

Oh? And how would they do that? No one even knows where you are.

She should have left a note. Or arranged some sort of signal.

Dear Lord, this wretched weather! No one had thought about notes or signals because they'd all been too concerned about Miss Drucy. It was hard enough keeping up with her on a clear, sunny day, but on a night like this . . . !

Easing herself down to the ground again, Ana winced at the pain that shot up her legs. By morning she'd be stiff as a board. For all she'd always been active, she couldn't recall the last time she had run so fast and so far, a large part of it up to her knees in water.

Catching sight of a glimmer of light, she caught her breath. Had that been a lantern or a firefly?

It was a lantern. And it was coming this way. *Thank you, Lord.* "Miss Drucy? Is that you?"

But hadn't all three lanterns still been hanging from their pegs when she'd left the house?

"Evard? Neil?"

The moon came out as bright as day, revealing the narrow, winding path worn by the ponies through the wild beach grass. She squinted, but still couldn't tell who was carrying the lantern.

Oh, God, what if it was James?

"Fallon, is that you?"

She went limp with relief. "Neil, thank goodness! Did you find her? I was so sure she'd be here. Just this morning she was talking about horses and shade and—"

"We found her. She was digging up her rosebushes, taking them up to the attic."

"She was *what*?"

"She said Noah told her to do it."

"Noah who?"

By then he'd reached her. While he held up the lantern it occurred to her what a mess she must look. Her gown was ruined. Her pretty new yellow Swiss muslin. Her hair, as usual, had escaped its pins and was streaming down her back.

He lifted a hand to touch her cheek. "Captain Noah of biblical fame. Your face is wet. I thought it was mud, but it's scraped."

"Ow, that stings."

"Salty fingers. Sorry."

"Then she's all right? Oh, for heaven's sake, I heard someone in the shed, but I thought it was you or Evard looking for her in there. We all must have passed right by her. Why didn't anyone see her?"

He shrugged. "Poor timing, I suppose. Simmy missed her in the attic, too. Saw the roses and told Maureen. Then I came back for a lantern and— How'd you hurt your face?"

"I haven't the faintest idea. I do know my feet won't ever be the same." She was trembling. Her knees felt weak as water.

Relief, she told herself, knowing that wouldn't explain the sudden hammering of her heart, the way her senses leapt at the sound of his voice, the scent of his skin—the warmth of his breath when he leaned closer to peer at her cheek.

He was going to kiss her. She wanted it so desperately she didn't think she could bear it if he didn't.

Or even if he did. So she stepped back, then set out to follow the path home.

And tripped and nearly fell. "Um—why don't you

go first with the lantern? There's not enough room for us to walk side by side."

Leaning his shoulders against the wet wood, Brand took his time in answering. And then he said quietly, "Neither of us is going anywhere for the next few hours."

She sent him a blank look. The moon was high enough now to cast shadows under those high cheekbones of hers. He tried and failed to tamp down the rush of exhilaration that coursed through him as he explained why they were trapped there together. "The tide's cut gullies in several places. It came in faster than usual tonight."

For a moment she looked as if she didn't believe him. He was tempted to let her go and find out for herself, but the temptation to keep her there—by force, if necessary—was even stronger.

"But it wasn't—I mean, I got here safely enough."

"Full moon, high wind, floodtide. Take my word for it, Fallon, you're better off waiting here for the next few hours."

Chapter Fifteen

They argued. Ana was too tired to argue. Even before the search began it had been an exhausting day. But she was afraid of the silence. Afraid of being alone with a man who attracted her, frightened her, puzzled her. A man who, above all, made her feel things no man had ever made her feel before.

Pushing away debris brought down by the lighting, she settled in the open doorway, arms crossed over her chest. She uncrossed them, buttoned her raincoat up to her chin, and then recrossed them, just as if buttons and a defensive posture would protect her.

Protect her from Neil?

Or from herself.

Silence stung out between them. The high whining sound of the wind and the roar of the nearby ocean fell away, unheard. She swallowed hard and tried not to twitch, not to call attention to herself.

Silly woman. He's not going to bite you.

Oh, but he knew exactly what she was thinking, probably even what she was feeling. At various times she had thought of him as arrogant, angry, kind, understanding. He was all of those things, but more than anything else, he was a man who made her regret.

She sighed, the sound unaturally loud in the darkness. She had far too much to regret.

Not all the years with her father. Remembering the way he'd been when she was a child, she could never bring herself to regret that.

But Ludwig—God, how she regretted Ludwig! Regretted ever meeting him. Regretted ever letting herself be talked into marrying him. Regretted not showing him the door when he'd come back a week after the funeral, demanding his inheritance.

His inheritance!

She hated what he'd done to her. Not the pain, the humiliation, and degradation so much as the fact that it had put an end to all her foolish dreams, the dreams every girl had of falling in love, marrying, having babies of her own, and living happily ever after.

And all that was before she'd even murdered him.

"Fallon? It won't be so bad. At least it's not cold."

Wasn't it? Without the sun, it was hardly warm, but it wasn't the weather that bothered her. She looked at him and thought, I wouldn't care if it was the dead of winter if I could warm myself in your arms for just one night. I would rather spend a single hour in your arms here in this sodden, deserted ruin than spend the rest of my life swathed in the luxury with any other man in the world.

Unfortunately, neither option was possible.

She stirred restlessly. "Don't go too far inside, it's dangerous," he warned her, and she thought, it's more dangerous than you know.

He was leaning up against what was left of the door frame, no more than a foot or two away. With the moonlight carving his face into chiseled planes and mysterious shadows, he was more than ever like that mythical god. The one with a fistful of thunderbolts.

Under the shadow of his craggy brows, he was staring at her, too. "You look different in this light," he said, his voice suddenly the voice of a stranger. Did moonlight affect voices? "Fallon, how long do you think you can keep it up?"

"Keep what up?" If her heart thundered any louder, it would burst right through her oilskin coat.

"The pretense."

"Pretense?" She could barely speak, her throat was so constricted.

"It's time to end the game. I've been here far too long as it is."

She shut her eyes, steeling herself against fainting, against crying. One way or another she would hang onto her dignity if it killed her. Calmly, she asked, "How long have you known?"

He leaned closer to catch her words, and she realized she'd spoken in a whisper. It was the best she could do at the moment. His face was so close she could feel the heat of his skin against her wet cheek, unbearably intimate.

Using her hands, she began to edge back, but he caught her by the shoulders and held her there. "No, don't try to run away again."

As if there was anyplace to run.

He swore. Anger and something else—something even more frightening came at her like waves of heat on the hottest summer day. His fingers bit into her shoulders as if she were naked. As if she weren't covered by layers of cambric and Swiss muslin and oilskin—and that blessed bust improver that no one had even noticed.

"Damn you, woman, you won't lie your way out of this. I know what you are—I hate myself for wanting you."

And then he was kissing her. Clamping her jaw between thumb and fingers, he ravished her mouth with a brutal strength that was shocking and exciting.

Yet, strangely enough, he didn't hurt her. She wasn't even frightened.

He tasted her, forcing a response, and then groaned as he gathered her into his arms, but he didn't hurt her. And she, who knew far better than most the kind of pain a man could inflict—knew how quickly his mood could change—made not the least attempt to run away. Far from wanting to escape, she found herself actually glorying in his masculine strength, in the way he made her feel.

Anamarie, it's sorry you'll be, a small voice persisted.

She refused to listen. Even knowing what was likely

to happen next, she felt only a heated rush of anticipation.

He was furious. There was no mistaking his anger, yet oddly enough, he wasn't using his strength against her. It dawned on her then that it was himself he was angry with, for wanting her. He knew all about what she had done, knew she was not who she pretended to be, yet knowing that, he still wanted her.

Don't hate yourself, she pleaded silently. *Hate me, if you must, I deserve it—but not yourself.*

She waited for him to denounce her, but he didn't, and she knew he was in control of a force far stronger than anger. She'd felt that same force back when her nightmares had first begun to give way to her daydreams.

Felt it tug gently at her senses the first time he'd kissed her, and even more the next time, and the next. Whatever it was, it was far more dangerous than the powerful currents that ripped through the inlet. They were barely visible on the surface, yet they were strong enough to carve channels, to move big ships—to drown anyone who tried to fight them.

She was drowning.

Somehow, her coat had unbuttoned itself. She didn't remember doing it, although she did know that she alone was responsible for the buttons on his shirt. She'd had to touch his naked skin just once before it ended. Before the current carried her away. Simply had to, or she would have died.

The feel of him was like nothing she could have imagined. Ludwig's body had been pale, flabby, and dry, with breasts that had reminded her of an old woman's.

Neil was hard. Slick, damp, hard, and hot. There was a neat patch of hair centered on his chest between his flat nipples. She combed her fingers through it, thought she heard him groan, and then she cupped the firm muscles on either side and felt his nipples harden into tiny peaks against her palms.

This time he did groan, a guttural sound deep in his

throat. He edged her back farther in the doorway and came down beside her, leaning over her, sliding her skirt over her hips.

"You're wet," he said gruffly, at the same time she felt the night air against the wet drawers plastered against her thighs.

Of course she was wet. It had rained. On her way here she'd blundered into so many creeks—puddles—something, it was a wonder she hadn't truly drowned.

But she was wet in places the tide had never touched, and that surprised her even more than it embarrassed her. Ludwig had told her on their wedding night that it would be her fault if he hurt her, that she was dry as an old maid. She hadn't known what he meant, but then he'd forced her legs apart and driven into her, cursing her and hurting her, hurting her and cursing her, until he'd flopped over onto his back, panting, still cursing.

She'd thought at the time that it had gone on and on and on, like an unending nightmare, but later she realized that it had been over quickly. He'd left her there, hurting and disappointed, shedding silent tears amidst the wreckage of all her foolish, romantic dreams.

She felt something tugging at her clothing. Neil was fumbling with the hooks on her corset. "What are you doing?" she gasped, trying to brush his hands away.

He refused to be brushed. "What the devil do you need with this contraption?"

"It's not a contraption, it's an improver."

The sound of his laughter was harsh against her ears. Suddenly wary, she tried to scramble away. It was the feel of his hand on her breast, sending quicksilver racing through her veins, that robbed her of the will to escape. She opened her mouth to protest, but he cut off the words before she could utter them. By the time she felt his hands on the bare skin inside her thigh, she was aching so sweetly she forgot all about protests. Escape was the very last thing on her mind.

And then, "What are you doing?" she cried, twisting her mouth away. "Oh, please, Neil . . ."

Oh, please don't stop. Oh, please, I can't bear it—!

When his mouth moved down to her breast and he began to suckle her there, she thought she might die. And then his fingers found her most private part and began a slow, circular movement and she thought she had already died. Her breath came in short, strangled bursts. She moaned and lifted her hips, rising to meet the splendor that hovered just out of reach, and then it broke over her, like shattering rainbows, like a tidal wave, and she screamed.

She wasn't even aware of when he opened his britches. All she knew was that he loomed over her— that something hard and blunt and hot was prodding her there, and then he took both her hands, lacing his fingers through hers, and held them over her head.

"Please," she begged, barely able to speak for what had just happened to her. Please don't hurt me any more than you have to, she would have said if she could have found the strength. Not that it would have done her any good.

She braced herself for what was to come, willing herself to endure. Yet, all the while, a strange, irrational part of herself that she didn't even recognize trembled eagerly on the brink of anticipation.

"Shh," he whispered, and then, slowly, deliberately, he thrust into her. Thrust, withdrew, and thrust again.

She held her breath and waited for the incredible tearing pain, but it never came. Instead, that same splendor began to glow all around her. She heard her own voice whimpering—mewling little sounds like a hungry kitten—and then it happened all over again, breaking over her like a thousand rainbows, drowning her under a crashing wave of sheer indescribable pleasure.

Years later she found the strength to open her eyes. Incredibly enough, he was still there, lying close beside her on the hard, wet floor. One arm was flung across his face, the other had gathered her to him so that her head was resting on his shoulder.

He had a large shoulder. Her neck was bent at an awkward angle. It hurt. Her conscience hurt. Oddly enough, the parts of her that had been so thoroughly and gloriously used, did not.

She would have to tell him. He obviously knew some of it, anyway, but before this went any further— not that it ever could—he would have to know everything.

He would turn her in, of course. What else could any decent, law-abiding man do? And she couldn't allow it to happen that way. That was something she would have to do alone. In spite of everything, she still had too much pride to let him see her being dragged off in handcuffs like a common criminal.

Not that she wasn't a common criminal, but all the same, she couldn't bear for him to see her in prison, to watch her being led to a gallows and hanged.

All this went through her mind—incoherent bits and pieces—as she lay there, her boneless body still humming faintly, like the sound of crickets in the distance. It was fading now. She didn't want it to end, but of course it would. Everything ended.

"Neil?"

Neil. He wasn't Neil, dammit, he was Brandon! Just once before this farce ended, he wanted to hear her call him by his name.

Something about his stillness must have alerted her. He could almost picture the doubts, the sudden wariness creeping into those honey-colored eyes of hers. "You know about me, don't you?" she whispered. "How much?"

Showdown time. Damn. He wasn't ready for this. "Just about everything, I suspect," he said grimly.

He heard a long, shuddering breath, silence, and then, "How did you guess?"

"I didn't have to guess. I knew enough when I came after you." It was like shooting fish in a barrel.

Damned if she wasn't making *him* feel guilty now, and that made him mad as hell.

"What are you going to do?"

"I haven't decided. When I do, you'll be the first to know." He was proud of the hardness he'd managed to hang onto.

The hardness in his voice, at least. Unfortunately, his body was beginning to stir again, a reaction to the feel of her soft, hot body next to his, the silkiness of her hair against his face—the scent of lavender and lemongrass, sex and salt air.

"I know I shouldn't have run away, but I was so frightened. I panicked."

"Frightened." He made a sound of disgust. "You knew he was gravely injured—dammit, it was your fault! And yet you walked out and left him there!"

"It was the blood. There was so much blood—it was all over my dress, all over my hands . . ."

He sat up suddenly, dumping her so that her head struck the floor. "Your husband was hurt—dying for all you knew, and all you could think of was your damned *dress*?"

It hadn't been panic that had made her flee. She'd stayed around long enough to sell off everything that wasn't nailed down before she'd deserted him. That was hardly the act of a panic-stricken woman. It was the deliberate act of a heartless woman.

And yet . . .

While she struggled to sit up, Brand tried to deny the shame he felt now that the white-heat of lust had cooled. Never in his life had he treated a woman this way. He had used her. He tried to tell himself that it was no more than she deserved. All the same, he knew it would gnaw at his gut for as long as he lived.

God, what a fool he'd been.

He couldn't look her in the face, not even in the darkness, and so he looked away, into the darkest corner of the ruined building, the darkness echoing the bleakness of his heart.

He heard her small wounded cry, sensed movement,

but was too late to catch her before she sailed out the door.

"Fallon," he cried. "Dammit—!"

Ignoring him, she staggered, gathered her loose clothing in both hands, and took off at a run.

"Ah, Fallon . . . I'm sorry," he whispered.

For her sake? For Liam's? For his own?

God, he didn't know.

He let her go. Watched her in the moonlight, but let her go. She'd left her oilskin behind. That had been the first thing he'd removed. They'd used it as a bed. The pale gleam of her ruined yellow gown quickly disappeared from sight. He thought about following her, but didn't. Lacked the energy. Lacked the will. Sex always left him feeling drained, especially when it was good.

This had been more than good.

It had also been more than sex.

Damn.

She wouldn't get far. He almost wished she would. Wished it was daylight, calm as a millpond, with the ferry just pulling into the landing. Wished he could wait here until she'd had time to pack her things and get away.

Because now that she'd admitted her guilt, he didn't know what the hell he was going to do.

He knew what he wanted to do. He'd done it. And now he was probably going to spend the next few years cursing himself for doing it. Cursing himself for wanting to keep her with him so that he could do it again and again, until he grew tired of her.

And even then—even if he could come up with a just punishment—he wasn't at all certain he'd be able to inflict it.

At least neither of his brothers would ever have to know. That should have made him feel better. Instead it made his burden of guilt even heavier. Swearing fluently in gutter French, compliments of two months served aboard a French freighter, he buttoned the front of his britches, tucked in his shirt, and set out toward the far end of the island.

Maybe if he stayed away from the castle long enough he could outwalk his devils.

By the time Ana made it back to the castle she was drenched to the skin and shaking so hard she could barely speak. If anyone mentioned her appearance, she would blame it on the tide. On the rain. Tell them she'd been taken prisoner by pirates and had barely escaped with her life.

Or tell them the truth.

"Lord love a sinner, child, didn't Mr. Neil find you? Sure and he set out looking for you the minute we found Miss Drucy."

Ana could only nod. She allowed herself to be shepherded into the housekeeper's room, where she was stripped of her sandy, sodden clothes, swaddled in a flannel sheet, and shoved down into a rocking chair.

"Now you just set right there while I fill the tub. Miss Drucy's sleeping like a lamb in her own bed with Simmy on a pallet beside her in case she wakes up and takes a notion to wander." She muttered something about ungodly weather and full moons as she came and went. This time, Ana noticed with bitter amusement, she didn't mention making wishes.

Docile as a sleeping lamb, she sat where she'd been put. If the heavens had opened and Gabriel had blown his horn directly into her ear, she doubted if she could have moved an inch. She felt numb, and welcomed the feeling.

"Give me a good, decent city anytime. Sure and if the good Lord had meant folks to live in place like this, He'd have built streets and bridges."

Ana swallowed a bubble of hysterical laughter. Streets and bridges, full moons and stormy weather— as much as she would have liked to, she couldn't blame what she'd done on any of those. She had sinned and then sinned again, and she would pay for it for the rest of her life.

Which probably wouldn't be very long, after all.

"Is Mr. Merry still awake?" she asked when Maureen came bustling back from the kitchen with a steaming mug of her potent all-purpose remedy.

"Mr. Hobbs hasn't—that is, the last I heard, he was still in the library."

"I need to speak to him."

"It'll keep till morning, young lady. What you're wanting is a good hot bath and then into bed with you. I'll lay on another quilt, for all it's not that cold, else you'll likely take a chill."

Nodding distractedly, Ana sipped the spirit-laced tea and tried to sort through all that had to be done, and done as quickly as possible.

First of all, she would have to tell Mr. Merry everything, or enough to make him understand, so that he could advertise for someone else to look after Miss Drucy.

Next she would have to pack her things. Not all of them. Just enough to get her through what she had to do. Even if her conscience had allowed her to accept Mr. Merry's generosity, she had only the single valise she'd brought with her.

Then, too, she thought grimly, where she was going she wouldn't need very much. She had no idea how women prisoners were dressed, but it probably wasn't in silk or Swiss muslin.

"Tomorrow, then," she murmured, allowing herself to be led into the servants' bathroom, which was considerably warmer than the one upstairs, as it was closest to the coal-burning furnace.

Nothing could be done until morning, at any rate. As long as the wind blew the way it was blowing now, driving the tide practically up to the front door, there would be no ferry. No way for Mr. Merry to advertise for another companion.

No way for her to escape.

Which meant she would be stuck here with Neil, who knew all about her and would tell everyone. As bad as the guilt had been, it couldn't compare with the shame once they all knew what she had done.

"No need to look like ye've lost yer last friend, me girl, nothing's all that bad. Things has a way of working out how the good Lord intends. A body can't argue with that, now can she?" Maureen poured something into the bathwater from a brown bottle. Something that smelled like liniment. Ana gasped and reached for a towel to blot her streaming eyes.

"What in the world—?"

"Me own ma's recipe, child. It'll ward off constipation of the chest better than any mustard plaster."

What could she do but laugh? And if her laughter ended up in still more tears, why then, she could blame it on the housekeeper's remedy instead of on treasures found and treasures lost.

The sky dawned a soft, rose-tinted pearl gray. The air was warm, the wind not quite so strong, but the water was still halfway up the boardwalk when Ana looked out her bedroom window the next morning. One whole section of boards had floated away in the night. Evard and Neil were dragging them back from where they had lodged against a bayberry bush and trying to secure them in place.

She lingered a moment, admiring the strength of Neil's shoulders as he swung the sledgehammer to drive down the piling Evard was holding.

Last night . . .

"Don't think about last night," she whispered. "Don't even think about it now."

She'd slept later than usual, probably due to Maureen's hot spiced camomile, honey and whiskey, but at least she hadn't caught a chill.

Just as she reached the bottom of the stairs, Mr. Hobbs, impeccably dressed as usual in his dark three-piece suit, emerged from the kitchen with a serving tray holding two cups and a coffeepot.

"Do you think I might have a few words this morning with Mr. Merry?" she asked. For half the night she'd lain awake, trying to decide how much to reveal. She still hadn't made up her mind.

"I'm sure he'll be pleased for the distraction, Miss Fallon. By now he's read every newspaper twice over and stared in on volume one of the Britannica again."

Ana forced a smile, braced herself, and followed the dapper gentleman's gentleman into the library.

More than an hour passed before she emerged, feeling limp but remarkably better for having finally unburdened herself.

Partially unburdened herself. She'd decided nothing would be served by sharing the whole wretched business. But at least now she'd be able to leave as soon as the weather cleared enough for the ferry to run again.

Miss Drucy would manage without her until someone could be found to take her place. Mr. Merry had assured her of that. It had been one of her biggest concerns.

"I believe we'll tell the others only that you've a bit of personal business that requires your attention," he'd said just as calmly as if she hadn't told him she had got herself in trouble with the law back home in Connecticut—something to do with an abusive husband—and that she'd run away and met a woman on the train south who later died in a fire, and adopted her identity for her own purposes.

"One does what one must under unexpected circumstances," he said. "I've come to know you well enough, my dear, to know that you've done nothing dishonorable. You were right to leave the fellow."

"Oh, but—"

"Shh. We all make mistakes, child. With the best will in the world, we sometimes compound those mistakes. You're to be admired for going back now to make amends."

She hadn't known how to take that. Hysterical laughter had seemed the most appropriate response, but she'd managed to avoid it. Just barely.

"Promise me one thing, Fallon," he'd said, and she'd paused on her way out the door.

"Promise me you'll deal with your husband only through a lawyer. If only it were New York, I could direct you to several fine attorneys who would be more than capable of dealing with the cad. Perhaps one of them can recommend someone. I'll give you a letter."

Ana thanked him sincerely. She had already dealt with the cad, but it would take more courage than she'd been able to drum up to confess to murder. She prayed these wonderful people would never have to know that about her.

"Thank you, but my father's lawyer will know what to do." She would sooner hurl herself in front of a train than throw herself on the mercy of Horatio Quillerby.

"Just be sure you deal only through the law."

"I will," she assured him gravely. *One on each side, holding my chains.*

She closed the door behind her, leaned against it, and closed her eyes, telling herself it would have served no real purpose to tell him the whole story. He'd be distressed, and the poor man had more than enough stress to deal with.

The sin was hers alone. She would bear it alone. Fear was an ever-present enemy, but one she had dealt with before.

One step at a time. She'd just taken the first one.

Hearing the sound of a closing door, she opened her eyes and thought, damn. Not now. Not Neil.

He'd just come inside, his face still flushed from exertion, his hair shaggy and windblown. He had to be the most beautiful man on the face of God's earth, jutting jaw, broken nose and all.

She could tell the minute he saw her. He grew unnaturally still. His eyes took on a hooded look. "Fallon," he acknowledged.

She steeled herself against running. Against dashing down to the wharf, stealing Evard's boat and sailing the thing across the inlet, or to China, which was just as likely.

She couldn't even sail a paper boat. Tom's boys had tried to teach her, but hers always sank.

And so far, theft was the one crime she had not committed.

Standing as tall as she possibly could, she smiled with every evidence of serenity. "Good morning, Neil. I see you've been busy. Is the tide beginning to fall yet?"

"Some. If the wind drops off, I expect we'll be back to normal by this evening, except for the low places."

There might as well have been a ten-foot wall between them. She could have told him things would never be back to normal. Would she even recognize "normal" if it hit her in the face?

Probably not. "You'll have to excuse me, I'm on my way to Miss Drucy's room. She'll be wanting to set out her roses again."

He bit off an oath. "Damn her roses! Fallon, are you all right?"

It was one of her prouder moments. She managed to look down her nose, despite the fact that she was a good eight inches shorter than he was. "Of course I'm all right, Neil. Why on earth wouldn't I be?"

"We have to talk." He raked a hand through his hair, leaving windrows falling wildly in all directions.

"I'm afraid it will have to wait. Miss Drucy has first call on my time as long as I'm here."

"As long as—"

But she was already past him, skirts swishing as she took the stairs with the regal grace of a duchess. Somewhat more haste, but all the grace.

Fallon?

Why had he called her Fallon when he knew very well who she was?

Chapter Sixteen

Ana had already made up her mind to catch the next ferry out. Three days later when she caught sight of the familiar sail, she was tempted to change her mind, but it would never do. Now, more than ever, she knew she had to get away.

"No mail nor papers today. The *Curlew* ain't running yet, but I thought I'd better see how ye're faring," Pam called out as he tied up. "I'm on my way to deliver to the station. If ye're running short of coal or Irish potatoes, I can let ye have a sack of each and make it up to the station on the next haul."

Simmy and Evard had come down to see her off. Maureen, red-nosed, red-eyed, had stayed in her kitchen. "I'd just stand there keening me heart out, child, making a fool of meself. I'd as soon get on with me baking."

To Ana's great relief, Neil had set out for the station with a surfman some half an hour earlier. It seemed that a body had washed ashore during the night and the captain wanted someone from the castle to take a look at him before they nailed him up in a pine box.

"Leaving out a'ready, Miss Fallon?" The ferryman tipped his hat and eyed her valise and the sack of biscuits and cheese Maureen had insisted she take with her.

"Cap'n Pam, I'm so glad to see you. Do you have room for a passenger?"

She sounded breathless. She *was* breathless. Ever since she'd glanced out an upstairs window and spotted the familiar sail in the distance she'd been racing around, gathering up what she would need for the trip north, saying her good-byes, and trying not to lose her courage.

She'd promised to write, and she would, if only to say she wouldn't be back. Earlier, when she'd had her talk with Mr. Merry, he'd asked her to return once she'd settled her accounts.

That was what she'd called it. Settling her personal accounts. Dealing with an unpleasant situation she'd left behind. She had toyed with the idea of confessing everything, but she simply lacked the courage.

Besides, it wouldn't do him a speck of good to know the worst about her, and there might come a time when she would draw solace from knowing that somewhere in the world she had friends who thought well of her.

Drucy was the only one who didn't know she was leaving. Mr. Merry had assured her he would explain when and if the occasion arose, but they'd both known that Drucy probably wouldn't even notice her absence. It was a lowering thought, but Drucilla Merriweather lived more and more in a world of her own construction. Ana had grown fond of her and would sorely miss her, but it wasn't as if there weren't enough people to look after her until yet another companion could be found.

She'd been distraught at the thought of having to face Neil after avoiding him for two days, but for once, luck had played into her hands. Not twenty minutes before she'd spotted the ferry in the distance, the surfman had knocked at the door. A few minutes later, the two of them had left together.

What was that cliché so beloved of the writers of purple prose? If she'd read it once, she had read it a dozen times.

Go now, and don't look back.

Well. She was going. She would watch until there was nothing more to see, and then she would turn and face forward and set about forgetting how close she had come to falling in love with a man who could only despise her.

Not that it was really love. Whatever it was, it couldn't have been that. Not on his part, at least.

Once Pam and Evard had off-loaded a sack of coal and one of potatoes, Evard swung her baggage aboard, and then it was time to leave.

She turned to wave at Mr. Hobbs, who stood in the doorway. He had given her a packet of feverfew for her headaches, and actually blushed when she'd tried to tell him how much his friendship had meant to her.

Now she hugged Simmy one last time, feeling like an older sister, or an aunt. Like a good friend, at the very least. "Don't fret, dear, you're young yet. You've plenty of time before you have to make up your mind," she cautioned. "Just see that you don't allow anyone to rush you into making a decision that will affect your whole future. Forever is a long, long time."

"Come back real soon."

"As soon as I possibly can," she promised.

She held out her hand to Evard—would have hugged him, too, but he'd have been embarrassed to death. She did know that much about young men.

"Mr. Neil'll be real sorry he missed you, ma'am. We were fixing to finishing anchoring down the board-walk this morning."

"Yes, I'm sure," she murmured.

Just yesterday the pair of them had been up on the roof repairing a leak. She knew very well Neil had been watching her working in the garden with Miss Drucy, trying to salvage a few drowned seedlings. She'd felt his eyes on her, but kept her own eyes focused on the ground. Only when she was sure he'd gone back to hammering did she dare to steal a glance, and then she'd looked away quickly so he wouldn't catch her.

As if the image of his black hair blowing across his brow and his bare arms glinting like bronze in the sunlight wasn't forever etched on her memory.

It was silly. It was downright childish, and yet as

long as the two of them shared the same island, she could no more stop being aware of him than she could stop breathing.

Any more than she could help taking one last long look back at the island now, hoping she would see him on his way back from the station.

Hoping she wouldn't.

"Good-bye, Miss Drucy," she whispered. Watching the tiny figure bustling back and forth between the shed and the castle, carrying the sticklike remains of her dead rosebushes from one spot to another and back again, she felt her eyes begin to burn. Blaming it on the wind, she turned away.

Pam shifted a few coils of line and an anchor to clear her a place up forward. "Here ye go, Missy. Set an' let the wind blow in your face. It'll keep ye from sickenin'."

It might prevent seasickness. She wasn't at all certain it would do much for heartsickness, but she smiled her thanks and stoically turned her face forward, allowing the wind to have its way with her hair.

Which it was bound to do anyway, with or without her permission.

Just before she'd left the castle, Mr. Merry had handed her an envelope with instructions not to open it until she was well away from the island. Knowing she probably wouldn't be able to read whatever he'd written without weeping, she'd tucked it into her reticule. She was fairly sure he had enclosed money for her journey north. He'd told her earlier that he would certainly pay her fare home, that she had more than earned it.

She hadn't argued with him because they both knew it was true. She had earned it. More than that, she desperately needed it.

Not that she wouldn't have been willing to stay on forever without a penny of salary, if only her conscience would allow it.

And if only—

Well. No more daydreams.

*   *   *

The hotel at Nags Head was less than half filled because the season had barely begun. Ana had no trouble securing a small room, and was assured that the *Curlew* had resumed her schedule and would arrive tomorrow.

She ordered tea, toast, and a coddled egg in the dining room, because it was cheaper than being served in her room, and she needed to hoard every cent she could toward hiring a lawyer.

Not that the best lawyer in the world could do her much good. She had murdered a man. Nothing could change that fact.

Back in her room, she reread the letter from Mr. Merry and cried until her nose was completely stopped up. He'd advised her to take a Pullman so as to arrive rested. He'd warned her against speaking to strangers and listed several names and addresses of friends along the way in case she found herself in any sort of need before she arrived in Pomfret. "I wish you well, and beg you to return to us as quickly as possible," he'd written. "For you must know we think of you as the daughter we might have had."

She wouldn't be going back, of course. She suspected he knew it, but was too much the gentleman to press the issue beyond a simple invitation.

All the same, she was deeply touched.

She blew her nose, washed her face, and turned her thoughts once again to what lay ahead instead of what she'd left behind.

Lawyers. She would have to think about it. The only lawyer she knew personally was Horatio Quillerby, who had doubtless lived for years on what he skimmed from her father's estate. He had to have had his greedy fingers all over Marcus Gilbretta's investments, else why had he guarded against her every expenditure?

No way on earth would she ever ask a single thing of Horatio Quillerby.

But did a confessed murderess even need a lawyer?

Too bad she'd spent so many years reading romances. She should have been reading tales of crime and vengeance. At least then she might have a better grasp of what was about to happen to her.

The *Curlew* arrived the next day. Ana was on the dock with the scattering of hotel guests who'd come down to greet the new arrivals, along with their dogs, pigs, cows, chickens, children, and servants. Evidently the thrice-weekly arrival of the *Curlew* was a great social event. It was certainly a noisy one.

She had woken up feeling almost a sense of anticipation now that she'd set the train in motion. Or at least, a sense of relief.

Although resignation might be a better word. Having burned yet another bridge, there was nowhere to go but forward.

To that end she had forced herself to order a sweet-potato biscuit and coffee for breakfast. She'd managed to eat half her biscuit and felt better for it. She had definitely sworn off crying. It clogged up her head and didn't do a particle of good.

Ignoring the curious stares, she stood off to one side, reticule dangling from her arm, her heavy valise leaning against a bench, and waited for the last few stragglers to move off so that she could board the steamer for the return trip to Elizabeth City, and from there catch a northbound train.

"Fallon?"

"Neil?" she whispered, every vestige of color draining from her face. Struggling against a mixture of dread and exhilaration, she turned toward the man who'd come up behind her.

"Oh, I do beg your pardon," he said.

Her shoulders sagged. She didn't know him. There was something familiar about his voice, but if she'd ever met him before she would have remembered. He was strikingly handsome, well dressed, but looked as if he might recently have been ill. There were shadows under his eyes, and his clothes hung from what must have once been a powerful frame.

"I'm sorry, but I'm not—" she began, when he shook his head.

"No, I'm the one who should apologize. For a minute there I thought you were someone else. You look remarkably like a woman I used to know. I meant no disrespect, ma'am."

Merciful heaven, was there no end to it? Ana wondered as she mumbled something under her breath and hurried past him to board the departing steamer.

First poor James and now this man. How many more victims had she left behind? For someone so young, Fallon McKnight had certainly cut a wide swathe through the male population.

On his hands and knees, Brand was leveling the last few replacement planks in the boardwalk when he sighted the ferry entering the slough. He hadn't been expecting her back so soon.

"Looks like there might be a passenger on board," he observed. Sitting back on his heels, he wiped the sweat from his brow. It was well before noon, but the day already promised to be a sizzler.

"Could be Mr. Gill." Evard dropped the sledgehammer and loped off toward the house. "I'd better fetch Mr. Merry. Far's I know, we're not expecting no other visitors."

The all-around man, Brand thought. Damned well time that gentleman turned up.

Waiting for the small sloop to come alongside, he stretched a few aching muscles. He'd been working furiously to finish whatever projects needed finishing so that he could leave with a clear conscience.

She'd gone, damn her soul. Left without even telling him good-bye. According to Mr. Merry, she had personal business back home to attend, and couldn't say for sure when she would be able to return.

"Personal business, my sweet ass," he muttered. "She's cut and run again."

Coming alongside with a precision borne of more than half a century of sailing, Pam dealt with the sails and secured the freight boat. Brand shielded his eyes against a brilliant sun, but didn't move. His gear was all packed, but he hadn't expected to be able to leave today. He'd finished the roof and most of the other chores that were beyond the scope of a sixteen-year-old fisherman, which wasn't to say he felt good about going. If anything went wrong, the nearest help was at the station, more than an hour away.

But he had to go, and the sooner, the better. Already she had a good head start. According to Merriweather, who obviously knew more than he was willing to share, she was bound for Connecticut.

He'd wondered about that. So far as he knew, there was nothing left for her there. She'd cleaned out the McKnights. Her own cousins didn't want her.

A thought struck him, and he smiled with bleak amusement. She'd claimed to be heading north? He'd do well to buy a ticket on the first southbound out of Elizabeth City. The woman had done nothing but lie from the very beginning, damn her big, innocent eyes. And even knowing it—knowing her for what she was—he still couldn't put her out of his mind.

Passing the open door of her bedroom just that morning, he'd caught a familiar whiff of lavender—clover—whatever it was she always smelled of. Before his brain could kick in, his body had reacted so enthusiastically he'd had to wait nearly ten minutes before he could go down and join the others for breakfast.

He'd blamed her for doing it deliberately. Leaving her scent for every rutting male in the area to follow. It was a damned good thing she'd left when she had, because if she'd still been there, he would have likely wrung her neck.

Oh, yeah—sure you would.

Evard leaned in the doorway and yelled at the top of his voice, "Comp'ny coming, Mr. Merry!"

Brand stood slowly, brushed the sand from his hands and knees, and set out to meet the incoming

passenger, glad of anything that would distract him
from the wretched mess she had made of his mind,
his life, and his plans.

"Brand?"

Shock slammed into him like a runaway freight
train.

"They told me at your office I'd find you here."

If there'd been a tree handy, Brand would've
wrapped his arms around it and hung on until the
world settled back on its axis.

He whispered a name.

"Like the old bad penny, huh? What I want to
know is, how the devil can a fellow get drunk and
celebrate his resurrection when his own brother won't
hang around long enough to help him bend an
elbow?"

There was no opportunity to talk privately. By the
time they did, at the rate they were going, neither of
them would be in any condition for a serious discussion. As soon as they'd entered the house there'd been
the introductions to be performed, which had led directly to the explanations.

Which had meant starting from the beginning and
trying to sort out the whole muddled business, when
Brand, for one, still didn't know what the devil was
going on.

All he knew was that Galen was back from the
dead. It had been years since he'd actively prayed, but
if the half-formed hopes, the fears, and longings he'd
carried in his heart for so long could be even faintly
construed as prayer, then he was a true believer for
life.

Maureen had wept a few tears when she'd learned
that he'd been brought ashore practically in sight of
her beloved Wicklow Hills by the fishermen who had
saved his life.

Evard had immediately wanted to know all about
the kinds of fish they caught and the rigs they used.

Miss Drucy had said there were bugs in the parlor.

Finally, Mr. Merry was able to steer the two men into the library, where he immediately proposed a toast to Galen McKnight, back from the dead.

They all drank to that, and then Brandon McKnight, shipowner, also known as Neil Dalton, civil engineer, launched into his own explanations.

"The Neil Dalton part is true enough," he admitted, feeling guilty and embarrassed and laying the blame on Fallon. "Brandon Neil Dalton McKnight, named for both my father and my grandfather. As the first son, I got saddled with the whole lot in case there weren't any others, but as it turned out, there were three of us."

And then, of course, he'd had to explain about Liam, which led directly to an explanation of Fallon, which led to yet another explanation as to what he was doing there in the first place.

The old man looked confused, which was no wonder. It was a confusing train of events, even for a man who knew the score.

Galen spoke up then, leaning forward, glass in hand. "That reminds me, Brand, I saw a woman this morning who looked so much like Fallon I nearly caught her up in a hug. Good thing I didn't. She'd likely have bowled me over with that satchel of hers."

"Well now, as to that, my wife's companion . . ." Merryweather broke off, a look of confusion clouding his eyes. "But then, our Fallon was really Ana Hebbel. She wouldn't have been married to your brother."

Ana Hebbel. Fallon was really Ana Hebbel? The woman who was buried in Elizabeth City?

Something didn't make sense here. "Then who the devil is buried in Ana Hebbel's grave? I was there. I saw it. The marker said Anamarie G. Hebbel, and I was told she'd been traveling with Fallon, posing as her sister."

Galen shook his head.

Mr. Merryweather looked thoughtful.

Brand reeled under the double-barreled assault of having one brother return from the dead and having

Fallon turn out to be someone else. He stared out the window as one assumption after another came tumbling down around his shoulders.

"Let me get this straight. You're saying Fallon isn't Fallon?"

Then what the bloody hell had that confession of hers been all about?

"Before she left, Miss Ana told me her story. I thought at the time there might be more to it than she let on."

Brand rose and poured himself another drink. Bypassing the scuppernong wine, he went directly to the hard stuff. The occasion seemed to call for it.

His hand shook. He spilled his drink on the table, stared at the mess he'd made, and shook his head again in disbelief. Galen, back from the dead. And Fallon—

No, not Fallon. Ana.

Galen leaned back in his chair, stretching his long legs out before him. There was a streak of silver in his hair that hadn't been there less than a year ago. A man couldn't go gray that fast, but then, a lot of things that weren't supposed to happen did, he mused. For a man whose good looks and easygoing charm had always made him a favorite with the women, Galen was too thin, too pale, but God, he looked good.

Galen caught his brother's eye. "Funny, the way things turned out, isn't it? The woman I saw boarding the *Curlew* looked enough like Fallon to be her twin, except for the age and a few other incidentals. Now, I ask you, what are the odds of something like that happening?"

"What are the odds of your coming back from the dead?"

"Hear, hear." Galen lifted his glass.

Mr. Merriweather said thoughtfully, "Do you know, I can't say I was completely surprised at Fa—at Ana's story. The woman I came to know was nothing at all like her letters. She seemed . . . more mature. More thoughtful. But then, one can't always judge from letters. Tell me, Mr. McKnight—"

"Galen, please."

"Galen then, and thank you. I'd be interested to hear how you managed to survive and eventually make your way back home."

"Tomorrow, I'd be glad to give you a full account," Galen promised. "Or at least, all of it I can recall."

They'd heard a brief version, but Brand was pretty sure there was more to it than that. At the moment, however, he was still wrestling with the mystery of Ana-Fallon.

"Gale, are you sure?"

"Am I sure of what? That I survived? God, I hope so. If not, this is a real waste of some first-class whiskey."

"No, I mean about Fallon. I know what she said— I know what she told you, sir, but—"

"I'm telling you, the woman I saw wasn't Fallon." Galen had settled into the castle as if he'd been a regular visitor all his life. But then, he'd always been something of a chameleon, with the rare ability to sun himself on any old rock.

Maurice Merriweather yawned. He was obviously tired. It had been an exhausting two days, what with Fallon—Ana's—leaving, the discovery of a body, Galen's arrival, and now this.

Whatever "this" was. Brand was still trying to piece together parts of the puzzle that didn't seem to belong anywhere now.

He was still pondering all the bits and pieces when something Galen was saying to Merriweather snagged his attention. Something about eyes.

"Whoever she was, the lady I saw had brown eyes."

Brand frowned. "So? The woman who called herself Fallon had brown hair and brown eyes and a brown mole on her—"

Yes. Well, that was neither here nor there.

"But you see, the real Fallon had one blue eye and one hazel eye."

Both men stared at him, dumbfounded. "The devil you say," Brand finally managed.

Galen shrugged. "I thought you knew. I thought everybody knew. It was hardly something one could overlook, even in a woman as beautiful as she was. Is. Was."

After that, there wasn't much to be said. Whoever she was, whatever she'd done, Ana wasn't Fallon, and Fallon wasn't Ana. One of them was buried in a grave in Elizabeth City. It wasn't Ana, so it must be Fallon.

God, the story had ended before it had even begun.

On the stroke of ten, Mr. Hobbs came for Mr. Merry, and Brand was left alone with the brother he'd thought dead. He didn't know where to start. After the last few drinks, he was dangerously close to bawling his bloody eyes out.

"Tell me about Liam," Galen said, stretching forward to pour himself another drink. With his coat removed and his shirt opened halfway down the front, he looked thin as a rail. Looked as if he'd gone through hell.

"First, tell me about Galen," Brand countered. "Where the devil have you been? Why didn't you send word? I searched the whole damned North Atlantic for you, brother, without hearing so much as a whisper. Was it that bad blow last August? We heard three of Shoemaker's ships went down, and two schooners out of Nova Scotia. God knows how many fishing boats."

Briefly, Galen described what had happened almost a year earlier. "You remember the mess we had with the deck cargo? How the damned stevedores did such a half-assed job of loading and then walked off before it was finished? One sorehead thought he had a grievance and they all stuck together like tar in a barrel. We were already more than a week late, so I ordered everything double-lashed, just to be sure. I examined the hold cargo myself. I swear it was secure, but five days out when the storm hit, all hell broke loose."

"You were hauling rice and cotton belowdecks, if I remember correctly."

"Couldn't have been worse. If we'd been hauling lumber, we might have stood a chance. It was that damned deck cargo. A single line went slack, a piece of machinery slipped and cut through two more lines, and then the whole damned mess came crashing down on the forward hatch. After that there weren't enough men in the king's damned navy to keep us from going down."

He sighed, swore, and it came to Brand that his brother looked a full dozen years older than when he'd last seen him.

"You can probably guess the rest. The rice started swelling as soon as it got wet. We managed to get a winch in position and started hauling out bales of wet cotton, but before we could get to it, the damned rice had already swollen up and sprung the hull. With the seas breaking over us the way they were, there was nothing to do but abandon ship. From the last position taken, I knew we were somewhere off the west coast of Ireland, maybe close enough for a fishing boat to spot us."

Galen was quiet for several minutes, staring into a place Brand could only imagine. "The first boat was swamped before she could even pull away. The second went down about a hundred yards abaft the port beam. I was still on deck, trying to launch the third when we rolled. Took a comber broadside. The next thing I knew, I was being dragged on board a fishing boat by a pair of Irishers who kept complaining they'd lost a net full of cod in the process of rescuing my worthless hide."

Brand swore. Galen shook his head. "They were good fellows. God knows, I wouldn't be here if they hadn't been quick to sacrifice the damned cod. Besides, it wasn't the fish, it was their mate. Evidently the poor guy dived in after a bit of flotsam that turned out to be my half-dead carcass draped over a hatch cover. They said he called out that it was a man, and that he was alive, and then he slid under and drowned before they could reach him. The cold, I guess. Damn, but that water's cold!''

Brand could only stare, his empty glass in one hand.

"They did go so far as to say the man had a bad heart, that he'd suffered seizures before, but Brand, I think they'd have thrown me back to the sharks in a minute if it would have brought back their mate. God, I felt wretched. That is, when I could feel anything at all. I was so numb for days I couldn't even remember my own name. Or maybe the gash on my head had something to do with it, I don't know.''

He raked aside his tawny curls to display a jagged scar that cut through the streak of gray hair. "Man, I hope you never find out what it's like to lie flat on your back in a fishing camp where most of the men don't even speak the king's English. I didn't know who I was or what I was doing there. I couldn't figure out why every man and his brother hated my guts.''

"They hated your guts?"

"Well, maybe that's putting it too strong, but it was pretty plain they thought it'd been a rotten trade. My life for the life of a decent, church-going, law-abiding family man who was kin to half the people in the village they all came from. There were only half a dozen or so there in the camp, all men, all poor as dirt, but I have to say they shared what little they had with me. Fed me the same tasteless glop they ate twice a day. I don't even want to know what was in it, but it kept me alive. That and the whiskey they dosed me with three times a day. The stuff was strong enough to peel the hide off a walrus.''

They talked far into the night. According to Galen, he'd been wild once his memory had been restored. He'd tried to bribe the men to launch a search for his missing crew, thinking it was possible a few of them could have survived and made it to another fishing camp somewhere along that rugged stretch of coast.

As it turned out, they'd already searched and come up empty-handed. "They put out the word and told me later that several bodies had been found and given a Christian burial. No way of identifying them. No point in it, either, I suppose."

"Which reminds me, an odd thing happened here yesterday." Brand went on to relate the finding of a body that had washed into the shallow inlet that separated Pea Island from the lower banks. "Young, male, no identification, but one of his fingers was missing from the first joint."

"Bit off?"

"I doubt it. It appeared to be healed over."

Galen shrugged. "Poor devil. Brand, I need to know about Liam. All I know is what I heard in your office, but there's got to be more to it than that."

So Brand repeated what Marshall Kondrake had told him about Liam and Fallon's disastrous marriage, and what he himself had learned about the woman during weeks of following her up and down the eastern seaboard. "There was some talk of a sister. As near as I was able to find out, the two of them traveled from Pomfret together. They said the sister died when the hotel in Elizabeth City where they were staying burned down, but it had to be Fallon who died, and Ana who took her place."

"So where did this woman come from? What made her lie?"

"'I don't know, but you can be sure I intend to find out."

They fell silent. Brand reached for the bottle, lifted a questioning eyebrow. Galen shook his head, and so Brand set the bottle back on the shelf, unopened. As it was, he'd had more than enough. He had some thinking to do, and for that, he needed a clear head.

He kept seeing that shriveled gray hand with the missing finger. There'd been bruises on Fallon's—on Ana's throat. Bruises that could have been made by a thumb and three fingers.

But why had someone tried to kill Ana?

Who was she?

What was the "personal business" she'd gone back to take care of?

He didn't know, but he damned well intended to find out. Whoever she was, whatever she'd done, she didn't deserve to be strangled in cold blood.

"Listen, Gale, I've got a proposition to put to you."

Galen passed a hand over his face. "Is your head as muffled—mean t'say, as muddled as mine is?"

"Probably. It'll wear off. Now, listen—"

"Poor Limey, he nev' did have much of a head f' whiskey. Weren't all that much better, y'self, Bran' ol' man."

"It's not the whiskey that's screwing up my head, it's the damned questions."

"T' many questions, t' many anshers," the tall, thin man with the gentian blue eyes mumbled.

"And none of them fit. One last question—dammit, wake up, Gale! What would you say to hanging around here for a few weeks? I've been earning my keep by filling in for a hired hand who's due back most any day now. How about taking my place while I see what I can find out about our mystery lady?"

"Whoa, better straight'n tha' floor b'fore I get sick. Think I'll jus' take a li'l nap."

"You can sleep later. Now listen to me, because tomorrow your head's going to be hurting too much to hear anything I've got to say. You can stay on here and rest up. I've already done most of what needs doing, and Evard's pretty capable."

"Ever' ca'ble. Ri-igh . . ."

"These are fine people, Gale. You'll like them once you get to know them."

"How come y're not drunk as a hoot oil—mmm, hoot—"

"Owl? Because I've got about thirty more pounds of flesh on my bones to soak it up. Come on, I'll pour you into bed. Splitting head or not, you've got some listening to do tomorrow."

Chapter Seventeen

For no better reason than that he was a methodical man, Brand decided to go back to the riverside graveyard in Elizabeth City. Her lies might or might not have started there, but whoever Ana Hebbel turned out to be, she damned sure wasn't resting six feet under the small marker that bore the name Anamarie G. Hebbel.

Inside his coat pocket he carried the wedding picture. It wasn't perfect, but it was the best tool he could come up with. He could hardly go around asking strangers if they'd seen a woman with dancing golden lights in her amber eyes, hair that curled in damp weather, and a way of biting her lower lip when she was trying to keep from laughing that could drive a man right out of his mind.

A woman who smelled of lavender and lemongrass and clover, who would chase wild horses with a seventy-year-old playmate, guarding her fiercely against all dangers, real and imagined. A woman who would set aside her own dignity just to bring a smile to an old woman's face.

"Just who the devil are you, madam?" he murmured as he waited to board the *Curlew* at Nags Head. "Where the devil are you hiding? And why?"

By the time he reached Elizabeth City, he was no closer to the truth. Among the regulars aboard the steamer he'd found two people who claimed to remember the woman in the photograph.

"Looks familiar. I've seen that face somewhere, not long ago. This must've been took a few years back, but I'd have to say she's held up better'n most. Now, you take my wife . . ." said a porter, shaking his head.

A man who traveled the route selling ices and cold drinks claimed he'd given her a glass of water when she'd asked the price of tea and then decided she didn't want it after all. He'd peered at the picture again and frowned. "I'd have thought a woman who wore a nice fur cape like that could buy herself a glass of tea, but you never know. No, sir, you never know. She weren't wearing that fur when she come through here day before yesterday."

Of course she hadn't been wearing the damned fur. It was practically summer.

Brand studied the photograph again. Now that he knew better, he could easily see the difference in the two women. His heart had known all along.

It was Ana G. Hebbel who interested him now, not Fallon McKnight.

Whoever Ana G. Hebbel was.

Wherever she'd disappeared to.

Whatever it was that she'd done.

Because she had done something, all right. He'd seen the fear in her eyes more than once. She'd all but confessed to a crime involving a lot of blood and running away, and women didn't change their names for no reason.

Then, too, she'd admitted to being a widow.

He left the docks and went directly to the cemetery. And then he stood there, staring down at the marker as if waiting for a divine revelation.

None was forthcoming. Not that he'd really expected to learn anything from a dozen or so graves, some old, some new, and a few big magnolia and cypress trees. It had seemed the logical starting place, though, so he'd started there.

Logical.

Damn good thing he wasn't a civil engineer, the way he'd claimed. Engineers dealt in logic, and at the moment, he was flat out of that particular commodity.

Dismissing the hack that had brought him there, he

headed for Water Street and began his search in earnest. It took three stops to locate the talkative young hotel clerk he'd met when he'd come through town a few days after the fire.

"The one with the colored eyes, she was something, all right. Uppity, but sweet as sugarcane when she wanted extra blankets or more hot water. The other one, she was real nice, like she wanted to apologize for her sister. Didn't tip worth diddly, but neither did the other one, come to that. Still and all, I'm sorry as anything what happened. It was a real tragedy, yessir, a real tragedy."

The ticket agent was more help. "Lessee now, about three days ago, you say? S'many folks comes through here, and half the time, I don't even look up. Ticketin's right complicated work, y'know. Most folks don't realize how important it is, but you take a man wantin' to go to Smith's Corner, Georgia, he sure as shootin' don't want to end up in Smith's Corner, Arkansas. Connecticut, you say? Well, now, I do seem to recollect there was a young lady come through here a day or so ago . . . Brown hair, brown eyes, sweet smile, but looked like she'd jump right out of her boots if you were to clap your hands."

Brand slid the photograph across the worn oak shelf. The man nodded. "Yessir, that's her, all right. Pomfret, Connecticut, she said. Small place. Not many calls for Pomfret. None I re'clect since I been selling tickets here. I sold her a one-way on the nine-eleven. She'll be halfway there by now."

Brand was almost out the door when the man said, "Seems to me, though, I seen another picture of her just lately. Pretty woman. Said to myself at the time, I said, Oscar, you know that face from somewheres."

It came to him then. The newspaper. Those day-trippers. Hadn't one of them mentioned a picture in a paper?

Ana, numb with fatigue but unable to sleep, stared at the hat worn by the woman in the seat ahead of her and thought about another hat, one with a heavy, un-fashionable veil. Thought about all that had happened since she'd first boarded the same train to come south and gotten herself entangled in a web of deceit.

Clicketty-clack, clicketty-clack.

"Peanuts, sammiches, papers, an' drinks! Here ye go, sir, that'll be three cent."

Clicketty-clack, clicketty-clack.

She was running away again. The first time she'd had no choice, not if she wanted to go on living.

This time she had no choice, either. She was tired to death of living a lie. Tired of being with fine, decent people who accepted her without question. Tired of having people like James Webster turn up and scare the living daylights out of her.

She still wasn't sure what he'd wanted with her. One minute he'd seemed to think she was Fallon. The next he seemed afraid she might somehow connect him to the fire that had taken Fallon's life.

Poor James.

Still, it was a shame to have to go back just when she'd found something to live for. Just when she'd discovered what love felt like.

Not that it had been love. Not on Neil's part, at least. What they'd done together had been based on . . .

She didn't know what it was based on. She only knew she could no more resist the man than the sun could resist rising in the morning and setting in the evening. If she'd stayed—

Well, she hadn't. Simply couldn't, and that was that. Neil would have been forced to choose between her and his own conscience, and not for a single minute did she doubt which would have won out in the end.

Even if by some miracle he were to choose her, he would quickly come to despise her. Sometimes she thought he already did.

Sometimes not, though.

At any rate, it was nice to know that for once in her life, even briefly, a man had wanted her for herself, and not her father's money. He didn't love her—didn't even particularly like her—but he had definitely wanted her. And she had wanted him right back. Still did. Always would.

However long 'always' turned out to be.

The train sped on its noisy, sooty, bone-jarring way north, and she stared out the window, wondering why everything looked so gray and dismal when here it was April. Almost May. Springtime meant the world was supposed to be bursting with color, didn't it? Sweet-smelling and filled with hope?

Instead it was gray, filled with clouds, soot, and coal dust. With sad-eyed old men and track-side shanties. Children with sacks collecting lumps of coal that had fallen from coal cars.

If she could have sprouted wings and flown over it all, she would have done it, even though it would mean a quicker end to her freedom.

Almost there. Almost home. She'd barely spoken to a single soul for two days except for the porter and the—what was it Fallon had called him? The butch.

The prisoner's last meal was an onion and sausage sandwich.

"Oh, for heaven's sake, Anamarie, stop being so melodramatic."

She dozed and stared out the window and parceled out her funds for the cheapest foods she could buy. Not because she couldn't have afforded better, but because she felt guilty for having accepted money she didn't deserve.

Connecticut was so much smaller than she remembered. The hills closer together, the hedgerows and low rock walls chopping up the landscape into neat squares, like a crazy quilt done in shades of brown and green, with the occasional splash of pink or yellow.

No pale sand beaches, no deep blue waters, no broad, flat vistas that went on and on forever. Traveling, Ana mused, did that to a person. Enlarged her perspective. In more than a few ways. After spending years dreaming of all the places in the world she would love to see, she had finally seen one.

Not that Merriweather's Landing on tiny Pea Island on the Outer Banks of North Carolina had ever figured in any of her dreams, but living there only for a few months had forever changed her perspective.

Forever.

Even her perspective of the word forever had changed.

Lord, she was so stiff she could hardly walk. And wrinkled. She'd worn one of her new outfits, for courage. The lavender silk. It was hardly practical for traveling, but it matched the silk violets on her new black-straw hat, and the hat had a veil in case her courage failed.

At least she wasn't hungry, only incredibly tired.

Following the handful of passengers getting off at her stop, she blinked at the harsh sunlight. Two redcaps sauntered over. Three hackneys were drawn up in case one was needed. A mule-drawn ice wagon clopped past, and then a small boy rolling a big hoop went whooping down the sidewalk.

Traffic, even in a small community like Pomfret, was surprisingly noisy.

The churches. There was no church at Merriweather's Landing. She had missed the neat, familiar spire of the Congregational Church. She used to come to town every Sunday morning with her parents and then have to sit still for what seemed days, but had actually been only a few hours.

Coming to town had been exciting to a little girl who lived in the country.

The sermon hadn't.

"Shh, don't fidget, darling."

"Not much longer, Sugarcake. Here. You can play with my pocket watch, but don't try to wind it."

Taking a deep breath, she caught the eye of a redcap who summoned one of the hacks. Recklessly, she gave the man a nickel for his trouble, climbed board, and said, "Take me to . . ."

To where?

The jailhouse? She didn't even know where it was, or if there even was one. Had never needed to know.

Well. That would come soon enough. Meanwhile, she still had a few hours to kill.

Oops. To spend.

Her own home would be empty. Locked. She didn't even have a key.

Or maybe Horatio Quillerby would have moved in by now to look after his late client's interests.

Ha!

Impulsively, she gave the address of the house where Etta's sister lived. She had no idea where to find Samuels. She was going to need a friend, and the old housekeeper was the only one she could think of.

But the sister's cottage was shuttered, the grass already straggling, and the flower beds overrun with weeds.

How strange . . .

Ana sat there while the horse chomped on a patch of newly greening weeds beside the road. Did hackneys charge by the mile, or by the minute? She didn't even know that much, having always had her own transportation.

Think, Anamarie, think! This may be your last day of freedom.

"Take me to . . ."

"Yes, Miss?"

There was no point in putting it off. By now she'd probably been recognized by someone in town. Word would spread quickly that she was back again. The police would descend with their handcuffs and their dogs, or whatever policemen descended with when murderers returned to the scene of the crime.

She leaned forward and said, "Take me to the Gilbretta place. It's out on—"

"I know where it is, Miss. Everybody around these parts knows where old Marcus's daughter did in her bridegroom."

Thank God for the veil on her hat. A wispy little confection, it was meant to be worn crushed down

around the silk violets; instead, she'd pulled it forward
in the fruitless hope that it would disguise her features
so that she wouldn't be pounced upon the instant she
stepped down from the train.

Even knowing it was hopeless, she continued the
charade. There was the Rectory School—and the
school where she'd gone as a girl, where her mother
had gone as a girl.

How small they were. How safe they looked.

She could turn herself in now, or she could spend
her last few hours of freedom driving around, saying
good-bye to all the places she had once known and
taken for granted.

The little mare clip-clopped along the narrow road.
Over there, a man was trimming the hedge, releasing
the crisp green smell of hemlock.

Ana soaked up every sight, every sound, every
scent.

Ten minutes later they turned in between a pair
of familiar rock gateposts. The gate stood open, the
hawthornes on each side neatly trimmed.

"This is it. You want to look around?"

"No. That is, yes. Wait here if you don't mind, I
won't be long."

Before she could change her mind, she climbed
down and set out along the flagstone walk where she
used to play hopscotch. The grounds were in surprisingly good condition. Someone, it seemed, was making
an effort to maintain the value of the property, heaven
knows who, much less why.

Civic pride? Promfet was a wealthy town filled with
good, solid, respectable citizens who would hate the
notoriety she'd brought upon them.

But the windows weren't shuttered, which was
strange. She hoped the furniture had been covered
against fading. Etta would have seen to it if she'd been
there, or at least drawn the draperies.

The brass knocker sparkled as if it had been polished only that morning. How very odd . . .

Compelled by something she didn't even try to understand, she lifted a gloved hand and gave the thing a good hard whack, and then she remembered Horatio Quillerby.

The wretched little man must be living here. Probably brought his whole wretched little family.

On the verge of turning away, she changed her mind. Before she was thrown into prison, she would give herself the satisfaction of telling the miserable little worm what she thought of him.

The door opened silently, and she opened her mouth to speak.

And then shut it again.

Samuels's face broke into a thousand wrinkles as, with one soft cry, she hurled herself into his arms. Over her own noisy sobs, she could hear him saying her name over and over. "Miss Ana, Miss Ana, Miss Ana."

She was home.

Dear Lord, she was home.

Brand unfolded the dog-eared newspaper and tilted it toward the light coming in through the soot-dimmed window. He must have read the thing a hundred times on the journey north. By now he could practically quote the entire story by heart.

CONNECTICUT SOCIALITE BURIED IN LOCAL CEMETERY? The question was posed in the attention-getting headline, above a photograph of a startled woman bearing a strong resemblance to both Ana Hebbel and Fallon McKnight.

The picture had been taken of the survivors of the fire. Under the circumstances, few of them had been looking their best. Nor was the reporter certain enough of his facts to go on record. The details were just too bizarre.

A New England woman once accused of murder in Connecticut might have been one of the unfortunate victims in the recent fire at a local hotel. According to unimpeachable sources, the accused murderess was a guest at Brokerman's Riverside along with her sister, who survived the tragedy. Mrs. Ludwig Hebbel, widow of the late Ludwig Hebbel of New York City and Canterbury, Connecticut, only daughter of the late Marcus Gilbretta of Pomfret, is reported to have left town shortly after the murder of her husband.

Police refuse to divulge details of the case while an investigation in underway. We have it on excellent authority, however, that while all evidence points to Mrs. Hebbel's guilt, a secret witness has come forth to defend the alleged murderess.

The question in the minds of all citizens of our fair city is this: Who lies buried in the grave marked Anamarie G. Hebbel? Rumor has it that the real Mrs. Hebbel, be she murderess or no, can be found in the mountain hideaway of a certain Prominent Politician recently implicated in the Donlevy bribery scandal.

Sweet bloody hell.

To think that until recently, his entire life had been lived without incident, barring a few minor exceptions. He still had a small gray mark on his left wrist where once a whore had stabbed him with a pencil. Nothing serious.

He'd spent two extremely unpleasant weeks in a jail in Portugal, but that had been a misunderstanding. Thanks to a shipmate, he'd been able to bribe his way out.

Years later he'd nearly lost a ship when the yard where it had been under construction had been bought out, the contract price raised by the new owners. After a few frantic weeks, they had arranged a compromise and the *Mystic Lady* was now gainfully engaged in the West Indies trade.

Orderly.

It was his nature. Galen had once accused him of having the soul of an accountant. "Thank God one of us does," Brand had retorted, "else McKnight Shipping would have gone down the drain and we'd both be back home mucking out stalls."

The question was, how did such a dull, orderly fellow manage to get himself into such a twist? Did it come from chasing a sister-in-law all over creation, veering off onto the trail of an accused murderess—and falling head over heels in love with her?

Because he had done all three.

Her feet tucked under a shawl on a needlepoint-covered footstool, Ana sipped her Darjeeling and waited for a beaming Etta to think of something else to ask her.

Or to think of something else to tell her.

"Mr. Quillerby was fit to be tied. Drinks, he does. Smelled it on him more than once. Heard he drinks all the time, since he caught that real bad case of the mumps. Like to've done him in, they say," she grinned.

Ana's grin was slower in coming, but just as broad. And then it faded. "Why was he so sure I'd done it?"

"Well, you did, didn't you?" the housekeeper asked, plainspoken as always. "Not that a single soul in his right mind could blame you, with that devil beating you half to death. I don't mind telling you—"

She had already told her a dozen times, but Ana didn't mind hearing it again. It was comforting, and she still was in sore need of comfort.

"I'd have shot him myself if I'd known that gun was there, and me not able to set a mousetrap. Samuels, too. It was him that went to the police that night, directly that evil man locked us out. I was so upset I couldn't think straight. Sam told me to go get Mr. Johnston to come break down the door before something awful happened, and then he hitched up and set out for town. I hadn't even got as far as the end of the drive path when I heard the shot."

Ana poured herself another cup of tea. It was no longer piping hot, but it was comforting, all the same.

"It was sleeting that night, Etta. I'm surprised you could hear anything at all."

"My eyes might not be so sharp anymore, but there's nothing wrong with my hearing. I heard what went on upstairs in that bedroom night after night, and how he caught you in your father's study right after the will was read and took his belt to you, and when I started to send for the doctor, he threatened to strangle me with my own apron strings. Mr. Hebbel, not the doctor. I heard all that, and I told them every blessed thing that happened, you can count on that." She shook her head to emphasize the point.

"I'm not sure I'll ever be able to hold up my head again. Everybody must know."

"Leastwise, your head's still stuck to your body. Nobody blames you, child. What with all that came out about Mr. Hebbel, it's a wonder somebody hadn't sent him to the devil long before. Did you know he turned off one of his fancy women, and her with a new baby, and she ended up dying right there on the sidewalk in New York City, with folks stepping o'er her body while she breathed her last? He did most of his wickedness there in the city. Thought nobody would find out about it up here."

Ana knew. She had heard it before. When Etta was wound up, she had a tendency to repeat herself. She didn't particularly want to hear it again, but she was too drowsy to interrupt.

"Lucky thing a ragpicker heard the baby. He took him to one of those places—a foundling home, I guess you'd call it. Some decent folks took him in, they said in the newspaper that come out about two weeks after you left."

Ana's teacup tilted. Etta reached over and removed it from her limp fingers. For a long time she gazed down at the slender woman dressed in a robe and slippers, her hair in a braid over her shoulders. "Lord love you, precious, you're home where you belong now. Nobody's going to take you away without walking over Etta's dead body, I can promise you that."

A soft purr reached her ears, and she called for Samuels, who might be old, but who'd have been mortally offended if anyone so much as hinted that he couldn't carry out his duties.

"Let's get the poor child up to her bed. With what I put in her tea, she won't be having no more nightmares tonight."

The two elderly servants gazed down on the girl— no longer a girl, but a woman now—who had been like their own child for twenty-eight years. "You take her by the shoulders and I'll take her feet."

The old man waved her away and lifted the slender burden in his arms, his face going a deep shade of red. The housekeeper puffed up the stairs right behind him, ready to catch them both at the first sign of collapse.

"It'll take a while, I guess. She won't say what happened to her since she left here, but it's plain as day something did. What she needs is something to take her mind off things."

"She'll have to talk to the magistrate."

"And to Quillerby."

"Miserable worm."

"I'll go to town tomorrow and see if the library don't have some new books in. I know just what would perk her up. Always did like a good love story, poor baby."

Chapter Eighteen

Ana was up to her elbows in Coalport china when Samuels came to announce a caller one morning. Over the past few days since she had arrived to find the very last thing in the world she'd expected to find, she had inventoried practically everything in the house, from attic to cellar.

Which was better than crying, of which she'd done far too much, for no reason at all, in between meeting with the scores of people waiting to pounce on her the minute they learned she was back.

It was contagious. Crying. Poor Etta had sobbed right along with her, while Samuels stood by looking helpless and miserable.

At least counting knives and forks, sheets and pillowcases and then starting in on the china and crystal helped her fall asleep at night.

Not right away, but eventually.

"If it's that newspaper person from Norwich again, tell him I can't see him. Tell him—tell him I've gone to Outer Mongolia. Tell him anything, but get rid of him."

She'd been pestered to death ever since word had spread that the murderess had returned to the scene of the crime. The Gilbrettas had once been a prominent family. Wealthy, reclusive—or perhaps eccentric was a better word—but now touched by scandal.

Aside from reporters who swarmed around her like a hoard of locusts, there'd been all the official interviews. Both Etta and Samuels had stayed with her the first time, guarding her or supporting her, she wasn't sure which. A bit of both, probably. They'd already given testimony, but more was needed in light of her own version of what had happened that night.

Self-defense. That was the official version.

The correct version. She'd framed it that way in her own mind, but hadn't dared to hope anyone would believe her.

After that there'd been the tedious business with the lawyers. Not Mr. Quillerby, thank heavens. She'd put her foot down on that front, insisting on having her affairs turned over to someone of her own choosing.

Not that she'd known any lawyers to choose from. Fortunately, the neighbors had rallied round. As it turned out, Mr. Johnson had a nephew only recently graduated from the law school at Yale, who was hungry for clients.

After that, Quillerby, as her father's executor, had dealt with him. It turned out that the only reason Quillerby had allowed Etta, Samuels, and the yard man to return was because when he'd tried to sell the house, he'd been informed that executor or not, it wasn't his to sell, and that what's more, an empty house didn't fare well over a New England winter.

He'd sent word through Mr. Johnson that, as a mark of his respect for her late father, he would be glad to find her a buyer, as the house was far too large for a single woman, and invest the proceeds of the sale for her.

And pigs would fly.

Finally, after dealing with all that, she'd thought she could close the door and allow the healing to begin. But the ordeal wasn't over. There'd still been the sensation seekers. People who wanted to stare at the woman who had murdered her husband and got away with it.

She could always tell when one of those had been poking around. Samuels would come away from the dust-up with a particular gleam in his eye, almost as if he were enjoying the challenge.

She was glad someone found something to enjoy.

The trouble was—from her perspective, at least—that little ever happened in a small, quiet town like Pomfret. When Etta's older sister had run away with a baker from Canterbury, it set the whole town on its ear for nearly a week.

Then Miss Hetty Oglesby had slid on a patch of ice and ended up with a black eye. The town had buzzed about that for a few days, but everybody liked Miss Hetty, and so the talk had quickly died down.

But then the notorious Ana Gilbretta Hebbel had come back home.

Samuels cleared his throat. "Miss Ana, about that gentleman? I showed him into the yellow parlor."

Still on her knees, she said, "Great Scott, don't tell me the governor's come to call." The yellow parlor had been her mother's favorite room. Not exactly a shrine, but not a room to be taken lightly. "Do we know him then?"

"As to that, I couldn't say, but I thought he'd be more comfortable in there. I left the French doors open so he can smell the pear trees."

"Oh, my. Whoever he is, he must be impressive. What if he walks out with a knickknack as a souvenir? Someone stole an umbrella right out of the front hall day before yesterday. The man from the *Gazette,* I think."

The elderly servant gave her a look he'd perfected years ago, when she'd tried to pretend she hadn't done whatever it was she shouldn't have been doing.

On her knees in front of shelves full of china and crystal that hadn't been used in years, Ana touched her hair, then untied her apron and rose to her feet. "All right, all right, I'm coming. Do I need to change into something presentable?"

"You look just fine, Miss Ana. You might want to wash your hands, though, and there's a speck of dust on your left cheek."

More than ten minutes passed before Ana was deemed presentable. Etta made her do something with her hair. Samuels said he'd serve coffee directly. There was something in his expression—almost a smugness—that she found puzzling.

Even unsettling.

"Samuels, is this some kind of a game you're playing? If you and Etta are just trying to make me stop and rest, I assure you I'm not the least bit tired."

She'd been up at dawn every day since she'd been home, and seldom went to bed until midnight or even later. It beat risking nightmares. Or waking up in the middle of the night with her pillow wet from tears she'd shed in her sleep.

"No, Miss Ana. Yes, Miss Ana."

She was no longer Miss Ana, but none of them cared to be reminded of that.

"Well, whoever you are, you'd better be worth all this trouble," she muttered, marching down the front hallway. Arranging her features into what her mother used to call a social smile—polite, but no warmer than tepid—she swung open the white-paneled door.

And then nearly collapsed at the sight of the man who turned away from the open French doors to stare at her.

There were shadows under his eyes. Everything about him shouted exhaustion, anxiety, or both. He'd lost much of his tan. The grooves beside his mouth had been there before, but they were deeper now. He was wearing a frock coat with a dark green silk vest, tan trousers, and highly polished shoes, a far cry from the way he'd looked when last she'd seen him.

This man, with his guarded slate-gray eyes, was a stranger. A stranger who had broken her heart and was going to do it all over again.

"Neil. How are you?" She was proud of herself. If he was trying to shatter what little composure she'd been able to scrape up at short notice, he was doing a remarkably fine job of it.

"It's Brandon," he said. "Or Brand, if you will."

She arched her eyebrows at that. Still standing just inside the door, she knew very well that Samuels and

Etta were hovering just outside. With no outward indication of the turmoil she was feeling, she turned and said, "Etta, Mr. Brandon might like something to go with the coffee Samuels is about to serve. Aren't you, Samuels?" she added pointedly.

Two pairs of footsteps hurried down the hall toward the back of the house. She knew very well what they were up to. Etta had already supplied her with several romantic novels, and even Samuels, who hadn't a romantic bone in his body, had mentioned once or twice that that new lawyer of hers was a fine-looking young gentleman.

Clear as glass, the pair of them.

Only what made them think Neil Dalton—or Brandon, or whatever he chose to call himself—would be a safe candidate? She could have told them that he was the *un*safest man in the world.

"Ana? Don't you have anything to say for yourself?"

Well. She had a lot to say. She had so much to say she didn't know where to start. If she had a grain of sense, she'd start by saying good-bye and show him the door.

"So it's Neil Brandon, not Neil Dalton? Would you care to explain?"

With all the dignity she could summon, which wasn't a whole lot, she seated herself in the button-backed chair by the window and nodded to its mate.

He appeared perfectly calm, which was more than she could say for herself. Avoiding his eyes, her gaze fell to his mouth, and before she could help herself she was remembering the way it had felt on hers, the way it had tasted.

Quickly, she looked at his hands instead, only to remember the feel of those same hands on her face, her hair, her body.

If she'd had a fan, she would have been fanning for all she was worth. Her cheeks felt as if she'd spent the day outside without her bonnet.

"So," she said, trying on another of her social

smiles. "How lovely to see you again. Are you visiting in the—"

Dammit, where the hell was the woman he'd come all this way to find? "Actually, it's Brandon Neil Dalton McKnight." He wanted the matter of who he was set straight first of all.

He wanted to tell her that he knew everything. That he knew who she was and who she wasn't.

That he knew what she had done, and why.

God, it was the *why* that nearly killed him!

He was embarrassed, ashamed to confess what he'd been doing at Merriweather's Landing, but there were too many lies between them, on both sides.

Too many to forgive?

He didn't know. He only knew he had to try.

"Ana, I'm a plainspoken man, so if I may, I'd like to—"

"Plainspoken!" Everything about her seemed to bristle. He could have sworn he saw her hair curl tighter right while he watched. Those little corkscrew bits that escaped because they were too short to pin up.

He definitely saw sparks fly from her eyes.

"McKnight? As in Fallon McKnight? Good Lord, you, too? Don't tell me she had another husband."

"She was married to my brother. Liam, not Galen."

"I didn't know you even had a brother." She crossed her arms over the modest swell of her bosom, not quite so calm and poised now.

It was a good sign. More like the Ana he had come to know and—

"I think I'd better start at the beginning," he said, wondering where the actual beginning was. "I'm the eldest. Next comes Galen, and then Liam. Liam died last winter. Our father bred racing stock near Litchfield."

And so, while Samuels brought in a heavy Georgian silver coffee service that weighed half a ton and set it on the low table by the sunny window, lingering until Ana cast him a warning look, Brand explained how he had come to be at Merriweather's Landing under an assumed name.

"But then, you weren't exactly flying your true colors, either, were you, Mrs. Hebbel?"

The lengthy and involved discussion that followed led to several conclusions, one of them being that in all probability, Fallon had not been legally married to Liam McKnight. Not if what James had claimed was true.

Poor James. She had wondered what had happened to him. Now she knew.

She shivered. "Yes, well . . . there are records. You could probably find out which one of them she was married to."

"What good could it do at this point? I know they went through the motions. I know Liam thought they were married. Whether or not it was legal, we'll probably never know."

They both fell silent, caught up for the moment in their separate memories. Brand recovered first. He flexed his shoulders. "If I never see another train, it won't bother me in the least. I've got kinks in places where there aren't even places." Their eyes met. They shared a smile, and there it was again—that familiar affinity that had sprung up so unexpectedly almost from the first.

Ana was first to look away. She cleared her throat. "You never did say how you found me."

"Yes, well . . . the first step was finding out that you weren't who you were supposed to be. I think Mr. Merry would eventually have told me what he knew, but as it turned out, Galen saw you at Nags Head. He was getting off the *Curlew* when you were boarding."

"The man who called me Fallon." She lifted her cup, only the whitened tips of her fingers hinting that she wasn't quite as composed as she wanted him to believe.

"He'd met her before she married Liam—if she did. I hadn't. Everyone mentioned the eyes. The colors, one man said, only I didn't pick up on it. I thought, purple, or maybe green. Something unusual. No one ever actually described them. If they had . . ."

"If they had, none of this would ever have happened. To think that something so simple—"

"So simple, so obvious, that no one ever thought to describe it."

She was staring down at her cup, not at him. He wanted to take the thing from her hand and pull her into his arms. He wanted to hold her, to shake her. Anything to get some kind of a reaction from her. This wasn't the same woman who had waded up to her knees or giggled with a couple of kids and an old woman when her paper boat sank.

"Damn it, Ana—!"

The cup clattered to the table. "Damn it, Neil, or whoever you are, don't you dare swear at me!" Her eyes were blazing, every bit as remarkable as any mismatched eyes could ever be.

A sense of relief came over him. A smile tugged at the corners of his mouth. This was more like it.

"Miss Ana, I brought you some sandwiches. I thought you might . . ."

Without looking away, she said, "Thank you, Etta. Oh, and Etta, close the door on your way out, and tell Samuels we don't need any more coffee."

Brand had risen when the servant entered the room. He stalked toward the open French doors and stood there, hands in his pockets, feet braced apart, wondering where he'd ever got the notion that he was an orderly, sensible, logical man.

Because, dammit, he *was* an orderly, sensible, logical man—at least he had been before he'd met Ana.

Still gazing out over the well-tended grounds, he tried out a few lines in his head. He'd worked it all out in his head—what he wanted to say—and gone over it a hundred times on the way north, before he'd even been sure he would find her.

But of course he'd have found her. He'd found her

when he hadn't even known who it was he was looking for.

*"I would be greatly honored, Miss Hebbel—Miss
Gilbretta—Mrs. Hebbel—my dear Ana—"*

Too dull. Boring. Get to the point, McKnight.

"Ana, listen here to me—"

*Too bossy. She wasn't a woman to take instructions,
not even from a man who loved her more than his
own soul.*

A bee explored the open doorway. He ignored it,
still going over in his mind the best way to get down
to brass tacks. Something brushed against his back.
Something warm, something soft, something that
made him think of lavender, lemongrass, and clover.

"Mama had them planted when she first came here
as a bride. The pear trees. They're lovely, aren't
they?"

He gave up on orderly, sensible, and logical.
"Lovely," he said, his voice gruff, not entirely steady.
"Lovely. Ana . . . ?"

And then there was really no more to be said. They
were in each other's arms, laughing, perhaps sobbing—at least one of them was. Brand was saying over
and over, "I thought I'd never find you. Oh, God, oh,
God, why did you run away?"

Everyone in the house pretended not to know what
was going on. Etta had sent for Sally, the daily maid,
and together they'd aired one of the guest rooms.
Samuels had unpacked the bag Brand had left by the
front door, and brought down a suit to be brushed
and pressed.

Laughing, Brand had confessed that most of his
clothes had been packed since February. He'd taken
out only what he needed for a few days and left the
rest at the train station in Elizabeth City.

Etta had outdone herself that night. A roast of beef,
done to perfection with parsnips, carrots, and roasted
potatoes, and one of her light-as-a-feather lemon
cakes.

It might as well have been last week's newspapers soaked in rainwater. One of them would start to say something and then forget what it was, and they'd end up gazing across the table.

Out in the kitchen, Etta said, "I declare to heaven, if I ever thought to see the day. Do you reckon he's got a decent job?"

"Does it matter? She can afford him, if he's what she wants. The old man didn't cut her off completely."

"Oh, he's what she wants, all right. A woman would have to be a fool not to want that one, and our Ana's no fool. Oh, my blessed, would you look at that, they're going upstairs together."

Samuels crossed stiffly to the door. He shook his head, then came back and opened the match drawer, where the cards were kept. "Gin rummy?"

"Might as well. Don't look like we'll be needed anymore tonight. Help me clear away first, though, and mind you don't drop that water pitcher. I'll make us some roast beef sandwiches to eat while we play."

There was never any question of where he would sleep. Ana led the way to her own room. Brand opened the door, and then they were in each other's arms.

"How did you know—?" she started to ask, but he shook his head.

"Later," he whispered. "For now, all in the world I want to do is hold you."

And then he grinned, and she thought again that, for a man who could never be considered truly handsome, he was the most beautiful creature on the face of the planet. Iron jaw, shaggy black hair, crooked nose and all.

"What are you smiling about?" She leaned back in his arms, smiling, too, because it was so very good to look into those slate-gray eyes and see no shadows, no anger, nothing at all but love.

And to know that love was hers.

"Because I lied. Holding you isn't the only thing I

want to do. All I've been able to think about since that night we made love is how I could manage to get through the rest of my life without you."

She suspected there were a few more things he'd thought about—he'd already mentioned several—but none of it mattered now that they were together. So close together that words weren't needed to tell her what was on his mind.

It was on hers, as well.

Gently, she led him over to her bed, thankful that Ludwig had insisted on using the master bedroom. Here, there were no bad memories, only lonely ones.

And that was about to change.

Slowly, with a restraint that only heightened the shimmering tension between them, they began to undress. Brand unfastened the buttons at the back of her collar while she held her hair out of the way, and then he drew her back against him, nuzzling her neck.

Feeling the rigid contours of his arousal against her bottom, she forgot to breathe. She knew now what desire was all about. Knew where it could lead.

She was already more than halfway there.

"I want to go the rest of the way," she whispered, turning to lift her mouth to meet his.

Much later, damp with the heat of their love, they lie entwined and talked in drowsy murmurs about this and that. "I like your home," he said.

"It's only a house." And it was.

"I've been meaning to find something larger. In Mystic, I mean." He shifted so that she fit against him even closer, her head on his arm, his legs entwined with hers.

"Etta would want to go. I'm all the family she has now that her sister's remarried. Samuels, too, of course, but he's not as young as he used to be."

"Are you sure? I can't give you anything so grand, not for years—maybe not ever. Being a shipowner's not too different from being a professional gambler." His fingers strayed from her hair to her breast.

"I'm sure. I'd rather make new memories than try to hang onto old ones."

"Galen might want the farm. Probably not, though. He's never been particularly interested in horse breeding."

"We don't have to decide everything right this minute."

She'd discovered the hollow of his navel, and hearing his gasp, began to explore further. He was so deliciously sensitive.

But then, so was she.

"Where do you want to do the deed?" he asked after several extremely interesting moments.

"Do the deed? I thought—why not here? Or there's the bathtub. It's big enough, only Papa never would pay to have hot water piped upstairs."

He began to chuckle. And then he began to roar. Rising over her like a conquering hero, he whispered wicked things in her ear, things that never would have occurred to her although to be quite honest, so much had occurred to her these past few hours that she wasn't at all sure she was the same woman who had spent so many hours making careful lists in her neat handwriting of every cup, hand towel, and teaspoon in the house.

Well, of course, she wasn't. Brand had changed all that.

On the marble-topped table beside the bed, a lamp burned brightly. They'd left it on at Brand's insistence because he'd wanted to watch her while he made love to her, and then neither of them had thought about anything but each other.

The light shone through his eyes, making them clear as rain as he smiled down at her. "Sweetheart, we can pipe hot water to the north pole, for all I care. We can do this particular deed"—he demonstrated with a deft movement of his hips that left her gasping aloud—"anywhere you want to. The sky's the limit, and if you've a mind to try ballooning, I'm game for that, too."

At that point, Ana was quite certain she could fly without a balloon if he kept on doing what he was doing to her with his hands and his lips and his . . .

"What I meant was, where shall we get married? Here's fine, if that's what you want. My only request is that you don't make me wait through a long engagement. I'm not sure your Etta and Samuels are going to give us too many nights like this before we make it official."

"Oh. That. Well, do you know, I'll have to think about it some."

"Think tomorrow," he advised, getting down to some serious lovemaking.

"Tomorrow," she said with a sigh, and joined in.

Epilogue

"You wouldn't think a house this large could be so noisy," Ana murmured, bending over so that Maureen could secure her hat. Festooned with pale velvet roses and crushed tulle, it was so splendid she was almost afraid to touch it. She'd bought it in Elizabeth City when they'd stopped there to arrange for a proper grave marker for Fallon.

They had visited the cemetery, and whatever Brand's thoughts were, he'd kept them to himself. Remembering all the grief and tragedy both Ana and Fallon had been involved in, Ana had felt guilty for being so utterly, deliriously happy.

Seeing her expression, Brand had thumbed away her tears, kissed her on the brow, the tip of the nose, and the chin, whispering that he was saving the rest for after they were wed.

All the way across the sound, he'd treated her as if she were a fragile porcelain doll. Of course, she wasn't, but she'd rather liked the novelty. It had been a long time since anyone had cherished her. She'd almost forgotten the feeling.

Had never known it was possible to feel so much love her heart swelled with the sheer joy of it, spilling happiness as if it were sunshine.

Now she smoothed her pale yellow silk gown over her hips and thought about another yellow gown she had worn for one memorable night.

Who would ever have dreamed where it would all end?

Sounds of mild revelry drifted up the stairs. Mr.

Hobbs had been serving wine since noon. Galen had promised to keep the bridegroom sober enough to say his lines, but Tom Merriweather and George Gill were under no such restraints.

Etta bustled in, carrying the flowers Galen had sent for, that were only slightly wilted from their journey across the inlet. "I freshened it up with some of them yellow flowering vines that's growing all over the shed. Now, don't forget to walk slow. Maureen, did you remember to tell the preacher he's welcome to stay the night?"

"Sure, and would I be forgetting me manners in me own house?"

There was a certain amount of rivalry between the two women.

Miss Drucy wandered in, clutching a paper-wrapped bundle in her arms. "It's a doll. It's for you. Her name is Alice, but you can't have her until after you're married. It wouldn't be proper."

Ana hugged her. She'd hugged everyone at least a dozen times since she'd arrived three days ago, even Mr. Hobbs, who'd turned a bright cherry red. Brand had teased her about it. He'd teased her gently about any number of things, which was one of the reasons her emotions seemed to spill over at the least thing.

No one had teased her in such a long, long time.

It made her feel wanted. Loved. Brand claimed he never teased, either, that as the eldest of three brothers, it had been his duty to be sober, serious, and sensible.

"I was, too," she'd confided. "Only for me, it was dull, drab, and dutiful."

He'd given her that look, the one that spoke volumes without saying a word, and she'd melted all over him.

The bedroom door opened. Simmy poked her head inside, looking splendid in her wedding finery, but not nearly as splendid as did the bride. "It's time," she said.

"Come on, Miss Drucy, it's time."

"Time for what?" asked her maid of honor, resplendent in brocaded silk and sandy slippers.

"Never mind, love, let's go downstairs."

And clutching a china doll in one hand and a slightly wilted bouquet in the other, Ana went to meet her love.

Please turn the page
for a sneak peak at
Beholden
by
Bronwyn Williams
coming in
September 1998
from Topaz

Chapter One

Galen tipped his deck chair, propped his feet on the railing, crossed his arms behind his head, and concluded that life, on the whole, was good. Not a single cloud marred the sky. Going to be a scorcher, all right. He liked it hot. The hotter, the better.

Out on the street a mule clopped past, pulling an ice wagon. "Fre-esh ice, nickel a block, git it while it's cold."

Three yelping, shouting boys raced along the wharf, chasing a dog. The dog paused to sniff at a drunk sleeping off the night's revelry. The boys dutifully waited to see if the mutt would cock a leg. When he didn't, the parade continued along the waterfront, ignoring a whore who sat morosely on a bench sipping coffee from an enamelware mug. Ignoring the two gambling boats moored bow to stern, their decks largely empty at this early hour.

From the vantage point of his private balcony on the top deck of the *Pasquotank Queen,* Galen surveyed his world with complete satisfaction. Growing up in Connecticut, he'd never expected to end up owning a gambling boat in a small Southern town.

But then, he'd never expected to end up in the icy waters of Blacksod Bay off the West coast of Ireland a couple of years ago, either. If not for Declan O'Sullivan, a fisherman with more courage than luck, he might still be there, six fathom under.

All things considered, life was damned good.

Two decks below, he could hear the sounds of another day getting underway. The dry rattle of dice.

The clatter of the roulette wheel. A gasp and giggle from one of the girls.

The girls were a compromise, one of several he'd made since he'd parlayed a small stake into fifty-one percent ownership of *The Pasquotank Queen.* He still wasn't certain Elsworth Tyler hadn't lost that hand deliberately as an excuse to ease out from under his daughter's thumb. Ever since then, the gentleman had traveled from one resort to another, reveling in his newfound freedom and spending his cut of the profits as fast as he received his quarterly checks.

And profits were up. It riled the devil out of Tyler's daughter, Aster, who had her own notions of how to run a successful operation. But fifty-one percent beat forty-nine percent every time, and when the lady was only managing her father's forty-nine percent, why then . . .

Yessir, life could hardly be better.

Galen shifted in the folding oak deck chair and heard the crinkle of paper in his coat pocket. The letter had come yesterday. Up to his ears in book-keeping, trying to make sense out of some of Aster's entries, he'd shoved it into his pocket and forgotten all about it.

The letter was from Brandon, his older brother. Probably three lines from Brand, who'd never been much of a correspondent, a few newspaper clippings, a note from his sister-in-law, and maybe a picture of the baby.

Galen was an uncle now. Damned if that didn't make him feel downright old. As if life was passing him by, and all he had to show for his thirty-three years on earth were a few scars, a streak of white in his hair that hadn't been there a couple of years ago, and the deed to a leaky old tub that looked more like a high-class whorehouse than a respectable gambling boat.

He slit open the envelope and unfolded a single sheet. No clippings, nothing from Ana. Just half a page of his brother's execrable handwriting.

"Gale," he read aloud, his gaze skimming down the crisp sheet of vellum under the McKnight Shipping letterhead, "you'll be surprised to learn that you've inherited two . . . two . . ." Galen squinted, trying to decipher the unintelligible scribble. Ladders? Letters? Ladies?

"Ladies! The hell I have!"

Scowling, he continued to read. That couldn't be right. Maybe it was "lackeys." Last February Brand had sent him a cabin boy who'd lost an eye. The kid was smart as a whip, a favorite with all the dealers. He was already learning how to run a table.

But what the devil was an Os—obs-osculation? Whatever it was, it was going to be arriving by rail on the fourteenth. "The fourteenth? Hell, that's tomorrow!"

Galen raked his fingers through his hair. Here he'd managed to get rid of Aster for an entire week and now his brother was sending him—

What? A couple of old biddies to take under his wing? What the devil was he supposed to do with them, dress them up in red silk and bangles and let them hobble around serving drinks and cigars in the billiard room?

Damned if he wasn't tempted to do it, just to see what Aster would say when she got back from visiting her old man.

And what the devil did Brand mean, he'd inherited them? You didn't inherit people.

"We'll just see about that, brother. I might feed your ladies and put them up overnight, but then your little surprise package is going right back where it came from, with my fondest regards."

Brand had his wife, Ana, to help him deal with life's unexpected twists and turns.

Galen had Aster Tyler, a sharp-tongued harridan who wasn't above fighting dirty to get what she wanted. Right now, what she wanted was to compete with the town's other gambling boat, the *Albemarle*

Belle, by offering dinner cruises, dancing, stage play-
ers, and three-day jaunts on the weekends.

It was all Galen could do to stay one step ahead of
her shenanigans, without having a couple of old ladies
land on his doorstep.

Sweet Jesus, and he'd thought life was good?

It was full of surprises, that much he'd admit, but
that was all he'd admit until he saw what showed up
on the four-fifteen southbound tomorrow afternoon.

Kathleen stood on the siding and waited for the gentleman to return, striving to look brave, mature, and
composed. Tara had insisted on going with him, and
the pair of them had walked off hand in hand, leaving
her to wait with the baggage.

The minute they'd been swallowed up by the crowd,
she'd wanted to go after them, but she'd forced herself
to wait. Probably couldn't have moved if she'd tried
to. Tara looked on everything that happened as a
grand adventure, but then, Tara was still a child. A
delightful child, but one who attracted trouble the way
heather attracted bees.

Six years ago when their mother had died, it was
Kathleen who had taken over the care of the family.
As she was both frugal and sensible, they had done
well enough. But then they'd lost Da, too.

Fishing had been dreadful, the men forced to go
farther and farther up the coast to fill their nets.
They'd been staying in a rough camp along a barren
stretch of shoreline some distance away when a fierce
storm had blown up. After three days they had set
out again and were on their way in when Declan
O'Sullivan had spied what he thought was a man tangled in a bit of flotsam. Before anyone could stop him,
he'd gone overboard, and had drowned saving the life
of an American sailor.

The entire village had been devastated by the loss.
The neighbors had been kind, but Kathleen knew they
had little to spare. She had taken to cutting peat and
trading it for food to families who could just as easily

have cut their own, but it had hurt her pride sorely to be so beholden.

Months later, when Mr. McKnight's letter had come offering his assistance and enclosing a monstrous sum of money, that same pride had urged her to return it. As if any amount of money could make up for the loss of a man's life.

It had been Tara who'd stayed her hand. Tara, who was growing out of her clothes faster than Kathleen could cut down one of her own few gowns. Tara, who wore out shoes even faster than she outgrew them. Tara, who was ever and always hungry.

"Oh, Kat, don't send it back. I want to go to Ameri-key, I do." The child had scrunched her eyes shut and commenced swaying, the way she did when the sight was on her. "I see a ship. Oh, she's a lovely thing, she is, with pretty tables all covered in green, and money like golden rain! Oh, let's do it, Kat, let's go to Ameri-key like Mr. McKnight says!"

"Well, to be sure, he doesn't come right out and say—"

"He says if ever he can be of service, we have only to ask. That's the same thing, isn't it?"

"That it's not."

"But it's what he meant to say." Tara had grabbed the letter, held it tightly to her flat chest and shut her eyes again. "He wants us to go to him. Why else would he have sent us the money? Sure and I can hear his voice clear as a bell, Katy, that I can."

Pride had urged her to return the money, but Kathleen, ever the sensible O'Sullivan, knew pride alone would never put flesh on Tara's frail bones, nor shoes on her growing feet. Declan O'Sullivan had jumped overboard to save the life of a stranger and lost his own. Sure, that stranger owed Declan's daughters something in return.

He'd been such a charmer, their da. A good man, a comely man, if never a good provider. They'd been left with no more than a moldy thatch over their heads, and that leaking and fit to fall down. But to be fair, it wasn't the first time Declan O'Sullivan had leaped without first looking. Feckless, some said, and him with a heart that had never been strong.

She'd prayed over it, and Tara, bless the child, never said another word, as if she knew all along they'd be going. Given the choice of emigrating to America or continuing to depend on the charity of neighbors, Kathleen had made her decision.

The ship had been old and ugly, not beautiful. As for the rest of Tara's blather, there'd been no tables at all, much less pretty green cloths. They'd eaten ship's fare from tin plates balanced on their knees.

At least Tara had. The very thought of food had made her own belly start to heave.

And gold? The only gold she'd seen or was ever like to see was the sunlight glinting off Tara's head, and that more copper than gold.

And now here she was, in a town called Mystic in America, still reeling from the six-week journey, and about to set forth on yet another one. And for all her sister's assurances, she was wishing they'd never left home.

Casting a suspicious glance over her shoulder at the puffing, snorting monstrous machine behind her, she thought longingly of the pony cart that had carried them all the way to Galway, where they'd boarded the ship.

America was big. Big and noisy and full of people who spoke with a funny accent and looked down their noses at the likes of the O'Sullivan sisters.

Not Mr. McKnight nor his lovely wife, never a bit of it, they were kindness itself.

Unfortunately, Mr. McKnight was the wrong Mr. McKnight. When they'd finally located the offices of McKnight Shipping, only to be told that Mr. Galen McKnight, the man who was beholden to the O'Sullivans, was no longer there, she'd felt as if the world had suddenly tilted under her feet.

But then, ever since they'd left Galway Bay she'd

been struggling to come a-right, more often on her knees than her feet, with a bucket clasped in her arms.

It was not Mr. Galen, but his brother, Mr. Brandon McKnight who took them in charge, offered them tea and biscuits and explained that Galen lived in a town four days' journey to the south.

Kathleen could have wept. Only pride had kept her despair from showing. The gentleman had taken them to his home, where his wife had made them welcome. Tara had fallen in love with their new baby daughter, and Kathleen had fallen in bed and slept the clock around and then some.

"Here we are," said the wrong Mr. McKnight, handing her two strips of cardboard. "Are you sure you won't change your mind and stay on here for a few more days? My wife would be glad to have you."

Brandon McKnight felt compelled to make the offer. The poor child looked so forlorn. Not the young one, who was as frisky as a pup, but the eldest. The one who looked as if she was hanging on by her fingernails.

Ana had opened her arms, her heart and her home, as he'd known she would when he'd showed up with two strange young females in tow. After they'd been fed and settled for the night, she had joined him in his study. "Brand, those poor shabby bags of theirs are mostly filled with books, can you believe it? They've scarcely enough between them to dress a scarecrow. First thing tomorrow I'm taking them both shopping."

"You do that, my dear. But first find a way to keep from hurting their pride."

"Oh, Lord, you would have to mention pride. Well, I'll work on it. What in the world is Galen going to do with them?"

"I'd give a pretty penny to be a fly on the wall when they step off that train. I sent off a note to warn him, but they might get there before it does."

"Kathleen's pretty, isn't she? With a few more pounds and the right clothes, and something done with her hair, she'd be beautiful."

       Excerpt from BEHOLDEN

"Somehow, I don't think Gale's in the market for any more females, no matter how lovely. He's got his hands full dealing with Tyler's daughter."

"I can imagine. Brand, do you think there's something a bit strange about that child?"

"Tara? Our old friend Maureen would call her pisky-mazed. Fey. Probably a hoax, but a harmless one. Although, come to think of it, she hadn't been inside my office more than five minutes when she broke in to tell me where that manifest was that I'd been looking for all week. The blasted thing was right where she said it was, so maybe it's not a hoax after all."

"Yes, well, she told me my sister was coming for a visit, and we both know I don't even have a sister, so maybe it is."

Now, as he waited for the train to begin boarding, Brand thought about all that had transpired over the past few days since he'd been summoned to meet an immigration official and take charge of a pair of incredibly green girls.

He thought about his younger brother, his only remaining brother, whom he'd come so close to losing. Galen deserved all the good fortune that came his way. And lately, fortune had smiled on him, in spite of his ongoing battle with that harridan, Aster Tyler.

Things were going to get interesting, mighty interesting, he mused, once the O'Sullivans were added to the mix.

The conductor stepped out on the platform. Brand collected the shabby valise, which was all the luggage they possessed in spite of his wife's best efforts. The books he had packed in a small trunk and shipped south, after reassuring the eldest girl they would be waiting for her when she arrived.

Kathleen took out a handkerchief and dabbed at a smudge on her sister's face. "There, now," she scolded gently. "Stay clean, for we want to make a good impression on Mr. Galen."

Oh, you'll make an impression, all right, Brand

thought, a few minutes later, as he watched them take their seats. Tara grinned through the sooty glass and waggled all ten fingers of her grimy little hands.

Kathleen managed a smile, but her eyes were shadowed with apprehension. Probably wishing she had a bucket handy, in case train travel affected her the same as travel by shipboard.

"Oh, yes, brother Galen, you're in for a rare treat."

It might even be worth a trip south once Ana and the baby were up to traveling, just to see how it all turned out.

PASSION RIDES THE PAST

☐ **TIMELESS by Jasmine Cresswell.** Robyn Delany is a thoroughly modern woman who doesn't believe in the supernatural . . . and is beginning to believe that true love is just as much of a fantasy. She hides her romantic feelings for her boss, Zach Bowleigh, until the intrigue that surrounds him thrusts into danger . . . and into 18th-century England. It should be a place that no longer exists, yet does with the flesh-and-blood reality of Zach's coldly handsome ancestor, William Bowleigh, Lord Starke. (404602—$4.99)

☐ **WILD DESIRE by Cassie Edwards.** Stephanie Helton contrasted starky with the famous "white Indian," Runner, adopted by the Navaho as a child and destined to be their leader. Tall, lithe, and darkly sensual, Runner immediately recognized Stephanie as the fire that set his blood blazing . . . and his sworn enemy. Runner felt his soul riven by conflict—he could not both lead his people and join his destiny with this woman. (404645—$4.99)

☐ **FIRES OF HEAVEN by Chelley Kitzmiller.** Independence Taylor had not been raised to survive the rigors of the West, but she was determined to mend her relationship with her father—even if it meant journeying across dangerous frontier to the Arizona Territory. But nothing prepared her for the terrifying moment when her wagon train was attacked, and she was carried away from certain death by the mysterious Apache known only as Shatto. (404548—$4.99)

☐ **WHITE ROSE by Linda Ladd.** Cassandra Delaney is the perfect spy. She is the notorious "White Rose," risking her life and honor for the Confederacy in a desperate flirtation with death. Australian blockade runner Derek Courland's job is to abduct the mysterious, sensual woman known as "White Rose" Australia to save her pretty neck, only she's fighting him, body and soul, to escape his ship and the powerful feelings pulling them both toward the unknown . . . (404793—$4.99)

*Prices slightly higher in Canada   TOP5X

Buy them at your local bookstore or use this convenient coupon for ordering.

PENGUIN USA
P.O. Box 999 — Dept. #17109
Bergenfield, New Jersey 07621

Please send me the books I have checked above.
I am enclosing $_____ (please add $2.00 to cover postage and handling). Send check or money order (no cash or C.O.D.'s) or charge by Mastercard or VISA (with a $15.00 minimum). Prices and numbers are subject to change without notice.

Card #_____ Exp. Date _____
Signature_____
Name_____
Address_____
City _____ State _____ Zip Code _____

For faster service when ordering by credit card call **1-800-253-6476**

Allow a minimum of 4-6 weeks for delivery. This offer is subject to change without notice.